Marriage on the Street Corners of Tehran

Marriage on the Street Corners of Tehran

A novel

Based on true stories of temporary marriage

Nadia Shahram

UNHOOKED BOOKS
an imprint of High Conflict Institute Press
Scottsdale, Arizona

Table of Contents

I do not remember the ride in the ambulance, but I do remember all that has happened since that Saturday morning in May of 1980, all of which had led me to become a *siqeh*. You may ask, what on earth is a *siqeh*? Basically, it is a temporary wife, a prostitute of sorts, but with a contract. I have been married ten times. My name is Ateesh. I am thirty-six years old and this is my story…

I'd never felt so much pain in my life as I did then, laying in the hospital bed recovering from Hassan's abuse. My husband had broken my ribs and given me a deep cut under my chin that hospitalized me for two weeks. Being beaten up by one's husband is not talked about publicly in Iran, so when my family took my unconscious body to Pahlavi hospital, they admitted me under the guise of a "mysterious fall." As I awoke to find my family at my side, observing my bloody, twelve-year-old body on a hospital bed, in a semiconscious state, I heard Modar sobbing as she said to Grandma Tuba, "Divorce is un-avoidable."

Her words were all I needed to hear. In a state of tranquility, I drifted off to sleep as words continued to flow from Modar's mouth.

After my stay in the hospital, I was taken back to my parents' home and promised by Modar and Grandma Tuba that I would never return to my husband's house.

The next morning, Modar woke up quite a bit earlier than usual.

Unlike my father, she was not an early riser. She made a large breakfast with all my favorite items: flat, whole wheat bread fresh from the bakery; local, yellowish sheep butter; and fresh honey still in honeycombs. The elaborate breakfast, along with Grandma Tuba's presence, revealed that something big was going to happen. My guess was that they were going to take me to the registrar—a notary and religious official—to inquire about a divorce.

I listened and peered through the slightly open door as Modar and Grandma Tuba conversed quietly in the porch attached to the breakfast room.

"I told him again last night," Modar said exasperatedly. "Ateesh can't go back to her husband. He is going to kill her one of these days and I'm not going to wait for that to happen. She is all I have left, and I am going to protect her with my life."

Grandma Tuba smiled sadly and said, "I wish you had told your husband so clearly and strongly about your broken heart when he told you of his plans to take a second wife."

They were both quiet for a moment. "So what did he say?" Grandma Tuba asked.

"What do you expect?" Modar replied. "He said, '*Aberue yeh man meereh*! We will lose face!' I told him, plain and simple, 'I will live without *aberue*, face, but not without my daughter.' So, I told him…." she began to sob, "I told him that I forgive him."

"Forgive him?" Grandma Tuba interrupted. "Azim destroyed you by taking a second wife!"

"I have to rescue Ateesh," Modar said, "I have to." Grandma Tuba reached over and embraced her.

My head was reeling. I didn't know what to think. Poor Modar. More than ever I resented Baba for causing her so much pain.

I stepped onto the porch and walked toward them. As I approached, I tried to say something to let them know of my presence, but instead I burst into tears. I began to weaken and felt as if I was going to collapse. I grabbed onto the chair and suddenly felt their arms around me, lifting me gently onto the day bed.

"God kill Hassan for what he did to you," Modar said.

"Just watch how his opium addiction will spread through his body and into his soul," Grandma Tuba said as she looked toward the sky with the palms of her hands in a prayer gesture. "His dead body will be taken to the funeral home!"

They both helped me sit up.

"Look here," Modar said, as she attempted a smile and pointed to a basket of freshly picked yellow roses on the breakfast table. "See what beautiful roses Grandma Tuba has brought for you, Ateesh."

"They are almost as beautiful as you," Grandma Tuba said softly, avoiding eye contact with me.

Thin and of medium height, Grandma's face was full of soft wrinkles and she had dark eyes that could speak volumes.

Modar had told me stories of her father bringing yellow rosebuds to her every Thursday on the way home from where he worked as a clerk in the local taxation and treasury department. He picked the flowers from a garden where the treasury building was located. They were always carefully wrapped in his handkerchief to prevent the thorns from pricking her delicate fingers. Modar loved roses and would wait expectantly at the front gate of their home for his arrival. As I came to know the story, yellow roses became my favorite flowers. Seeing the roses now, I gave Grandma Tuba and Modar a faint smile as I felt the tears run down my cheeks.

"Eat some breakfast," Modar said as she pulled out a chair for me.

I adjusted my pajamas and sat down.

"Where's Baba?" I asked Modar, although I was sure of the answer.

"He had to go to the restaurant early to talk to the accountant," Modar replied, avoiding my eyes.

"Baba is ashamed of me," I said crossly. "I know he is, but what does he want me to do? He can kill me himself, instead of letting Hassan kill me!"

"Don't say that!" Modar said.

One day I had asked him, "Baba Joon? Would you have been more proud of me if I was a boy?" He told me I was equal, but I knew that was a lie. It was so obvious he loved his sons more than me—the two sons he had with his second wife. Only a daughter could bring this kind of a shame to a family, and that was why he was avoiding me.

"Modar, is today the day we are going to the registrar?" I asked. "You both promised me in the hospital that you would get me a divorce with or without Baba's approval. Please don't make me go back to Hassan…please!" "Yes, Ateesh *Joon*," Modar said, "today is the day. We are going to free you. Grandma has the name and address of the registrar who will help us get a divorce. Now eat your breakfast and take a shower. Then we'll go."

Grandma Tuba walked over to the samovar and poured tea into my favorite teacup.

"Here is your tea, my princess," she said, bowing gracefully. "Shall I spoon feed you, too?"

All three of us burst into laughter. Grandma Tuba always rose higher in spirits to comfort us, especially lately.

"Are you coming too, Grandma?" I asked, my happiness deflating as quickly as it had come. "You don't have to. I know that divorce is not…is not a proper thing…even to talk about, but you know this isn't my fault. You don't want to be seen going to a registrar's office, right?"

Without hesitation Grandma Tuba replied, "Right now, my child, the most important thing is to save your life, get you a divorce, and get you out of that house. I can handle *mardom*, people, but not losing you. *Allaho Akbar!*" she exclaimed. God is great!

Modar nodded in agreement.

Grandma Tuba would wait at home for our return while Modar and I went to the registrar's office.

After we finished breakfast and washed up, Modar and I took a short taxi ride to the main street. As we rode in the backseat, she held my hand gently, though I wasn't sure if this was for her comfort or mine.

"Ateesh," she said, pale as snow, "I believe in fate and that our path in life is written when we are born."

Her hands were soft and reassuring, but I could feel her pulse racing.

"Modar," I said, admiring her strength and courage to rescue me,

"I will make you proud."

I wasn't sure at the time exactly what that entailed, but as my modar affectionately squeezed my hand, I knew it was the right thing to say. I looked at her sad yet determined face. In her late twenties, Modar was attractive and used to having people comment on her beauty. Her beautiful long, dark, curly hair decorated her dark eyes with a perfect set of white teeth. I took pride in hearing that I had taken after her. But at that moment, sadness overwhelmed her beauty.

As we rode, I tried to remember the last time I saw a glow on her face and a genuine smile on her lips. She had been heavy with sadness for years now. I rested my head on her shoulder and suddenly recalled one night when I was about four years old, when I had been awakened to the sounds of screaming and shouting, as if someone was being chased.

"Modar!" I had screamed.

She was already in my bedroom, clearly shaken up.

"Metarsam!" cried, "I am scared! What's going on?"

"Ateesh Joon." she said, attempting to be calm, "there's nothing to worry about. Baba will take care of it."

"Take care of what?" I asked, bewildered.

That's when we were startled by a sudden flash of light through my open window, where our gardener, Qolam-Ali, and his eldest son had appeared.

"Khanoom; Ma' am" he said calmly, "Aqa is awake and is on his way. He wants to know if you are all right. He is checking the pool house, but it looks as if the intruders have left the same way they came in."

As he finished his sentence, Baba appeared next to him with a shotgun in one hand and a flashlight in the other. "Go back to sleep and close the window," he said with authority. "Everything is under control."

His presence triggered something in my mind. Why wasn't Baba already in the house? Something was wrong.

As Modar closed my bedroom window, she stole a glance at Baba, and though no words came out of her mouth, her eyes asked a thousand questions.

At that young age, I knew that Baba had a second wife, and that she hated us and we hated her, but I hadn't realized until that moment that he wasn't living with us any longer.

Before Baba had taken a second wife, Modar would play with me in the garden pool during the hot summer months. We had so much fun together, until Baba married again and she refused to go with me. "I don't want to run into *her*," she would say.

That's when she began to stay inside and watch me from the window. Was this what marriage did to women?

I thought of my own husband, and a shiver ran through me as I remembered my wedding night, that first time I had met him…

"Wait here for your husband and stop crying, or Baba will get angry," Grandma Tuba had said sharply.

I looked up at her. I had never heard that tone in Grandma Tuba's voice before. I searched her face for comfort, for an answer, but she turned away from me, walked out of the room and closed the door behind her, leaving me alone in a strange room. I stared at the closed door, praying that it would open and she would come back to me, but nothing happened. Everything was still. I wanted to run to the door and pound on it, scream out her name, but I was too frightened to move.

Suddenly the door opened. I held my breath as a tall, thin man with cold, dark eyes stepped in and closed the door behind him. He smiled at me, but it wasn't a real smile. It was more of a smirk. I turned away. He was older than I, but I wasn't sure exactly how much older. Maybe 19 or 20? My heart raced as he came closer. I didn't know anything about this man who was about to touch me.

I watched as he placed a square white cloth on the bed, and then reached for me. I tensed as he removed my clothes, lifted me up and placed me on the bed on top of the white cloth he had laid out, which was much longer and wider than my hips. Before I could say anything or make a move, he forced himself on top of me. I felt a sharp pain as he smiled down at me with a pleased look on his face. I squeezed my eyes shut and prayed it would end.

The next thing I remember I was naked, lying in blood next to this stranger.

I squeezed my eyes shut again. This had to be a nightmare I was having.

Where was Modar? Where was Grandma Tuba? My ears searched for their familiar voices, somewhere out there, but there was nothing. As weak as I felt, I promised myself I would never allow what happened to me to happen to my own daughter.

He sat up and held the white cloth under the night lamp. With the same smirk on his face, he looked down at the white sheet under me, which also was stained with blood. Then he returned to bed, laid his head on the pillow, and turned his back to me. I lay still, my heart pounding, and stared at the back of his head until I heard snoring. I wanted to get up and run out of the room. But that would have brought shame to my family. I had already lost my virginity. My only choice was to remain. My marriage had been arranged. I was legitimately where I belonged: with this strange man who was now my husband.

I laid there feeling numb until he woke up and forced himself on me again. As he entered me, my mind began to race. I heard Grandma Tuba's voice saying, "Stay away from boys. They will hurt you." Why was it okay for this man to hurt me? This man they call my husband?

"This is what girls must go through to become women," Grandma Tuba explained to me the first time I got my period, as she put a warm towel on my tummy and joked about the real pain awaiting me. "Ateesh Joon, delivering a baby is a lot harder than this. This is only practice to prepare you for the real pain."

What about this pain? She hadn't mentioned this. If what was happening to me now was normal, why hadn't anybody ever talked about it?

When he tried to force himself inside me again, I squeezed my legs together. He forced me onto my stomach, and before I know what was happening, I felt a sharp pain in my rear. He pushed my head and neck down into the embroidered white bridal pillow filled with swan feathers. I struggled to turn my head sideways and cried out.

"You are my wife and I can do anything I want with you," he

whispered into my face. "There is no limit to how I can use your body for my own pleasure. It is my right."

"I will never love you," I spat. "You disgust me."

He laughed and said, "You will learn to love me."

Never, I thought.

I didn't sleep at all that night. As sunlight gently crept inside the room and warmed my face, my husband caressed my cheek and said, "You are even more beautiful now that I have deposited my juices in you." Then he sat up and said, "God forgive me! I've missed my morning prayers!"

In my exhausted yet attentive mind, it occurred to me that God could not and would not forgive him for hurting me so badly. I did not believe then, and I do not believe now, that religion would justify hurting others, not even one's wife.

Everything still felt unreal. This had to be a nightmare. It had to be. I kept squeezing my eyes together in a desperate attempt to wake up.

Almost immediately after he left the room, Modar and another woman I came to know as my modar-in-law came in. I turned away from them, holding back tears. I felt shattered and angry, especially at Modar and Grandma Tuba.

"Ateesh," Modar said, "it is alright."

Her beautiful, dark brown eyes were puffy and red. She appeared pale and fragile.

My modar-in-law looked pleased at the bloody sheet that had been left on display by her son on the edge of the bed. "The doctor's virginity certificate was genuine," she said with a smile.

A virginity certificate? It was then I understood why Modar had taken me to the doctor a few days earlier. The doctor had examined my private parts and gave Modar a piece of paper. When I asked Modar what it was, she ignored me, but now I knew.

As my modar-in-law left the room, Grandma Tuba walked in, closed the door behind her, and came over to me.

"I know you feel betrayed by us Joon, dear," Grandma Tuba said, "but you will learn the truth one day why your modar and I had to accept this marriage proposal without your knowledge. He is a good boy and has promised us he will treat you kindly."

I felt her hands on my head, and my tears surfaced. Then for the first time, I remembered where I saw him before: at Baba's second wife's house.

"You both betrayed me!" I shouted.

∿ ∿ ∿ ∿ ∿

The taxi came to an abrupt stop in front of the five-story office complex. It was not far from the main street, which connected the harbor to the city of Abadan where my family lived. The building was hidden behind a shopping plaza frequented by young men and women looking for the latest fashions inspired by European designers. Modar and I had visited some of the boutiques in that plaza, but we had never noticed this unimpressive office complex before. There was also sweet shop where we stopped every Friday afternoon for traditional-style ice cream. Although I hadn't cared much for the pistachio nuts in the ice cream, I would swallow them whole since I was told they were good for me. I was so fond of ice cream that I wanted to marry the ice cream man so I could have ice cream all the time. If only I had had the choice of whom I would marry.

"How much?" asked Modar.

"Five *tumon*," said the taxi driver. Modar handed him the money, and we stepped out onto the street.

We walked toward the dreaded building. Modar pushed the main door open and it made a cracking sound similar to seagulls preying for food. Trying to stay calm, I counted the fifty-four dusty, marble steps up to the fourth floor of the building. A short hallway led us to the entrance of the registrar's office. My heart was pounding so fast I feared it might jump out of my chest and claim a life of its own. I looked at Modar, who was trying to remain composed.

The registrar was the only one who could end my marriage. I imagined him to be a cleric with a white beard, a clear sign of a halo above his holy head, and rosary beads in his hand. Grandma Tuba had a picture of her religious guru, Ayatollah Boroujerdi, on the table in her sitting room along with photos of her parents. Those visions in my mind were comforting.

An old sign on the registrar's tinted, glass door read, "Registry of Marriage and Divorce since 1950." The door bore a religious name and his title, *Hajji* Mohammad Al Jabar. Only men who had been to Mecca were referred to as "*Hajji*," and the title warranted respect. Still, his name concerned me.

"He's Arab, Modar?" I asked. "Can he speak Farsi?"

"I was told by Grandma Tuba that he is the one who performed my religious wedding ceremony," Modar said, whispering so quietly I had difficulty hearing her. "Maybe his father is Arab. Let us go in and see. It shouldn't matter; he can still help us with the divorce."

I guessed she was concerned that somebody might hear what we were talking about. After all, the word divorce itself is taboo in our culture, and even speaking of it could bring shame. Modar took a deep breath, then knocked before turning the doorknob. A deep voice asked us to enter and take a seat.

The office was cold and impersonal, furnished with office-type leather fixtures. There was a long wall unit holding many files. The white walls were decorated with Islamic calligraphy bearing the ninety-nine virtues of God: God is Great, God is Merciful, and God is Forgiving. These were some of God's attributes, I was told. Knowing what I've been through, I thought, God will help me.

The registrar was on the phone but motioned for us to sit across from him on a black sofa. His beard was jet-black, same as the hair that was showing under his turban. On two of his fat fingers, right next to each other, were rings with enormous stones.

My grandfather had told me that religious men usually wear a ring decorated with a precious stone called aqiq as a sign of piety. Grandfather always wore a ring with aqiq.

The second ring was decorated with a large Mediterranean blue sapphire, signifying wealth, and a special religious affiliation as a direct descendant of Prophet Mohammad. Modar and I glanced at each other. As soon as we sat down, I felt the weight of his eyes on me. I looked to make sure my blouse was buttoned and I straightened my skirt over my knee.

As he talked on the phone, he lifted his eyeglasses off the desk, put them on, and started appraising my modar and me. "We will continue this conversation another time," he was saying, "but I want to make clear that I will not allow this kind of indecency in my neighborhood."

He hung up the phone, cutting short the voice on the other end.

"What is the purpose of your visit?" he asked, as he fiddled with the collar of his shirt.

"We are here to request a divorce for my daughter," Modar said, her voice shaking with nervousness.

At the word "divorce," his eyes turned to me.

"We were told you can effectuate a divorce," Modar continued. "Is that true?"

Fixing his eyes on me like a hawk, the registrar stood up, walked around his desk and stood right in front of us. I shifted in my seat and tried to appear more like a grown up, by crossing my leg in front of me and holding my head up.

"How old is your daughter?" he asked Modar, without removing his eyes from me.

"She is turning thirteen on the eleventh of July," Modar said.

"She looks as if she is seventeen or eighteen," he said. "Where is her father? We need his permission to do it."

"Is her father's presence absolutely necessary?"

"Of course it is," he answered. "According to Islamic law, as long as the father is alive, he is the legal guardian of his children."

"What if he is dead?"

Her question startled me. I turned and looked at her. To get my divorce Baba needed to be dead? But surely the registrar must have heard of Baba's cholo-Kababys, restaurants. The registrar observed her for a moment then asked her to step out into the hallway.

Modar hesitated.

"I need to ask your daughter something," he said. Something in his voice had changed. It seemed to have gone from authoritative to sympathetic.

Modar must have felt the change in his voice too, because without a word, she sheepishly stood up and walked toward the door. Just before she left, she lifted her sad eyes to gaze at me. The fiery sparkle, which had once illuminated her beautiful face, had long since been extinguished. Instead, pain and suffering were etched onto her drawn visage.

Desperately I questioned her departure with my eyes, and with her eyes, she replied, "No choice." She stepped out of the room before I could ask, "Why?"

As the door closed behind her, the registrar went back behind his desk. I followed him with my eyes. He was well into his fifties and had a bulging belly that suggested good food and a comfortable living. His mustache covered his upper lip and most of his mouth. He reached into a drawer and took something out. Then, without taking his eyes off me, he opened a small perfume bottle, dabbed a few drops on himself and closed it. He affixed his light cotton, black religious robe over his shoulders.

His robe reminded me of the one Grandfather put on every time he left the house. Grandma Tuba always helped Grandfather put it on, making sure it hung evenly on all sides.

"If your grandfather leaves the house untidy, I, as his wife, will look bad in front of people," Grandma Tuba explained.

If Grandma Tuba wasn't around to fix his robe, I would follow him to the front door, adjusting it to make sure it hung evenly. Grandfather told me I would make a good wife. The robe indicated status and piety for men like Grandfather, and, presumably, for men like *Hajji* registrar.

Counting the beads on his rosary, the registrar walked toward me. My heart was pounding, but nothing compared to the first time my husband had walked toward me. As the registrar came closer, I smelled his cologne. Unlike Grandfather's heavenly smell of wild roses, the registrar's perfume smelled like rotten fruit. I held my breath as he came closer.

"I will get you your divorce. It is going to be very hard without your father's permission. But, out of the goodness of my heart, I will get it for you, on the condition that you become my *siqeh* for a year."

His smile revealed stained, ugly teeth. His cold eyes stared at me, and I could smell his lust. Suddenly the halo I had imagined around his carefully wrapped white turban disappeared, and I sat there feeling nauseated.

Siqeh? I had never heard that word before. But that is what the registrar wanted in exchange. It must be something valuable that I possessed, but I didn't know what it was or how to respond. I looked at the door where I could see Modar's shadow. It didn't move.

"Think about it for a minute," he said. "It's your only way out."

I stared at the doorknob, hoping it would turn by force of her hand, but it didn't. I wondered if it would've turned if Grandma Tuba was there. I thought of my wedding night, when I had stared at that door, waiting for Grandma Tuba to come back in, and suddenly felt a resurgence of pain from my almost-healed injuries. I squeezed my eyes shut. I didn't know anything anymore.

Only a few days earlier, Grandma Tuba and I had visited the rug market. It had been crowded with all kinds of people, especially elders looking to purchase rugs for their children's soon-to-be brides or grooms. It is customary for parents to include fine rugs as wedding presents. Grandma Tuba and I were looking for a runner to replace the old worn-out one she had in her stairway. The aroma of delicious long grain rice, *dom syya*, from nearby restaurants was mouthwatering. But I forgot about eating when I noticed the glances I kept getting from the salesman who was trying to convince Grandma Tuba to purchase a particular runner.

"You bastard," Grandma Tuba suddenly spat, as she hit him on the head with a newspaper, "Don't you have a modar or sister?"

The salesman quickly apologized. He placed his right hand on his chest and lowered his head in a subordinating gesture, and said, "Forgive me, Modar."

To call an older woman "Modar," who is not your Modar, shows respect and sincerity. Of course, if you call a woman Modar who is not older than you it has the opposite effect.

Grandma Tuba then gave him a short lecture on righteousness and the consequences of impure thoughts on the soul.

As we walked out of the shop, I asked her if she believed all of what she had said to him. She explained that she had heard many times in sermons that our thoughts are heard by God, and written down by angels. On Judgment Day, it will be read and we will be judged. "We'll be sent to hellfire or paradise," she said, her tone indicating she believed.

But now, Grandma Tuba was not with me. Avoiding the registrar's eyes, I noticed the framed lithograph on the wall near the exit. In Arabic, it said "*Allaho Akbar!*" God is great! Grandma Tuba used that particular phrase all the time.

I turned back to the registrar and asked politely, "*Siqeh?*"

He smiled and muttered something. He moved so close to me that I could smell his body and the strong odor of tobacco on his clothes. The strong feeling of *Allaho Akbar* was vanishing as he stood there leering at me, in his old-fashioned black suit, with a crease on his carefully ironed white shirt, and the rosary around his wrist. He reminded me of that pushy salesman in the rug market.

The registrar's smile had the opposite of its intended effect. Grandma Tuba would say that he was going straight to hell for his evil thoughts. I felt as if I were standing in the room with my husband again. But this time I didn't feel as scared and weak. I knew more and was learning quickly about life.

"How does that work?" I asked in a very soft voice.

He explained that it would be exactly the same as a permanent marriage contract, but with a fixed, shorter duration. The look on his face made clear what he expected of me in exchange for granting my divorce. Still, I did not completely understand.

"If you agree to be my *siqeh* for a short time, I promise to get your divorce," he repeated. "As a sign of good faith I also agree to pay you a marriage gift of five gold coins, plus monthly maintenance." He stopped to take a breath, and then in a low, desperate voice, he said, "Say yes!" as spit escaped his mouth.

"*Chi?*" I asked. "What?"

In exchange for my divorce, I would be his temporary wife, and he would pay me five gold coins plus monthly living expenses. Maybe

I would bring less shame to my father this way. But what would I be losing in exchange?

He then went on to explain that, as a minor, I wouldn't be allowed to divorce my husband without my father's consent, although my husband could divorce me without my knowledge, or even my presence.

"Why is that, *Hajji*?" I asked, intentionally calling him *Hajji* to appear respectful.

"It is all in the Quran," he replied with authority. "It is of course for the protection of the weaker sex: women." He looked directly into my eyes and continued, "You need my support and protection and I will help you. Let me handle your father. We men understand each other better. He will agree."

The more he talked on, the less I understood his rationale for temporary marriage and why this arrangement would even be called marriage and how it would protect me. Bewildered, I noticed saliva beginning to collect in the corners of his mouth and the edge of his mustache. He looked less like a cleric and more like a decrepit old man eyeing a mouthwatering pastry.

Maybe, just maybe, I was in control, just as Grandma Tuba was in the rug market with the salesman. But it was me that they desired.

No longer feeling weakened by his presence, I stood up and looked straight into his eyes for the first time. "Thank you," I said. "Let me convince my modar and I will come back." And without hesitation I stood up and walked toward the door.

I was still nervous and couldn't fully feel my legs, but I wasn't going to let him know that.

"Shall I talk to your father?" he asked, following close behind me.

"Oh, no," I said. "He would kill me."

I quickly stepped out of the room and closed the door behind me.

"Let's get out of here," I said to Modar, who was still waiting right outside the door.

I saw the registrar's outline recede from the tinted glass of his office door, and I was relieved that he wasn't going to come out and repeat his proposal. Perhaps he was worried for his *aberue*, face!

Though I could not have explained it then, the registrar taught me one thing in his office, and it had nothing to do with the Quran. I think it was then that I began to learn about sex and power. This was my first time in a registry office, but subsequent events would take me to similar offices again and again. Like other young temporary wives, I found refuge in a place of devil's practice. I learned to think of my sexual ability as a sharp sword in my hand. The word, *qarardud*, contract, became one of the most frequently used words in my vocabulary in the coming years.

"Ateesh, what happened?" Modar asked. "What did he say? I was worried to death standing there and leaving you with that dirty old man. He was no man of God!"

I didn't share with Modar the details of the conversation, but simply told her, "He will not help us." I was sure Modar had heard his evil proposal, which is why she'd referred to him as a "dirty old man."

As we stepped out onto the street, we found Grandma Tuba waiting for us.

"Grandma!" I cried as I ran into her open arms.

"I was too nervous to wait at home," she said.

"That *be pedar*, bastard, asked Ateesh to become his *siqeh*," Modar said to Grandma Tuba.

"*Be pedar!*" said Grandma Tuba as she spat with disgust onto the pavement.

No further words were spoken between us, but a few meaningful looks exchanged between Modar and Grandma Tuba told me that another plan was needed to get my divorce.

I held Grandma Tuba as we rode home, and as the taxi driver pulled away from the dreary office building, I saw the registrar standing on his balcony, watching us.

Inadvertently, I glanced through a boutique window in the plaza. The dress on display had changed. The solemn black one displayed earlier had been replaced by a beautiful red dress with tiny straps on the shoulder, two rows of pleats with an uneven hem, and ruffles at the bottom. I kept looking at the dress until the plaza and boutique were no longer in view. I imagined dancing barefoot to a Persian rhythm, wearing that dress, in our garden by the pool. In the taxi, paying no attention to the whispers of Grandma Tuba and Modar, I wished I could own that red gypsy dress with the uneven hem.

◇◇ ◇◇ ◇◇ ◇◇ ◇◇

"Modar, why can't I live here anymore?"

"Baba thinks *mardom*, people, would say you are spoiled child and we did not teach you how to be a wife."

"Is that what you think, too, Modar?"

"I might have thought that the first couple of times you complained," she said. Then she turned toward Grandma Tuba and said, "Right?"

Grandma Tuba nodded. "But that *haywon*, animal, turned out to be a no-good drug addict, and your Baba's second wife must have known this."

"What exactly was her role in my arranged marriage?" I asked.

"No need to get into that now," Modar said. "We have more important things to take care of."

Grandma Tuba offered the solution. "Ateesh will come and live with us."

Modar looked at me and waited.

"Sure," I said. "But what about Grandfather?"

"Let me handle him."

"What about Baba?" I asked. "Who is going to convince him?"

Modar and Grandma Tuba just looked at each other.

For days after that, there were arguments between Baba and Modar. I stayed in my room and anxiously awaited the outcome. I was sure Baba wished he had never had me. His sons probably never gave him any problems at all.

I was four years old when Baba's first son was born. He was named Karim, which means "blessing," and always referred to as one of God's virtues. One year later Baba's second son, Alireza, was born. Things got a little better for me then, because as Baba's second wife was busy with Alireza, Karim would come into the garden and play with me. I was a tomboy as a child and he and I became great playmates. We would swim for hours, run around the garden, and climb trees. We were always in competition over who could reach the top first. Our favorite trees to climb were right next to one another, and every time I saw those trees as an adult, I thought of him and how much fun we used to have.

As Alireza got bigger, he came into the backyard and followed us around. Many times we hid from him, hoping he would lose us so we could run faster without worrying about him. Karim and I became his babysitters. His modar, like my modar, would watch us from the window. Karim and Alireza had been told by their modar to call me *Khohar*, sister, and my modar, *Zan Baba*, wife of the father.

I remember even at that young age feeling guilty for having fun with the children of a woman who stole Baba from us and hurt my modar.

The fun didn't last, though.

One day when I was about eleven years old, I overheard Baba say to Modar, "Ateesh should not climb trees like that."

"She is a tomboy and loves to climb trees," Modar said. "There is nothing wrong with it. This is our orchard. She should be free to do what she wants."

"What if she falls and loses her hymen?" Baba said. "She has reached the age of womanhood!"

"Did your precious wife plant that in your head?" Modar asked. "I am shocked to hear such words coming out of your mouth, Azim."

"She shouldn't swim with Karim and Alireza anymore, either," he said.

Modar slammed the cabinet door shut.

"Maheen will no longer allow it," he continued. "According to the Quran, all men except a father, brother, and uncles are *haram* after the age of female maturity."

"*Haram?*" Modar asked.

"*Haram* means forbidden," Baba explained, "They are forbidden to see Ateesh without her full clothing."

"I know what *haram* means!" Modar snapped.

This *haram* idea stayed with me in the back of my mind until years later when I took a serious interest in understanding my religion.

The news traveled quickly to my grandmodars. Both visited the next morning for breakfast before Baba left for work.

I could hear everything from my room where Modar thought I was still asleep.

"Ateesh is still a child!" Grandma Tuba said to Baba. "She has not even matured yet. The Quran does not say mature girls have to cover in front of younger children. She may have to cover up in front of mature men, but not from her six- and seven-year-old stepbrothers! And anyway, nobody in this household follows religion so strictly, so how come this poor child has to?"

Without waiting for his response, she continued, "How about Maheen? Does she cover? No? How about you, Azim? When was the last time you went to a *masjid*? Since when has Maheen become the religious scholar? Jamileh, what do you think of all this?"

I knew Grandma Jamileh, Baba's modar, was in the room and wondered what she was going to say. She said nothing about religion or covering up, but bitterly said to Baba, "It is all Maheen's doing. She is jealous of Ateesh's beauty and you are being a fool."

There was no sound. I tiptoed downstairs and looked into the kitchen from the bottom of the staircase. Baba rested his head on his hand and pondered for several minutes. I will never forget the look on his face. It was that of a tired man, caught up in his own battle.

Then he turned to Modar and said, "I am afraid that Ateesh may take our family *aberue*, face, away."

"How?" Modar asked, "She is only a child!"

"I hear that boys follow her to school and remark on her beauty. Instead of cursing them, she smiles at them. I hear…"

"That stupid woman has affected your thinking about your own child!" Modar interrupted. "Are you forgetting Ateesh is a part of you and not just anyone's daughter? Have you ever heard me complaining about Maheen's boys?"

"They are boys," he answered. "There is nothing they do can make me lose face in the community."

That was when I understood the difference between me and his sons. I could make Baba lose face in the community, and they couldn't.

"Azim Joonam," Grandma Jamileh said, who usually added *Joo-nam* to his name as a sign of affection and love, "are you eating well? You look sick. You look tired and worried. You do not visit me any-more. Maheen must be giving you the meat of a dead body!"

Grandma Tuba nodded emphatically, confirming, I guessed, that Baba must have been given the meat of a dead body. Whatever that meant.

"You are a fool, Azim," Modar said. "She is feeding you non-sense." She walked out of the room and headed toward the staircase. I ran to my room and jumped into bed before I was caught.

That same night when we were alone in our beds on the balcony, Modar explained to me that when a husband has been fed the meat of a dead body it means he is under the total control of his wife, which makes him uninterested in any other woman but her.

"I have no idea how they came up with that," she said. "I only know what I've been told."

Despite the darkness, I knew she was crying. It seemed that with every tear she cried, her body became smaller. My mind was working quickly to comprehend everything. I was beginning to feel light-headed. "So it is because Baba has been given the meat of a dead body that he does not sleep with you anymore?"

She didn't reply. Instead, she gazed up in despair at the beautiful clear sky and said, "I want to be born a man in my next life."

"Stop it," I begged, but she continued.

"Men do as they please and women simply must bow down to them and kiss their feet. All these years of kissing his feet, I cannot stand it anymore."

"But why do women have to listen to men?" I cried. "Why?"

"That is the way things are," she answered gloomily. Several min-utes went by before she stood up, wiped away her tears, and caressed my hair affectionately. "Go to sleep now, Ateesh," she suddenly said, her tone unusually brisk. "It is getting late."

"I am not going to listen to any man," I told her defiantly, and hid my face under the covers before she could scold me. I am not sure how much I really understood about everything that was happening, but one thing I knew for sure was that men were mean. I remember that night well, because it was one of the rare occasions that Modar and I had had a conversation about Baba.

The next morning I looked over the balcony to see if Karim was there waiting for me, but he wasn't. Not even Alireza had come out. The next few days were the same. I woke up every morning and looked for them, and every night I went to bed wishing for things to be as they were before.

Several months went by before I saw Karim again. One night as I was lying in bed, I heard him calling my name. I jumped up and ran to the balcony.

"Karim!" I said joyfully.

He looked cold and distant.

"Are you sick?" I asked. "Where have you been? I missed you so much. What happened?"

"Your modar is not a *Zaneh Kamel,* because she could give birth only to a girl and not a boy!" he said. "I hate you!" Then he ran into the garden and disappeared.

The next morning I woke up with Modar by my side with a cold towel on my forehead. She placed a thermometer in my mouth and said, "Joonam, your body is hot like an oven. I have called the doctor and he is on his way." I closed my eyes and hoped to wake up from the nightmare I was having.

~ ~ ~ ~ ~

Now here I was, almost thirteen years old and married, listening to Baba and Modar argue over what to do with me after the shame I had brought to the family.

I asked Grandma Tuba why Grandfather couldn't come and talk to Baba about my new living arrangements. Maybe he would listen to a man. She agreed, but explained that Grandfather would never argue with Baba in front of us. He might talk to Baba privately in support of the idea, though.

I was so happy when I heard Grandma Jamileh's voice. "I had to hear from Maheen that Ateesh is here!" she was saying. "Ateesh is my grandchild too!"

As I ran toward her voice in the kitchen, I crashed into Modar, who was walking out. Modar wasn't ever happy to see Grandma Jamileh. She wasn't welcome in our home because she had supported Baba's second marriage.

"Grandma Jamileh!" I shouted as I ran to her.

She opened her arms and held me. "*Bacheh Joon*, dear child, I am here to help in any possible way. No one should be allowed to hurt you."

I felt the warmth of her words and her touch was comforting. But none of these women, not Grandma Tuba, Grandma Jamileh, or Modar, had done anything to prevent my arranged marriage. Instead, they went along with tradition and culture. As strong and loving as they were, I felt I was breaking away. I wanted to become stronger than the traditions that had bound me to an arranged marriage.

I don't know the details of what was discussed that day between my grandmas, Modar, and Baba. All I know is that was the last day I lived with my parents. I went to stay with Grandma Tuba and waited for a resolution.

My new living arrangements suited me just fine. The important thing was that I was far away from Hassan. Though my absence from home saddened Modar, we saw each other nearly every day.

Prior to my marriage, Grandma Tuba had been more like a modar to me anyway, sometimes even more so than Modar. Ever since the day I got my period, when I was eleven years old, she had been teaching me how to be a proper woman. "You must avoid boys altogether," she told me that day in her deep voice as she made jasmine tea to help my stomach cramps. Whenever she was serious, she had a tendency to deepen her voice. I think she was trying to sound like a man.

"But why, Grandma?" I asked, mischievously imitating her deep voice.

"They are only after your body and they can hurt you," she said.

"But Baba would never hurt anyone," I said.

Impatiently, Grandma Tuba shook her head. At that age, I didn't know the extent of the pain Baba put Modar through by taking a second wife.

Though Grandma Tuba's plaits were usually hidden by a headscarf that matched her clothes, her beautiful long locks of black and gray hair were always braided neatly into two sections that fell to her shoulders. On this day she wore her favorite colors, a dark blue skirt that came below her knees, dark leggings with stockings over them, and flat black shoes. She wore a loose-fitting, dark blue blouse with a few lighter colors as accents around the edge of the sleeves and collar.

Grandma Tuba's dark eyes were speaking volumes, but I could not read them now as we stepped out into the bright sunlight and walked toward the garden.

"You silly girl!" she suddenly laughed. "I don't mean Baba!" Then becoming serious again, she added, "Just remember, you must not be alone with boys. They are not to be trusted. You must remain a virgin or you will bring disgrace to your family."

"Disgrace? How?"

"You don't have to know everything now, but you must stay indoors after coming home from school. Most importantly, stay away from boys. Boys are like fire and girls are like cotton balls. If they are left unsupervised, the cotton balls will catch fire."

I frowned. "But Modar Bozorg, I'm not a cotton ball!" I said, remembering that she had used the word fire when describing my cousin, Saeed, my father's nephew. Grandma Tuba always loudly disapproved of me playing with Saeed, but Grandma Jamileh hadn't been as strict and often invited Saeed when I stayed overnight with her. I never told Grandma Tuba this, of course.

Four years older than me, Saeed was absolutely my favorite cousin, and I think I was his. Whenever he came over to Grandma Jemileh's to visit, we spent hours looking up at the sky, making up stories and chatting. Many times we'd tried to count all the stars, though all of our attempts were fruitless.

"Ateesh, how many stars do you think there are?" he asked, as we lay in our separate beds on the balcony.

23

"I don't know how many stars there are, but some sure are prettier than others," I answered.

"Ateesh, you are the prettiest of all the stars," he said.

Thinking back now, I don't know why we never kissed. I wanted to kiss him and I could feel he wanted to kiss me too. We felt so close to each other but perhaps what we shared was more like the love and friendship of siblings. It certainly was strong and beautiful.

In Farsi, *Saeed* means blessing. He was a blessing to me, but unfortunately I saw little of him after my marriage.

～～ ～～ ～～ ～～ ～～

Now that I was away from my husband and living with Grandma Tuba, I found myself curious about everything. I had so many questions I was anxious to have answered.

"Grandma, did you have boys as friends when you were growing up?" I asked as I watched her cut slices of watermelon in the backyard.

She didn't answer me at first. She just continued slicing.

"Have some," she said, as she placed the plate in front of me.

As we ate our watermelon in the gentle afternoon sun, Grandma Tuba shared something about herself with me that I was surprised to hear: The first man in Grandma Tuba's life was not Grandfather.

One day, shortly after her ninth birthday, when Grandma Tuba came home from school, her modar, Naneh Mashady, handed her a favorite doll to play with.

"Go wash up and change into this dress," Naneh said to her as she handed her a beautiful white dress with red polka dots.

"We're going to a party?" Grandma Tuba asked.

"No party," her modar said. "It is a wedding ceremony."

"A wedding? Whose?"

"Yours."

Grandma Tuba started to cry, because she knew that meant she would have to leave her parents' home and go live somewhere else. That was all she knew.

She was not present at the religious part of her own wedding. A photo of her husband was shown to her after the fathers on both sides signed the marriage certificate.

"Who is this?" she asked.

"I think that's your husband," an older cousin said.

"How sad, Grandma!" I exclaimed, thinking of the first time I saw my husband, when he walked into that decorated room.

"In some arranged marriages at that time, grooms were only a few years older than brides and truly did not know how to consummate the marriage. They would hear a little from their friends, but they knew the most important thing was to produce a bloody handkerchief," Grandma Tuba said. "Of course, in my case, Saeed Mohammad was older, and he knew a lot more. Though only through religious literature available through the *masjid*.

"After the religious ceremony had taken place and I was dressed up, I sat on a beautiful white pillow in the middle of our living room," Grandma Tuba said. "A few of my friends sat around me wearing beautiful dresses and holding their favorite dolls. I wanted to hold my favorite doll, too, but Modar took it away. I cried and begged, but she said no."

Grandma Tuba sat quietly for a few minutes, staring out, as if remembering. I tried picturing her as a little girl, crying for the doll that her modar wouldn't give her. She must have felt the same way I had felt that night in the decorated room, when I was reaching for her but she wouldn't come.

"Several women were sitting around me," Grandma Tuba continued. "They appeared to be happily celebrating a wedding. I would have been happy, too, if it was not my own wedding."

I nodded in agreement.

"In the next room were the men," she said, "smoking and enjoying drinks especially made for the occasion. I remember my father and uncle on one side, and a strange young man and his father on the other. Next to them, a cleric recited lines from the Quran. An older cousin on my modar's side told me that I should sit quietly and poised. Nothing was expected of me. I remember being so sad that I had to leave my home. Some words were exchanged between my father, uncle, and the cleric. Then everybody clapped, and sounds of laughter and conversation filled the room. Nobody said a word to me."

I sat still and anxiously waited for Grandma Tuba to continue. She had gone through the same thing I had! I felt so sad that Grandma Tuba went through that as a little girl, and at the same time I wanted to ask her why, if she knew how scary it was, did she allow it to happen to me? I didn't say a word, though. I just sat there and listened quietly as she continued.

Right from the start Grandma Tuba was very frightened to be left alone with her husband. She cried and pleaded with her modar-in-law to let her sleep with her instead. Her modar-in-law had no daughter of her own and allowed her to stay. "Tuba is only a child," Grandma Tuba heard her modar-in-law telling a woman who Grandma Tuba came to know as her great aunt. "I know how frightened I was at that age. She'll stay a few nights with me until she feels comfortable."

"I can hold her head until the marriage is consummated," the great aunt said, but her modar-in-law said no. "We will wait until Tuba is ready," she said. "I still remember, Auntie, you held my head as I cried and screamed with pain. I was the same age as Tuba."

"Held her head?" I asked.

Grandma Tuba nodded and said she shivered under the covers as she listened to them speak about this. These head holders, Grandma Tuba explained, are usually women unrelated to either side of the families whose job it is to accompany the young child bride into the bedroom and keep her still for the groom. For so long, she explained, young girls were told to stay away from men because they might violate their honor. So, it was reasoned, when these young girls are pushed into a decorated room to be with their husbands for the first time, a head holder was sometimes necessary.

I was glad Grandma Tuba had such a kind and gentle modar-in-law. My modar-in-law didn't care how frightened I was. She would never have let me sleep in her bed, not that I would have wanted to.

"My modar-in-law was my first religious teacher," Grandma Tuba said. "Her favorite verse was on the creation of people, and it went like this: 'God created man and woman equally, and it is only righteousness which sets them apart.' That one became my favorite too."

I nodded and wondered, if God has created man and woman equally, why weren't we treated equally? I had a lot to think about! But first I wanted to hear all about Grandma Tuba's first marriage. "So what happened with your husband?" I prodded.

Grandma Tuba said that every time he came into the decorated room, she Tuba began weeping and sweating. Then she started to complain of severe stomach pain every time he approached her. A truly religious and understanding man, he let this go on for a year. During this time, Grandma Tuba slept in her modar-in-law's bed, where she was treated with kindness, like a daughter. The marriage was never consummated.

After a year, Grandma Tuba's severe stomach cramps were not getting any better. First, she was treated with herbal medicines. Then the family attributed the pain to her menstrual cycle. They took Grandma Tuba to a physician, but the medicine he prescribed was of no help. Finally, after two years, they came to the conclusion that she was suffering from an incurable disease. They had no choice but to divorce her and marry their son off to another young bride. She was sent back to her parents' home, still a virgin!

It was two years before my Grandma Tuba would be married off again. Grandma Tuba said that although a divorce tarnishes a woman's life forever, it did not affect her as much because she had remained a virgin. At thirteen, she was married off to my grandfather, a widower who was ten years older than she.

Although she had claimed to be a virgin, a physician's certificate was no longer enough because she had been married before. To verify her claim of virginity, Grandma Tuba had to go through a humiliating experience. Before her marriage was consummated, three elder women from the bridegroom's family came to her home with a mission. They wanted to examine Grandma Tuba themselves to make sure the story they were given was true. Grandma Tuba was told by her modar to lay motionless with her legs wide open.

I wasn't sure exactly what they were looking for, but asked Grandma Tuba, "What if you failed the examination?"

"Either my marriage would have been canceled, causing my family to suffer, or his family would have demanded a more substantial *jahizeyeh* and would not have paid any *shirr baha*," Grandma Tuba explained.

"No presents but ask for more money?" I asked, somewhat confused.

"*Jaheziyeh* usually consists of household items, and can sometimes be enough to furnish the couple's first house. *Shir baha* is paid to the girl's family at the time of marriage. Elders on both sides decide the exact sum. The fathers of the younger and prettier girls usually get the most *shir baha*. They use it to buy some or all of the *jahizeyeh*, which is given to the bride to take into her matrimonial home."

Then, lowering her voice, she added, "Before the Prophet's time, money was paid to the girl's father as if he was selling a commodity! Then Prophet Mohammad changed the Arabic custom and required that the bride money be paid directly to the bride-to-be, instead of her father or male guardian. Unfortunately, what is happening now is not what the Prophet had envisioned."

"Did you get paid directly, Grandma?"

"I was married off at the very young age of nine, and had no say. I had no idea I was even getting married. What did I know about bride money? No, I did not get paid."

Another thought occurred to me. "What about your incurable disease, Grandma?"

Her beautiful face lit up, and smiling mischievously, she replied, "Eventually it did go away."

I was relieved but puzzled. I had so many questions and wanted Grandma Tuba to keep talking.

The only other thing she told me that day was that if a young girl dies a virgin, she would go to heaven. I definitely wanted to go to heaven. But I was no longer a virgin.

~~ ~~ ~~ ~~ ~~

"Maybe we should visit another registrar for my divorce," I suggested to Modar at dinner one night when Grandfather was listening to the evening news and not paying attention to us. I had been living with Grandma Tuba for weeks and the status of my divorce was still unsettled. I felt I couldn't relax until I knew that horrible marriage to Hassan was completely behind me.

"I've already visited two more registrars and was told it is the law," Modar said. "The father must file for the divorce of his minor child."

"Have you heard anything from Hassan or his family?" Grandma Tuba asked Modar. "Has the second wife told Jamileh anything?"

"They're negotiating a settlement with her in-laws to buy Ateesh's freedom," Modar said. "That bastard knows that without his approval or Baba's filing a request we cannot get a divorce. He may end up getting the house we gave them at the wedding."

"What about his addiction to *teriyak*, opium?" I asked. "Why can't we use that?"

"What?" Modar asked.

"I read in the newspaper that there was a case in Tehran's family court in which the judge granted the wife a divorce based on the husband's addictions to drugs," I said.

"I remember, Joon" Grandma Tuba said, "but the bastard won't go for blood work, and without the certified lab results from the hospital, we cannot prove his addiction. Anyway, because you are a minor, we still need Baba to file."

"Why can't he be ordered by the court to go for a drug test?"

Modar and Grandma Tuba both looked at me. Then Modar smiled and said, "Ateesh Joon, I am so proud of you. You are only thirteen and so smart. You are not going to make the same mistakes we made."

Grandma Tuba nudged her to be quiet.

I hoped Modar was right. She had to be.

"Speaking of smartness," Modar said, "Ateesh has to finish high school. Evening classes are going to begin in early fall."

At this, Grandma Tuba laughed loudly and said, "Ready for another fight with your Baba?"

Modar leaned closer to us and whispered so Grandfather wouldn't hear, "As soon as we're done with this divorce, we're probably going to receive marriage proposals. Baba is going to say that Ateesh is too young and beautiful to remain unmarried."

"Ateesh can say she wants to finish school," Grandma Tuba said. "This will buy her time, and then when she is older maybe she can decide if she wants to marry again."

"Ateesh Joon, it is marriage or education," Modar said. "Do you want to become independent from Baba?"

"Oh yes, Modar!" I answered.

"But before anything else, we must get this divorce," Modar said.

That was a wonderful evening. I found myself filled with hope for my future. After dinner, when Modar was leaving, we held each other at the door.

"Modar," I said softly. "Thank you."

"Ateesh Joon," my beautiful modar said as she held my face in her hands, "forgive me for not standing up to your father about your arranged marriage."

Grandma Tuba and I spent the following days chatting, preparing food for Grandfather, and receiving friends at home. I tried to stay busy and away from dark thoughts of my marriage. I filled my mind with thoughts of the future—of an education and independence. It was the middle of the summer, and the aroma of fresh grapes on the vine filled my grandparents' courtyard.

"What are we going to make, Grandma?" I asked. "Can we pick fresh grape leaves and make *dolmeh*?"

"Why not? I will also make some shish kabob for Grandfather. He is a man and must eat meat for protein." Grandma Tuba bent down and kissed my cheek. "I bet right now, in that little head of yours, you are asking why a man should eat meat."

"Yes, why do you always give the best part of our food to him?"

"Well, Ateesh Pareh Joon, dear sparkle of fire, he is the man of the house, so he must get the best of everything. Why don't you pick some fresh leaves, and make sure to pick the large, yet delicate ones. I will go prepare the stuffing. And not another question from you, unless it is about stuffing!"

I ignored her request. "When we have dinner parties, why do men get to eat first, then women and children? Why do I have to be quiet when Grandfather is napping, but not when you are?"

"Where are you, Grandmodar of Ateesh?" Grandfather called out from the other room. "I have brought in three guests for dinner!"

"Why doesn't he call you by your name, Grandma?" I asked impatiently.

"*Baseh! Baseh!*" Grandma Tuba replied. She hurried toward the kitchen, holding her hands to her ears.

I hated when Grandfather brought guests home for dinner unannounced. Now we had to prepare a first-class, five or six course meal for them. But Grandma Tuba told me I wasn't allowed to complain. "It's just one of those things that men do," she explained.

Other than Grandfather's dinner guests, I noticed that fewer visitors were coming by since my arrival, probably to avoid the uncomfortable topic of my divorce. Despite the efforts my family made to keep my divorce quiet, everyone must have heard about it. So Grandma Tuba and I were surprised a few afternoons later when we were sitting outside in the yard having tea and Grandma Tuba's friend, Batul, and her daughter, Farah, came for a visit.

Grandma Tuba, acting as if my presence was nothing out of the ordinary, invited them to sit with us on the garden chairs.

I was beginning to learn that little lies were an important part of being considered grownup.

"Ateesh Joon, please go and get us the *qalyan* and some lemonade," Grandma Tuba said.

It would take me at least twenty minutes to make fresh lemonade and to prepare the *qalyan*, hookah, and I didn't want to miss anything. I hurried inside. First I went to get the *qalyan*. It was kept in the kitchen, clean and ready to be filled with fresh cold water at the bottom. I put a few pieces of charcoal on the stove to get them burning hot. As always I would get Grandma Tuba to put the tobacco on the top portion under hot charcoal, which I was told not to touch. Then I went to the kitchen, where I was relieved to find fresh lemonade. I cut up small cucumbers and arranged them on a plate with fresh mint leaves and lemons. Grandma Tuba would be pleased.

With both hands, I carried a silver tray with four tall glasses of lemonade, a plate of lemons, cucumbers, and mint. To fit everything on the tray, I placed the pastry platter on top of the glasses.

"Modar Bozorg, I think the charcoal is ready," I said. I learned to call her Modar Bozorg in front of company, which is more formal, and means, "great mother."

"Were you afraid you were going to miss something, Ateesh Joon?" Grandma Tuba laughed, knowing full well that was exactly the motivation for my balancing act. Farah and Batul Khanoom laughed with her.

Farah stood up and went into the kitchen. After I put everything down, I followed behind her and watched as she assembled the *qalyan* and placed the charcoal on top.

"Ateesh, why you are living here instead of with your husband?" she asked.

I was caught by surprise. Grandma Tuba always answered such questions.

"I did not love him," I said.

She laughed. "That is your reason? I never heard of that one before! Love comes after marriage. My husband almost killed me on my wedding night, but I love him now."

I stopped arranging the fresh fruit on the serving platter. "Did you say killed?" I asked.

"On my wedding night, after we were done, my husband turned on the light and wiped me with the white cloth. You know, the one that's placed under your hips?"

I nodded.

"He was looking very carefully at it, so I leaned closer to see what he was looking at, and saw there was nothing there. That's when he slapped me really hard and yelled, '*be aberue!*'"

I hated that phrase, "*be aberue.*" It was so unfair that it was used for girls but never to describe a boy's behavior. The white cloth under me on my wedding night was filled with blood but I was called "*be aberue*" on many occasions anyway, like when I told my husband that if he ever touched me again I would kill him. His answer to that was, "Good wives are obedient!"

"Farah," I said softly. "You are not *be aberue.*"

"Oh God, Ateesh, no blood means *be aberue!*"

I didn't say another word.

"My aunt and sister-in-law came running into the room and saw him waving the cloth in front of my face." I figured Farah's aunt was there in place of her modar. Modars were hardly ever present on the wedding night, to avoid any kind of confrontation.

"'No blood?' my aunt said. 'Maybe there is a problem!' She sounded worried. Maybe she thought there was a medical reason, or that I wasn't a virgin.

"My sister-in-law shouted, 'No blood means your bride is not a virgin!' and they all started arguing. My husband was sitting on me, as if he was going to slaughter me like a sheep. He was yelling about the honor of his family. 'I will kill you,' he kept repeating. 'You are nothing but a whore!'

"I was crying and pleading with him, 'I swear I am a virgin! No boy has ever touched me! I swear on the eighth Imam. Please have mercy on me!'

"But nobody listened to me. 'Shut your mouth!' he said, and he put his hands around my neck. My aunt rushed over and tried to pull him off me. His sister came to help, but she looked at me with such anger."

Farah sighed. "Finally, it was decided that I would go to the emergency room for a professional to determine my virginity. My husband reluctantly accepted, and as he released me from his grip, he pulled my hair, forcing my face close to his. Then he threatened to cut my throat."

My head was spinning. He threatened to cut her throat because she wasn't a virgin? What about him? I wanted to ask her. What about his virginity? Why doesn't any of that matter? But I didn't dare say a word.

"I remember trembling as I put on my clothes," she continued. "Instead of the bright, colorful outfit that was purchased by his family for me to wear the morning after our wedding night, my aunt handed me the jeans and blouse that I wore the previous day. I looked at Auntie's face. I looked for hope, but saw only shame."

"So many thoughts were racing through my head. Maybe I wasn't a virgin. But what could've happened to my virginity? Was my husband going to kill me? I was never touched by a boy. I was even afraid to touch myself!

"I saw my family gathered outside the bedroom, with looks of disappointment and shame on their faces. His family looked at me with condemnation. Nobody said a word. I kept my head down and didn't look at anyone. Then the four of us drove to the emergency clinic. My aunt and my sister-in-law walked over to the nurse sitting at the reception desk and whispered something to her. The nurse looked at me, where I was standing behind my husband. It seemed as if everyone was looking at me. I could feel them thinking 'this bride is not a virgin. How could that *jendeh khanoom*, slut, do this to her family? She deserves to die.' And I did want to die. Right there."

I knew how she felt. I remembered thinking about death on my own wedding night. I couldn't imagine being shamed like that in front of all those people.

"So then what happened?" I asked.

"There was a nurse there," she said, "She placed her hand on my shoulder and smiled kindly at me, as if she didn't know the reason I was there. I walked with her into the examination room, and auntie and my sister-in-law followed behind. The nurse handed me a sheet and told me to remove my clothes. I looked at my aunt and sister-in-law to see if they would turn around. They didn't. It seemed the only compassion and kindness I was going to receive was from the nurse, who was a stranger to me. I removed my clothes and lay on the cold examination table with the sheet around me.

"I closed my eyes and silently recited verses from the Quran: God is merciful, God is great, God is forgiving, God is—until I felt the doctor's cold hand force my legs apart. It took everything in me not to scream or cry.

"Then I heard the doctor's voice, 'She is still a virgin. The mucus wall has not been pierced. It is unusually thick and just needs stronger penetration. Go and bring in the groom.'"

"I thanked God, opened my eyes and thought, 'I am not going to be killed. *Allaho Akbar!*

"My husband came in and the doctor repeated, 'She is still a virgin. If you wish to send her back I could give you a new certificate of virginity.'

"My aunt and sister-in-law shook their heads, and one of them told the doctor, 'Bite your tongue. It is sinful to send back a virgin bride.'

"My husband handed me my clothes. 'Let my wife have privacy,' he demanded. As he led everyone to the exit, the doctor whispered something to my husband with a wink, and a smile appeared on my husband's face.

"All I could think was, '*Allaho Akbar!*'

"When I walked out of the room, I saw my aunt smiling proudly. Everyone in the waiting room seemed happy. As we passed through, I heard a few wedding wishes, '*Mobarak basheh.*'

"We walked out of the hospital together, my husband in front like a soldier having won a war!"

Farah took a long puff at the *qalyan*, looked straight into my eyes and said, "Now you see what I went through, Ateesh. I would have been killed if the doctor couldn't prove I was a virgin."

I didn't know what to say. My husband was a monster, too, but the difference between myself and Farah was that there was no way I could say I loved him.

"Farah, are you talking or making *qalyan*?" Batul Khanoom's voice interrupted. "Are you smoking it yourself? Bring it out right now."

"Ateesh," Farah said, as she placed her hand on my arm, "please don't tell anybody I told you this. My modar thinks the fact that I did not bleed right away is not normal and somehow is not a good thing."

I managed to nod my head.

When we sat down with Grandma Tuba and Batul Khanoom, Farah took more tobacco and placed it in a small round opening above the hot charcoal at the top of the *qalyan*. Taking the hose into her mouth, she inhaled deeply. I watched the smoke fill the tube, and watched as it came out of her mouth in the shape of rings. Exhaling contentedly, Farah passed it to Grandma Tuba, then sat back in her chair, and looked at me.

"Farah Joon, *mobarakeh, mobarakeh,*" said Grandma Tuba after a long inhale. "Ateesh, did Farah tell you she was pregnant?"

"Pregnant?" I tried not to show a reaction.

"Yes, pregnant!" said Batul Khanoom. "Isn't that what you girls were talking about?"

I nodded. "Yes, pregnancy." I looked at Farah, who was taking another puff of the *qalyan,* and I said, "We were talking about tobacco and its harm on a baby."

"Have you thought of names?" Grandma Tuba asked.

"My husband said we have to choose a boy's name because it has to be a boy," Farah said. "He does not want a girl."

"He is right," Batul Khanoom added. "The first one has to be a boy. After the first child, then daughters are welcome."

Grandma Tuba's eyes questioned my silence.

I felt sick to my stomach. I had to get out of there. Noticing some empty glasses, I went to get the pitcher of lemonade. By the time I came out, the talk had changed to other topics.

～～ ～～ ～～ ～～ ～～

"Do men also have to remain virgins until they marry?" I asked Grandma Tuba later that evening, as I helped her clean the *qalyan.* "Do they get killed if they aren't?"

"If God wanted men to remain virgins until they married, he would have given them hymens too," Grandma Tuba said.

"God makes all these decisions?" I asked.

She shook her head at me. "Farah told you about her wedding night, didn't she? Did she tell you how close she came to death?"

I nodded.

"Do you still question the way things are, Ateesh?"

"Would Farah really have been killed if she wasn't a virgin?" I asked.

"Yes, she would have been killed. It has happened many times. *Mardom chi megan,* Ateesh. Haven't you heard this? What people perceive is all that matters."

"What does that mean?"

37

"Women are considered the face of the family honor, and if *mardom* come to know that she has broken the rule of chastity, it is the end of the family's honor. Killing her supposedly cleanses the stain. I know it is painful, but it is the reality of our lives."

In the past, before I was married, we talked about *Mardom chi megan*. Grandma Tuba told me the tragic story of Masumeh, the daughter of one of her neighbors. Masumeh was a beautiful young girl and an excellent dancer. People would watch her body move in awe at family gatherings. She was fifteen years old, and had four brothers who watched and guarded her every move. When she was caught talking over the phone with one of the neighborhood boys, her brothers decided Masumeh needed to be taught a lesson. They cut out her tongue!

At the time, I thought Grandma Tuba was exaggerating to scare me, but now, several years later, after hearing Farah's story, I knew she was not.

"Such violence is not sanctioned by the Quran, Ateesh," Grandma Tuba said, perhaps, as I thought then, to comfort me. Years later I learned she was right. "Those who say it are following the interpretation of bad practitioners, not the Quran. These are not the words of God. You have to read the Quran for yourself to learn that God is our protector." Then she recited the verse on kindness and justice:

O Mankind
We created you
From a single (pair)
Of a male and a female
And made you into
Nations and tribes,
That ye may recognize
One another
(Not that ye may Despise each other).
Verily, the most honored of you
In the sight of GOD
Is the best in conduct
(49:13)

"You will find out for yourself that not everything in life is as you wish," Grandma Tuba said. "However hard it might be, when it comes to religion, sometimes you have to accept what wise elders tell you, even if you disagree with them. Do you want to be labeled a crazy young woman questioning God's Prophet?"

"Oh no, Modar Bozorg! I believe in God and the Prophet from within me." Tears began to well in my eyes. "But you told me that forgiveness is one of God's ninety-nine virtues. I do not think God is vengeful. God will forgive our mistakes. To stone a woman to death for what people perceive as misbehaving is unjust. God has to be just or God cannot rule people!"

Grandma Tuba pulled me close to her chest, caressed my hair, and kissed my head.

"*Joonam*, I do not understand why you are so eager to learn about such painful subjects. You will never face such a situation in life. Your marriage and divorce are legitimate. You are a good girl. I will shut *mardom's* mouth!" Soothed by Grandma Tuba's touch, I fell asleep in her lap.

While asleep, I dreamt I was at the corner market talking and laughing with a group of boys. It felt as normal as it did before my eleventh birthday and my marriage. It didn't feel forbidden or strange. I felt at ease with them, flipping my long hair from side to side. Then, in the distance I heard the deep, disapproving voice of Grandma Tuba. "Ateesh, are you talking to boys?"

I told the boys to run away. When Grandma Tuba approached me, I asked her, "What if nobody sees the girl talking to boys, Grandma? Should she be killed?"

"Perhaps not," she said, as she looked directly into my eyes, "but these things have a way of becoming public."

"So, Grandma, it is for the public that she gets…"

I was awakened by Grandma Tuba's gentle kisses, "Wake up, Ateesh *pareh*, you are asking questions even in your sleep!"

I was so relieved that she hadn't really caught me talking to boys.

~~ ~~ ~~ ~~ ~~

Even though Grandma Tuba didn't approve of Grandma Jamileh's ways, she let me visit her often. I always had fun with Grandma Jamileh. When I was younger, she would take me to Cinema Iran, a movie house owned by a friend of Baba's, Aqa Shahpareh. Since we always got in for free, Grandma Jamileh would often take me more than once a week. The movies were usually Persian or Indian, and once in a while, Western. The Indian films were my favorite. There was singing and dancing, romance and love, death, friendship, and betrayal. Even though they were tragic stories, they had happy endings. Every half hour the vendor would pass through with Coca-Cola and different sweets and nuts, and Grandma Jamileh always bought me something.

After my bad marriage, I could have used the movies with their happy endings, but shortly after my divorce, the cinema burned down. We didn't go out as much then anyway, since I was being hidden from public view.

The last movie I saw there was *Ten Commandments*. It was the longest movie I had ever seen. Grandma Tuba loved it because it was full of religious historical facts, which confirmed her belief that Prophet Abraham was the grandfather of Islam.

I had fun at Grandma Jamileh's house, and often got my favorite dish there: A sweet and sour dish made with ground lamb shaped into hamburger-sized patties. Usually we sat on Grandma Jamileh's comfortable day bed in a small parlor with many windows that revealed her tremendous garden. Grandma Jamileh was well-read and had memorized thousands of stories and poems from renowned writers and poets. Her favorite book was *Shahnameh*, written by Ferdosy, the great Persian historian and poet, around 1000 A.D, which became the national epic. The *Shahnameh* relates the mystical past of the nation, from the creation of the world to the Islamic conquest of Iran in the seventh century. It took Ferdosy about thirty-two years to write it.

One day while I was visiting Grandma Jamileh, she let me play with her hair and tweeze her full eyebrows. I had been asking my grandmodars a lot of questions about their lives, and today I asked Grandma Jamileh about my grandfather, whom I never knew.

"Your grandfather, Rahim, was a good husband and a good father," she said sadly. "The day I received the news of his death, I had no idea what to do. I had four children and was all alone. My family was from Kermanshah, and they disowned me after I married your grandfather without their permission."

I couldn't believe my ears. Grandma Jamileh married without her family's permission? I wanted to hear more about that! Then I realized how sad it must have been when he passed away and she was left to raise her children all by herself.

"His father was the village chief in Daqda-Abad, in the state of Hamadan," she said. "He ordered me to come to the village with the children, so I collected our belongings and followed him. They handled everything for me."

"What were they like?" I asked.

She shrugged. "They were okay. Very religious. Too religious for me, but I had no choice but to do what I was told. I was powerless.

"They decided to bring Rahim's body home and have a large funeral for him. After all, he was the eldest son of the chief of the village. At first, they told me it was not Islamic for me, as a woman, to attend his funeral."

"Why?" I asked.

"I don't know the religious justifications," Grandma Jamileh said. "You should ask Tuba Khanoom. But I rebelled, Ateesh. In the end, they could not stop me. Islamic or not, I was going. And let me tell you this! A woman, Hager, the modar of Ishmael, founded the origins of the city of Mecca. I heard this on the radio from a Moslem scholar. So, if a woman is the founder of the house of God, it doesn't make sense to forbid a woman from going to her own husband's funeral. Remember, Joon, things have to make sense, especially when it comes to religion. Just because it is claimed to be from the Quran does not mean we cannot question its misinterpretation."

I nodded in agreement. She sounded so strong and independent. It made me proud.

"I lived with them for the next ten years," she said. "I was required to be with them at all times. Ateesh, your grandfather and I were not religious at all. We even had Jewish friends that we shared meals with and confided in. But my in-laws were very religious and were raising my children to be religious. I didn't like it, but I was powerless."

"Grandma Tuba has Jewish friends too," I said.

"Oh, Tuba Khanoom!" She said, dismissing Grandma Tuba's religious beliefs before she went on. "My father-in-law was a kind man, but controlling. He kept insisting that I marry your grandfather's younger brother so that I would continue to live in his house. He told me because I was no longer his daughter-in-law, I was *haram*, forbidden, to him. He wanted me to marry my brother-in-law in order to remain in the pool of people who are not *haram* to each other."

"So did you?" I asked.

"No. I didn't want to marry after your grandfather passed away."

"Why not, Grandma? Is it bad to marry again?"

"No, child. No. That is not what I said. A woman should marry only if she wants to and not because she needs the shadow of a man over her head. My in-laws believed I must have a man to keep me from committing, *zina*, sin. They said, '*mardom chi feker mekonand*. What are people going to think?' Meaning I should remarry to keep peoples' mouths closed."

They were just like Baba! I thought.

"I asked my father-in-law to allow me and my children to go back to the city. I wanted to open a business, anything to be financially independent from him. 'You can go,' he said. 'But the children will remain with me. If you work it will bring shame to me. People will think I am not providing for you.'

"As a young widow, I was not to talk to any man. All of my female friends had to meet my father-in-law's standards. My life became my four children, and I was content with that, but I still desired to escape his control."

I nodded. I knew that feeling! I was still waiting to hear more about how Grandma Jamileh married a man that she wanted to marry.

"How did you and Grandfather meet?" I asked.

At my question, her face lit up. "Well, he was from the village and I was from the city with some Qajar blood on my modar's side. We met at the rug market in Hamadan. I was with my parents and he was with family as well. It was love at first sight. Our families couldn't stop us, and we had a good ten years of marriage before he died suddenly of tuberculosis."

Their families couldn't stop them from getting married! They didn't listen to anyone but themselves. I admired her so much for this.

"Eventually, your father, Azim, turned eighteen. I started planning to take my children and move here to Abadan where I belonged. Your father knew of my plans. He also wanted to move here to the city, go to the university to become an engineer like his father."

"My father, an engineer?" I asked, surprised.

"Oh yes. Village life never really suited him. He had many dreams of education and success, Ateesh. He wanted to come here, where we used to live with your grandfather. I told your father that the idea must come from him or his grandfather would refuse to allow us to move away."

I never saw a side of my father that rebelled against authority, and was shocked to learn that he did not always want to run a restaurant. For the first time, I saw a likeness between us, but I kept this to myself.

"To my surprise, your father's request was accepted and my father-in-law asked me to follow along to look after him. I pleaded to take the rest of my children. Azim finally convinced his grandfather to allow all of us to live in the city, but only under Grandfather's close supervision. He provided us with monthly support and made unannounced visits until he died, shortly after our move. But in his will my children were disinherited."

"What does that mean?" I asked.

"It meant things became harder for us. Your father had to quit his classes at the university and take a job at a restaurant. Eventually, I opened a bakery, first at home and then outside. It took a few hard years before your father decided to quit the university and start his own restaurant."

"You became a real businesswoman, Grandma?!" I asked in excitement.

"Sure, why not? Prophet Mohammad's first wife Khadigeh was a successful businesswoman when they met. She was a widow and much older than he was. She hired the Prophet to work for her in the early sixth century. Of course, my religious in-laws never would have approved, but the way I saw it, my life here was like what I knew of the Prophet's examples."

I had to ask, "Modar Bozorg, did you ever fall in love again after Grandfather's death?"

She frowned and said, "No."

"Did you ever think of having a male friend?"

"Ateesh, what has gotten into you? Are you going to make me beautiful or what? Enough about men and love and get busy with those tweezers!" Then she paused and said, "I did think of marriage again, but nobody was good enough compared to your grandfather."

Her eyes glistened, and I knew I had asked too many questions.

After composing herself, she said, "If there is one thing you can learn from this, Ateesh, it is that you do not need to have the shadow of a man over your head, no matter what people say. I heard it all the time. *Mardom chi megan!* Over and over! To hell with *mardom!* Where were they while I was suffering? I devoted myself to the business and raising my children. I lived my life the way I wanted."

"You are the best, Grandma. Thank you for telling me these things," I said.

"*Khoshgelam kon,* make me beautiful!" She said with a wink.

To that we both laughed. Poor Grandma Jamileh. I kissed her chubby cheek and continued to pluck her eyebrows.

I drifted off to sleep that night with thoughts of Grandma Jamileh running her own business and refusing to marry. The thoughts comforted and soothed me. I was sleeping so much better than I did when I was living with my husband. I shivered at the thought of him. It must have been nice for Grandma Jamileh to sleep with a man whose touch didn't repulse her.

~~ ~~ ~~ ~~ ~~

The next day Grandma Tuba and I went to the *masjid,* where one of Grandma Tuba's younger friends, Sedikeh, joined us after prayers. She was in her mid-twenties and had three young children. I overheard someone say she was recently divorced from the same man for the third time!

"Does that mean they visited the registrar's office three times?" I asked Grandma Tuba, remembering my own dreadful visit.

"Why don't you walk with Grandfather back to the house?" she said. "Sedikeh and her husband will be coming over this afternoon. Put some fresh fruit on the table and don't forget the pistachios."

"But—"

"You will find out later, I promise," she interrupted. "It's about their irrevocable divorce."

"Irrevocable? What does that mean?"

"Not another word here in the *masjid*," she said sternly as she put her hand gently over my lips. "Now go and get Grandfather before he calls us."

They were coming over to discuss their "irrevocable divorce," and we were serving tea and fruit as if we were celebrating. I didn't understand and could hardly control myself.

I joined Grandfather at the main gate. "Grandfather," I asked, "do you know Sedikeh Khanoom from the *masjid*?"

"No," he said.

"Are you sure, Grandfather?" I prodded. "She is a tall, skinny woman with three rowdy children. They came to our sermon at home last year."

"Oh, them!" Grandfather said. "You should have said that! I know those children! They ate all the sweets that Grandma put on the table, and anything they didn't eat, they threw on the rug!"

He stopped walking, looked at me and asked, "Why are you asking? Grandma has not invited them to the house again, has she? I told her not to! What is she doing at the *masjid* that kept her from walking with us, anyway? Your grandmodar should look after me and my needs more. She spends too much time with all those women who have problems."

Grandfather went on like this for a while. He was no longer accustomed to having small children around the house and had little tolerance for them. Sometimes he himself acted like a baby. He needed to be looked after all the time. Grandma Tuba took care of him like he was sick or something. Sometimes it angered me that she pampered him so much.

"I don't want those children in the house!" Grandfather said.

"I heard Sedikeh Khanoom telling Grandma how she was ashamed of her children's behavior in your house," I told him.

"She should be!" he said. "Well, at least she is realizing it herself."

I had no idea if the children were coming or not, but I didn't want Grandfather to ruin this by giving Grandma Tuba a hard time.

Grandfather acted tough, but it was more of an act than anything else. He was so dependent on Grandma Tuba and couldn't do anything without her. I tried to think of a time he did anything on his own. He went to his pension place once a month to pick up his retirement check. Then he would hand it to Grandma Tuba, who in return gave him a small portion. That was his pocket money. He used his money to buy cigarettes, newspapers, and a lottery ticket. "Ateesh," he would say as he handed me the ticket, "this is the winning ticket and we will share it." We never won anything.

Also, at the end of every year when it was time to pay *zekat*, alms, Grandma Tuba would calculate the required *zekat* for the *masjid*. Then Grandfather would take it to the nearby *masjid* they belonged to and give it to the Imam.

Other than that, Grandma Tuba did everything herself, though she let him think Grandfather was in charge.

"You are the man of the house! What would we do without you?" Grandma always told him.

⋀⋀ ⋀⋀ ⋀⋀ ⋀⋀ ⋀⋀

Once we were home, I raced around the house and prepared everything as Grandma Tuba had instructed me to.

Grandma Tuba and three of her friends arrived home about an hour after we did. Then Sedikeh Khanoom and her husband arrived. Shortly after that, a man in his fifties came to the house. He was short and bulky with a funny mustache that twisted on both sides. He looked sort of happy, as if he were getting married. I wondered who would marry such a funny-looking man. I had never seen him among my grandparents' friends, and wondered who he was.

I walked over to where he sat and asked if he wanted tea. As he nodded yes, I followed his gaze to Sedikeh. She had her head slightly bent, avoiding any possible eye contact; and she looked sad and withdrawn from the rest of the people.

As I poured the tea, Sedikeh's husband and my grandfather came to sit by the strange man, leaving Grandma Tuba standing by herself. I quickly went to join her.

"Grandma, what is going on?" I asked.

"According to the Quran," she said quietly, "when a man divorces his wife three times, and then decides to take her back, he cannot do it so easily. I do not like what I am going to tell you, but you see that man over there with Grandfather, with the funny mustache?"

Without looking in the direction she was pointing, I nodded.

"Sedikeh's husband hired that man to marry his wife for one night. The morning after the consummation of the marriage, the new husband was to divorce her so Sedikeh's first husband could remarry her again."

"What?" I blurted out. I wasn't sure if I heard Grandma Tuba correctly. "Sedikeh Khanoom and her husband cannot be husband and wife again unless she marries that man?" I stopped, took a long breath and exclaimed, "This is too difficult for me to understand, Grandma."

Grandma Tuba explained that the second husband is called a *mohalal*. He gets paid to marry a woman for a short duration, usually one night. This has become a profession for some men.

I remembered the registrar, when he asked me to be his *siqeh*. *Mohalal* and *siqeh* seemed very similar to me.

In Sedikeh's case, after the marriage was consummated with the *mohalal*, he refused to divorce her the next day, as agreed upon. The funny-looking man had enjoyed the one-night union and negated his verbal agreement with the first husband. He was told by the community to honor the agreement but he said, "I quit this profession. I have found the wife I've been looking for."

The community loudly disapproved and told him it was not right to renege on the agreement. He defended himself, saying that based on the interpretation of the verse, he could divorce if he wished, but he did not have to.

"Is he right about that?" I asked.

"I believe the verse in the Quran has been interpreted that it is up to the wife and *mohalal* to make their union permanent," Grandma Tuba answered.

Grandfather called Grandma Tuba and she went to join him. Their three friends joined in as well, and Sedikeh Khanoom was left sitting by herself. She obviously wasn't included in whatever negotiation was going on. I wondered how she felt about that. I wondered how she felt about sleeping with another man. Had she been given a choice in the arrangement? Probably not. Did she even want to go back to her first husband?

Sedikeh looked up at that moment and caught me staring at her. I quickly turned away and looked for something to busy myself with. A little while later, when she was still sitting by herself, I walked over and sat down next to her. "Can I ask you a question, Sedikeh Khanoom?" I asked.

"Yes," she shyly responded, "and just call me Sedikeh."

"But Grandma told me to call all her friends Khanoom," I said.

She shook her head, "No, that's okay. Please ask me your question."

"Do you want to stay with the *mohalal*?"

At this she smiled brightly, as if I asked the question she had been hoping someone would ask her.

"I had no idea a husband could be so nice!" she gushed. "Ateesh, swear to God you will not tell anyone?"

"I promise."

"Not even your grandma!"

Reluctantly I agreed, even though I felt guilty keeping secrets from Grandma Tuba.

She told me that Grandma Tuba had been called by both families to bring Sedikeh Khanoom and the *mohalal* to their senses. Being an elder in the community, Grandma Tuba was looked upon like a family judge.

Sedikeh felt ashamed, but she had experienced a relationship with the *mohalal* that she had never had with her husband.

I thought of my own husband and wondered if I, too, would ever experience something different than what I had experienced with him.

I admired Sedikeh for finding happiness with the *mohalal* when she couldn't find it with her husband. "You should stay where you're happy," I said.

But she would have to wait for others to decide her future.

Grandma Tuba tried not to judge them too harshly, especially in front of me, but she said that what they had done had been unheard of in recent years.

"After all," Grandma Tuba said, as she turned to Sedikeh's husband, "it was your fault. This shall serve as a lesson for men not to divorce their wives in such a hasty manner. You should be afraid of God."

The room was suddenly quiet. Grandma Tuba had crossed a boundary in scolding a man in front of his wife. I was so proud of her and I knew the Prophet would have been also.

After much discussion it was decided that Sedikeh Khanoom would remain with the *mohalal*. The funny thing was that nobody ever asked Sedikeh if she wanted to go back to her first husband but me. It was just assumed.

Later, when Modar was at the house, Grandma Tuba told her what had happened with Sedikeh Khanoom.

"Do you remember the Faramands?" Modar asked.

"Yes."

"They practice the same thing but they aren't Moslems."

The Farahmands were Zoroastrians, Parsees. Grandma Jamileh had told me that all Persians were Parsees before Arabs invaded our country.

"Mrs. Farahmand's pregnancy was the result of her brief marriage to a *mohalal*," Modar said. "Mr. Farahmand was not the baby's biological father because he couldn't father a baby. After she got pregnant, the *mohalal* divorced her. Thereafter she remarried Mr. Farahmand.

"In Sedikeh Khanoom's case, the goal was to allow the husband to get his wife back after a one-night union with the *mohalal*," Grandma Tuba said sternly. "For Zoroastrians, it is different. It is a service offered by the community to a husband who is infertile. Mrs. Farahmand's husband chose the man to father his child.

"Either way, it is the husband who chooses!" Modar said.

"You sound like Ateesh now!" Grandma Tuba said. "What is it with you two? Don't you realize it is easier to accept the way things are?"

Modar and I didn't answer.

"Well if you are determined to change it," Grandma Tuba continued, "then do it carefully, with caution. Don't stir up too much at once. Look for the good. There is plenty of it!"

"Let us now talk about Ateesh's school," Modar said, obviously wanting to change the subject.

Since my divorce, I had been expected to remain invisible, especially to my father. I remained in Grandma Tuba's house and went outside only with her. Now that summer had passed, it was almost time to start school, and I really wanted to go.

"Are you ready to talk to your Baba?" Modar asked me.

I nodded. I was ready. I decided I was not going to back down from men and let them make all of my decisions.

~~ ~~ ~~ ~~ ~~

"Why do you want to go back to school?" Baba asked me.

"Why not?" I asked.

"You are a divorcee!" he exclaimed. "You should not be out there in the public eye. What will people say?"

"People will say" I shouted, "that here is a girl whose father arranged her marriage to an abusive husband!"

Before I could say more, he slapped me. I staggered backward a bit, but I still stood strong. I was determined not to accept blame for something I had no control over. I wanted to go to school and make sure I would never again find myself in an abusive marriage. Someway, somehow, I was going to make decisions for myself, and I would follow through on those decisions one step at a time. I had Modar and my grandmas to help me.

Later that evening, Grandma Tuba came upstairs to tell me that Baba had finally agreed to let me go to school, under two conditions. One was that either Grandma Tuba or Modar ride with me in a taxi to school and back, to make sure I entered and exited the building safely. The other condition was that I start wearing a chador.

"He wants me to wear a chador?" I asked in disbelief.

She nodded. "Yes," she said, as she held it up.

"Modar Bozorg, I do not want to be invisible. I didn't do anything wrong! What should I be ashamed of?"

"Just put it on," she prodded gently.

"But even Modar does not cover! Why should I? You are just like Baba! He wants me to disappear!"

She pulled me close and held me gently for a few minutes until I calmed down. Then she sat next to me, held my face in her hands, and looked me straight in the eyes.

"Ateesh *Pareh Joon*, dear sparkle of fire, listen to me carefully; many times we women use the chador to be able to move freely everywhere without being seen and harassed. This is an advantage for those who wear it. Once you put it on, you become one of many. Men cannot see you, but you can see everyone. Do not be afraid to become invisible. It offers many advantages, especially for a beautiful young woman like yourself."

I thought about what she said. "Does that mean if I cover I can go wherever I want?"

"No, my child. But I want you to see that some situations can be turned into advantages. Look at it from a different angle."

"Is that the reason the Prophet's wife was covered?"

"Yes," she said. "The Prophet used to receive many male visitors from all over, unannounced, right at his house. The first of a series of verses on covering was directed only to his wives."

"Wives?" I interrupted.

She placed her hand over my mouth.

"It is a clever idea, and it was actually for this reason that the verses on veiling were revealed. Prophet Mohammed wanted to protect women who were out in public without a man. Women from good families always covered to remain anonymous," she said. "No more arguments with Baba. Let him think, by covering your body, you are obeying his wishes."

I nodded and finally gave in. "Okay," I said. "I'll wear it."

As Grandma Tuba placed a beautiful, black, silk cloth with large, inlaid flower patterns on me, she said, "This chador makes you even more beautiful. I think we should get you a plain cotton one with patches, something like Cinderella wore!"

Before I could protest, she said, "Just kidding!"

The next day, Modar took me to register for school. I felt anxious as we sat across from the school official.

"A divorcee or a widower cannot attend regular day schooling," the woman said. "Young girls like you who have experienced matrimonial life cannot mix with girls who are still innocent."

Modar shifted uncomfortably in the chair next to me.

"You can attend only evening classes. You are lucky that you are even allowed to continue your studies," the woman continued.

"We are here to register my daughter for school," Modar said. "Not to listen to a sermon!"

Dealing with Baba and school officials hadn't been easy, but I was finally registered for school. I couldn't wait to get started.

There were a handful of other girls in my classes who were in my situation. Some, but not all, were being controlled as carefully as I was. They all had been married before, which was the main reason they were attending evening classes.

"What about men who have been married before?" I sarcastically wondered aloud one night at home, knowing the answer well. "Do they also have to be restricted to evening classes?"

"Oh, Ateesh Joon, not everything has to pass your equality test!" Grandma Tuba said. "But to answer your question, no, I don't think they have evening school for boys. Boys are always older than the girls they marry, and after they divorce, they are no longer of school age. So, don't worry, Ateesh. There is no discrimination here!"

Grandma Tuba laughed as she finished her sentence. I didn't laugh with her. Sometimes I couldn't understand how Grandma Tuba could find humor in such things as this. Girls and boys should marry in their own age group. Baba was ten years older than Modar. Same with Grandma Tuba and Grandfather. On average, husbands are ten to fifteen years older than their wives. How strange and sad, I thought.

In one of my classes, there was a beautiful girl named Behrook, whose husband had died in a car accident. She was a few years older than I, but we were in the same grade because she had stopped attending school during her marriage. She was friendly, and we enjoyed talking between classes.

When Behrook told me that she was having sex with our Arabic teacher, Mr. Shamsy, I literally fell to the ground.

"Are you crazy?" I asked. "You could be killed! You could get pregnant! You could go to hell and burn!"

"Don't tell me you don't want to have sex!" she said. "You know you do! Once a girl experiences sex, she cannot control her desire to have more."

I thought of sex with my husband, and shook my head in disgust.

"Tell me, Ateesh," she insisted. "I won't tell your family. I promise." Then in a quiet, raspy voice, she whispered, "Don't you wish to be touched by a man?"

"No!" I said, and then turned and walked away.

I didn't want to talk about this with her. She seemed so at ease in the very same world in which I felt so stifled and constrained. Why? Was it because she was older that she was more comfortable with sex? Or maybe sex is different when a woman loves her husband. Was I even a woman? I was thirteen. Sometimes I was referred to as a child and other times a woman. I was so confused.

Lying in bed that night, I kept thinking about her question: "Don't you wish to be touched by a man?"

My husband of six months never asked me if I wanted to be touched. It was never a choice of mine, but an obligation that came with marriage. No, I did not miss that.

Then I wondered if it would be different if I was touched by another man. I thought of Sedikeh and the *mohalal*, the way she gushed and blushed when she spoke of him. I thought the experience must have been good! Even though I was no virgin, I was still like most girls my age. Whenever I felt a hint of desire, I repressed it. A shiver took over my body as I allowed myself, perhaps for the first time since my divorce, to feel desire, if only for a moment.

"Shame on you, Ateesh," I said to myself. "After what you have done, you are *be aberue* to think about other men!"

A battle ensued between my conscience and body.

"I am not *be aberue!*"

Other than school, the only place I was allowed to go was to the *masjid*. It was one of the very few places women could go by themselves, and I always looked forward to going. For me, it was a chance to socialize.

Every Thursday night, as well as all the nights during *Muharram Ramadan*, school was closed, and I walked to the *masjid* along with Grandma Tuba and a few of her friends. Even now, when I hear the beautiful Arabic lyrics of the *muzzin* calling the faithful to prayers, I stop to listen, just as I did then. It makes me think of Grandma Tuba and the many women with whom we walked. From these women, I learned as much as I did at school. I saw them all as my teachers.

Batul Khanoom always joined us en route to the *masjid*, along with Zaynab Khanoom, another friend of theirs. Whenever we saw them come through the alley, Grandma Tuba and I would slow down for them, as Grandfather continued on without us.

As always, I trailed behind them and listened.

"He put his fist right through one of our walls!" Zaynab said one night. "When I bandaged him up later, I told him he deserved all the cuts and bruises he got, for going after his wife like an enemy on the street. I was liberal in applying alcohol to those cuts. You should have seen his face!"

The others laughed at her cleverness. Zaynab's husband could be cruel, but what he dispensed with his fists, she usually matched with her merciless tongue.

Grandma Tuba usually advised women like Zaynab to be more patient and kind to their husbands. Tonight, I caught her smiling at Zaynab.

Batul Khanoom also suffered from abuse. She was beaten by both her husband and her grownup son. Every time her son misbehaved, her husband blamed her, and every time her son didn't get his way with his father, she was blamed too. Batul was sandwiched between two abusive relationships. Now her daughter Farah also was in an abusive marriage. The three of these women, Zaynab, Batul, and Farah, all spoke of this as if it were normal.

"*Dandon ru jigar mizareh ama hechi nemegeh*, bite your tongue and don't say anything." I heard this phrase often on those walks. It was a phrase I had also heard from Modar during my marriage. In line with such exhortations, women remained in abusive relationships. Perhaps they were simply resigned, and laughter helped them cope. I sensed that if leaving their marriages were an option, they would have walked out a long time ago. But it wasn't, and I felt both blessed and guilty at the same time that Modar and Grandmodar were fighting to give me some options in my life.

Muharram commemorates the martyrdom of Imam Hussein, a grandson of the Prophet. During the seventh century of Arabia, he was slain in Kufa, Iraq, in a bloody battle between him and the religious leader, which took place on the plains of Karbala. This event contributed to the split of Islam into Shi'i and Sunni sects, intensifying an already existing division. After the usual prayers, loud outcries, and beatings on the chest by the more orthodox Moslems, food and refreshments were served.

While I was usually fairly attentive during the sermons, today I was thinking about the small gathering that was to take place at Grandma Tuba's house after the service. I began to welcome and love these gatherings, and I was especially excited about this one, because Grandma Tuba let me help prepare the rice.

Making saffron-flavored rice is considered an art in Iran. I had been watching Grandma Tuba and her helper, Naneh Fatemeh, for quite some time, but this was the first time I was supervised in its preparation. We chose long grain rice, *dom seeya*, from an area near the Caspian Sea. First, we soaked it in plenty of salted water. The next day, I drained the water and poured the rice into a large pot of rapidly boiling water. Grandma Tuba and Naneh Fatemeh stood next to me the entire time, making sure I could handle it.

Grandma Tuba had purchased sweets from the sweet shop that morning, and she had let me arrange them on large, beautifully hand-decorated plates. Naneh Fatemeh was making a few other dishes that Grandma Tuba had requested. I tasted each dish, and based on my liking, she added more herbs or spices. Grandma Tuba always said that receiving guests at home was a privilege. *Mehmoonhabibeh Khodast,* a guest is God's gift. I was taught to treat guests with the utmost hospitality and generosity, even those who came unannounced.

As soon as the sermon ended, small children began running between the men's section in the front and the women's section in the back, moving the curtain that separated the sexes.

I peered in to catch a glimpse of the men's side. This was one of the few instances during which girls might catch a glimpse of boys or even talk to them and arrange secret meetings.

Decorated with many fine Persian rugs and exquisite chandeliers, it was much more colorful and elegant than the women's side.

That's when I saw Behrook. She was walking toward the men's section.

I hadn't seen her since we'd been out of school on holiday, and I wanted to invite her to Grandma Tuba's house. I asked Grandma Tuba to pack my prayer rug, rosary beads, and prayer stone in my bundle for me so I could catch up with her.

As I hurried toward her, I nearly collided into Grandfather as he came out of the washroom, swearing loudly. Swearing in the house of God was a sinful act, and Grandfather knew it.

"What happened?" I asked him.

"Nothing," he replied angrily. "Where is your Grandmodar, and why are you alone in the men's section? You cannot trust anyone, anymore. This is the end of humanity, and the twelfth Imam, Mehdi, has to appear."

To invoke the presence of the twelfth Imam means something immoral enough to shock the conscience of humanity has taken place. As Grandfather walked toward the hallway leading to the women's prayer section, he gestured for me to come along with him. I turned back to find Behrook, but she was gone.

Grandfather then opened his prayer abaya and brought it close to his right side where I was walking, signaling me to get close to him. Then he placed part of his abaya on my shoulder. That's when I caught a glimpse of Hajji Asghar, an acquaintance of my grandparents, hurrying out of the washroom. A boy, even younger than I was, came out behind him.

Grandfather's face was red with anger as he mumbled some swear words under his breath. I didn't dare ask any questions. I would have to ask Grandma Tuba later.

Back at the dinner party, my saffron rice was a great success! Preparing a good rice dish is also often jokingly associated with the readiness of a girl for marriage. Preparing rice and other delicious, colorful dishes showed a wife's ability to keep her husband satisfied at home.

Traditionally, Persians sit cross-legged on beautiful rugs as they eat. A white cotton tablecloth, *sofreh*, is spread in the middle of the eating room, and everybody sits around it. Plates, glasses, and utensils are placed all around the tablecloth, and food, salads, bread, and soft drinks are spread throughout the middle. I was proud, and I knew Grandma Tuba and Modar were too. Even Grandfather, who was typically stingy with praise, commended me on my hard work.

Later that night, after everyone left, I did my homework as Grandma Tuba and Grandfather were having tea and listening to the evening news on the radio. They spoke in hushed voices, and I knew they were talking about what had upset Grandfather so much at the *masjid*. I became unable to concentrate on my homework. My curiosity was brewing.

"That *be pedar* had taken the boy…"

I couldn't hear the rest of the sentence. I moved closer to the room where they were sitting and stood quietly in the doorway.

"Ateesh should never go to the men's section," Grandfather said.

"Never again, I assure you Hajji," Grandmodar said softly. That's when she looked up and saw me. "Ateesh Joon, time to go to bed." Her eyes signaled me to leave right away.

"Okay, Grandmodar," I said, and left the room quickly.

When Grandma Tuba came in to kiss me goodnight, I asked her to tell me what had happened to make Grandfather so upset. "Grandfather swore in the *masjid* and invoked the presence of Imam Mehdi, Grandma," I said. "Why?"

With a resigned look, Grandma Tuba said, "I promised your Grandfather that you are not to be seen in the men's section, ever. Don't take this lightly, Ateesh."

My question remained unanswered as, much to Grandma Tuba's relief, we were interrupted by Grandfather's voice asking Grandma Tuba to give him a glass of warm milk. Grandma Tuba kissed me lovingly and placed her two fingers on my lips.

"So much to learn and you have so much time ahead of you, my child."

~ ~ ~ ~ ~

I got my answer from another source — Behrook. "I bet your grandfather caught Hajji Asghar doing forbidden things to a boy in the bathroom!" she said.

"What do you mean, forbidden things?" I asked.

"What do you think I mean?" Behrook said. As if that answered my question, she went onto say, "Can you imagine? Grownups doing forbidden acts right in the house of God!"

Sensing my complete incomprehension of what she was trying to tell me, she grabbed her history book and flipped through the pages.

"Look here," she said, as she pointed to a picture of Nasser al-din Shah Qajar, the King and Shah of Persia, who ruled from 1848 until 1896 when he was assassinated. He was the third-longest reigning king in Persian history, after Shapur II of the Sassanid Dynasty, and

Tahmasp I of the Safavid Dynasty. I recognized the Shah right away, sitting in front of the Peacock Throne in Golestan Palace, Tehran. Standing next to him, in an identical uniform, was a young, chubby, red-cheeked boy.

"Who is the boy?" I asked.

"Malijac," Behrook said. "The Shah and Malijac had a strange relationship that nobody ever questioned. Maybe Hajji Asghar and that young boy are like that, too! Some men are like animals, Ateesh. They are looking for a hole to deposit their juice. They are born like that. They cannot help it. Oh, Ateesh, why are you curious about this, anyway? Forget about that! Let's talk about a man and woman! Come on, tell me the truth. Don't you feel sensations when you think about a man?"

"Oh, Behrook," I said. "Enough!"

Her question didn't make me as uncomfortable as it had the last time, but I still didn't know how to answer.

"Do you know where I was headed at the *masjid* when I was walking toward the men's section?" she asked.

Preparing myself for something scandalous, I asked, "Where?"

"To walk by Mr. Shamsy and pretend not to notice him," she said. "Why?"

"We're through," she said. "I don't want a married lover. I want a real husband, not a temporary one."

"Temporary?" I asked. "What do you mean? Like *siqeh*?"

"Exactly! He wanted me to be his *siqeh*! But I said no."

"You did the right thing, Behrook! *Siqeh* is not good."

"Well, for one thing, it's not bad. It would legitimize my relationship with him."

"But he is married!"

"Married men can make *siqeh* with as many single women as they want," she said. "Didn't you know that?"

"No. What about married women? How many can they make *siqeh* with?"

"Women are allowed just one husband at a time."

"Why are the rules different for women?"

"I don't know and I don't care," Behrook answered. "Let me finish telling you about what happened with Mr. Shamsy!"

I sat back and listened as Behrook went on about how she wanted a real husband. My guess was that she wanted a man's shadow over her for the legitimization that only a man could offer, but she also needed a man who would not disapprove of her pursuing an education and career. Behrook wanted this man to be Mr. Shamsy, but soon began to realize that he was never going to leave his wife for her. To prove this to herself, Behrook went to the *masjid* to get a good look at him with his family. Seeing him there with them made it clear that she was never going to get what she wanted and needed from him.

Mr. Shamsy begged her not to end their relationship. He wanted to keep everything the way it was. She told him she wanted a husband, and that's when he asked her to be his *siqeh*. She became angry and told him that was not enough for her. "Then he had the nerve to threaten my grades! I told him if he tries that, I will go straight to his wife! I would too! He knows I mean that. That was the last we spoke."

"Good for you, Behrook," I said. "You shouldn't have to be anyone's *siqeh*!"

※ ※ ※ ※ ※

"Ateesh, put on your chador!" Grandma Tuba said as she headed toward the front door. "We have to go see Khanoom Berenji."

I did as I was told and followed her outside.

"That good-for-nothing nephew of Hajji Berenji has thrown Mrs. Berenji out of her house!" Grandma Tuba said as we walked briskly down the street. "Mrs. Berenji shared that house with her husband for forty years! But because they have no children, her husband's nephew inherited everything that should be hers! She has been left with nothing!"

Mrs. Berenji was Hajji Berenji's third wife. He'd married and divorced two women prior to Khanoom Berenji, before he finally learned it was he who was incapable of fathering a child.

Hajji Berenji's nephew lived in another state and had lost all contact with the couple many years earlier, but when Hajji Berenji died, the nephew inherited three-fourths of the entire estate.

"A widow, a wife with no children, gets one fourth of her husband's estate," Grandma Tuba said. "The other three-fourths get divided between the other family members, be they near or far. If there is more than one wife, the fourth of the estate is shared by all the wives."

The nephew evicted Mrs. Berenji because she could not afford to buy his share. Out of desperation, Mrs. Berenji would have to sell her share to her husband's nephew and rent a small house. She had no other assets left to survive on.

"I'm worried about her," Grandma Tuba said, "We're going to meet Mrs. Berenji and then we're going to our local Imam. Maybe he'll know what to do."

It is customary practice for religious people to consult with the Imams or respected religious figures on all matters, but especially on such personal matters as inheritance. Sometimes there are even lines of people waiting to ask for advice.

In what seemed like record time, we came upon the *masjid*.

"You won't believe what else!" Mrs. Berenji exclaimed as we approached her. "That ungrateful bastard has inherited the orchard too! He gets the land, Tuba, while I get the trees. What good are trees or the fruit on them if they are out of my reach? If they are on land I cannot set foot upon?"

Grandma Tuba embraced her. "Mr. Berenji never would have wanted this," Grandma Tuba said. "If anyone can help, it is the Imam. Let's go in."

I followed them inside. It infuriated me that the wife never seems to have legal rights to anything. Even after being married for forty years! It all came down to the man, even if it was a nephew that had been estranged for years! It was wrong! I couldn't wait to hear what the Imam had to say about this.

"The wife does not inherit agricultural land," he said.

"Why not?" Grandma Tuba asked.

"Because women do not know what to do with such properties. It is unfortunate that you did not produce a son, because he could have taken care of the land."

Grandma Tuba leaned forward and said, "Prophet Mohammad's first wife was a businesswoman who hired the Prophet and several other men to work for her. Where did this idea that a woman cannot take care of agricultural land come from?"

I felt like applauding her!

"Hajji Berenji was not plowing the land himself as a man, nor is his wife going to," she continued. "This kind of interpretation of the Quran is shameful. The Prophet's tradition of equal treatment for women should be respected!"

The Imam was quiet for a few seconds. "The widow can remain in the house for a year after her husband's death," he said. "Before that, she cannot be asked to leave unless it is her desire to do so. How long has it been?"

Grandma Tuba looked at Mrs. Berenji.

"It has been nine weeks, Hajji Aqa," she answered. "He wants me out before winter."

Winter was only three months away! I looked at Grandma Tuba, who silenced me with a single glance.

"Where is she supposed to go after forty years of marriage?" Grandma Tuba asked him.

Imam Razani looked away from Grandma Tuba, and turned to face Mrs. Berenji.

"Did you keep any of your personal and real property under your own name?" he asked hopefully. "Women who keep their personal and real property separate from their husbands, under their own name, do not have to share it with their husbands."

"Hajji Aqa, what are you talking about?" Mrs. Berenji asked, as she began to cry. "We were married forty years ago! Whatever my parents gave me at that time was given to my husband to be spent on us!"

"I suppose you have no income of your own either?" he asked. "This you could keep as well."

Mrs. Berenji wiped her tears with her chador, turned to Grandma Tuba and said, "Let us go, Tuba Khanoom. The death of my husband is also the end for me."

As she turned and walked toward the exit, Grandma Tuba straightened her chador and signaled me with her eyes to move. I followed them, but not without looking back at the Imam. I wanted him to stop us from leaving and tell us something different.

He shook his head in a regretful way.

"Your grandfather tells me that you are continuing school," he said instead.

I nodded.

"My middle daughter lives in Germany and teaches at the university. Teaching is a great profession for women. Women descended from the Prophet are held with the highest regard in Islam. You should go into teaching. It is a respectable profession for women. Good luck."

I turned and followed Grandma Tuba and Mrs. Berenji outside, thinking more highly of Imam Razani than I recently thought of any other cleric.

As Grandma Tuba tried to comfort Mrs. Berenji, I thought of the cherry trees that filled my parents' backyard—the same trees that Karim and I used to climb. My modar would eventually inherit a small portion of those trees, Baba's second wife would inherit another equally small portion, and I, an even smaller portion of those cherry trees. But it would only be Baba's sons who would inherit the land that holds the trees and their life-sustaining roots.

The tension between Baba and me increased as we came nearer to my graduation from high school. He knew how badly I wanted to go to the university, but going to any university in the city of Abadan was out of the question for a young divorcee. Baba was well-known in our community. The popularity of his restaurant brought me the misfortune of belonging to a high-profile family. Change for me would only be possible in the capital city, far away from people who knew us. That was exactly where I wanted to go.

"You are single and men will harass you, Ateesh!" Baba said. "Why don't you get it? You need a man's name on you, to protect you! Your only way out of this mess is to get married. It is the only way. Maybe under the shadow of a husband you can go to the university."

"I am not *be aberue*!" I exploded. "I refuse to be like other women in your culture! I don't want this! The only thing I want to do is continue my studies! I hate you and all men!"

He slapped me hard across the cheek. I staggered backward and almost fell, dazed for a moment. When I regained my balance and composure, I stood tall in front of him and looked him in the eye defiantly. Looking directly into his eyes, I didn't see any love, only shame.

I knew his feelings of shame had not diminished since my divorce. But his ill thoughts had lost their effect on me. I knew I didn't do anything to deserve what he thought of me.

"Go ahead and slap me again," I said firmly. "I am not going to stop telling you that I want to go to the University of Tehran! People like you make up this culture of yours and I have no respect for it. I would rather kill myself than remarry."

Modar rushed in and positioned herself between us. "Over my dead body, if you ever touch Ateesh again!" she said.

Those four short words, "Over my dead body," were used only once before by Modar. The day she fought him for my divorce. I was so tired of having to fight him for what I needed! But the fact remained that I did need his help. Although I was still living with Grandma Tuba, he remained my guardian. Any major changes still required his permission, and I needed his financial support.

"Why do you even want to go to the university?" he shouted. "To become more arrogant and disrespectful? You know that girls go to university to increase their chances of getting married! You are lucky that you even have any marriage proposals even though you are a divorcee!" He stepped back and started walking toward the door. Then he stopped and turned around.

"She is all yours!" he said to Modar. "You deal with her. I am through supporting her. She is not stepping back into my house."

After he slammed the door shut behind him, I turned to Modar and said, "I will never get married again!"

Modar opened her mouth as if to say something, but then didn't. I could point to countless women all around me—beautiful, talented, and wise women—whose lives might have been so different, so much happier, if marriage hadn't been compulsory for them.

My desire to attend university presented me with financial problems for the first time in my life. It was then that I understood why many of Grandma Tuba's friends stayed in abusive, loveless marriages: money. They had no choice. In a way, Modar had done the same. I was determined not to become my modar. Her culture took her soul. I needed a way out. I had to move to Tehran, the capital city. But how? Without Baba's permission and financial support, it would be impossible! I didn't know what to do. Once again, I began to fear for my future.

～～～～～

Modar and Grandma Tuba continued to reason with Baba for me, but I could tell they were running out of steam.

"Is there another way?" I asked, even though I knew the answer.

"Actually," Grandma Tuba said, "The answer might lie with your father's second wife."

"Maheen?" I asked. "How?"

"She has a great influence on him. She is also very clever."

"But she hates me!" I said. "Why would she want to do anything to help me?"

"Well if she believes she is getting something out of it, she will. If she believes your Baba would disown you and write you out of any inheritance. You should talk to Grandma Jamileh. She knows Maheen better than all of us."

The surprise must have shown on my face.

"Regardless of how I feel about Jamileh, I know she loves you and would want to help you," Grandma Tuba said. "Let us not wait any longer. We have to handle this with full force."

Before I could respond, Grandma Tuba stood up and said, "Let's leave now so we can catch Jamileh before she leaves for one of her many evening engagements." Sarcasm dripped from her voice. I guessed, by the way she perceived her, Grandma Tuba thought Grandma Jamileh would be more skillful in using any means necessary, deceptive or otherwise, to convince Baba to let me go.

"Modar, aren't you coming?" I asked, when she didn't get up from her chair.

"No, I do not want to go to her house, but Grandma is right. This might be our only option." Then, pointing to the door, she said, "Go on. Don't waste any time. I will go back home and wait to hear from you. Call me as soon as you get back."

It was early evening. It was a fifteen-minute walk to Grandma Jamileh's house. Grandma Tuba and I took a shortcut and passed through a number of small alleys. As we were walking fast, Grandma Tuba was talking. "Ateesh, remember never to come to this alley by yourself. You never know what could happen. Also, when we get to Jamileh's house, you do all the talking. I do not want her to know I suggested this idea. I also do not want her to think that just because I think you should ask her advice and help in this particular situation, that she can advise you on everything else. Especially not on religion!"

"Yes, Grandma."

As I hurried to keep up with Grandma Tuba, I realized how firmly she supported my decision to go to Tehran University. I was excited and nervous.

When we arrived at Grandma Jamileh's house, I gently pushed open the unlocked front door. She was sitting on her daybed in her sitting room, next to a large window, where she had a full view of her lavish garden, full of flowers. Her legs stretched out in front of her and, as always, she was reading a book. She was dressed in her usual bright colors. Bright blues and greens were her favorites. Sometimes she wore a dark green headscarf to show her once-removed Sayeed blood from her father's side. This showed that grandma was a direct descendent of Prophet Mohammed. Today, she loosely wore a more casual green scarf.

When she saw us, she smiled warmly, placed the book she was reading on the bed, stood up and opened her arms. "*Khosh amadeed, safa awordeed,* welcome, you brought pleasure by your arrival."

I glanced over at Grandma Tuba and could see that she looked annoyed. Before she could say anything unpleasant, I stepped forward and embraced Grandma Jamileh.

"Please, be a little serious," I whispered gently into her ear.

I loved to hold both of my Grandmas tight to my heart. Unlike Grandma Tuba, Grandma Jamileh was plump and stocky in the loveliest way.

"We are here for a *kareh vajeeb,* a serious matter," Grandma Tuba said, "Ateesh has a plan and we have to help her." Then she looked at me and signaled with her beautiful eyes, "Speak up, Ateesh! Do not waste time!"

But Grandma Jamileh wasn't done with her pleasantries.

"*Hajjieh Khanoom,*" she said to Grandma Tuba, "please don't stand up like that! You must sit and I shall serve some refreshments."

"*Modar Bozorg*," I said, "I want to talk to you about convincing Baba to let me go to the University of Tehran."

She was quiet. I put my arm around her and we sat down together on the daybed. Grandma Tuba made herself comfortable in a nearby chair.

"Of course women should go to universities," Grandma Jamileh said, more to herself than to us. Then she turned to me and proudly said, "Do you know your grandfather was in favor of higher education for women? He was the first man in our neighborhood who said that women should be able to walk in public without a chador. I was one of the first women to do so on the day that Reza Shah Kabier ordered women to remove them."

"We are in a different time, Jamileh!" Grandma Tuba loudly interrupted. "You talk about the past. I am talking about the present. Azim is only the first hurdle to Ateesh's education."

Grandma Jamileh still looked wistful.

"How can you sit here and lecture on women's rights and freedom?" Grandma Tuba continued. "You are the one who supported your son's marriage to a second wife and ruined my daughter's life. My daughter is deeply depressed because of what you did!"

Grandma Jamileh opened her mouth to say something but Grandma Tuba wasn't finished. "And the removal of the chador brought nothing but disrespect for women!"

Oh my God. This was the first time that Grandma Tuba criticized Grandma Jamileh to her face. Since Baba's second marriage, there was always an uncomfortable silence between them, but this was worse. I knew I had to stop them, but how? I didn't want it to seem as if I was taking sides. The truth was that I loved them both. They were both strong and wise. Both wanted what was best for me as a woman, even if it meant defying the culture.

"Please stop!" I shouted, interrupting my grandmas for the first and, as I remember, the last time in my life. "Each of you has told me that you love me and want to help me to succeed in this man's world. Please! I need both of you to convince Baba to allow me to go to the

University of Tehran. If I remain here at home, where everyone looks at me like secondhand goods, I will not survive."

They were both staring at me now, open-mouthed. But at least they were quiet.

"I will never marry again," I solemnly added. "I need your love as my grandmodars, but also your strength and wisdom."

Although I felt overwhelmed with emotion, no tears came. Probably because I had none left after weeks of fighting with Baba. Fights that always ended in tearful frustration.

"Please Modar Bozorg, I need both of you to cooperate with each other to help convince Baba. If I stay here I will die!"

Then I felt their arms around me, embracing me in a warm hug.

"We will help you," Grandma Tuba, said. "We love you. Do not worry." Then she looked at Grandma Jamileh and said, "Right?"

"Without a doubt," she answered. "Whatever it takes."

The three of us held each other. I was glad I told them that I needed them. "Let's have some tea while we talk," Grandma Jamileh said. "Ateesh, why don't you go and make us some?"

∿∿ ∿∿ ∿∿ ∿∿ ∿∿

I walked into the kitchen to make tea. Local, fresh dates were in season, and a bowl filled with yellow ones were on the kitchen table, inviting me to eat them. I put one in my mouth, then poured some fresh, cold water into the samovar.

Grandma Jamileh was meticulous and artistic in her tastes. I pulled out three stylishly designed tea glasses from her decorative showcase cabinet and placed them next to the bowl of dates on a serving tray. I browsed through her collection of teapots and chose the one with the figure of goddess Anahita, who is known in Iran as the source of life. She was pictured as a tall, beautiful goddess, and is widely known to be as powerful as the two male gods, Mithra and Ahura Mazda.

Looking at the portrait of the goddess, I noticed that there was a strong resemblance between Anahita and Grandma Jamileh. They shared the same round moon face, thick dark hair, and joined eyebrows, which traditionally symbolize feminine beauty in Iran.

The sound of water coming to a full boil interrupted my thoughts. I turned the brass knob on the samovar and poured hot water into the teapot in which I had already placed some tea leaves. The leaves swelled from the temperature and force of the hot water, and I watched as one tea leaf swam on the top by itself, instead of remaining at the bottom with the rest.

I placed the teapot on the top of the samovar and peered into the sitting room to check on my grandmodars. It appeared that they were in a deep discussion, sitting very close to each other. If they couldn't agree on anything else, I was glad they had me in common.

Not wanting to interrupt them just yet, I stopped and read a short poem, which was hanging on the kitchen wall. The poet, Padishah-khatun, was a queen who had ruled Kerman, a state south of Tehran. Grandma Jamileh told me many stories about the queen while I was growing up, and how she became one of the most accomplished rulers of Iran beneath the shadow of her husband. Grandma Jamileh especially admired Padishahkhatun's poetry.

I am the woman who does all good deeds
Hidden under my veil
Not everyone who wears the veil is a lady
Not every man who wears a crown is a leader.

I wished I had seen the poem earlier, before I'd given poor Grandma Tuba such a hard time about wearing a chador. Padishah-khatun's poem made me feel better about wearing it. Grandma Tuba was as wise as the queen who had once ruled the country!

It was time for me to pour tea into our glasses and serve it before it brewed for too long.

As I carried the tray into the sitting room, Grandma Tuba got up, took the tray from me, and set it on a nearby table.

"We have a plan," she said, in a rejuvenating voice. "Jamileh and I think you are going to like it. The way to get to your father to agree is to convince Maheen that it is financially better for her and her sons if you move away. We know that she cares more about your Baba's money than anything else, so we have to convince her that by mov-

71

ing away, you are letting go of your inheritance and right to financial maintenance by your father."

Grandma Jamileh took one of the tea glasses and passed it to me. "We know what you are thinking now, Ateesh," she said. "Who is going to pay for your expenses? We will do as much as we can. Tuba and I have some savings. But the first step is to get Azim's permission. As your father, he does have the power to stop you."

"We don't want it to get to that point," Grandma Tuba intervened. "We would rather see you go with his blessing."

Her expression suddenly changed and she looked as if she were about to say something funny. She took a sip of her tea. "Ateesh, you make the best tea! I believe it is time for your marriage!"

Both Grandmas burst into laughter, then stopped abruptly when they saw the frown on my face.

"I will drop the hot tea tray on the lap of any suitor who dares to walk through this door!" I said.

"That's my girl!" Grandma Jamileh replied.

Typically, when a suitor and his family come to a girl's house to propose marriage, the girl enters the room with a tray of either freshly brewed tea or cold sherbet, depending on the season. This is an opportunity for the prospective bride and groom to look at one another. In more traditional families this step is skipped, as parents on both sides negotiate the whole marriage contract without the tea ceremony.

"Speaking of marriage," Grandma Jamileh said as she turned toward Grandma Tuba, "Azim needed to have more children. You know that. Regardless of what I may have said or done, I never wished to see your daughter suffer. What else could my son have done? One child is not enough. He would have taken a second wife even if I had not supported the idea."

Grandma Tuba's face softened, but she did not say a word.

It was true. Baba would have taken a second wife even if Grandma Jamileh hadn't supported the idea. He did it even though it hurt my modar. It did hurt her, because she really loved him. Modar never talked to me about it, but I heard bits and pieces from Grandma Tuba.

When Modar first saw Baba, she fell in love with his dark, curly hair. Traditionally it was not allowed for a young couple to go out together, even with a chaperone, but Baba asked Modar anyway. Apparently, tradition became more important to Baba after I was born.

Grandma Tuba agreed to chaperone them. "Every time we went out, your Baba asked me if he could be alone with your modar for a few minutes," Grandma Tuba revealed to me one day when we were talking about courting properly.

On one of those walks, he asked Modar if she would consider marrying him. At first she didn't answer, but he kept insisting until she finally confessed that she had been in love with him since the first time she laid eyes on his dark curls.

It was so difficult for me to imagine all of this. I wondered why Baba had opposed my education so strongly and why he wanted to force me into another marriage, when he had been allowed a love marriage.

I've seen a number of pictures of them, which had been taken during their courtship. In all the black-and-white photos, Modar looked shy, with her head down, but they both seemed happy. There were a few pictures of both of them with Grandma Tuba in the far background.

It was when I was born that something went wrong with Modar's ability to carry babies. That's when their marriage took a drastic turn. She was told that she was not fertile any more. Soon after she had me, Modar felt the pressure to have more children, especially a son for my father. My modar's sister in-laws started to pressure Baba to marry a second wife who could bear more children for him. Modar hoped that Baba would decline the idea, but he didn't. It was his sisters that introduced the second wife's family to Baba.

So, it appears that sometimes even happy marriages don't turn out so well.

I held up the tea tray. "Tea, anyone?" I asked. "I promise not to pour it on you."

Both Grandmas smiled, and we were back to the subject of convincing Baba.

~~ ~~ ~~ ~~ ~~

By the time we left Grandma Jamileh's house, it was dark. Grandma Tuba did not want to go back through the same alley.

"But Modar Bozorg, it will take us twice as long and Grandfather will be back home from the prayers at the *masjid*. You know he gets upset if we are not home when he gets back."

"Fine, but I have heard that young women unaccompanied by men are touched in these narrow dark alleys. Stay close to me and walk fast."

I walked as fast as I could and stayed close to her. Grandma Tuba made me swear on Modar's head that I would never walk that alley by myself. I knew that my divorce—now six years in the past—increased my chances of being harassed on the street.

I could not wait to go to Tehran. I was prepared to show everyone in Abadan who shunned me that it is what people do with their lives that makes them honorable, not whether you are a man or woman, or what people think of you.

When Grandma Tuba and I arrived back at her house, Modar was waiting there for us. Though her deep depression had never subsided, she'd been in higher spirits lately. Despite all of the fighting between Baba and me, she seemed to be energized by this fight for my future. But I could see by the look on her face now that there was a problem.

"I contacted the University, Ateesh," she said. "We need much more money than we thought."

All of my hope deflated. "How much money?" I asked.

"Don't worry about it," Grandma Tuba said. "We will support you as much you need."

I did not want to exhaust Grandma Tuba's savings. One day, she and Modar might need her money. Many of Grandma Tuba's friends relied on Grandma Tuba for occasional borrowings too.

"Maybe we should talk to Zari," Modar said.

Zari was my modar's cousin, the only family I had that lived in Tehran. She lived with her husband and three young children in a house that was given to her by her parents at the time of marriage.

She worked at a bank, and if it had not been for her husband, I would have asked to stay with her. Nobody liked her husband. As Modar told me, Zari had married Housheng to save face because she had lost her virginity to him. To make matters worse, she'd gotten pregnant.

Housheng was an uneducated high school dropout who hung around her family looking for occasional handyman work. When her family came to know about Zari and Housheng, they preferred to have Zari marry him, despite his low status, because that was the only way to save her honor. Housheng took advantage of her parent's concern with *aberue* and their public image. He started threatening Zari physically, trying to extract more money from her family. After some time, he made good on his threats. Zari remained miserable in her marriage, resigning herself to the commonly held belief that her unhappiness was her fate.

"You cannot escape your fate," she told me, the day she learned about my marriage and divorce. "It was meant to be."

I have never found this way of thinking satisfactory.

Over my long telephone conversation with Zari, I told her about my plans. Modar was right. Zari was more than willing to help me. She told me about the bank's short-term money lending program designed just for women. In exchange for the sum lent to me, the bank would take three to four times the value of the money in eighteen and twenty-four-karat gold jewelry.

I thought of all the gold jewelry I'd received from my family and friends at the time of my wedding. I immediately got excited. Most of it was never worn. We received it in great quantity from both sides of the family. At least I could use that for a good cause!

Zari explained that after the due date, there was a grace period with penalty, and after the grace period, if the money hadn't been paid back, the bank would take over the gold deposit.

"Remember," Zari said, "only gold, and no stones. Good luck, Ateesh!"

"Thank you, Zari," I said.

I hung up the phone and told Modar and Grandma Tuba about the bank's requirement of the gold deposit.

"I will give you all of my gold jewelry," Modar said, "including my wedding ring with three diamonds. And I've saved cash, too."

"What about my *mehreeh* and *jahizeyeh*?" I said excitedly.

Modar was quiet for a minute, and then said, "We don't have that. We had to return everything as one of the conditions to get your divorce."

"What?" I said in disbelief. "You had to pay them to get my divorce?"

"Why are you surprised? That is the way parents buy their daughters' freedom," Modar said.

My blood boiled in anger. I couldn't believe all the money and gold that was given to that bastard. My stay at the hospital could not get me a divorce. Even Baba's consent was not enough. It wasn't until my abusive husband was bought out by my family.

"Modar, I had no idea," I said. There was so much I didn't know about my own divorce. Once I had moved in with Grandma Tuba, I was happily sheltered from the realities that my modar faced every day. Though I resented my powerlessness, I realized then that Modar and Grandma Tuba had done more than get my marriage dissolved; they had given me back my life.

"What is important is that you are finally divorced," Modar said. "You know what finally convinced Baba to agree to your divorce? I told him I would forgive him in my heart for taking a second wife. That's when he agreed to go to the registrar. If he had not gone, we would never have gotten the divorce."

"Oh, Modar," I exclaimed with much sorrow and gratitude. I held her hands in mine and saw her eyes look like they were going to overflow with tears. "How can I ever thank you?"

She gently took her hands and caressed my hair, smiling lovingly.

"Don't you ever become a second wife," she said. "If your husband remarries, walk away without looking back. You hear me, Ateesh? It is a slow death sentence. The thought of knowing your husband is with another woman is like the beginning of an incurable disease which spreads slowly all over your body. It kills you from within."

I didn't know what to say.

"Promise me, Ateesh," she said.

Without any hesitation, I promised.

"If it ever happens to you, walk away. Don't stay," Modar repeated. "I will support your decision if I am alive. And if I am not, you are strong enough to leave and not put up with the pain."

I nodded in agreement. "*Man khelly dosat daram*," I said. "I love you very much."

We gave all of the family jewelry we had, but Zari informed us that the bank was not going to accept most of it because of the mounted precious stones on them. Between Modar's, Grandma Jamileh's, and Grandma Tuba's gold, I would be okay for the first couple of years. After that I didn't know what I would do, but I was satisfied for the time being. All I needed to do now was to get Baba's consent to leave Abadan.

Grandma Jamileh had set a date for me to talk to Baba's second wife.

"I don't want to do the talking," I said. "I hate her!"

"Listen, Ateesh. She will take it better from you than from any of us," Grandma Jamileh said. "You must make her think it is a defeat on your part, leaving your family behind and going to Tehran for the unknown. Then when she consults with me, I will say it is the best thing for her and her sons."

Grandma Tuba nodded in agreement. "We have to rehearse every sentence that comes out of your mouth, Ateesh," Grandma Jamileh said. "*Allaho Akbar!*" Grandma Tuba exclaimed. Both Grandmas appeared confident. Modar seemed less certain. I kept quiet and did what I had to do to make it happen. And so began a new chapter in my life.

Suzan was my first friend at the University of Tehran. She was a tall, beautiful girl with proportionate curves. She was from an affluent family and lived in one of the most exclusive neighborhoods there. She had a classical Iranian look and a warm smile that showed off her straight, white teeth. She wore amazing clothes, exuded self-confidence, and was charming and also fluent in English. Her presence was immediately noticed in any gathering. I wanted to be like her.

I lived at the dormitory and Suzan lived at home. She didn't want to live at home, even though her parents gave her many freedoms—much more than my family had ever given me in Abadan.

We were having tea and delicacies in her well-decorated room, when Suzan first told me she had a boyfriend.

My experience with Behrook taught me not to act surprised when I heard of an unmarried girl in any kind of relationship with a boy.

"Have you slept with him?" I asked, trying to sound casual.

She smiled and looked as if she were trying to stifle laughter. "Where did you come from, Ateesh?" she asked. "Of course I did!"

I nodded and tried not to show a reaction.

"But don't worry," she said, "I'm still a virgin when I want to be!"

Suzan waited to see what I would say to that, but I still said nothing.

She lowered her voice and continued in a whisper. "I went out with a surgeon," she explained. "We broke up on good terms. He sewed me back up. Poof! Virginity restored!"

"Are you serious?" I asked, no longer able to hide my shock.

"Then I went out with Professor Parsaee," she continued, "our chemistry professor. When we broke up, I was sewn back up. Then we got back together. You should have seen his face when he realized I was a virgin again! I just played innocent the whole time!"

I couldn't believe what she was telling me. She was talking and laughing about the same virginity Grandma Tuba and I had such painful conversations about. Conversations that always ended in tears! Farah had nearly been killed on her wedding night over it! My head was filled with contradictions about the importance of a girl's virginity.

"Sewing up hymens is big business here in Tehran. Ateesh, all men, even our liberal professors, want their girlfriends to be virgins," Suzan explained. "My ex-boyfriend, Akbar, the surgeon, does not charge me anyway, and even if he did, it would be worth it. I give Akbar's number to all of my friends. You should have his number, too, just in case. He is great for a short-term relationship. He is not the type you want for a long-term relationship."

"No," I said. "That is fine."

It angered me that girls would get themselves sewn up again and again just to please men.

She sat back and leaned against the high back of the chair, gazing at me with both sympathy and satisfaction.

I stared back at her with a million questions I did not dare ask. I did not want to appear provincial or prudish to this girl, who was one year ahead of me in school and obviously worldlier. She reminded me so much of Behrook!

Suzan seemed to be reading my mind, as if she knew I was about to get on my soap box. I did have a lot to say about the unrealistic demand of an intact hymen until the wedding night, and about the high value placed on that small piece of tissue.

"You know, Ateesh, men want virginity from women," Suzan said again, casually. "Why not play along and give it to them?"

Men are so childish for wanting to be fooled, I thought.

"So tell me," I said, wanting to change the subject. "What was it like? I mean, the first time?"

"Well, the first time wasn't the best, but he was gentle and really knew what he was doing," she said. "After the first few times, we were more comfortable with each other and it just got better and better from there."

Better and better? It wasn't like that for me!

After nearly seven years, I was aching to tell someone the story of my rape and my crazy husband. I had kept silent for so long, not wanting to bring further shame to my family, but I suddenly wanted to blurt it out. I wanted to tell this open-minded and sophisticated girl.

"I was married once," I muttered.

Her mouth fell open. Being affluent and living in Tehran meant young girls didn't get married at twelve years old. Abadan was more conservative than Tehran, and my family was definitely traditional and strict when it came to marriage.

"What do you mean?" asked Suzan.

Then it came out. I told her about my arranged marriage, my husband's addiction to gambling and drugs. Thoughts of the first time he raped me— yes I referred to it as rape—literally brought a physical discomfort to my body. I spared her some of the details. She listened in disbelief.

"Ateesh, I had no idea. I never would have gone on and on like that" Suzan said.

"It's okay. I never really talked about it with anyone. I feel like a weight has been lifted," I said.

For the first time since that tragic night when he first forced himself on me, I felt no shame for what had happened. I had absolutely no control over the events that had affected me in such a major way. Yet I did not want to think of myself as a victim. Victims were weak. I was not.

I felt relieved. For the first time in a long time, I felt light and free. My eye-opening friendship with Behrook had enabled me to think a bit more about boys and be more comfortable with my own desires. I found myself wanting to experience a satisfying physical relationship with a man as she and Suzan did. I wondered if I could. I had a lot of unpleasant memories to unload first, I supposed.

"When you feel sad, what makes you feel better?" Suzan asked. Without waiting for an answer, she stood up and put on some music.

"That is what makes me feel better," she said. "I have all of the latest dancing music!"

Persian music filled the air. She started moving charismatically toward me. She held her arms out in front of her, inviting me to join in. I hesitated only a moment to think of Grandma Tuba. Grandma Tuba was such a good dancer and she used to always get everyone dancing. I thought of how she would take off her scarf and open her braids...

It had been so long since I had danced. I pulled off the bow that was holding my hair back and let myself go. Persian dancing involves moving the hips and waist much like in belly dancing. It is very sensuous and seductive, though not necessarily in a sexual way. I let my long hair swing free and gracefully in front of my face and around my shoulders and back.

Soon we were both laughing and singing along with the singer. "You mesmerize me, and God is my witness," we sang. "I am in love with you and I will sacrifice my life for you, so come to me and let us celebrate our love!"

Suzan and I both were startled as her mom opened the door and looked inside.

"Do you girls realize what time it is?"

"Mom, we are celebrating our freedom and womanhood!"

Her modar smiled thoughtfully, looking at us with an unconvinced expression on her face. "What freedom?" she asked. "It is all make-believe! *Shab bekhar!*"

"Good night!" we responded in unison.

That night Suzan and I stayed up late and talked about our lives. According to Suzan, she was not the only classmate with a boyfriend. Almost half of our classmates had boyfriends. Some were even having affairs with married men. They went to expensive restaurants and received flowers, jewelry, and other gifts. Suzan also told me that she had traveled out of town with Professor Parsaee on several occasions when he was attending conferences. She also told me he was married at the time but divorced later on.

"Girls expect to be pampered and to receive presents," Suzan said. "Boyfriends are very generous with their girlfriends. Especially the married ones."

Probably more generous than they are to their poor wives, I thought.

After Suzan fell asleep, I kept thinking about the past. My arranged marriage to a man seven years my senior had been a disaster. Somehow, in the end, his family considered this disaster my fault, never understanding why a twelve-year-old girl would be unable to put up with or cure his addiction. But then I learned that it was a commonly held belief that a man's bad behavior was always attributed to either his wife's inadequacy or his modar's failure to raise a good son.

From all I suffered in my marriage, I had developed ways of defending myself. When my husband got in one of his many rages and started throwing objects at me, I stayed out of his range. Because our house shared a courtyard with my parent's house, I often crept home in the quiet darkness and spent many nights sleeping in Modar's bed with her. My husband would often be too high to notice my absence.

"Sometimes love comes later, Ateesh," Modar would tell me before she sent me back to the matrimonial house. "*Dandon ru jigar mizareh ama hechi nemegeh*. Things will get better. Wait until you have a baby."

Looking back, I realized Modar herself didn't sound too convinced at the time. She was probably repeating what she was always told, what she was still trying to somehow believe, herself.

To get through those walks back, I would recite poetry in my head. Hafez's poems were, and still are, among my favorites.

In hopeless situations there is hope, the end of a dark night is a bright morning if your goal of walking through the desert is to get to Kabeh, do not mind and worry about all the thorns on your way.

Those poems saved me from losing my sanity. Now I shared

Hafez's point of view and felt darkness to be a temporary situation, which eventually would become the brightness of day.

~~ ~~ ~~ ~~ ~~

It was a sunny day in late autumn and the university grounds were filled with colorful leaves. Suzan and I were on our way to meet our friends Azita, Marjon, and Roya, for a late lunch at the cafeteria just outside the main gate of the university. I had been up all night studying for mid-semester exams and had skipped breakfast. I was famished, but felt reinvigorated with each breath of fresh, cold air. We walked briskly to keep ourselves warm. I jumped on every pile of leaves I came across so I could hear the crisp sound of leaves breaking. It brought me back to when my cousin Saeed and I were kids and would roll around on an open field with the colorful fall leaves crunching under us.

"Come on, Ateesh," Suzan scolded me, "behave like a university student!"

As we reached the main road on campus, one of our professors, Dr. Parsa, slowed his silver two-door Ford Mercury Cougar alongside us, and lowered the passenger-side window.

"Good afternoon," he said as he slowed the car to a stop.

As soon as I heard his voice, I froze.

"Good afternoon, Professor," Suzan replied.

"You know, I've been very impressed with both of you so far this semester," he said. "Have you had lunch? I was just on my way."

He seemed to be addressing both of us, but he was looking right at me. My heart started beating fast. He was my professor of poetry and literature. When he'd walked into the lecture hall on the first day of school I immediately felt a weakness in my knees. He had the longest eyelashes I had ever seen. His jet-black wavy hair, which he kept neatly parted on one side, complemented his perfect, high cheekbones and full lips. I couldn't stop staring at him that day—or any day after that.

After that first class, I always arrived early so I could find a seat right up front. In a large lecture hall filled with four hundred students, I wanted to make sure I had a good view. This was the first time I had ever been attracted to a man. Every time I saw him, I thought of Behrook's words, "Don't you want to be touched by a man?" I chased her words away during the day, and didn't go back to them until I was in bed, in the darkness of night, when I knew Grandma Tuba was sound asleep and couldn't hear my thoughts.

"Ateesh?" Suzan nudged me. "I was just telling the Professor that I can't go to lunch with you because I need to finish some work. Why don't you go ahead with him?"

I felt my face flush. I knew what she was doing. She was lying in order to send me off alone with him. She had been telling me that finding a boyfriend would be a step toward my recovery from my painful past. She had even bet that this professor would try to get close to me.

"He does this every semester with a freshman," she'd said.

Those words rung in my mind as I stood there, not knowing what to say. It turned out that I didn't have to say anything because Dr. Parsa was already out of his car. He came around to the passenger side and opened the door for me.

"Please," he said, gesturing for me to get in. I looked at Suzan. She had a big smile on her face.

"Get in, Ateesh," she said. "You don't have that much time for a lunch break, and of course, the Professor has to get back to his office."

Then Suzan sort of gently pushed me toward the car. I stepped forward and got in. I watched as he closed the door, walked around the front of the car, and turned to wave to Suzan. I felt as if I were doing something very wrong. If Grandma Tuba saw me here in the car with this man, what would she say? What was I doing? What was I thinking? Apparently I wasn't thinking! I wanted to open the door and run away, but I couldn't move.

When he sat in the car, his arm brushed against mine and I realized how close we were to each other. I looked at Suzan. She winked at me and then gestured, with her hand on her lips, for me to smile. Was she kidding me? How could I smile? All I could think of was the ever-watchful eyes of the community. How disappointed my poor Grandma Tuba would be with me if she saw this. I couldn't do it.

I must not have looked well because Suzan suddenly leaned into the window and said, "Professor, do you mind giving me a ride to the library? I feel too tired to walk."

"Sure, get in."

She opened my door and said, "Move over just a little, I don't take much space."

She pushed herself in next to me, pushing me even closer to the professor. His car didn't have much space between the two seats up front. I was practically on top of him. He smelled so good. Again I felt that weakness in my knees.

As he turned on the radio, Suzan whispered in my ear, "It's just a lunch. You look like you're going to the slaughterhouse. It's just food. Think of delicious charcoal-broiled kebab over mouth-watering saffron-flavored rice, with a side order of grilled tomato and fresh basil and mint. If you don't stop it, I am going to go with him and drop you off at the library, you old maid!"

The car came to a stop in front of the library. "Here you go," the Professor said.

"Ateesh," Suzan said, "Do you want to join me in studying or would you rather go to lunch with the Professor?"

I looked from her to the Professor. They were both staring at me and waiting.

"I know a quiet place we can go for some traditional dishes before they close," he said.

I nodded. "Okay."

Suzan got out of the car quickly, but not before she whispered, "*Khosh begzareh*, have fun!"

Relieved that I had a little more room now, I slid closer to the passenger door.

The pleasant fragrance of his cologne scented the air in his car. Music of the French singer, Charles Aznavour, played in the background. Modar used to listen to his records. I always felt moved by his deep, passionate voice.

What was I doing? I thought again. People are going to say I am *be aberue!*

It was strange being in the car with him. I had never been alone with a liberal, highly educated man. I felt I should be intelligent and witty, as I sometimes was in class. I wondered what he expected from me now that we were alone.

Men are only after your body. Was that Modar or Grandma who had said that? Grandma Tuba or Jamileh?

"If you do not like it, I can change it," Dr. Parsa said politely, interrupting my thoughts.

"Oh, no," I said. "He is one of my favorites."

"You are familiar with his music?"

"Through my modar," I said. "She loves his voice. I've read his memoir. I hope he continues giving concerts."

Aznavour's singing reminded me of the poetry of Forugh Farrokhzad, who had died tragically in a car accident in 1966. She was a controversial, Iranian woman who had refused to hide her love for a married man. Her words defiantly exposed the hypocrisy of a culture that preaches virtues and virginity for women but not for men.

I was nervous, but this was very different from what I had experienced with my husband or that old registrar. This nervousness was not unpleasant, but it was still uncomfortable. I looked at him from the corner of my eye.

"Please don't be so nervous," he said.

I shifted in my seat. I didn't realize I was being so obvious!

"We are just going for lunch," he said.

I opened my mouth to explain myself, but I didn't know what to say. Suddenly I felt his warm hand lightly touch my thigh, right above my knee. I jumped so high that my head hit the roof on the car.

"I am sorry," he said as he immediately removed his hand.

My mind was all over the place. No, I had never been with a man like this before. From the first minute I was left alone with my husband, I hated being in his presence. Every time he had attempted to touch me, I tried to get away. But now here I was sitting in the professor's car, and it was because I wanted to. I'd felt attracted to him since day one.

Again, I thought of Behrook's question, "Don't you wish to be touched…?"

"Are you okay, Ateesh?" he asked.

I nodded.

"Almost there," he said.

~~ ~~ ~~ ~~ ~~

He took me to a small section of Tehran known as Tajreesh. Suzan went there all the time with her boyfriends and often spoke of its picturesque setting. Although it was late afternoon in the middle of the week, many people were still having lunch. He chose a small restaurant that overlooked a creek. The owner greeted and called the professor by his first name, Bejan. Musicians played softly from another room that was attached to where we were, by the open area right on the creek. Only the scent of homemade cooking was familiar, and it reminded me of walking through the market with Grandma Tuba as a child.

Without asking me, he ordered kabobs and rice with grilled tomatoes, and a few side dishes. It was the best food I had tasted since arriving in Tehran. With little money to spend on luxury items, I did most of my eating on campus. The combination of this scrumptious meal and my famished state made me forget myself. I ate with vigor until I noticed Dr. Parsa looking at me, amused.

"Shall I order some more?" he asked, smiling. "Ateesh, slow down. Enjoy it."

I smiled back at him. I found his good humor calming. After that, we talked mostly of academics. I found myself relaxing as we discussed the Shahnameh. He must have sensed this.

"Ateesh," he asked, "how profound do you think the effect of works like Ferdowsi's *Shahnameh* has been on today's literature?" His voice sounded authoritative, just as it did in class, but now he was looking directly into my eyes.

I remembered what Grandma Tuba had said about Grandma Jamileh, "Instead of reading the Quran, Jamileh reads *Shahnameh*, as if it's a replacement for the Quran!"

"I think Ferdowsi's *Shahnameh* has had the most lasting, and profound cultural and linguistic influence on our modern literature and language," I said. "Professor, hasn't studying Ferdowsi's masterpiece become a requirement for achieving mastery of our language by our poets?"

"I agree with your statement, but Ateesh, how do you know so much about *Shahnameh*? You are just what, eighteen, maybe nineteen years old?"

"My paternal Grandma, Jamileh knows the book by heart. I have heard all sixty-two stories at least a few times since I was born. Instead of lullabies, she would tell me about the legend of Rostam and Sohrab, and a thousand or so verses of his tragedy."

Because of the early, informal teachings by Grandma Jamileh, I'd been fascinated with poetry and literature since childhood. I wondered if this was one of the reasons I was so attracted to him.

He smiled and asked, "What else besides poetry are you interested in?"

"Professor—"

"Oh, please," he interrupted, "call me Bejan. Stop the professor talk or I'll start to feel really old."

"Okay," I said. "Well, I'm interested in justice. For women, especially."

As I spoke these words, I found myself sitting up straighter and looking him in the eyes. By the end of our lunch, I had enjoyed myself so much that as soon as he asked to pick me up for lunch next day, I accepted without hesitation.

He drove me back to the university and pulled his car into a discreet spot in the back of the dorms. Since our lunch lasted into the late afternoon and students were not around, there wasn't much of a chance of us being seen, but he was being cautious. I appreciated it.

Before I stepped out of the car, he leaned toward me. Putting his hand gently through my hair and around the back of my head, he pulled me to him. The warmth of his hand on my neck and the smell of his cologne was sensational. Suddenly, thoughts began to swarm around in my mind: *How easily you forget that men are the cause of women's suffering! He is going to use you!*

I pulled away, thanked him for lunch, and stepped out of the car. I walked into the dorm in a daze. Everything happened so fast. I felt a certain amount of shame, but there was a part of me that felt as if I should not feel any shame at all.

I saw my roommate, Roya, in the hallway. She smiled at me knowingly and turned to follow me into the dorm room. Suzan must have told her about my lunch with Dr. Parsa.

Roya was a beautiful girl from the outskirts of Khoramabad, a provincial area, south of Tehran. Her father was an educated man, a professor of physics. He had established a successful research laboratory, but he knew that Khoramabad was no place for his daughter to continue higher education. He had insisted she attend the University of Tehran and live on campus.

Despite this vast difference in our upbringing, Roya had known many girls from very traditional families. When I talked to her, I didn't need to explain myself as I sometimes did with Suzan.

Once we were safely in the dorm room, I locked the door and sat on the bed. "After so many years of trying to make myself indifferent to men, I fell, Roya," I said. "I fell hard!"

She smiled softly. I knew I could trust her not to tell anyone about my afternoon.

"I have never felt so vulnerable and good at the same time," I said. "He touched my hand, and he touched my hair…"

"And?" Roya asked, searchingly.

With no answer from me, she added, "Ateesh, please be careful. This professor has a reputation for being with a different freshman every semester."

I don't think I internalized the last part of her comment. But it could've been that, or maybe it was something from my past, perhaps even some remnant of worry for my *aberue*, that made me stop short of telling her I was going to see him next day. I also didn't tell her he'd asked me to call him Bejan.

As much as I wanted to tell Suzan, I knew how easily she shared with me the secrets of other girls' relationships with different professors. I could not take a chance on telling her.

For the past six years, I had been an observer. I observed women like my Grandma Tuba's friends who took great pride in dodging their husbands' fists. But then, I had met women who took pleasure in the company of men, women like Suzan and Behrook. I was learning to be more like my friends.

I couldn't concentrate on anything for the remainder of the day. That night I had the same dream that I was talking to boys on the street, flipping my long hair from side to side, when I suddenly heard Grandma Tuba's voice.

I sat up in bed crying. I had this feeling of pity for myself, and I hated it.

"Stop acting like a baby!" I said to myself, "You wanted to be here and you got it. From now on you cannot blame anybody else for anything but yourself! Grow up."

∿ ∿ ∿ ∿ ∿

Bejan picked me up for lunch in the same spot he had dropped me off the day before. I had avoided Suzan that morning because I didn't want to answer any questions. Regardless of what Suzan was trying to do to make me feel comfortable, I continued to feel an undeniable shame for meeting a man in private who was not related to me. But my desire and attraction to him were taking over.

He took me to a trendy bistro on Pahlavi Street, across from a beautiful park. He was wearing a white jacket over a white turtleneck, with black trousers. His dark brown sunglasses reminded me of the sunglasses Baba wore in the photographs I had seen, when he was courting Modar.

"We'll place the order for food here but we'll go upstairs to eat," he said. "It is more private."

We walked up the narrow steps of a spiral, gray metal staircase. The room upstairs was decorated beautifully with matching gray metallic, bistro-type, round tables and chairs. There were only two other tables occupied with other couples having lunch.

"Sit anywhere you'd like, Ateesh," he said. I pointed to a table by the large window that overlooked the park. When we sat down, the waiter came upstairs with two carbonated bottles of buttermilk, opened the bottles, and handed them to us. When he left, Bejan raised his bottle and said, "To your beauty and intelligence."

Catching notice of his perfectly shaped lips, I blushed and looked away.

"Come on, Ateesh," he said, "it is bad luck not to do this with your buttermilk. Lift up your bottle and let us make a wish."

I smiled and held up my glass.

"That is my wish as well, Ateesh," he said, as if he knew what was going on in my head.

I was quiet during lunch. There were all of these feelings going on inside of me. I kept hearing his words, "To your beauty and your intelligence." My desires seemed to be piling up and trying to climb out. It was as if they had a life of their own.

After lunch when we were in his car, he pulled me gently toward him. My heart was racing and I was sweating. My initial reaction was to resist him, as I always had with my husband, and I immediately tensed up. But something magical was happening inside me. I can't quite articulate it. All I can say is that after a short minute of being held by him like that, my guard came down. He stared at my lips, tracing them with his fingers as if he was going to slip his finger into my mouth. I didn't know what to do. My heart must have been beating loud enough for him to hear it, because he whispered, "*Metonam ghalbeto bebosom,* May I kiss your heart?"

I felt flushed, hearing his words and feeling his breath.

"I think we should go back," I managed to say. "I think I may faint."

He held my hand through our ride back to the campus. I could hear him talking but I had no idea what he was saying. I felt feverish.

Before he dropped me off at our spot, I agreed to see him for dinner the next day.

Again, I was restless for the remainder of the day and all through the evening. The next morning I awoke feeling anxious and nervous. I had been so afraid that I would never experience those feelings for a man that Behrook always talked about. But Bejan's scent was in my head. This was exactly what she was talking about. I wanted to call Modar and Grandma Tuba to tell them what was happening to me. But I couldn't.

By the next evening, when I was getting ready to meet Bejan, I was still a nervous wreck. It didn't help that I had no idea what to wear. I jumped when the phone rang.

"Ateesh, I just left the campus," Bejan said. "The whole area is very busy tonight because of a couple of seminars. There are people everywhere. How about you take a taxi and I meet you on Pahlavi Street by the park? Just give the driver the information."

"Okay," I said.

"Be careful and don't get lost," he said. "Make sure you only take a commercial taxi."

Suzan and I usually took rides with non-commercial cars. I had learned from Suzan that many private cars were willing to drive passengers if they were going in the same direction. This was a way for boys to pick up girls in hopes to get to know them. They wouldn't usually charge money, and they would take us anywhere we wanted, even if our destinations were far away.

I would never ride in a non-commercial car without Suzan, though. Unlike me, she knew what to say and how to hold conversations with the boys until we got where we needed to go. She was the one who took their phone numbers. I just followed along.

I was still avoiding Suzan. I had even cancelled dinner plans I had with her tonight. I knew I couldn't continue like this. She was my friend. I hated being so secretive all the time. It made me feel worse. Maybe I would just take a chance and tell her everything.

I looked out the window. A light snow had fallen during the day. I thought of the long, stylish, fall jacket I saw Suzan wearing that day, and wondered if she would let me borrow it.

I knocked at Azita's door, where Suzan was staying.

"Suzan?" I called.

Some shuffling noises followed, but no response.

"Suzan?" I called again, louder.

Still no answer. I gave up, and decided to go without the jacket. I promised myself I would fill her in on everything another time.

I walked around the back of our residence hall, which was used less frequently. I kept my head down and walked quickly, hoping I wouldn't run into any of my friends. I didn't want to have to explain why I was so dressed up.

When I turned the corner, I nearly collided into a man who was standing there with his back to me, shivering in the cold. He didn't have a coat on, and his shirt hung untucked from his pants. I recognized him immediately from a picture Suzan had shown me. It was her surgeon! He turned and began to walk very purposefully away from the building. When he disappeared around the corner, I followed his newly made footprints in the snow back to their origin, which was the door of Suzan's friend Minoo.

It looked like I wasn't the only one with a secret! Between the shuffling inside Azita's room, and a half-naked surgeon running through the snow from Minoo's room, it seemed as if everyone was trying to hide something. I wondered how many hymens the surgeon had sewn free of charge on campus alone!

I felt nauseated knowing how he took advantage of everybody's obsession with hymen.

※ ※ ※ ※ ※

I asked the taxi driver to drop me off in front of the park on Pahlavi Street. There were sure to be many people milling around, and I could easily blend into the crowd. Bejan was to meet me on the corner by the streetlamp, which lit one of the many entrances to the park.

Thursday night traffic in Tehran forced us to crawl to our designated spot. The driver apologized several times, but I told him I understood. I was glad for the delay. To calm my nerves, I talked with him about some of the famous landmarks as we passed them. When we stopped at one traffic light in particular, not too far from our destination, I noticed several women standing around Shahyad Monument Square. Around its central, vast, white marble structure stood a woman with her chador inside out. I thought perhaps she had been careless when she put it on, but then I noticed about three or four other women who also had their chadors turned inside out.

Further away from the monument, families were strolling along, stopping at the many vendors that dotted the streets, and some police officers were patrolling the area.

"What is this?" I asked the driver, who had been liberal with his answers up to that point.

He explained to me the history of the famous site.

"No, not that," I said. "The women."

The driver cleared his throat a few times and hesitated before he said quietly, "*Siqeh meshan*, available to be temporary wife."

"How can you tell?"

"Their chadors are inside out."

"Just by that you can tell?"

"Yes, and of course, these are the areas where they hang out."

The light changed, and we drove on.

I did not dare turn back to take another look. Suddenly that visit to the registrar's office nearly six years ago became fresh in my mind.

Siqeh meshe? He had asked. The memory of his gruff voice and sour cologne made me feel queasy all over again.

"Khanoom, we are here," the taxi driver said.

"How much?" I asked. As he took the bill from me and gave me my change, I remembered Modar handing the driver the money that day in front of the registrar's office. I thought of the boutique with that red gypsy dress, and the registrar standing on the balcony of that dreadful building. There was nobody next to me this time whose hand I could hold. I was on my own.

"Khanoom are you okay?" the driver asked.

"Thanks, I am okay."

All of that was in the past. This was the present. I was in charge.

I stepped out of the taxi and onto the crowded sidewalk.

I didn't know if I felt sick from the memory of the registrar's proposal, or if it was because I knew what was going to happen between me and Bejan. I knew I could no longer resist the overwhelming desire I had for him.

As I stepped onto the curb, I heard his voice. "Ateesh! Here I am."

He was sitting in his car with the passenger-side window open. He was all smiles and had a fresh bouquet of flowers next to him on the seat.

"Come on in before the traffic police give me a ticket."

His smile put me at ease and I quickly got into his car.

Soft music played, and he reached for my hand and held it as we drove to his apartment.

Roya's words crossed my mind, "Be careful, Ateesh…a different freshman every year." I wondered if he expected me to be a virgin. I was sure he would never guess that I had been married. The feeling of shame began to surface again but I forced myself to ignore it.

"You can tell any man that if he pays for it, you could become a virgin every Friday night!" Suzan joked during a recent dinner with all the girls. The thought eased my mind a bit.

His apartment was on the tenth floor in a very private and exclusive neighborhood. In the elevator, I met one of his neighbors, Professor Yaquby, also a professor at our university. I almost died! I was introduced to him as Ateesh.

"Bejan has an incredible library of poetry books," he said. "Volumes you wouldn't even find at the university library."

"Oh, yes," I said ineptly. "Professor has told me much about his books. He has offered to lend me some."

He gave Bejan a knowing smile, and got off the elevator on the eighth floor. When the elevator door closed, I looked out the corner of my eye at Bejan. He turned to me, put his hands on my waist and pulled me to him.

I couldn't believe how much I wanted this. When the elevator door opened, he led me out, his hand still on my waist. I never thought that being touched by a man could feel so good.

"Please, after you," he said, as he opened the door to his apartment.

As I went inside, I saw that Professor Yaquby was right about his veritable library. I wondered if Grandma Jamileh would approve of him now.

Bejan closed the door behind him and put down his black brief-case. Then he took off his jacket and placed it on the chair by the door. He kept his eyes on me as he removed his shoes and placed them under a chair. I didn't know what I was supposed to do. I stared at the buckle on his black shoes. I guessed I should take off my own shoes before I stepped into the main area onto the beautiful handmade rug. Before I could take them off, he bent down and began to take them off for me. He touched and massaged my foot as he gently removed each shoe. He touched every toe. Then he reached higher to remove my black nylons. I put my hand on his to stop him from reaching beyond my knees. He stood up.

"Ateesh," he whispered into my ear. Then he began to kiss me lightly around my ear, tickling me. I pulled away nervously. He smiled down at me.

"How about some Shiraz?" he asked.

"Wonderful," I said, trying to sound casual and worldly, but wondered why he would be talking about the city of Shiraz at a time like this. He must have heard my thoughts.

"You know Shiraz?" he asked.

Again, mindlessly I nodded. He disappeared into the kitchen and returned with two empty glasses and a bottle.

He held up the bottle and said, "This is Shiraz."

"Oh, to drink?" I said, feeling very stupid.

"No, not to drink, Ateesh Joon."

He set the bottle and glasses down on a table. "Maybe to take a shower in or perhaps to wash your feet in or..."

I was backing away from him with each step. Before I knew it, I fell back onto his couch. He followed and brought his body close to mine. It was electrifying.

I remembered Behrook's words, "When you are touched by the right man, you will feel electricity run through your body."

My pulse raced as he kissed me. He must have felt my heartbeat. He lowered his head and started kissing my chest.

Before I knew it, he had expertly opened my blouse. As his lips got to my breasts, I felt a sensation I had never known. Dizzily, we slid off the couch and down onto a beautiful rug. A rug similar in pattern to the one the salesman at the bazaar was trying to sell to Grandma Tuba. I remembered the lust in that salesman's eyes. I smelled the registrar's body odor mixed with the scent of sour fruit, and I saw my husband walking toward me, smirking. All three of them were dancing in front of my eyes.

"Ateesh, are you all right?" Bejan asked. "You're so tense."

I realized then that I was closing my eyes tightly. I was so afraid if I opened them that I would find Hassan there instead of Bejan. What if this was all a dream? What if I was stuck there in that life?

"Ateesh… Ateesh…" I felt soft kisses on my closed, wet eyes. Hassan never touched me softly.

"Nobody is here but you and me, Ateesh." Bejan's voice was reassuring. Then with great tenderness, he undressed me and carried me to his bedroom. I tried not to think of the first time…and let myself go.

My body was on fire. It was what I had been waiting for. It was as if his touch were lighting a fire. The joy of making love again and again was intoxicating. We turned our bodies in ways I never thought possible. He kissed me in places I never knew were kissable. The more he touched me, the more I wanted him.

We made love until the sun came up the next morning.

I laid my head on his chest.

"Have you ever had an alcoholic beverage?" he asked.

I shook my head.

He got up and left the room, returning a few seconds later with the bottle and two glasses. "Although I can tell I already gave you what you were really desiring, how about tasting this?" he asked.

"This is Shiraz?" I asked.

He laughed and nodded. He poured some in a glass and brought it to my lips. I opened my mouth and let him pour in a little, and then he kissed my lips. I didn't like the taste of Shiraz but the taste of his lips was sweet. He took a large sip of the wine and then began to kiss me with his lips and tongue again, all over my body. I never wanted him to stop. I had discovered the intoxicating joy of making love.

~~ ~~ ~~ ~~ ~~

We spent every night after that at his apartment making love and reading poetry. I confessed to him my love of poetry and told him that I felt like Shahrazad, reading to him and making love night after night.

"That doesn't make me King Shahriyar, does it?" he asked playfully.

"I don't know," I said, smiling.

A couple of months passed and the fall semester was almost over. My classmates were talking about going home. I hadn't given much thought to beyond the first semester. I hadn't given much thought to anything, except for being with Bejan.

Roya and, of course, Suzan, were the only two who knew about us. They made excuses for my many absences and always quashed rumors before they started.

"What have you done to that man?" Roya asked me. "I think you've broken a record!"

I was aware of Bejan's reputation, and I'd heard that the black sofa in his office had indeed been used for purposes other than "tutoring" freshmen. But none of this bothered me. He wasn't Hassan. All I wanted was to be in his arms.

"What will I do without you?" Bejan asked me over dinner at his apartment before the break.

I didn't want to go home for the break. I missed Modar and my grandmas, but I wasn't sure I could face them now, especially Grandma Tuba. Of course, it was also the plane cost and other expenses.

"I decided not to go home for break," I said. "I'm going to stay with Suzan instead."

"Stay with Suzan? Don't do that," he said.

"I don't have any other choice. The dormitories are closing and I can't afford an apartment on my own. I can't ask my family for help," I said.

He put his hand over mine. "If I rented you an apartment, would you stay?" he asked.

I didn't answer. I took his hand and gently pulled him to a standing position. For the first time, I led us into his bedroom.

Up to that point, the only lies I ever told Modar and Grandma Tuba were those of omission. Of course, I never told them about Bejan, my escapades with my very worldly girlfriends at school, or even about some of what I was learning in classes that might contradict Grandma Tuba's traditional beliefs. When we spoke on the phone, I talked about my studies and classes, leaving out anything contradictory, and I asked a lot of questions about Grandma Tuba's friends. I became a former version of myself, but perhaps a lot more confident than I ever felt in Abadan.

When I moved into my new apartment, paid for and leased under Bejan's name, I delicately explained my move to Modar and Grandma Tuba. It was much cheaper than living on campus, I reasoned. Yes, the building was secure. Yes, of course they could come visit and stay with me I told them, though, not without some dread. They liked the idea of visiting and staying with me. I was comforted by the fact that it was unlikely they would. The driving distance between Abadan and Tehran was about one thousand kilometers. Neither of them drove cars and flying was the only option, which was costly.

And no, I exasperatedly told Modar and both Grandmas again and again, men were not harassing me!

During the break from school, I spent my days exploring the city, meeting up with Bejan for lunch or dinner, and I spent my nights with him at his place or mine. Being with him and doing things as simple as drinking tea together was so liberating. I loved it. He was the first man in my life. I refused to consider Hassan, the man I was deceitfully left alone with six years ago, the first man in my life. My life was so different in Tehran than it had been in Abadan. I tried not to think too much about my past and made a conscious effort to live in the moment, and enjoy every minute of it.

One day, as I walked past the famous bookstore on Pahlavi Street, "Katab Khaneh Pahlavi," I noticed a book in the window, *Tales from the Thousand and One Nights*, the same book that lay on Grandma Jamileh's table, by her daybed, where she spent most of her days reading.

Bound and covered with a vivid and colorful jacket, the book stood seductively in the window display. I was mesmerized by Shahrazad's stories, and loved it when Grandma Jamileh read them to me. Grandma Tuba loved them, too, and described Shahrazad as witty, intelligent, and resourceful to survive a king's harsh punishment. Grandma Jamileh emphasized Shahrazad's head-to-toe charm, beauty, and unmatchable cleverness. They were both right.

When I asked the clerk for the book, he pulled a brand-new one from a tall stack behind the register. The one in the window display, I imagined, had looked unflinchingly at so many customers who walked by it. Its colors somewhat faded from the sun, seemed, in its secondhand appearance, to resemble Grandma Jamileh's book and to have more stories to tell than this new copy that I held, one which had only seen the inside of the box in which it was shipped.

I asked the clerk to give me the copy from the window. He protested, telling me that the sun may have caused fading, but seeing the determined look on my face, he relented.

As the clerk went to retrieve the book, I thought of how Shahrazad told stories to entertain, and how that entertainment enabled her survival. Stopping the flow of stories would have meant death for her. King Shahriyar had been betrayed by the queen, which drove him mad enough to behead not only his queen and her lover but also all the virgin girls in his kingdom after spending one night with each of them. Shahrazad knew no other way to stop the killings, and she wanted to prove that women were not just created for sex, but were also intelligent, strong, and capable of surviving. What set Shahrazad apart from the other virgins was her refusal to become another victim. She took charge of the situation with creativity and wit; never for a moment letting the king suspect that it was he who was under her control.

Night after night, for the next thousand and one nights, Shahrazad came down from her quarters, situated a few stories up in the castle, to the main courtyard where the king and his followers were waiting. Since the first night, Shahrazad had taken the duty upon herself to entertain the king, so she carried on her back a baby calf. By the last of the thousand and one nights, it had grown into a full-sized cow. Because she carried it each night, her strength grew along with calf's size and weight. Her physical resilience grew alongside her wit and creative prowess. Her ability to tell stories earned the king's heart, but her wisdom to save the conclusion until morning, thereby buying herself another day to live, earned his respect. In the end, she also won her freedom.

I wanted to be like Shahrazad.

I left the bookstore with the *Tales from the Thousand and One Nights*. Excited by my purchase, Bejan and I spent the next three days reading different passages to each other. I felt as if I was living in Shahrazad's shadow. Words seemed to take a life of their own as they danced out of our mouths.

"Her strength came from her desire to survive," Bejan said.

"And it was her unique approach to survival that kept her alive."

"And, of course, her charisma and beauty."

"It was her intelligence. More than any other characteristic, it was her intelligence that set her apart."

I looked at Bejan. His arm brushed against mine as he turned the page, and I watched as he read quietly. I wasn't sure if what I was feeling toward him was love. Whatever it was, it was great, but I began to wonder if I was depending on him too much. He had become my family in Tehran. I was addicted to him and his touch. That concerned me a bit. I didn't feel as shameful as I had before, though, when I stepped into his office for more than advice on school matters. I was so lost in my world of Bejan and Shahrazad, that I hadn't realized that Grandma Jamileh, Grandma Tuba, and Modar were trying to reach me. For those three days, I hadn't been home to receive their calls.

"Stay one more night with me," Bejan said as he kissed my neck and gently traced my shoulder with his tongue. "Just one more night. You know I have to leave early in the morning for a conference out of town."

"I can't," I said. "Tomorrow I have to go to the bank, and that will entail a visit with my cousin, Zari. I haven't even picked up any gifts for her kids. They'll be expecting something. Also, what if my family tries to get in touch with me?"

He looked at me pleadingly.

For a second I saw the registrar's face looking back at me.

"I'll see you when you get back," I said. I kissed him on his forehead and stood up. As I walked out his front door, I felt more in control than I had in a long time.

~~ ~~ ~~ ~~ ~~

I nearly tripped over my own feet when I saw Modar. There she was, sitting in the lobby of my apartment building. It was close to midnight. "Ateesh, *Kojaboody*, where were you?" she asked, as she stood up and opened her arms. "We were worried to death!" I walked into her arms and hid my face in her embrace. I was filled with shame, but it felt so good to be in her arms again. We walked upstairs to my apartment. Did she notice my disheveled hair? Could she smell his cologne? Polo, by Ralph Lauren, was all over me, and at that moment the smell of it was making me sick to my stomach.

After much fumbling with my keys, we went into my apartment. Bejan had bought things for my apartment and I had decorated it beautifully with different art effects.

"You have done a good job in decorating this place," Modar said.

I studied her face and could see she knew everything. I looked around at my apartment and all I could see in its decor were signs of my guilt.

She didn't ask questions. As she fell asleep in the bed next to me, I felt shame that was worse than any physical injury I could ever endure.

She knew without asking that her little daughter was no longer so innocent.

The next morning, we did not speak of the previous night and my whereabouts. I went into the kitchen to make Modar some tea, only to realize I had none. I had become a coffee drinker. I offered Modar a cup of Nescafé and she gracefully accepted it.

As I sat across from her, I saw sadness in her face.

"What is it, Modar?" I asked.

"It's Saeed," she said. "He was in a car accident."

"A car accident?" I waited for her to say he was okay, but the look on her face told me that he wasn't.

"Oh my God!" I said, as I felt tears rush to my eyes.

"I wanted to give you the news myself," Modar said. "We all knew you and Saeed were close. The funeral was held two days ago but the seventh-day reception is in five days at the *masjid*.

I wiped at the tears on my face, as I pictured him next to me on the balcony, pointing out the stars.

"We were so worried for you, Ateesh Joon, when you didn't answer the phone for three days. That is why I came. Grandma is missing you, but she said you come home only when you are ready to come. Here is an open plane ticket."

She handed me the ticket, then opened her suitcase and took out a large package.

"What is that?" I asked.

"Grandma sent some of your favorite snacks. Grandfather sent some money. Grandma Jamileh also sent you some money and a book you might like."

I knew I couldn't face them now. There was no way I could do it. Even if it meant missing my favorite cousin's funeral.

Modar and I talked the rest of the afternoon. She updated me on everyone back home. I showed her around the campus, trying to tell her, without many words, that I had not changed much since coming to school, and that my first priority was still my education.

All afternoon I waited for an interrogation that never came. She never once asked me where I was those three nights, and who knows how many other nights when I failed to answer the phone. She never asked who was buying me all the things in the apartment.

"*Movazeb bash*, be careful, Ateesh," she said, as we said goodbye at the airport.

"I will," I replied, embracing her with my heart and soul. "Please don't worry about me anymore. I am fine and I'm going to be fine. I am in charge of my life."

"Don't be fooled by the appearance of things," Modar said as she pulled me close to her one last time before boarding the plane. I said a prayer for Saeed that night and I cried loudly. Standing outside my balcony, I looked for the stars. There were none I could see.

"You are the prettiest of all the stars," he had told me. I missed him and my innocence. My tears were for both.

I never made it to my meeting with Zari, and my monthly bank payment was overdue. That was the reality of my situation. I needed much more money to remain in Tehran. I had been looking for jobs, but there was nothing available. The transportation would cost more than the jobs would even pay.

I wondered what Shahrazad would have done.

Bejan was returning in two days. I needed some time to clear my head. Modar's visit had me rethinking everything I was doing.

～～～～～～

My friend Tanaz was an artist who lived in Tehran with her husband and two children. We met during one of her shows at the university. I hadn't known she was the artist. In fact, having shown a great interest in my studies, I thought she was a professor. We talked for a while that day and it wasn't until the end of our conversation that she confessed to creating the masterful pieces before us. I was impressed with her right from the start. As we said goodbye that day, she slipped her business card into my hand.

"Call me, Ateesh, and we will go for Nescafé," she had said.

We met a week later for coffee, and that's when she came right out and told me she was a lesbian.

"Really?" I said, in shock. "I didn't know we had that here!"

"Had what here?" she said. "You cannot even say the word?" She seemed disappointed in me. "I thought...when you took me up on my invitation, that you were one too."

"Tanaz, I do not even know the name in Farsi!" I said. "Lesbian is an English word, right?"

"I am sorry to hear that," she said.

"But you're married?" I asked.

"Yes. I have to save family face, *aberue*. No choice."

I nodded. I knew how that was.

"So you aren't a lesbian anymore?"

"You are so naive, Ateesh! This is not something that can go away with marriage. And no one questions the time women spend together," she explained. "Besides, my husband is out of town a lot on business, and my children are at school all day. It's easy to manage being with my female friends who are married and in the same situation."

I was fascinated by what I was learning from her.

"Wow," was all I could say.

"I knew I was attracted to women long before I was married, Ateesh," she said, as if she had anticipated the question I had no intention of asking.

"My family interpreted my disinterest in men as a sign of my good character. When my husband's family came to ask for my hand, I did not even look at my future husband. They thought that was the way a virgin girl should behave." I laughed at this, and she began to laugh too. Tanaz and I became good friends. She was one of very few people I was close with outside of my circle of university friends. Now, I needed her candor and empathy about my relationship with Bejan.

"Ateesh," Tanaz said when she saw me. "It is so wonderful to see you!"

She kissed me on both cheeks before sensing that this was more than a simple social invitation.

"What's going on?" she asked.

I told her everything. All about my relationship with Bejan, how it had progressed, Modar's surprise visit, and my feelings of shame. She listened attentively.

"I feel as if I've let Modar and my grandmas down," I said, as I wiped at the tears that were rolling down my cheeks.

She handed me a tissue. "When was the last time you went to a *hammom*, public bath?" she asked.

"What?"

"You heard me, Ateesh. *Hammom*. Let us go. It will be refreshing." She stood up.

I thought what an unusual thing that was to do. We have showers right in our homes now. Back home, in Abadan, I used to go about once a week, or once every two weeks, with Modar or one of the grandmas for a serious bath. Otherwise, we washed up in our plain and modest bathrooms. As a child, I spent more time playing in the water than I did washing. My grandma would put shampoo in my hair and direct me to wash it. Then she would take a bucket of tap water and pour it over my head. After all the shampoo was gone, it was time for me to be washed all over again. I remembered the gossip that was shared between Grandma Jamileh and some of her preferred *dalock*, washing women.

"Why, Tanaz?" I asked again, "This is so… so…"

"Call it whatever you want, but we're going."

"Okay."

I didn't see how this could have anything to do with Bejan and where my relationship with him was going.

We took off our clothes in the changing room. Out of a habit developed during my childhood visits to the *hammom*, I left my underwear on. I kept talking as Tanaz and I walked down a narrow hallway that led to a large room with multiple showers, water fountains, naked women and children, and *dalocks* waiting to be hired.

As the *dalocks* washed our bodies with washcloths made from special fabric, I talked more intermittently. Since the changing room, Tanaz had listened to me go on and on about Bejan and she didn't interrupt. Now that I was sure I covered everything and there was nothing more to tell her, my mind started to drift. I was distracted by the *dalock's* firm strokes. I thought of Grandma Jamileh and how she liked to be scrubbed. When I was a child, even the gentlest strokes could sometimes be too painful. Today, I felt purged by them.

"Let's go, Ateesh," Tanaz said, interrupting my thoughts.

The *dalocks* were finished. Tanaz and I walked to an adjacent room and got into a large pool to rinse. I remembered something Modar would say: "Never rinse your body in the rinsing pool. It is filthy."

"Talk to me about something," I said. "Anything."

"Okay," Tanaz said. "One day when I was about fifteen, I came here with my friend, Parry. I was rinsing her hair for her. We were fooling around and splashing, and I accidentally touched her breast. She blushed, and I'm sure I did too. We moved to a shower that had a lock from the inside." Then she lowered her voice to almost a whisper, "Then without any words, under the running water, we just started touching each other."

Had anyone else been telling me this story, I would have thought it scandalous. From Tanaz, it seemed okay.

"Eventually, we heard someone pounding at the door, yelling that we were taking too long. We quickly ran out of there without a final rinse, got our clothes, dressed and left the *hammom*. After that, Parry and I used to go to each other's houses every day after school and experiment. We promised each other that we would never get married and that we would remain friends for the rest of our lives, but after high school, our families arranged our marriages. Parry left Tehran with her husband."

Then Tanaz was quiet. I had never seen such a sorrowful look on her face. It revealed pain and resignation, two emotions I hadn't often associated with her. I wasn't sure what to say.

"Ateesh, you have more options than Parry and I did," she said, suddenly becoming serious. "If you love Bejan and you are happy with where this relationship may take you, make your decisions based on that. But remember, you are just beginning your life and career. In my opinion, no man is worth sacrificing your career. From what you are telling me, this man is a playboy. Is that the kind of character you are interested in?"

Before I could answer, she continued, "He is the first man in your life and you really do not know much about him. Don't settle. For all we know about this professor, he is complicated and he might dump you, even though he says he loves you."

"I think I love him," I said.

"This would be a good test of your abilities as a strong woman. If you can walk away from this first love, then no man can ever hurt you. I truly believe that."

"I can't leave him."

"This is a test of your strength in relation to men. Not to become a prisoner of their superiority means walking away from perfect situations."

As I walked back to my apartment, I thought about what Tanaz said. I was a prisoner to a man once. I never wanted to be one again. Here I was saying things like, "I think I love him," and "I can't leave him." Isn't that what Modar said? What Farah said?

I spent the next day cleaning my apartment and listening to music.

When Bejan returned the following day, we made love passionately at his place; then I ended our relationship, as hard as it was for me. I told him about Saeed's death and what had happened with Modar. He held me as he listened.

"Ateesh, I'll give you as much time as you need," he said. "But I hope you change your mind."

"About the apartment..." I stammered.

"Don't worry, I will pay until the end of the year when the contract expires," Bejan said. I looked at him. He knew where I needed help the most. I wanted to tell him, no, I don't need you to do that. But I couldn't.

After leaving his apartment, I wandered around the city, thinking about what had happened over the past few months. It all seemed a blur. As I walked, I passed Shahyad Monument Square, that was right near our meeting spot on our first—or was it our second date? It became our meeting spot for every date until I had moved into my apartment. I stopped for a moment and looked ahead.

There they were: The women who wore their chadors inside out. The *siqeh*.

What possible life situation would make these women become *siqeh*? How did they feel about being sexual objects?

That night back in my apartment, I woke up a number of times, sweating. I walked to the balcony and desperately searched for a star in the sky, but there wasn't one. Close to sunrise I finally fell into a fitful sleep.

The next night, I walked to the monument square. With every step I took, my heart beat harder and faster. I slipped into a nearby alley, and with trembling hands, took my chador out of my purse. I hadn't worn the chador since I was in Abadan. I flipped it inside out and placed it over my head.

With the chador on my head, I could not take another step. My legs were numb and my heart felt as if it had stopped. I removed the chador and placed it back in my purse. For the first time since I had left Baba's house, I hated the strong desire I had to be independent.

I went back to my apartment and collapsed on my bed.

One afternoon as I was walking past the newspaper kiosk located by the main gate of the university, a headline caught my eye: "Siqeh Keeps Society Clean."

I stopped next to an older man who was reading the paper. He was wearing the traditional dark brown cloak and white turban that identified him as a registrar. He was larger in frame than the dirty old registrar whose office I had walked into years ago. The memory of that registrar made me uncomfortable in the presence of this man, and I suddenly found myself inching away from him.

Then I stopped myself. It was time for me to grow up. How long was I going to hold on to all of that? It was time for me to stop being a victim.

The man looked at me and smiled. His smile was nothing like the one I remembered.

"Look at this," he said, as he pointed to the bold headline.

I nodded.

"It is not a profession for all women," he said, "but some could benefit from it."

"How?" I asked.

"Well, a woman can get the financial support she needs."

"And the men?"

"Well, they get what they need too."

I thought again of the old registrar.

"How does it keep the society clean?" I asked.

"Well, men's natural desires are controlled," he said. Then he lowered his voice and asked, "Are you interested?"

I saw in his eyes then that there wasn't much of a difference between the old registrar and this one. For a brief second, I was haunted by the same feeling of powerlessness I had that day, when I was twelve years old.

"No," I finally said. "Society is doing pretty well without my help." Then I turned and walked away.

"Wait, I'm sorry," he said as he ran after me. "I didn't mean to insult you."

I stopped at the entrance of the campus and turned toward him. He held out his business card. "Take it," he said softly. "Maybe you're doing some kind of research or something. I am a registrar and could provide you with statistics and information on *siqeh*. *Bebaksheed*, forgive me."

I looked around to see if anybody was watching. Quickly, I took the card, closed it in my hand and walked away.

I didn't feel good for the rest of the day. My friends assumed it was because of my breakup with the professor, but that wasn't the only reason. Yes, I missed Bejan tremendously and wanted to run and hide in his arms, but I resisted the temptation of allowing my feelings to take over. I made the decision that I would control my emotions. It was difficult, though. Sometimes I felt as if my heart was bleeding.

Every night since the breakup, I cried for hours alone in my bed and called out Bejan's name. I felt so alone and ached to be with him again.

Tonight, I looked at my tear-stained face in the mirror. I stared into my eyes, which were red and swollen from crying.

"Ateesh," I said, "learn from all around you. If you are not independent, the chances that men will use and abuse you are great!"

I thought of Modar and how she had been stuck in her marriage all these years. I remembered Grandma Tuba's friends, one by one, and how they felt so miserable and helpless...

"Ateesh," I said, "don't pity yourself. You have a choice. You are not a child anymore. You wanted to be in control of your life. Here you are."

When I closed my eyes, Baba and Hassan stood before me. When I opened my eyes, their images faded. I was going to use men to reach my goal of independence from them. "*Mardom chi megan*, what would people say?"

"Grandma?" I remembered asking years ago, "what if people don't come to know about a girl's inappropriate behavior?"

I wondered, could I become a *siqeh* without anybody knowing? To be a *siqeh* means to be a prostitute, no matter how many religious justifications there were. For the next few days, Grandma Tuba, Modar, and Grandma Jamileh kept popping up in my mind. If they only knew what I was thinking!

There was only one time Grandma Tuba had ever defended, and even arranged, the act of *siqeh*. It was for Khanoom Berenji, after her husband's nephew took the home she lived in for forty years. Grandma Tuba helped her become a *siqeh* to a widower Hajji, who was in his seventies. The arrangement, as Grandma Tuba explained, was to "provide her with a home and him with companionship and someone to look after him."

Being a *siqeh* provided Khanoom Berenji with what she needed after she lost it all. I wasn't old and destitute and didn't need a shadow of a man like she did, but I had my own reasons. One was to be financially independent, and the other, to become emotionally indifferent to men. Reasons that Grandma Tuba would neither understand nor approve of.

On Friday, October ninth, I picked up the phone and called the Hajji Registrar.

"*Salam Azizam*, Hello my dear!" he said. "I was hoping I would hear from you!"

"How exactly does this work?" I asked him.

"Well, men would contact me and I would provide them with information about you," he explained. "Then they would call you directly."

"Who determines the duration and prices?"

"We have guidelines, of course, but ultimately it would be between you and him."

"Guidelines?" I asked.

"Yes, the price depends on your age, and of course your physical appearance."

"How do you make it legal?"

"I issue a marriage license, just as you would get if it was a permanent marriage. I would need your photo, not only to show the prospective client, but also to place into the certificate booklet."

"What do you require of him?"

"Of course the financial ability to pay, but his photo has to go into the certificate as well."

I took a deep breath before I asked the next question.

"What about any diseases he may have?"

"What?" he asked.

"What if he has some transferable disease?"

He was quiet for a minute, then snapped, "I never had a *siqeh* ask me so many questions! Are you sure you want to do this? You sound more like a *mohaqeq*, researcher! Don't fool me, Khanoom!"

I gripped the phone in my hand and waited for him to calm down. I needed answers to these questions if I was to go ahead with this. "Sexually transmitted diseases are to be taken seriously," I was told by Suzan.

"No, I am not a *mohaqeq*," I said. "So what is your share, Hajji?" I took another deep breath.

"I see you are a businesswoman, *Khahar*, sister!" he answered, "My share is fifty percent of the contract price."

I was silent. Fifty percent of the contract price? That's half!

"Remember, you need me to find the clients," he said.

I was silent.

"Are you there?" he asked.

"This is not for me," I said.

Before he could respond, I hung up the phone. I ran into the bathroom and threw up.

What was I thinking? What was I becoming? When I climbed into bed that night, Grandma Tuba's stories ran through my mind again and again. Stories all about the unacceptable behavior of girls. Never once had I heard a story about the unacceptable behavior of boys.

"Why not God?" I shouted.

I felt so lonely.

~~ ~~ ~~ ~~ ~~

For the next few weeks, I focused completely on my studies, avoiding Bejan on campus. Suzan told me he had already started going out with another student.

"Good for him," I said. "I really don't care." Pain was inside me, though. That very night I dreamt about him. In the dream, I walked into a coffee shop and he was sitting there, facing the entrance. Our eyes met. My first instinct was to run to him. In my dream I didn't fight it. "Hold me and don't let go," I said to him. Everybody and everything had disappeared. He was the only one present. I woke up crying and aching for his touch. But I could not have him and still remain in control of myself and my life. I was still vulnerable to him and I didn't like it. He was my weakness and I had to overcome it.

One day right after afternoon classes, Roya and I went to the bookstore on Pahlavi Street. As she was looking for a book for her English class, I went to the religion section and browsed through the different books written by Moslem authors. One book in particular that attracted my attention was a translation of the book *La femme dans l'inconscient musulman* by Fatna A. Sabbah. *Woman in the Muslim Unconscious*. I browsed through it for a while, then noticed another book on a shelf nearby that someone must have misplaced.

As I reached for the book, there was another hand reaching for it at the same time. As our fingers touched, I noticed his hands were just like Baba's. His fingers were long and thin, his nails neatly and evenly cut with a slight hint of shine. His hands were soft like Baba's, and I suddenly remembered holding onto Baba's hand tightly as he helped me climb one of the fruit trees in the orchard. I was about three or four years old. "You can do it, Ateesh," he had said. "Just concentrate on the climb."

"I am sorry," the man's voice said gently, bringing me back into the present moment.

I smiled at him. He was a cleric of medium build with a pleasant smell of cologne. My nostrils filled with a jasmine-like flower scent. He was wearing a long, light-gray gown down to his ankles, with about five buttons down the side. His lightweight, black cotton religious robe was hung loosely on his shoulders exactly the way Grandfather wore it. He had a fine, white turban around his head with a white curl in the front that sat right above his light brown eyes. He looked like the high-ranking clerics I had seen on TV during the month of Ramadan, the fasting month.

I opened the book and pretended to read it. I felt my face flush when I saw the title, *Pleasing Your Sexual Urges*.

The way he looked at me, without any words, said it all. He looked right into my eyes, instead of gazing down as is religiously required from a "believing man." He fit right into the stereotyped image of men who practice temporary marriages: religious clergy who believed in having more than one wife. He had a similar look as the old registrar. I could see his desire, although this time it wasn't vulgar.

Discreetly and gently, he took his business card from his pocket and placed it on the bookshelf. Then he apologized again and walked away. My eyes followed him as he exited the bookstore. I picked up the card and read his name, Hajji Aqa Ayatollah. The jasmine scent from his cologne remained in the air. I stood there for a few minutes longer gazing at the book we both had reached for.

If I was going to become a *siqeh*, Hajji Aqa Ayatollah was going to be my first temporary husband. I had a feeling then, which was confirmed later on by him, that he was hoping for the same.

For the next several nights, I went to the square where the *siqeh* women stood, waiting. They were dependent on men. My goal was the exact opposite.

Was that possible?

Several weeks passed before I picked up the phone and dialed Hajji Aqua Ayatollah's number.

A whole new chapter in my life was about to begin.

"Allo."

"Salam Hajji."

"Salam?"

"We met at the book store several weeks ago."

"Oh, yes of course! I've been hoping you would call. How are you?"

"I am fine."

"Would you like to meet at the bookstore to talk?"

"Okay," was all I could say.

We met the next afternoon in the same spot at the bookstore. As soon as I saw him, I took a deep breath in to inhale his fragrance. As we made small talk about the weather, my studies, and books I liked to read, I felt his desire for me, and I wasn't appalled by it in any way.

"Have you read any of Ayatollah Boroujerdi's books on Islam?" he asked, as he pointed to several writings by the Ayatollah on the bookshelf.

"Not really," I said, as I recalled the framed photograph of him that Grandma Tuba had on her table in the sitting room, "but I know of him and his philosophy on different issues through my grandmodar as her disciple."

"There are several others who share his philosophy on Islam, advocating for the separation of powers between state and religion."

The more we talked, the more I realized how much I could benefit from his vast knowledge on religion. If I was going to learn by selling myself, this was a good beginning. We were dancing around the idea of *siqeh*, until finally he asked directly: "Do you know how much you want?" He had a twinkle in his eye.

"Not really," I said, "but I heard there is a going rate."

He laughed and said, "What else did you hear?"

"I heard that the religious clerics like yourself are the main practitioners of it, because they know these religious practices, whereas the average person may not know about its existence."

"You are smart and beautiful," he said. "Why do you want to do this?"

I remained quiet. I was not exactly sure yet myself.

"You don't have to do anything you do not wish to do," he said softly. "Then it would become *haram*, a forbidden act, which negates the purpose."

I recalled my mother's voice, when she snapped at my Baba, "I know what *haram* means!"

"Please don't ask me why," I said. "Just guide me from here on what to do, Aqa Hajji, to consummate a legal *siqeh*," I said. "I am a fast learner."

My directness surprised him. "I like your straightforwardness. It is refreshing."

We set a date for him to come over to my apartment, then we parted.

My mind was totally numb.

I spent the next several days focusing on my studies and, now, avoiding all my friends.

Later on that week, he came over to my apartment. He brought sweets and a bottle of Diorissimo by Christian Dior for me.

"This is my favorite scent, Jasmine," he said, "and I would like you to wear it whenever I come here." Then he handed me a box that contained a lavender dress with an open back and low neckline. It was ruffled below the chest and flowed at the bottom.

I was surprised. "This looks like the dress Marilyn Monroe wore in *Some Like It Hot*," I said. "Where did you get this?"

"I bought it on a recent trip to Europe and kept it," he said. "I knew I would be meeting you. Please, put it on."

I picked up the dress and went to the walk-in closet in the bathroom to try it on. He followed me.

"Hajji," I said, "please, first the wedding vows."

He apologized and waited in the bedroom until I came out in the dress. I felt as if I was ready to be wed. Then we sat on the bed in the bedroom and he recited the required religious verse: "Would you be my wife for a period of one year in exchange for one million tumon per month, Ateesh?"

"I accept," I said quietly. Then I asked, "Is that a good price?"

He laughed and moved toward me until our bodies touched. He lifted my chin with his hand until our eyes met.

"Money won't be an issue between us," he said, then he gently pushed me and I fell back onto the bed.

"Can you pay my rent too, Aqa Hajji?" I asked. As he took over my body, I kept my eyes closed to hold back tears that threatened to come.

~~ ~~ ~~ ~~ ~~

Hajji Aqa Ayatollah, my first temporary husband, was not only familiar with the practice of temporary marriage, but he was well-versed in the Quran. The main difference between the men who practiced *siqeh* when I was a child, such as the registrar who propositioned me when I was twelve, and the men who practiced it by my early adulthood, was simply that they were growing in numbers. More and more men were encouraged publicly to practice *siqeh*.

Among the ten temporary husbands I've had, at least five of them were high-ranking clerics who were well-educated in the theology of Islam. Along with my professors at the university, these clerics became my teachers, enabling me, whether they always knew it or not, to understand how easy it is to abuse women under the guise of God's will. I will always remember Hajji Aqa Ayatollah, not only as my first temporary husband, but as a religious teacher.

So began a major chapter and a turning point in my life—my double life, as it turned out. Of course, as a young girl, I had learned about pretenses through listening to my Grandma Tuba's friends and acquaintances. The majority of women presented a perfect picture of a happy marriage to the outside world, but I'd heard the bitter truth as they confided to Grandma Tuba.

Behind closed doors I was a *siqeh*. Out in the world I was a serious student. I lived in total celibacy. I had people believing what Tanaz's family thought about her—that I didn't even like boys. Keeping secrets and pretending to be someone else is quite easy in a culture that

119

promotes keeping up appearances at any cost. If anyone asked me why I became a *siqeh* I don't think I could have quite articulated my reasons, at least not at first. Of course, money was a concern, and this gave me financial independence. I did not want to rely on any man for rent ever again. But that was not the only reason.

A few months into our contract, Hajji Aqa gave me two new copies of the Quran, each with Farsi translations and the author's explanations. He offered them to me after one of our more heated conversations, and I had graciously accepted.

"First lesson," Hajji said, "Never trust one translation. These revelations are from God, through Gabriel, to Prophet Mohammad. Then through him, to his companions, and through them, to scribes."

I tried not to seem confused. He smiled, pulled me closer to him, and, as our bodies touched, he kissed me on my lips.

"Ateesh, why have you become a *siqeh*?" he asked. "It cannot be just for financial reasons. You would have no difficulty in finding a permanent husband who could support you."

After a moment of silence, he continued, "You are too intelligent to remain a temporary wife. Why not consider a permanent marriage?"

I pulled away from him gently, and looked into his eyes. "I have already been married, Hajji," I said. "One marriage that was supposed to be permanent was enough. Husbands do not treat their wives well. I will never put up with abuse like I did with him. I have more respect for myself now."

I came to realize that as a *siqeh,* I had more control of my destiny than I ever had as a wife or a daughter. I felt comfortable with Hajji Aqa, and although I never felt passion for him the way I had felt for Bejan, I was unafraid to ask him questions about anything. I asked him why he practiced *siqeh*. I also asked him if I was his first *siqeh*. He said I wasn't.

"If temporary marriage was not allowed and encouraged religiously, I would not have married you," he said, matter-of-factly.

I did not believe in what he was telling me, but he appeared sincere. Hajji truly believed that his temporary marriage to me earned him *savab*, blessing.

"Imam Sadeq has highly recommended that men should marry temporary wives as often as possible," Hajji Aqa explained.

"As an educated religious man, Hajji, tell me how having sex with a woman could be related to *savab*?" I asked. "What kind of blessings can you get from this? Pleasing yourself, encouraging the economic dependency of women, and hurting your wife? Marrying another woman can earn you *savab*?"

We had frequent conversations like this one, and he sensed my frustration. I tremendously enjoyed this part of our relationship. He tried to answer all my questions about Islam and it was because of him that I realized there was a big gap between *dean* and *deandar*, religion and its followers.

After a while, he stopped defending temporary marriage as a religiously divine duty. I think I may have created a doubt in his mind about the whole idea of having sex for *savab*.

Hajji paid me well over our contracted price. I was even able to save money.

He asked me to move closer to his house, but it was too far from the university, so I didn't accept.

"Now I can come over only two nights a week," he said. "I was hoping for four nights."

"Is there a customary time, like per week or month, Hajji?" I asked.

"Yes, but too bad for you, Ateesh, you did not make it clear at the time of the contract," he said, with a pleased look on his face. He crossed his legs, put his hands on me, looked into my eyes and smiled.

"Well, Aqa Hajji," I said. "The Quran forbids taking advantage of the weaker sex." Then I asked softly, "Isn't that what you did?"

He almost fell over. "You are Ateesh *Bala*, Ateesh *Pareh*, sparkle of fire."

We had conversations like that often, which he seemed to like, because they always ended with him all over me.

These debates continued, especially as I was learning how to read and think critically in my classes. Although I had learned much about the rules and restrictions of Islam from my Grandma Tuba, Hajji was patient with my questions, and always thorough in giving me the rationale.

"Why is it always the case that the subsequent wives are younger?" I asked him once, thinking of Baba's much younger second wife.

"If it is done according to Quran, the age should not be a factor at all," he said. "This is a historical fact and it is written in Quran that after the war of Uhud, the Moslem community was left with many orphans, widows, and some captives of war. Their treatment was to be governed by the principle of the greatest humanity and equity. The revelation came solely to protect that class of women and orphans in need of men's support and protection. Remember Ateesh, we are talking about the sixth century."

His last sentence hit me like a thunderbolt. "So what was justified under social necessity in the mid-sixth century is encouraged now in the twenty-first century?"

"There is no harm in that," he said. "Ateesh, a temporary wife's job is to please her husband, not to read newspapers and get analytical," he would tease. "Aren't you my *siqeh*, Khanoom?"

Being a *siqeh* was more like a part-time job for me. That was how I looked at it. On a typical week he would come to my apartment two to three times per week. He came after lunch and stayed until late evening. We would generally start our time together by having tea and talking about the news headlines. I couldn't wait to discuss these cases with him.

"Ateesh, sometimes I feel as if you are blaming me for all the ill doing of some Moslems," he said.

"Aqa Hajji, you are one of the teachers in a faith that promotes social justice, right? Look at this story." I pointed to the back of the newspaper he was reading.

A teenage woman had defended herself and stabbed the young man who had attempted to rape her. And yet, now she was on trial for committing adultery.

"If a religious leader like you doesn't have an answer, can you imagine how ordinary people like me feel?" I asked.

Then I walked to the kitchen and turned on the samovar to make some tea.

I felt his arms around me. It felt good to be held.

"Ateesh, marry me," he said.

"We are married," I said.

"I mean…," he said.

"You mean for real? Not temporary, right?" I said.

"You don't make it easy at all, Ateesh."

"Aqa Hajji, my job is to keep the society clean, not to make it easy for you." I pulled myself away and busied myself with the tea. "I'll be in the bedroom in a second to continue our discussion on cleansing the society by attending to your needs," I said.

"You are the devil herself in flesh," he said, as he walked toward the bedroom. In many writings of well-known religious leaders, women have been referred to as devils.

That night as he said goodbye, he looked into my eyes and said, "Ateesh, don't confuse a religion with its practitioners."

I was learning a lot about Islamic law at the university, but even more importantly, about how it was being practiced, and I wanted Hajji to give me further insight. I wondered if his permanent wife was challenging him on religion as well.

As our marriage continued on into the second and third months, he did not seem to mind my inquisitiveness as much. Though our marriage was encouraged in the Quran, at least according to his interpretation, I was sure Hajji wasn't telling his wife about our relationship, or our conversations. How could he justify his needs to have a *siqeh*? In my Baba's case, he justified his second marriage with Modar's inability to conceive more children after me. Culturally, it is well-accepted for a man to do so. In Aqa Hajji's case, however, he already had several grown children, so Baba's reasoning wouldn't work for him. And if his wife had some incurable sexual disease, he would not be justifying his actions under "religious duty." It looked to me as if Hajji was doing this solely for his pleasure.

As I was reading yet another incident of stoning in the newspaper, he explained patiently. "The Hadith, the Sunna, and the Shariah have been interpreted as prescribing stoning as the punishment for adultery," he said, in answer to my question. "Unlike the Quran, which is the direct revelation, the Hadith and the Sunna are commentaries on the Prophet's life traditions and sayings. The Shariah refers to laws compiled and interpreted by jurists after the Prophet's death in 632."

"In other words, these three sources are the result of human interpretations of historical events. Is that correct, Hajji?" I asked.

"Yes," he said, looking at me the way teachers look at prized but impertinent pupils. "But before you jump to any conclusions, you must understand that the Hadith and the Sunna were compiled and then carefully screened by righteous jurists before they were written down as authoritative."

"But Hajji, how can we trust an interpretation that prescribes such a harsh punishment for one gender alone?" I asked. "Were any of these interpreters women? 'God is fair,' 'God is forgiving,' I hear that all the time!" I continued, my voice getting louder, "Show me the fairness in how some of these verses have been interpreted!"

Hajji Aqa could not, or perhaps chose not to answer me just then. Instead, he told me that he found my inquiries into religion admirable and, at times, sexy. Then he became serious. "You have to promise me not to make these inquiries with anyone else, Ateesh," he said, "I will answer any question that you may have about Islam, but no discussions of this sort with others. Do you understand? People will think you are a *Kafir*, a non-believer."

I nodded. I remembered promising Grandma Tuba the same thing when I was a young teen. But I was not a young teen anymore, I was twenty-one years old.

"Hajji, why can't we just reinterpret the misinterpreted verses to bring back the social justice that Islam was built upon?"

~~ ~~ ~~ ~~ ~~

A year later, Hajji renewed our marriage contract. By this time, I was accustomed to his schedule and most of his ways. For example, he never stayed for dinner on Thursday nights because it was an important night for prayers and sermons. It is believed that praying on

Thursday nights brings more blessings to men who are believers. We always had sex in the shower on Thursdays, because he had only a couple of hours before prayers, and he had to shower before prayers.

One Thursday night, I was in the kitchen turning on the samovar for tea when I heard his panicked voice calling my name from the shower. I ran in and found him standing there in the stall, naked and dry.

"There is no water," he said. He sat down on the shower bench and put his face in his hands.

"No water?" I asked. Then I started laughing, but quickly stopped myself when I saw his face. He was looking at me like a frightened child.

"Ateesh," he said, "I must perform ablution before I can pray! What am I going to do?"

"Yes, I know," I said. "Let me see." I tried to think without laughing. One of the most respected and educated clerics was sitting naked and helpless in my shower, not knowing what to do because there was no water to cleanse himself. He sat there with his face in his hands, cursing himself.

I heard noises from outside. I quickly dressed and went outside to see if it was related to water pipes. There I found streams of water running down the street in front of my house. Apparently, a nearby water line had broken.

When I went back inside, I found him holding onto his rosary, asking all the religious figures to mediate between him and God to find a way for him to perform ablution.

I only had a couple of water bottles in the refrigerator, so I suggested he go home and take a shower.

"Don't be foolish, Ateesh," he snapped. Had he gone home, his wife would have known that he had sex with another woman. Culturally, taking a shower is associated with having sex, especially during the day.

I suggested *tayammum*, a less frequently used purification procedure that did not require water. He angrily refused, and explained that *tayammum* can only be used after touching, not penetration and reaching climax. A full ablution was required before he could lead prayers at the *masjid*.

"Let me see if I understand this," I said, as I felt myself beginning to lose patience with him. "We can kiss and touch and do everything else, but only a full penetration requires ablution?"

"Ateesh!" he yelled. "This is not the time for your reinterpretation of Quranic verses! Stop it. This is vitally serious. Not another word from your mouth unless it is about water."

I felt sorry for him, and felt the need to rescue him from his helplessness. I suggested driving him to a private bathhouse not far from my apartment, but he said there were the same implications of taking a shower in the afternoon.

Then I had an idea. After he was dressed, I handed him one of my chadors to put on, instead of his usual white turban. Ignoring his protests, I drove him to a public *hammom* with private showers. There I waited for him to finish his ablution.

As we drove back to my apartment, he was quiet and deep in thought. I could see he was deeply ashamed of dressing up as a woman and saw it as a signal from the higher divine power. We went back to my apartment where he quietly changed into his religious cloak and turban. The *masjid* where he was leading the prayers was not far from my apartment.

As he stepped out, I called out to him, "*Qaboul basheh,*" wishing his prayers would be accepted by God.

He did not look back, nor did he say a word in reply. He walked with his head down. I closed the door and went back inside.

For the next few days I didn't see or hear from him. I knew he must have been incredibly embarrassed. I didn't know what to do. I couldn't call him for fear that his wife would pick up. In the nearly eighteen months I had been married to him, it was he who always called me.

It was the end of another semester, and my friends came over to my apartment to study. I had given them the same explanation for my apartment that I gave to my family: It was cheaper. I got a good deal. None of my friends knew about Aqa Hajji *Ayatollah*.

My friend Azita cooked a fabulous dinner, for which all of us, Roya, Suzan, and I, were grateful. Though I no longer survived on university cuisine, nor had the money to eat in restaurants, as they did, I never really bothered to cook for myself. I only cooked when Hajji came over. Having grown up in Tehran, Suzan was not a cook. Suzan had, in fact, introduced Roya and me to the best restaurants in the city. But I went to them only with Bejan.

Azita grew up in a middle class family with four siblings. Her parents met in *Boroujerd*, a small town in eastern Iran, best known for its pleasant spring and summer weather. Her baba was a Lebanese-born Arab, and her modar was from Abadan. Such mixed marriages were common in *Khosastan*, where they lived. Mixed-blood Iranians from this region have distinctive features and accents. When I first met Azita, I immediately found her exotic and unconventionally attractive. Together, we often went to the nearby shrine of *Hasrateeh* Fatemeh Masumeh (sister of the eighth imam Reza) in Qom, one of Iran's holiest cities. Though I respected *Hasrateeh* Fatemeh, Azita's reverence for Fatemeh as a great model of sacrifice and martyrdom was much deeper than mine. My ideal had become *Hasrateeh* Zaynab, the granddaughter of the Prophet. She was known for her fierce sermons to mix crowds of men and women to keep the spirit of shii's up at the time.

So, for more than her basic mastery of kitchen skills alone, we often asked Azita to cook when we met at my apartment. Her creations were unlike anything available to us in Tehran, despite many international restaurants. Unlike most university women I knew, she took pleasure in cooking. For most of my married friends, cooking in the kitchen was an essential part of being a woman, and especially a wife. If they took pleasure in it, that was a bonus.

Azita was quieter that night. She wasn't buzzing around the kitchen as excitedly as usual, and I wondered if something was wrong.

Her baba, like mine, had two wives, one much younger than the other. Azita was from his first wife. His second wife had a son, Majid, from her first husband. Her first marriage had ended in tragedy when her husband had died unexpectedly in a crash. After their parents married, Azita and Majid were raised as brother and sister in the same household until she was ready to leave for university. Then, just before Azita left for Tehran to attend the university, Majid expressed a romantic interest in her.

Commonly, families justify such unions by explaining that they know exactly what their children are marrying into. Azita's parents were so excited when they learned of his interest, that they started spreading the news of an engagement without even asking Azita if this was something she wanted. "This is the way it should be," her parents told her.

"This is not what I want!" Azita said. She simply could not even imagine marrying her own brother, so she had refused and threatened to kill herself.

I felt horrible for her. Baba's second wife would have done the same thing if she could have, but getting rid of me by sending me off to Tehran proved even more attractive to her. I was lucky. We assumed that Azita was lucky, too, because her parents let her go to the university and didn't press her about the marriage.

"Is everything okay, Azita?" I asked, as I finished setting the table and sat down next to her.

She shook her head and tears came to her eyes.

"What's wrong?" Suzan asked, as she sat down with us. "Is it Majid?"

Suzan hadn't been raised with such conservative cultural practices, and this situation between Azita and Majid had shocked her when Azita had first told us about it.

Azita nodded, as the tears rolled down her face.

"But your family let you come to the university," Roya said hopefully. "Isn't that all over now?"

"About a month ago, when I went home over break, I saw Majid," Azita said tearfully.

We all held our breath. I knew where this was going, and I wondered if the others did too.

"He knew I would never marry him by choice," Azita said. "So he raped me." She finally broke down. "He came to my room one afternoon when nobody was home. I fought him. I bit him and scratched him. I tried everything to stop him, but he was too strong for me."

No one said a word. I wanted to tell her she should have told us sooner, but I knew why she hadn't.

"When he was done, he kissed me and told me to go and wash myself."

Then she picked her head up and her eyes met all of ours. "I scrubbed myself head to toe with a rough cloth! As he was walking out, he told me 'you cannot say no anymore. You are mine.' He took my virginity, my *aberue*! He knows no other man will marry me now!"

Suzan reached out and held Azita's hands in her own. She said nothing. We all sat there quietly, but I was screaming inside.

Customarily, when a girl is raped in Islamic societies, the rapist is given the choice of marrying the girl he has raped. If he does so, little is often said afterwards. At the university, I even heard of "rapes" being planned by the man and woman, forcing families to allow what amounts to a love marriage. I knew that these cases were rare though, and I knew this wasn't what had happened in Azita's situation.

At worst, if Majid ever changed his mind about marrying her, Azita would be seen as the criminal who committed *zina*, sex outside of marriage. For her, as a daughter in a conservative family, this would literally mean a death sentence.

"My parents are forcing us to marry."

To save their own faces, I thought. I had lived through it myself. A girl's behavior is seen as a reflection of the family's honor. Azita's parents, no doubt her baba especially, would become her executioner instead of her protector, just to save the rest of the family from dishonor.

"I did not have any choice," Azita confessed with sadness. "I agreed to the marriage if I could come back and finish the semester."

Azita's parents agreed, and told her that it was in her fate to marry her stepbrother.

"I thought by coming back to the university, I could think of a plan, a way out," Azita said. "Now that the semester is over, I don't know. I see no way out. I would rather kill myself than marry him."

"Azita, life does not have to end for you," I said.

The three of them looked at me. That's when I told them my arranged marriage story. When I was finished, Roya looked horrified. Azita looked at me like she had a new respect for me.

"I was twelve," I said. "My modar and grandmodars supported me all the way through my divorce and the stigma of it. You are an educated young woman, Azita, and you have us to support you emotionally."

We all agreed that running away or simply staying in Tehran would not help. Azita's family would surely hunt her down. I wondered suddenly, could Grandma Tuba's incurable disease work for poor Azita?

I shared the story of Grandma Tuba's mysterious cramps, and they were so impressed they started applauding. Grandma Tuba was a great heroine to them! I reminded them that she was only nine years old at the time, yet she was still able to make this work. But even as I was speaking, I knew this wasn't going to be easy. I knew that the influence of Azita's family and culture had a much stronger effect on her than they did on me. Azita gave into that pressure and the marriage date had already been set. I thought the next best thing would be to try to protect her rights under the marriage contract. For this, though, I would need to talk to Hajji. I promised her I would help her. I told her I had a friend I could talk to. I just needed to get more information.

I waited impatiently for Aqa Hajji to call. It was two more days before I finally heard from him. When he finally came over, he looked pale, as if he hadn't slept for days. I put my arms around him and led him to the couch.

He handed me a small, velvet, maroon box with gold trim around it. The box was attached to a gold chain, making it look like an oversized pendant. Hanging from the bottom of the pendant box were four gold pieces, attached to a short chain, with a dark blue stone in the middle of the row. Such dark blue stones are commonly used by believers to keep evil eyes away from the carrier.

I opened the box, and inside there was a miniature Quran inlaid in gold. I was puzzled. Hajji knew, as strongly as I felt about the presence of God in every aspect in my life, I did not believe in rituals. Yet, I felt emotional and unnerved. I looked at him curiously.

"My modar received this pendent at the time of her marriage," he explained. "My baba was also a religious cleric like me. After my parents died, I kept it for myself. I could not part with it until now. I did not think I would find a woman worthy of wearing it."

He was giving this pendent to me. Wearing it meant that God was watching over me. Hajji was protecting me from evil eyes.

"Is your answer still no, Ateesh?" he asked gently. He had already renewed our contract once, and we had four months left on it. I could see that the recent events had shaken him. Perhaps he had taken another look at his actions, which almost led to him losing face in the community. Having a *siqeh* wife, though religiously encouraged, was still frowned upon by some. Whereas men who take a second wife could eventually go public, men who had *siqeh* usually remained in secrecy.

As I had been in the past, I was blunt with Hajji. I felt sad about letting him go, but I knew it was time for me to move on. My answer to his permanent marriage proposal was a clear no. I took him to bed with me, then offered to cook him a meal, which he gratefully accepted and that's when I decided to bring up Azita and seek his advice. Deferring to his religious authority always made him feel comfortable and easy to talk to. Of the many roles he played in his life—those of husband, temporary husband, and baba to his children—the role of religious authority seemed to suit him best. He generously told me what Azita needed to do to protect her rights as a wife.

He told me that at the time of marriage, every bride has the right to insert certain conditions into the marriage contract; conditions to which both families must agree. These conditions, Hajji had explained, to my surprise, could range from the woman being allowed to work outside of the home, to having custody of the children beyond the religious and civil practices at the time of divorce. If the husband broke any of these conditions, then the wife had the right to divorce.

"Ateesh, please consider marrying permanently instead of what you are doing," he said, suddenly. "I am worried for you."

When I didn't say anything, he sighed, then continued. "If you decide to continue being a *siqeh*, you must at least work through a registrar and write your own contracts. That is the only way to protect your religious rights as a *siqeh*, and it is safer."

"I am grateful, Aqa Hajji," I said, as I held his hand in mine.

I had no idea the same contract could be used for permanent as well as temporary marriages.

"If you ever need money, call me," he said. Those were among the last words he said to me before he got up and left. I felt sad saying goodbye to him. But that made it all the more clear that it was time to go.

Later, I found an envelope he left for me. It held enough money to pay my rent for a year, and a card with the name and number of a registrar.

Throughout the years, I have seen Hajji mostly in the news media. He tries to promote equality between men and women as the basic philosophy in Islam. Wearing his religious cloak and beautiful, finely woven, white turban, he always looks powerful and in control.

I continue to admire his affection and conviction for his religion.
***

Later on that week, Azita and I sat down together and wrote all her conditions. She was to be permitted to continue working toward her degree in civil engineering, to choose the place of residence, and to work after the completion of her degree. I told her to make sure that all the above conditions were written down as part of the marriage contract, and that Majid acknowledged it in front of witnesses.

With only a few days until the end of the semester, we then went to see a pharmacist friend of mine so that Azita could secretly start taking birth control pills.

Azita returned to university the next semester as a married woman. Majid had chosen to stay behind in Khosastan and await her return there.

"He agreed to the contract right away, Ateesh!" Azita said. "He must not have taken it very seriously. He told me before I left that I must return home at the first sign of pregnancy."

At that, we smiled. He would be waiting a long time.

Just as Grandma Tuba had those terrible stomach pains, Azita became a crazy, religious fanatic who considered sex unnatural and ugly. She did this by reading from Imam Burkhart's book, *Al-Shih*, and Imam Gazelle's book, *Good Practices as Regards Marriage*, advising that God be invoked not only at the moment of orgasm, but also at the beginning of the sexual act. Both of these books were given to me by Hajji.

"God's presence was not only to be acknowledged in all steps, but most importantly, shouted out at the time of ejaculation," Azita told her husband, insisting that he follow all instructions verbatim.

It did not take long before Majid grew tired of her irrational behavior. The following year, Azita came back to school a divorcee. As a righteous woman, she didn't like to be divorced, but the relief she felt was evident. She was told by many in her family and hometown that it was in her fate to be divorced.

"*Allaho Akbar!*" I exclaimed.

"Ateesh, I owe you my life!" Azita told me as we celebrated her divorce over glasses of cold buttermilk. "How can I ever repay you?"

"Get your degree, Azita," I said. "And try to help women who need it."

Azita graduated after two years and found a good job, which enabled her to move out of her parents' home. Shortly after, her family disowned her.

I wondered what my family would have done if they knew about my decision to become a *siqeh*.

⁂ ⁂ ⁂ ⁂ ⁂

Hajji Aqa Ayatollah had given me three great gifts on our last night together: the pendant which had meant so much to him, the advice for Azita, and guidance for me as a temporary wife. I took that advice and called Hajji's Registrar. Together Hajji's Registrar and I wrote a tight contract that would protect my rights and me, as much as was religiously allowed. As a result, Hajji Registrar, as I called him, became my business partner for years to come. I never had to turn my

133

chador inside out and put myself on display in the street, after that one and only time that I almost did.

The contract Hajji Registrar and I had written helped me to be selective in my choice of husbands. He knew I was not in the business for financial reasons only, as many other women were, but to escape the reality of gender inequality in Iran. With most of my temporary husbands after Hajji Ayatollah, I let men think they were in control of me. The reality was the opposite. Under the pretense of needing them to survive, I remained in control of my own destiny.

I usually met with a prospective husband in Hajji Registrar's office after he had first been screened Hajji Registrar. At my insistence, the marriage had to be done according to the strictest interpretation of temporary marriage. My *mehreeh*, marriage price, was set at one million tumon per month for a minimum of three months, and could last anywhere up to a year or more. I required a health certificate, indicating that the applicant had tested negatively for certain diseases. On the last two pages of the marriage booklet, there was a blank area left for any conditions I might insert before marriage. I am certain that for many brides those pages remain blank, though mine never did.

My marriage contract included five conditions, and if any of the first four were breached by my husband, I had the power to nullify the marriage before the contract's expiration date. If that happened I would lose any remaining money that was owed to me, but I could immediately break ties.

The first condition was for one half of the *mehreeh* to be paid up front. From this, I paid Hajji Registrar twenty percent. The remaining half was due after the consummation of the marriage, in installments based on the duration of the marriage. From each installment, Hajji Registrar was also paid his twenty percent. If for any reason the husband did not want to remain married for the contracted period, he could simply walk away, but he had to pay half of the remaining amount. If I decided to walk away, I was free to do so as well, but again, would lose any unpaid balance on my contract.

As a Moslem wife, I was required to wait three months before I could remarry again. Of course, none of my husbands had to wait any period of time to remarry. They could, in fact, marry several women at the same time, temporary or permanent. As most of my husbands were married men, nothing really was religiously required from them but to pay. For the wife, the required waiting period of three months and several days was to insure that she would know who the father of her child was, in case she should happen to be pregnant. At that point, the child could become the legitimate child of the father if he recognized it as such.

For this reason, my second condition mandated that if I became pregnant, my temporary husband had no rights to the child. Each of my temporary husbands happily consented to this condition, as none wanted to be stuck with a child from a temporary marriage that was most likely undisclosed to his first wife.

My third condition was that my husband could not stay overnight more than twice a week and would have to notify me twenty-four hours in advance. I still had my classes and friends from school to think about.

The fourth condition was that he could not ask to have sex more than three times on each visit. If any of the above four conditions were broken, I had the right to a divorce without his consent.

The fifth condition was that my husbands had to be cleanly shaved, showered, and use my favorite cologne, Polo, with the scent of wildflowers. I kept a bottle in my apartment. The scent reminded me of professor Bejan, and my time spent with him. To my surprise, all my husbands seemed to be fine with it.

～～ ～～ ～～ ～～ ～～

Although I saw little difference between myself and women like Suzan, I still kept my life as a *siqeh* secret. Suzan often received presents from her boyfriends, usually professors who always gave her high grades. I received cash and kept my independence. No doubt, I put myself at greater risk than she ever did, but the payoff was greater. Ironically, I earned both respect and, usually behind my back, jeers from my friends. Azita respected me for what she thought was my resistance to the temptation of dating the most illustrious professors. Of course, most of the dating between boys and girls remained in secret. Families like Suzan's who allowed open relationships before marriage were in the minority, even in a fast-growing modern city like Tehran.

It was difficult to fight the urge to just let go and fall in love and follow my heart. I was bottling so much desire inside me that I had to think of some way to replace it.

I was gaining a reputation as one of the university's most promising undergraduates, and I sometimes wondered if I was denying myself further opportunities by rejecting the professors' propositions. Roya had known about Bejan and was simply baffled at my newfound disinterest in dating. I felt guilty for lying to my friends, and of course, to my family. For a while, Suzan fished for information. Was I dating after the professor and if not, why not? She was usually the first to inquire about my unexplained absences from university happenings and my weekend whereabouts. It wasn't in her nature to accept my newfound veneer of celibacy. Of course, regardless of my religious justification for being a *siqeh*, I did not believe even for a short second that the practice kept society clean. Deep down, I was not proud of what I was doing, but my independence from men made up for some of the shame I was feeling.

My second temporary husband was a pharmaceutical salesman who spent his weekdays working in Tehran, and his weekends in Qom, Iran's second holiest city, with his wife and children. Well-mannered to a fault, I got the feeling our union was his way of proving his manliness to himself or perhaps some of his sleazy colleagues. I wondered how he ever managed to sell anything, though I never asked him about it.

Sex with him was dutiful and businesslike. I felt neither excitement nor disgust at his touches, and this utter absence of emotion was a problem. It gave me time to think. Only once did I let myself tear up as he was on top of me. He sensitively stopped to ask me why I was crying. What could I have told him?

"It is nothing," I said. "Tears of pleasure."

This seemed to please him.

Eventually, I had to shield myself from my own judgment. I

learned to think about other things besides what was actually going on in the bed. I understood that as a temporary wife, my job was to give guiltless pleasure to men. My duties were no different from those of a common prostitute, but my fee was much greater. My temporary husbands, even Hajji Aqa Ayatollah, had paid dearly to think of their transgression as a sanctified act. I wasn't about to disappoint them.

I practiced reciting famous poems from memory, a skill that is held in high regard in Iranian culture. To please my husbands, I recited passionate love poetries. At the same time, it helped me to distract myself. Many times, as I was lying beneath a man I barely knew and most certainly held no feelings for, I silently recited poems of strength and resilience, never forgetting for a moment that my life depended on his utmost satisfaction. Poems by Kayam, Molana, and Hafiz became my mantras. I had heard these as a child whenever I visited Grandma Jamileh, and subsequently learned them by heart.

The one I knew best was one of Grandma Jamileh's favorites, from the thirteenth century epic of Shahnameh Ferdosy. One of the major heroes in the epic is Rustam, who unknowingly injured his son, Sohrab, in a battle with a poison-laced sword. Sohrab was the child that resulted from a single night spent many years earlier with his temporary wife, the princess Tahmineh. After Rustam had left his temporary wife, he continued on with his responsibilities as a Hercules, never learning that he had a son, Sohrab, until he injured him in battle. By the time the antidote arrived, it was too late to save his son.

Centuries later, the poet, Shahriyar, drew an analogy between the late arrival of the antidote and his own lover's return.

You came back and I sacrifice my life for you; but why now?
Unfaithful, why now that I am crippled of life, why now?
You are the antidote coming after the death of Sohrab,
You came back and I sacrifice my life for you, but why now?

I suppose I recited this poem fearing that by the time I became totally independent and did not need to devote myself exclusively to my profession, it might be too late to fall in love. Many times as I lay next to any of my temporary husbands, I often thought of the first time I was in the arms of a man by choice. It was only at such times that my longing for independence was weakened by desire and I felt like the poet for his lover or Rustam for the antidote.

I always wondered if Grandma Jamileh loved Ferdosy's epic because she had lost her husband at the young age of twenty and never remarried. Was she longing for love or a husband? Poor Grandma Jamileh. Trapped in a culture that associates love with lust, I considered myself lucky never to have been in love. I had broken it off with Bejan before I could find out if that was what it was.

~ ~ ~ ~ ~

I knew that with each new husband came new risks. My business partner Hajji Registrar screened all of my clients thoroughly, but the fact remained that I invited men who were complete strangers not only into my home but into my bed. Even so, by my senior year at University, I had been in the business for almost three years, and in that time, I often only had to defend myself against the possible spread of rumor and my own judgment. That changed with my sixth temporary husband, Akbar.

By this time I was living in a larger, more comfortable apartment. My commute to the university was long, but the distance was necessary to keep my two lives separate.

About a week into my marriage to Akbar, I was home reading some papers and listening to soft instrumental music when there was a sudden pounding on the front door.

"Ateesh!" Akbar yelled. "Open the door!"

I jumped up and ran toward the door. "Akbar?" I asked.

What was he doing here? He was never supposed to come unannounced.

"Let me in!" he shouted, as he continued pounding on the door.

Against my better judgment, but fearing the wrath of my neighbors, I let him in. He practically fell in when I opened the door, and he smelled like vomit and whiskey. While some of my husbands drank, I never dealt with anyone as drunk as he was.

Catching me by surprise with his fervor, he pushed me toward the bedroom and shoved me on the bed.

For a second I was totally shaken by what happened. I was taken back in time to that first night with Hassan. I became furious and screamed so loud that I startled Akbar. Before he could move, I jumped on top of him and began pounding him with my fists as hard as I could. I was no longer a helpless, little twelve-year-old girl.

In his condition, Akbar was clumsy, but he was still stronger than I. I kicked and punched him as he tore off my clothes and began undressing himself. Then he grabbed hold of my hair and kept me pinned to the bed.

I couldn't fight him anymore. I had to think of something else. That's when I stopped fighting him and became totally motionless, hoping he would think I had given up. He smiled malevolently, and began telling me that I was beautiful, that he wanted me.

In silence, I waited for an opportunity. The minute he let go of his grip on my hair to open his zipper, I rolled out from underneath him with all my strength and reached toward the silver alarm clock on my nightstand, which had been given to me by my grandfather as a going-away present when I left for the university.

Akbar grabbed me by the legs and tried to turn me onto my stomach. We struggled, and then with one lucky swing, I struck him on the head with the clock, knocking him onto the floor. He laid there motionless, with blood running down his forehead into his eye. I ran out of the bedroom and locked the door from the outside.

There I paced back and forth, not knowing what to do. What if I had killed him? I didn't want to go back in there and find out.

I went to the balcony and looked at the mountains, tall and strong in front of me, yet motionless.

Oh my God, I wondered, what am I going to do if he is dead?!

"But your honor, he tried to rape me!" I would say.

"Rape? What do you mean?" The judge would ask. "You were his wife. What he expected is perfectly legal, and especially in your kind of a marriage, which is meant to be for his pleasure alone."

Rape does not exist in marriage. Even if he stayed and finished what he came to do, I would have no legal or religious recourse.

I went back inside and stood near the closed door. Then I pressed my ear against the door. There was no sound at first. I peeked in through the keyhole. There he was, holding his head and moaning in pain. As he writhed on my bedroom floor, he seemed more pathetic than dangerous. He moaned an incomprehensible mix of curses and nonsense.

Akbar was a film director, and what was happening between us at that moment might have seemed quite cinematic, except for the very real pain he felt.

"I am opening the door, Akbar," I said. "Please don't make a move or I will hit you again."

I opened the door. I stood over him with the clock in my hand. Realizing my seriousness, he seemed to become a weak, defenseless creature before my eyes.

"I must have had too many drinks," he said. "Come on, let's have sex to make me feel better and I promise I will make it up to you."

Disgusted, I left the room and closed the door. I didn't lock it. I thought he may just leave after sobering up. I felt numb. I needed time to recuperate and think. I went to the guest bedroom, locked the door, and placed a chair under the doorknob. I removed the clothes he hadn't torn off, got into the shower and stood under the hot running water. The water did not make my head feel any better.

The first time I was hit by Hassan was one week into my marriage, when I refused to sleep with him. He went out and got high on opium, then came into the bedroom. The next day I walked to Modar's house and told her.

"What do you mean, he raped you? You are married."

"I know I am married, but it was against my will! It was *tajavoz*."

"Ateesh Joon, be patient. You are a newlywed. He wants you. Let him have you."

And I went back to his house. After a few similar episodes, my husband got rougher with me. I tried desperately to figure out what I was doing to cause it, but I couldn't think of anything. I knew I couldn't blame myself. I hated him, and the smell of him and his sweat made me throw up right in his face. As time went on, he became more and more angry and violent until I finally ended up in the hospital.

Now, again, I found myself staying awake all night, fearing for my safety, just as I did back then, although I remained somewhat comforted most of the time by Akbar's loud snoring all the way from my bedroom. I got up twice to check on him from the keyhole, and he seemed okay.

The next morning, I heard him get up and start making coffee in the kitchen. I knew he was making it for me. Because like most Iranians, he always started his day with freshly brewed tea instead of coffee. Suddenly I was unafraid to face him. I walked into the kitchen. My body ached with every step I took. I was bruised everywhere, and especially in my heart.

"Good morning, Ateesh," he said, as he held out the mug of steaming coffee. His eyes were bloodshot and swollen. His forehead above his left eye was bruised. "Here is your coffee, just the way you like it."

Without making eye contact, I took it from him and walked outside onto the balcony. From where I sat, I could see the great Alborz Mountains, a mountain range in northern Iran stretching from the borders of Armenia in the northwest, to the southern end of the Caspian Sea, and ending in the east, at the borders of Turkmenistan and Afghanistan. This view so often gave me strength and tranquility. I replayed the previous evening's events in my head until I heard Akbar's voice from behind me.

"Ateesh," he said, "I was drunk. I will make it up to you. I promise."

He seemed quite calm and sweet as he said this, and he sat down next to me. For a moment, neither of us said anything, but just stared ahead at the great mountains. I thought about the money I was about to lose. I knew that some Iranian wives would receive flowers or jewelry after such an occurrence. Less fortunate women would find themselves being reprimanded for having brought the assault upon themselves. That is what an obedient wife is led to believe. I wasn't obedient anyway, so I couldn't take any blame for the incident.

"I want to take you overseas to Europe," he said.

"Listen, Akbar—" I said, as I turned to face him.

I saw him looking down at my left arm, which was covered in bruises.

"It will never happen again," he interrupted, as he put his teacup on the table. "I was drunk and you made me really mad by not opening the door. If only you hadn't done that, I would have come in as always, and after having sex, things would have been normal. But it's okay. Things are okay now. I am not angry with you."

I looked at him. I thought of Grandma Tuba's friends who felt proud after evading their abusive husband's fists and kicks. I thought of Grandma Tuba reading from the Quran on patience, and Modar's constant use of the word patience. In practice, the word had become gender-specific. It teaches tolerance of domestic violence toward women.

"If you do not want to see me, that is fine," he continued, "but I am not paying for the rest of the contract if you cancel."

"Fine," I said. "I cancel our marriage contract. You don't have to pay the remaining balance."

He got up and dumped his remaining tea over the balcony into the street.

"For what I am paying you, I could get two younger women. There are more of you than you could possibly imagine," he said.

He was right about the availability of women. I knew he was trying to be hurtful, but I also knew why a man like him had paid such a high price for a *siqeh*. His high profile in Tehran invited scandal as it was. Hajji Registrar had no doubt assured him of my professionalism and discretion.

"You are absolutely right. There are many more women like me," I said. "If it wasn't for your money, none of us women would tolerate men like you. I rescind our contract."

"I can snap my fingers and be with two girls like you tonight," he said. Then he got up and left, knocking over the table on his way out.

After I locked the front door, I went back to the balcony and thought for a long time about what I was doing. I looked through the sliding glass doors at my apartment that contained many fine things I could never have afforded on my own. But what was I achieving? Akbar would simply move on to another woman and pay her much less, I was sure, to satisfy his needs. My head was still hurting and as much as I tried to get strength from the mountains, tears began to spill out.

Later that day, I called Hajji Registrar to give him my version of the story. Unsurprisingly, Akbar had been to his office already and conveyed a very different rendition of events.

"If word gets out that you rescind contracts, that would not be good for you," Hajji warned me. "And these men do not want a woman with a sharp tongue!" But he assured me that he would continue to screen my clients as carefully as before. "Ateesh, don't look at *siqeh* so analytically," he advised.

Sometimes, the shame of being someone else, and not myself, and not being truthful about everything that was going on in my life was so painful that I would go into seclusion and cry for days. But I always came back feeling justified.

For the next few months, I devoted myself wholly to school, and I even took graduate courses upon the recommendation of some of my instructors. As in my personal life, my professional interests concerned justice for women, especially their rights at the time of divorce. My friends were well aware of my interest and the help I had been able to give my friend Azita. At least among my friends, I became an authority on marital rights.

Just before my graduation, I received a call from my friend, Marjon. Marjon and I began our studies at the university at the same time, but Marjon's parents had arranged a marriage for her just prior to our senior year.

"Ateesh, I need to talk to you about a problem," she said. Her voice was low and sad.

Marjon had recently been wed to a well-known cleric, and precisely for that reason, she could not continue her studies at the university and remain in such a high-profile marriage.

"What is the matter, Marjon?"

"It is hard to explain… my husband… he…can I see you somewhere? Please," she asked, her voice cracking.

"Sure," I said. "Just tell me where you are and I'll be there as soon as I can."

It was an hour taxi ride from the university to her parents' house.

What kind of marital problem could she possibly have? I wondered. Was it physical abuse? Psychological abuse?

I thought of the several walks I took as a twelve-year-old newlywed to my parents' house. Marjon was at her parents' house, and this meant it must have been serious, if she was calling someone outside the family for help.

As soon as the taxi dropped me off in front of a big house in the upscale neighborhood, Marjon and her modar greeted me by the wide-open gate. Marjon looked pale and her eyes were red. I held her close and felt her heart beating rapidly. I remembered how much I just wanted to remain in Modar or Grandma Tuba's embrace when I felt hurt.

"Let us go inside," Marjon's modar said, as she rushed us inside. "If people see Marjon broken up like this, what are they going to think?"

Not much had changed since I first heard those words, *mardom chi megan*, what would people say.

We went inside and sat on a sofa by the bay window that overlooked beautiful grounds. The wall surrounding the window was framed in diamond-cut mirrors, accentuated with smaller cuts of lightly colored glass, which effected the distribution of light evenly.

As Marjon and I sat next to one another, her modar went into the kitchen for refreshments.

I held Marjon's hand and said, "You are a young, intelligent, and sophisticated woman with a lot of potential. No matter what the problem is, there is a resolution."

"Ateesh, he only wants to have anal sex," she said in such a low voice that I wasn't sure I heard her correctly.

"What did you say?" I asked. "Only what?"

She started sobbing. Her hands were ice cold in mine and she was shivering. "We don't have sex the normal way," she said. "I mean… you know, Ateesh."

Her modar came back with a tray of pastries. "*Bebakhsheed*, Ateesh Khanoom, forgive us for taking your time. We did not know what to do and whom we could tell. When Marjon suggested you, I said, fine. We don't want this news to get out of this house—"

I interrupted her before she could say the "M" word, *mardom*. "What is more important than *mardom*," I said, "is Marjon. Let them say and think what they want. None of those people care about your daughter as much as you do. Are they sharing your sorrow with you right now?" Then I turned to Marjon and asked, "Have you talked to him seriously?"

"A number of times," she answered. "He says it is his right to approach me in any manner that pleases him."

"I told Marjon to tell him to be afraid of God," her modar said. "He responded that it is well within the parameters of rights given under Islam. Is that true, Ateesh Khanoom? The verse he is citing does say, 'approach your wife in any manner,' but is this what it really means?"

I knew they were referring to Chapter 2 Verse 4, but I had no idea if this interpretation was a commonly held belief among men. Then all of the sudden, it hit me. The night of my wedding at the age twelve, my husband forced himself on me that way and he used the same verse. But then, he did that as a punishment to me because I was resisting him.

I didn't know Marjon's husband, but I had heard he was a man of God, and I was burning with mixed emotions of anger and disappointment in him.

At the prospect of putting up with his uncompromising behavior for the rest of her life, Marjon was desperate for an answer and had even contemplated leaving him and staying at her parents, despite the possible consequences.

I told them I would get back to them as soon as I could.

I consulted my advisor, Dr. Behi Goodarzi. One of the minority of female professors at the university and an advocate of women's rights, Dr. Goodarzi had become my mentor and friend. Since I took her course as a freshman, we had become good friends. Medium height with short, wavy, dark hair, she resembled Natalie Wood, the great American actress. She was very smart and I hoped that one day she would become the first female university president. But women were not allowed to run for the presidency.

With much sympathy, Dr. Goodarzi explained that unlike Sunnis, Shi'i Moslems believe that a man can enter his wife's body in any way he pleases.

"But," she said, "this belief is a minority view in Islam, although I know some Sunnis practice this as well."

Even Dr. Goodarzi could not offer any religious grounds for Marjon to deny her husband—at least none that he would accept.

"She better be careful," she added. "If she leaves and stays for too long at her parents, she might be found guilty of *tamkin*."

I already knew that leaving one's husband home without permission is a criminal offense punishable by imprisonment and, sooner or later, Marjon would have to return to her husband if she left. So we tried to find a legal way to get Marjon out of her marriage. As we did our research, I couldn't help but remember what a promising future Marjon seemed to have before her marriage. She loved children and wanted to be a teacher, but her husband had prohibited her from pursuing even this innocuous career path.

Marjon's only way out of her marriage was for her husband to agree to a divorce. She had been staying with her parents under the pretext of helping her modar care for her ailing baba. But her husband, already suspicious of her intentions, could subpoena Marjon through family court and force her to return at any time. If she ignored the subpoena, the court would issue a warrant for her arrest.

Unless her family supported her decision to leave her husband, she would be forced to return. Even in Marjon's case, her parents were advocating mediation towards reconciliation, not divorce. "I think Marjon can change him slowly," her modar had naively and desperately said. She reminded me of the commonly held attitude that no matter what flaws the husband has, the wife ultimately has the responsibility of changing him.

"The priority attributed to men over women is best understood as originating from their greater responsibility as protectors and maintainers within the socioeconomic context of Arabian society during Prophet Mohammed's time," Dr. Goodarzi explained. "Because men defended and supported their extended families, they were given higher status as a result of these responsibilities."

She knew this wasn't new information to me.

"As you know, Ateesh, 'protection and maintenance' in practice have been used to oppress and abuse women," Dr. Goodarzi added, sharing my frustration. "The Quranic verses that were intended to limit men's power over women have been misinterpreted by men to justify the ill treatment of women."

For now, I had no solution to offer Marjon. I felt like a failure.

~~ ~~ ~~ ~~ ~~

A few months later, I completed my thesis and my undergraduate degree. I wrote about the Quran as a text intended to liberate women from lives of subservience in sixth century Arabia. I wrote that the spirit of the Quran was feminist in nature and should be seen in this light in modern times.

Dr. Behi Goodarzi had been a tremendous influence on my work. Her work had contributed greatly to the fight for women's rights. I was so happy to receive a scholarship to continue graduate school under her guidance.

"Ateesh, I want you to assist me in a case right away," Behi said to me in her office, right after graduation.

"This is the file on the case of 'killing prostitutes'" she said, and she handed me a large yellow folder with rubber bands around it. "The trial starts in a week."

A married man in his mid-thirties had been arrested and put on trial for murdering six women, between the ages of 18-25, in a period of one year. This happened in Qom. Being the second most sacred religious place for Shi'i Moslems, Qom was frequented by pilgrims from around Iran and other Moslem nations. Behi, on behalf of the state, was representing the families of the victims.

"Have you talked to the victims' families?" I asked as I was reviewing the file.

"No. I have tried unsuccessfully several times. You know how it is, Ateesh. Their families are too ashamed of their daughters to acknowledge their murders by being present in the court."

I thought of my Grandmas and Modar back in Abadan, and felt an uneasy feeling in my stomach.

"Although all six women were practicing *siqehs*, which is a legitimate profession under Islam…" Behi was saying.

Practicing *siqehs*…that was me. I could have been one of those women killed and dumped by the curb. I felt lightheaded and dizzy, and I grabbed onto the back of the chair to keep myself steady.

"Are you okay, Ateesh? I should have warned you about the gruesome photos. Sit down here."

I felt her hands gently guiding me to a chair. I heard the phone ring…

"Allo," Behi said.

I felt relief as she continued chatting on the phone. I had a moment to center myself. I had heard about the murders, but never dreamed I would actually be involved in the case. While I was ecstatic to be asked to help the prosecutor convict this killer, I felt sick as I looked at those pictures, thinking about my own practice of *siqeh*. I knew I had to assist Behi in bringing justice to those who were killed.

"I cannot pay you." Behi said.

"You're talking to me?" I asked. I cleared my throat and sat up straighter.

"Yes, you Ateesh. Your face is so pale, as if you know those women. Are you all right? We have to start working on this right away."

"I am okay," I said. "I want to do this."

The next day, I asked a colleague to take over my teaching and workshop schedule in exchange for the salary I would have been paid.

The trial first began in Qom, but after two days it was adjourned and moved to Tehran, due to the highly publicized nature of the killings. All the murdered women were runaways from different states throughout the country. Such killings were the first in the nation and it attracted a lot of attention. All six female victims had started as temporary wives but apparently did not keep up with the entire religious requirement, such as the waiting period between the marriages. All the women were strangled to death and left near the shrine they used to find the needy traveling husbands. There was a note left on each victim, "*Jendeh bayyad bemereh*, prostitute must die."

I was thrilled to accept.

~~ ~~ ~~ ~~ ~~

"*Jenabeh Qazis*, your honors, he killed those women because they were dishonoring Islam and the defendant as a Moslem," his attorney said in his opening statement in front of a panel of three male judges. "These were indeed Honor killings."

My jaw almost dropped. I looked at Behi. We both turned to look at the family of one of the victims who were in court. They kept their heads down. The five other families of the murdered women were too ashamed to be present.

"The bastard is defending under honor killing. And not even his own honor directly but in the honor of his religion," Behi whispered. "This is absolutely crazy!"

Then the defense put on evidence that the six women who were murdered were indeed prostitutes, not religiously endorsed "temporary wives."

My head was spinning. It was as if I was on trial myself. I was so disturbed that I didn't even hear the testimony of the first man who took the stand. He sat there with his head up, as he described having sex in exchange for money with two of the victims, without the required religious pronouncement.

I looked at the family of this man who was sitting in the audience. His wife was sitting right there as her husband described his sexual encounter with two women, and she was looking at him as if he was the victim.

She had her head held high, just as he did, as if this was justifiable.

Then I heard the name of the next witness.

"The defense calls the next witness: Dr. Ayatollah as a religious expert in temporary marriages," the defense attorney said.

"Oh my God, no!" I said to myself and looked down at the ground. This "Dr. Ayatollah" was my Hajji Aqa! *Allaho Akbar*, I thought.

I took a deep breath and opened my eyes. I looked at Behi. She was saying something to me but I couldn't hear her. I could see her mouth was moving but I couldn't hear any words.

I watched as he came out from the door behind the judges and walked to the witness stand.

Suddenly all I could remember was him lying next to me, his arms around me. "Ateesh, why did you become a *siqeh*?"

As soon as he sat on the chair, our eyes met. I had not seen him for nearly five years. I could see he was clearly in shock, seeing me sitting next to the prosecutor, directly across from the witness stand. He moved uncomfortably in his chair a few times before looking at the defense attorney.

I took a deep breath as the defense started reading Hajji Aqa's long list of credentials.

"Please walk us through the requirements of a properly conducted *siqeh*, Doctor" the defense asked.

I remembered the first time Hajji Aqa asked me, "I want you to be my wife for one year in exchange for five million *tumon*. Do you accept?"

Back in the court, the defense asked, "What other stringent requirement does a *siqeh* have?"

"A woman must wait for a period of three months before she can remarry."

"Anything else?"

"No."

"So it is pretty straightforward and clear, is it not?"

"Yes."

"In your opinion why would a person not follow such clear, straightforward requirements?"

"I am not sure."

"Why not? You said all it takes is an offer, acceptance, fixed duration, and exchange of a sum of money and the waiting period."

"Yes."

"So the question is, if one skips one of the requirements, like the waiting period, can't we assume she did not believe it was important or necessary?"

"I can't be certain but it is possible."

"So it is possible that these women didn't wait for three months before remarrying because they did not believe what they were practicing was temporary marriage?"

"Yes, it is possible."

"If what they were practicing was not temporary marriage, what was it? Do you have opinion on that, Doctor?"

"No."

"No?" The defense asked. There was some tension and noise in the audience.

"*Saket basheed,* be quiet," the judge ordered.

"I am asking a simple question: If what was practiced was not temporary marriage, what had it become Doctor?"

"I am not sure. God is merciful and forgiving,"

"Thank you Doctor. I have no more questions, *Aqayeh Qaiz,* Your Honor."

"Do you have any questions for the defense witness, Dr. Goodarzi?" the judge asked.

I passed my notepad to her with written questions. She looked at me. I nodded in confidence.

"How did *siqeh* come about?" she asked.

"We believe that during Prophet's time, some men were taking advantage of women who were in vulnerable situations, like widows and orphans. By requiring a contract between the parties it was the Prophet's intention to lessen the possibility of the abuse of the weaker sex and to insure some accountability on the part of men."

"By weaker sex, you mean women?"

"Yes."

"What accountability?"

"Well, for example, the requirement of the waiting period is to ensure that the woman is not pregnant, and of course, if she is, then the father would be responsible for child support."

"Is that why a single woman can contract only one husband at a time?"

"Yes indeed."

"What is Islam about, in one line, Doctor?"

"Of course, it is about social justice and equality. That is the core of Islam."

"You agree that it is to ensure social justice, especially for the weaker sex, that we have rules to protect them? Not the stronger sex?"

"Yes, no doubt."

"So if the weaker sex does not exactly follow the very rules which were put in place to protect her, she should be punished?"

Aqa Hajji shifted uncomfortably in his seat. "What do you mean?" he asked.

"Simple. If the woman breaks the very rule which was intended to protect her from abuse by a man, should he benefit from it?"

Aqa Hajji looked at me and our eyes met. He was the most righteous man I had come across, and had no doubts that he was a true believer. I missed our many great challenging discussions about Islam and Moslems.

"No," he said. "Those laws were intended to protect and benefit women who were economically in a vulnerable situation. Not the men."

"In your opinion, as a religious leader, should the families of the six victims be entitled to *qisas*, blood money?"

"The Quran is clear on those who can claim *qisas*, and the families of all six victims qualify under that category. May God forgive our sins."

"*Saket basheed! Saket basheed!* Be quiet," the judge said as he gaveled loudly.

"Hajji Ayatollah, is this your final opinion, that *qisas* is recommended?" one of the judges asked directly.

"Yes, based on the fundamental premises of justice and equality on which Islam is built, this is my final opinion."

"Do you have any questions for Dr. Ayatollah?" The judge asked the defendant's lawyer.

"Yes, your Honor."

"Doctor, in similar cases that have occurred in two other states, the verdict has been that if a woman does not follow the simple yet stringent requirements of what constitutes a *siqeh*, it nullifies the contract. And if the contract is nullified, then the union falls into the category of *zina*. And if it is *zina*, adultery, then it is punishable by death. Correct?"

"No."

There was unrest again in the court.

"Ateesh," Behi whispered, "do you see what he is trying to do?"

"I am not sure," I said.

"He is trying to show that those women have committed *zina*, which is punishable by death. Either way the women deserved to be killed. His logic is sick." She held her head in her hands. I looked at Ayatollah and once again recalled his question for me, "Ateesh why do you practice *siqeh*?"

"Because this way, I have more control over myself," I had answered.

"Here is a name of a reliable registrar," he'd said. "Make sure everything is done within the parameters of Islam. Be careful."

Back in the courtroom I heard the defense attorney's voice. "No?" The defense attorney asked the Ayatollah. "What do you mean?"

"The Quran is very clear on the requirements of having four reliable witnesses to *zina* in order for there to be any punishment. To accuse a woman of *zina* is not to be taken lightly. You need eyewitnesses, not mere hearsay."

"Doctor, are you defending the six women accused of prostitution?"

"God is almighty," he answered. "Islamic law is clear on the punishment of those who are indeed convicted, but that can follow only after producing clear and convincing eyewitness testimony in court. That is what I am saying."

"No more questions, your honor."

"How did you predict he would recommend *qisas* if I followed your line of questioning?" Behi whispered.

"Because he is a true believer and a religious teacher. After all, he is an Ayatollah," I said.

By the end of my second year of graduate studies, I was completely broke. I had managed to save a bit from my previous husbands, but the rent had increased. I had grown fond of my apartment and couldn't bear the thought of leaving it for something cheaper. I was willing to sacrifice neither my privacy nor the view of the mountains.

So I picked up the phone and dialed Hajji Registrar. I asked only two favors of him. First, I wanted a marriage that would last no longer than three months. Second, I wanted a higher price.

"You are getting older and you're demanding a higher price?" he asked.

"Hajji, I have become a courtesan. That is much more than a *siqeh*."

"You are what?"

I knew he wouldn't agree with me, but that's what I was. I had learned of it when I was reading about King Louis XIV of France and his first open official courtesan, Louise de La Valliere.

"Ateesh, don't you dare to call yourself that. You are a *siqeh*, doing what is allowed under Islam."

"Yes, Hajji," I agreed, wondering if he caught the sarcasm in my tone.

A week later, I found myself accompanying my new husband, a general, on a trip to Khoramabad, located in Southwestern Iran.

157

Despite not being a major tourist destination, it is still quite scenic and situated in the Zagros Mountains, which is the largest mountain range in Iran and Iraq. While I seldom traveled with any of my temporary husbands, I made an exception in this case. I did not know anyone from Khoramabad, so there was a low risk of running into anyone I knew. The trip would last most of the summer, and after hearing Hajji's high praises of me, the General was willing to pay my price, in its entirety, upfront.

For the first time in recent memory, I could stand my profession. The General was a gentleman, and more than anything else, he simply desired the companionship of a woman while he worked at the army base, running a series of meetings of some of the high-ranking military officials. He also wanted me to accompany him to some of the dinner functions while he was there. It was fine with me.

"How am I going to be introduced?" I asked him.

He thought for a second and said, "I don't think there is anybody here who knows my family back in Tehran. You come as my wife."

"Which I am, but of course just a temporary one!" I said with a wink.

"Hajji said you are a witty one," he said. "I like that."

I raised my right arm and saluted the General.

He laughed, "Let us see if you are as good in bed!"

"I am sure there are things I am going to learn from you," I said. "After all, you are a general and in control."

For personal and professional reasons, I was eager to visit Lorestan, in the outskirts of Khoramabad. After the trial I was even more curious about *qisas*, an Arabic term describing the crime and its punishment, and I knew they were practiced among the clans and tribes in this area.

According to the Quran, *qisas* is allowed for a very precise type of retaliation: the infliction of an equivalent bodily harm by the victim or his family against the perpetrator of the crime. Often ignored, though, is the latter part of the same Quranic verse, which encourages the perpetrator to offer compensation to the victim's family instead. According to the verse, the latter method of justice is the one more highly encouraged and favored by God.

There had recently been a case, in Khoramabad, in which the sister of a murderer was given to his victim's brother as a wife, and as *qisas,* she was considered compensation to the victim, and of course, this punished the murderer and his family.

This reminded me of a story Grandma Tuba told me once, after my divorce, when I was still living with her.

Batul Khanoom's niece married a young man from Baluchestan. He was a hardworking laborer, but he had been accused of making sexual advances to the unmarried sister of one of his clients, a family of a higher class. He was found guilty, and the community tribunal had declared that his younger sister, at twelve years old, be given in marriage to the female victim's brother. The decision of the tribunal was final.

"That's not fair!" I said to Grandma Tuba.

"It is brutal, is it not?" Grandma Tuba had said. "Ateesh, this is not Islam. The holy book never says a girl has to be sacrificed for the wrongdoings of a man."

Now, all these years later, I was given the opportunity to visit Khoramabad, where this kind of *qisas* was still being practiced.

Every morning, after the General left for work, I went to the teahouse, *chay khaneh,* located on the first floor of our hotel. The hotel we were staying at was named after Shah Abase, the king of Iran, and the greatest ruler of the Safavid dynasty. He was only sixteen when he was named the Shah, and he was given the throne in 1587.

The hotel was located in the middle of a garden with fountains, beautiful bushes, and trees surrounding its grounds. The teahouse was connected to the lobby through a narrow walkway covered with vine leaves hanging down from the ceiling on the sides. The vines reminded me so much of Grandma Tuba's house.

As much as I missed my family, I was happy to be away from Abadan. Modar was right about me when she said that I was like a fish born in a river but I really belonged to the ocean.

I was told that the *chay khaneh* was frequented by university students, and this was obvious from the first day I spent there. With some persistence, I hoped I could learn from some locals about the fate of the girl and her family.

I could have spent days in the hotel's *chay khaneh*. It was a beautiful, old-fashioned teahouse decorated with all kinds of tea glasses, teapots, and many white and golden samovars of all shapes and sizes. Ornate calligraphy unique to Moslems covered the walls surrounding the teahouse. Some walls contained Quranic verses right alongside intimate poems by Omar Khayyam. I found my favorite spot in the corner that faced the rose garden, adjacent to the tearoom.

From Grandma Jamileh I had learned that Khayyam was a mathematician and philosopher. Years later, however, through Edward Fitzgerald's celebrated translation and adaptation of Khayyam's quatrains, (*rubaiyaas*) in Rubaiyat of Omar Khayyam, I found that he was also one of the most famous Eastern poets in the West. Seeing a depiction of him with his women, I could not think of the poet himself uncritically. In portraits, he is often shown as an old man with a much younger woman, and a wine decanter with glasses. The depiction of an aging man with a much younger woman has been used to uphold the standard of men marrying women who are anywhere from five to twenty years younger than they are. I wondered if any of the beautiful, young women in pictures with Khayam and his old friends had chosen to be there. Through experience, I learned that no matter what age any of my temporary husbands were, they all wanted pleasure from me and not along with me.

Once in the *chay khaneh,* I ordered a pot of tea with fresh dates. I also ordered the local newspaper, hoping for some news on *qisas*.

For the entirety of our stay in Khoramabad, I spent each morning outside, enjoying the weather and scenery. In my new surroundings, I realized I had needed this break from Tehran. Despite the method by which I found myself on this extended vacation, the respite from the fast pace and noise of the city, and even the time away from my friends, was well worth it.

Three weeks passed and I still hadn't heard anything about the young girl who was given as *qisas* to another family. I was looking for an opportunity to strike up a conversation with someone local, but hadn't had any luck. Then one day I noticed a group of young women, university students, at a table not far from mine. I listened in as one of them complained about her parents' refusal to let her travel out of town to attend the University of Tehran.

That's when I got up, walked over to their table, and introduced myself as a researcher from the university. The women were shy at first, but greeted me and invited me to sit down. We talked for a little while. They seemed to warm up to me when I told them I was originally from Abadan. Leaving out many of the harsh details, I told them that I, too, had struggled and fought for my father's permission to attend the university. To gain their trust, I listened to them and their stories about the injustices they faced right in their homes in the way their parents raised them. Miriam, an eighteen-year-old girl, came from a military family.

"I have to clean up after my brother because he is younger," she complained. "But I also have to listen to him and respect him because he is a boy! I want to be born a man in my next life."

"Why is that?" I asked.

"My father believes men are superior to women," she said.

The other girls nodded their heads in agreement. Their fathers were the same.

"What do you believe?" I asked.

They hesitated before answering, probably as I would have, if anyone had bothered asking me that question at their age.

"We believe what men tell us about religion," a delicate-looking girl named Pari said. "My parents told me it is in my fate to get married and have children."

I wanted to quote them verses directly from the Quran about equality between the sexes. I wanted to tell them that the answers they sought could be found there. But I hesitated. Khoramabad was known for its conservatism, and I didn't want to get these girls in trouble at home. Ultimately, any decisions would be their fathers' to

161

make. I groaned inwardly at the thought of that.

I told them I was in town with my husband and asked if we could meet the next day at the teahouse for breakfast. There was no school that day so they eagerly accepted.

That night, as I lay in bed next to the General, I couldn't stop thinking about those girls. Every instinct I had in the teahouse was to teach them, offer them new knowledge, new ways of reading the holy book that could liberate them. But the strength and desire to fight prejudice has to come from within. In my case, I was lucky that I had strong women around me to lift me up. As horrific as my own childhood had been, I realized how far I had come. I felt removed from the powerlessness of my childhood. These women were five or more years younger than me. So little had changed.

"Ateesh, where are you?" the General asked. "Aren't you going to take care of my needs?"

"Oh yes, master General, your needs!" I said, then dimmed the light.

I dared not tell the General anything about my life outside of his world.

I thought about calling Grandma Tuba. She thought I had gone to stay with a college friend in another city. No, I could not tell her where I was or what I was doing, but I wanted so much to talk to her.

The next morning, I met my new friends bright and early for breakfast. I told them to order whatever they wanted. It was my treat. Conversation was awkward at first, but by the time our food came, we were speaking more comfortably.

Then Pari asked a question that I was wholly unprepared to answer.

"Did your family arrange your marriage or was it a love marriage?" she asked.

I hesitated, and slowly sipped my tea before answering.

"Arranged," I said, then I hypocritically added, "Sometimes love comes later."

"You are lucky then," Miriam said, unknowingly rescuing me from having to explain anything further. "All of my cousins are married and have children. Some of them are even younger than me. No one asks about love when they arrange our marriages."

That's when I saw an opportunity. "I've heard about this custom of marrying a girl into a victim's family to cleanse the bad blood," I said. "*Qisas?*"

"Oh, yes!" Pari said. "You heard about it in Tehran? We didn't know the girl personally, but she went to our school."

"Menejeh, I think, was her name," Miriam said. "She was actually from Nahavand, but for some reason she stayed with her uncle here in Khoramabad. He is a landowner with a lot of influence in town. That's why everyone around here knows about it. One of his sons got in a fistfight with the son of another influential landowner. I forget his name. The son from the other family was killed when he was pushed onto the asphalt. Photos of his bloody body were all over the newspaper. Everybody expected a horrible confrontation between the two families."

Pari, Shahnaz, and Yasmin nodded in agreement. I was relieved that they didn't mind talking about it.

Nayereh spoke up, adding to Miriam's rendition of the story. "The head of the village of Nahavand called a meeting between the two families to judge the correct provision of *qisas*. Everyone in the village showed up."

"Why?" I asked, silently condemning those in attendance for what I assumed was a spectacle, a mockery of justice.

"Khanoom, if there was going to be *qisas*, everyone wanted to know," Nadereh explained. "It affects them. Everyone in the community wanted to know what to expect."

"It sets precedence, just like courts," I said, making sense of it all.

"Yes," she agreed.

"My parents told me it is more than that," Pari chimed in. "Leaving their nice, fancy homes here, to see a respected head of a primitive village, sets an example of humility and humanity for all. Poor and wealthy are judged and treated equally. That is what *qisas* is about. God has given us the right to harm the one who has harmed us, but also recommends forgiveness as a sign of strength for a true believer."

Then Shahnaz, as if she was reading my mind, spoke up. "I say only God gives life and only He should be taking it. I leave it for the *Akherat*, Judgment day."

I could hardly believe what I was hearing. These girls were taking me by surprise. I wanted to know more.

Sara, the only one in our group of six women wearing a headscarf, was also the only one who had not spoken up. I asked her what she thought.

"The Quran says I, as the victim, can make the decision to seek revenge or to forgive," she said carefully. "People must look deep within their hearts when they are faced with such a decision."

Miriam and Pari exchanged glances, but only Shahnaz spoke up.

"I don't know about any of you, but I want my wedding night to be happy. I want singing and dancing," she said. "These stories make me wish that I had not been born a girl. *Qisas* only brings misery and makes the girl another victim. I would rather die than live with such a label on my forehead."

"Some things are in our fate," Sara bravely argued back. "We cannot fight everything."

"It is not justice!" Shahnaz persisted. Then she turned to look at me, and waited.

I had to say something. "I don't know if two wrongs always make a right," I said, wanting to agree with Shahnaz, but also to be careful not to offend Sara. Other people in the teahouse were looking over at our table. I quietly suggested we continue our discussion another time when the *chay khaneh* wasn't so busy.

Before we left, I asked Shahnaz for the easiest way to get to the town of Nahavand.

"You don't want to go there, Khanoom," she said. "It is backwards."

"Oh, I've got nothing but time while I'm here," I said. "How far is it?"

"About an hour by taxi," she said. "Anyone willing to drive you there will know the area well, and maybe the story too."

We parted ways. I wished them luck, and gave them my phone

number in Tehran in case they ever needed anything.

~~ ~~ ~~ ~~ ~~

After a quick cup of tea the next morning, I headed over to the main street where a number of yellow cabs were waiting in line near the curb.

"How much to Nahavand?" I asked one of the taxi drivers. He smiled at me then replied, "*Tehranyeh*." Literally, he was suggesting that I was from Tehran, but the term also implied that I was easy, or had money.

Not wanting to waste any time, I moved on to another driver, a man probably about my father's age, who was gesturing me toward his cab.

"*Bfarmayyed*" he said. "Please come. You pay me whatever you want and I will not question it." Even though I knew he may not have meant it, I liked his good manners.

I thanked him and got into the car. As we headed toward the mountain roads, I sat there, silently taking in the scenery, until the driver finally spoke.

"Khanoom, you are from Nahavand?" he asked, probably guessing that I was not.

Glad that he was up for conversation, I replied, "No Aqa. I'm just visiting." Grandfather's family was actually from Hamadan, which is the province that Nahavand is part of.

Remembering that I was not in Tehran and around the familiar grounds of the campus anymore, I thought about my safety. "A friend is expecting me this afternoon. I'm here with my husband for a few weeks while he works on the military base," I said. "I'm from Abadan."

"Ah, so it is your first visit?" he asked good-naturedly.

"Yes," I said. "What about you? Are you from here?"

He explained that he had grown up in Nahavand, but now lived closer to Khoramabad with his wife. His three children, who were all about my age, he said, lived nearby with their families.

"And how many grandchildren do you have?" I asked.

He said he had six, so far. I told him he was very lucky, and we chatted some more. He seemed to like talking about his family. I wanted to know more about Nahavand. He told me that life in Nahavand was very different, even from life in Khoramabad. Houses usually did not have much furniture, but were usually outfitted with mattresses, cushions, and handmade rugs. But elders were nice, hospitable, and welcome guests with open arms.

I remembered what Grandma Jamileh had said about Hamadan, where she lived in Daqda abad, a nearby village. "According to local Jewish traditions," she had said, "the City of Hamadan is mentioned in the Bible as the capital of Ancient Persia, in the days of King Ahasuerus, in the Book of Esther. It was then known as Shushan."

"What about young people?" I asked the cab driver. "What are they like?"

"What do you mean, Khanoom?"

"Well, the young people. Do most of them stay here to live? Do they leave? What do people do for a living?"

He explained that most families were agricultural. And yes, many generations of families often remained in Nahavand, or in nearby villages and towns. People born there often stayed and had their own children there.

Finally, I decided to stop beating around the bush. Clearly, this man was harmless, and I felt that he was enjoying our chat. I told him that I had heard about *qisas* being practiced there, and understood that all the locals seemed to know the story involving the girl I had read about, Menejeh.

"These decisions are made by elders," he said. "They do what is best for the families. But you do not have the whole story, Khanoom. The family of the dead boy received a girl in marriage from the murderer's family. Then they decided to give a girl in marriage to the murderer's family in exchange. This was decided by the elders on both sides to assure the fair treatment of the girls by each opposing family."

I was quiet. How could that possibly contribute to justice for anyone?

"They should have done that in the first place," Aqa driver said. "It is fair. This is the only way to make sure no retaliation on either side will happen, not now and not ever. God is merciful and wise."

I understood, but I couldn't stop myself from protesting. "Desiring such a peaceful outcome is admirable," I said. "But the cost to the girl is high. Wouldn't you agree?"

"Khanoom, you have to look at the bigger picture," he explained. "Sacrificing oneself to avoid bloodshed between families is a more important goal."

"It's always girls that are sacrificed for the mistakes of boys!" I protested. "Have you ever heard of a boy paying for the mistakes of a girl?"

"You are looking at it the wrong way, Khanoom. It is a family decision. Consider the community's welfare, and not just the individual. That is what Islam is about. Community and social order above individuality."

He reminded me of Hajji Aqa Ayatollah. I liked talking to him.

"You are a wise man and I admire your conviction," I said. "But this custom affects girls more drastically than boys. It is simply unfair. That is what I have an issue with."

He smiled, then began to talk about the scenery and what it was like growing up in the mountains. He obviously didn't want to argue with me anymore. I listened patiently until we arrived in Nahavand.

"Where to?" he asked. "What is the name of the friend you're visiting?"

Not wanting to admit that I had lied to him, I gave him a made-up name.

"I don't know of any family here with that name," he said. "Are you sure?"

We drove on for a while, until we saw a woman walking down the road with her children. Aqa driver pulled over, and I got out to ask her if any family by that name lived in Nahavand. I felt foolish, but I didn't know what else to do.

When I went back to car, Aqa driver was standing outside, smoking and stretching his legs. I explained to him that I must have been mistaken. He nodded. Perhaps he saw through my lie, but if so, he didn't say so. More than anything, he seemed amused by me.

I stood next to him and looked around me, suddenly realizing how long I had been surrounded by the drab colors of an urban setting. Here, patches of colorful flowers and trees in bloom surrounded us, seeming to grow more vibrant in the distance. For the first time in a long time, I felt close to God. I can still see the beauty of Nahavand on that perfect summer day.

We spoke very little on the ride back to Khoramabad. At the end of our journey, I thanked him and paid him generously. He made the usual polite customary comment, *qabel nadareh*, it was nothing. But unlike most of those who use this phrase, he appeared sincere.

I asked him if he might drive me through some other local villages the next day. I told him he could pick the destination. I just wanted to see the beauty this place had to offer. He agreed. Before I stepped out of the taxi, I asked him a question.

"Aqa, what about the difference in blood money if a girl is killed?"

"What do you mean?" he asked.

"I mean, if a girl is killed and her family decides to revenge the death of their daughter, and they do not settle it by receiving money, then what?"

"Well," he said, "the killer would be put in prison, and if still the girl's father doesn't agree to receive blood money from the boy's family, then the killer would be punished as if it were intentional homicide."

"But what about the difference in the value of a woman versus that of a man?" I asked. "I know that it has been interpreted that the value of a woman's testimony is half that of a man. But there is no verse I know of in the Quran that assigns different value to their lives."

"The difference of value between a woman's and a man's testimony was assigned when establishing the procedure for witnessing business transactions."

As Aqa finished his sentence, I saw an army jeep stop and the driver come to the passenger side to open the door. Quickly, I said goodbye to Aqa and hurried back into the hotel.

The next morning, as soon as the General left, I rushed downstairs and out the front door of the hotel. Sure enough, Aqa was waiting for me by the curbside.

"Good morning," I said as I stepped into the car.

"Good morning," he replied. "Khanoom, we are going to visit my cousin's neighbor not far from here."

I nodded and decided not to ask any questions. "I am sorry I left in such a hurry yesterday," I said. "My husband likes to have me in the hotel before he arrives."

"Your husband's request is understandable, Khanoom. After all, you have the whole day to tend to your business."

On the way there, he told me the purpose of our trip: An eighteen-year-old boy was sentenced to death for killing a girl with whom he had been in love with two years ago, when he was sixteen. He had proposed to the girl, but when her family didn't agree to the marriage, he killed her and then tried to kill himself. When apprehended, he confessed to the crime. His family had been trying to convince the girl's father to forgive their son and receive blood money as compensation. Her family refused, and now that the boy had reached the age of maturity, he would be put to death unless the girl's father changed his mind and accepted the blood money. Aqa said we were going to meet with her family.

I felt queasy. "We are going to meet with her family to say what?" I asked.

"Khanoom, you want to know about *qisas*," he said. "Perhaps by talking to the families directly you may understand it better. I tell you, though, it is not going to be easy."

In just a short few minutes, we came to a stop. "From here on we have to walk," he said. "These small alleys are not built for cars."

As we made our way through the alley, I remembered walking through similar alleys with Grandma Tuba. "Never pass through alleys alone without a man," she instructed me. I moved closer to Aqa.

After about ten minutes, we walked up to the door of a small house. He knocked at the wooden handle attached to the outside lock. Old-fashioned houses that haven't been renovated had this kind of lock from the outside. If the lock was on, it meant the people were not home. As we were walking, I noticed that all the houses in the neighborhood were the same.

Promptly, the door opened and a tiny woman stood there. She was clutching her chador under her chin with one hand, and holding the door with the other. Her worn-out chador had sky-blue flowers on it.

"*Khoshamadeed, Bfarmayyed,*" she said as she moved to the side so we could enter.

We took two steps down and entered what appeared to be a small courtyard, and then followed her into a small room. "*Bfarmayyed, Bfarmayyed,*" she said again as she guided us.

The woman, whom I came to know later as the dead girl's modar, offered me a seat on a worn-out rug by the wall and placed a small cushion behind my back.

"I know it must be uncomfortable for you," she said, kindly. "Please forgive us."

I appreciated her generous hospitality and apologized for the intrusion. I had no idea what Aqa had told her. I looked around while Aqa and the girl's modar went to get her husband. This was perhaps the poorest house I had ever been to. There was nothing of value in the almost naked, damp room. The rugs were in poor condition, too, but everything was kept neat and clean. Above a carved opening in the wall, I noticed a photo of a beautiful school-aged girl. She looked happy. The door from which we had entered was covered with a long, worn material, acting as a drape, separating the room from the small courtyard.

I was still feeling queasy. A few minutes passed before a white-haired man of about fifty entered the room with Aqa. As a sign of respect, I stood up and extended my hand. "I am so sorry for the intrusion," I said. He gently shook my hand and asked me to sit down.

"Your cousin told me," he said, as he sat down next to me, "that you are a professor writing about *qisas*, and that you might be able to help us."

Confused, I looked at Aqa, who sat across from me. Our eyes met for a second and I tried to read his face.

The man said sternly, "I will not permit the boy who took my daughter's life to go free. His family and friends have been trying to convince me by offering blood money, but I will not accept it. I am a religious man and I believe in the Quran. The holy book says that if I revenge my daughter's death, God will forgive me. I am exercising what is right for my family and me. And no amount of money will bring back the daughter I loved."

His voice began to crack and tears came to his eyes. I didn't know what to say.

The woman walked in with a tray of tea and placed it in the middle of three of us. She sat behind her husband quietly.

"How can I help?" I managed to ask.

"As you know, Khanoom," the man said, "the worth of my beautiful daughter's life is half that of the boy who took her life. In order for *qisas* to be done, I have to pay the difference in value to his family before the state executes him. We do not have the money."

I felt a shiver through my body. Is this what Aqa meant when he said I could help? I looked at Aqa again, but he was gazing downward. Did he think I was angry with him? I thought so. Was I angry for being put to the test like this?

"Khanoom," the woman said, as she looked at me sadly, "I say let us get the *qisas* money so we can buy the things we need for our two sons, who are close to marriageable age. It will be expensive to marry them off. We have to think of our children. What good will it do to revenge our daughter's blood?" With this, she burst into tears.

The father raised his voice angrily and said, "I cannot forgive the boy who took my only daughter's life! I do not want any money. Only his blood can put this to rest. The Quran gives me that choice, and God is forgiving."

The woman began sobbing louder as she hid her face in her chador. Aqa looked at me, then at the father.

"How much money do you need, Hajji?" he asked.

"Five million *tumon*," he answered.

Aqa and the man both stared at me. They wanted me to help

them have the young man in prison executed. Five million *tumon*. That was all of my income from the General. That would enable them to pay the difference in the worth of their daughter to the boy's family, after which the state would execute the boy. How could I do that? I was angry with Aqa for doing this to me.

～～ ～～ ～～ ～～ ～～

"Why did you put me in such a position?" I said to him on the way back.

"Khanoom, you wanted to learn about *qisas*, not me. I only want to show you that it is not such an easy decision, as it may seem to be in your research paper. It is a test of belief and endurance."

"I'm not going to help him have the boy executed!" I said angrily.

"Why not, Khanoom? You want equality and fairness in treatment of men and women. The boy killed the man's daughter, is it not fair according to you that the boy be put to death?"

I still felt sick. "Can you take me back to the hotel now?" I asked.

Once back at the hotel, I headed directly to the garden. I needed time to clear my head before I had to face the General. But my mind was too active to enjoy the beauty the garden offered. The verse on *qisas* is clear on empowering the victim's family with the decision on the defendant's fate. But the second part of the verse emphasizes the fact that God prefers forgiveness. The father loved his daughter so deeply that he had closed his eyes to his family's desperate financial needs, even that of his sons. I liked the father and his stand, not only for his love of his daughter, but his religious reasoning. He couldn't afford what was religiously recommended because it was a girl that was killed and not a boy.

It was then that I realized why in poor families fathers usually take the money. Not because they believed in forgiveness, but because they could not afford to pay the difference in price. Is this really what the intent of the verse on *qisas* was from in its inception? From my reading and understanding of the verse, there is no mention of, nor inclination towards, attributing a girl's worth to be half that of a boy.

What had started out as simple research was fast becoming a lot more than I expected.

Later in bed, as the General was on top of me, I thought of the young boy in prison, and how this time he was going to pay for his crimes as a man. Too bad for him he did not have an unmarried sister to give to the victim's family in exchange for his life.

As soon as the General left the next morning, I dressed quickly and went outside where I found Aqa again, waiting by his car at the curb.

"Where to today?" he asked. "To the prison?"

I looked at his wise, kind face. "No," I said.

"Khanoom, let us go and see the boy who has killed," Aqa suggested.

I got into the car and closed the door, without replying.

He sat quietly for a moment before he started the car, "Where to, Khanoom?" he asked politely.

"Take me back to the father's house," I said.

He looked disappointed, and waited for me to explain.

Instead, I looked out the window at the picturesque Zagros mountains, which created a geographic barrier between the flatlands of Mesopotamia.

Aqa respected my silence, and we drove quietly until we came to our stop. Then we took the same narrow alley as the day before.

I asked Aqa to wait outside. His eyes questioned me, but he agreed.

The same woman as before opened the door and welcomed me in again. As I followed behind her small frame, which wasn't covered fully as it was the day before, I thought of Grandma Tuba. Oh, how much I missed her! Since leaving Abadan, I had been searching every old woman I saw for a resemblance to her.

When I entered the small room, I sat across from the father, who was holding his head down as a sign of shame and sadness.

"I never told my daughter I loved her," he said. "If I let her killer go, she may never know how much I loved her."

I thought of my own Baba, and remembered how he used to take me everywhere with him until he took a second wife. Then it just stopped. All these years I had been trying to understand that.

I pointed to the holy book the man was holding in his lap, and said, "I don't claim to understand it all, but I know this much for sure: To do what is 'right,' we have to think about the Prophet's intention before we can apply these verses to our situation. Our Prophet turned his other cheek when he was slapped in the face by a non-Moslem. The satisfaction of not using your power to take a life, which only God should take, is more humane, as our Prophet showed by example."

The room was silent. I could hear my heartbeat and thought I almost heard theirs. With shaking hands, I took out a large envelope containing five million *tumon* from my purse, and placed it in front of both of them. "The decision is yours," I said. "*Allaho Akbar.*" Then I got up and left quickly, before either one of them had a chance to say anything. I felt as if I was about to break down.

I found Aqa waiting outside. "Let's go," I said, as I raced past him through the alley.

We were silent for the ride back. When we arrived back at the hotel, I got out of the car and said to Aqa, "I have some things to take care of for the next few days." Then I walked into the hotel, through the lobby, and out the door, which opened into the garden.

⁂ ⁂ ⁂ ⁂ ⁂

I didn't go back to the teahouse for the next few days. Instead, I spent that time going for walks in the hotel garden and writing in my journal. I visited the beauty parlor, and stopped at a fortuneteller who told me my future by reading my coffee cup, *faleh qahveh.*

"Your fate is to marry overseas and leave Iran," he said. Then the small, fragile-looking old man looked up at me, adjusted his glasses, and continued, "But that won't be your only marriage."

At night, of course, I tended to the General, who did not know about my daily adventures and never asked.

A few times, I peeked outside to see if Aqa driver was out there waiting. He was, even though I had told him not to. I wasn't ready for him yet.

A few more days went by, then late one morning as I came downstairs, there was a message for me from Aqa to meet him at the curb.

It was a gorgeous Thursday afternoon toward the end of summer. I walked to the curb and smiled at Aqa who was standing next to the passenger side with the door opened.

"How are the interviews going, Khanoom?" he asked me.

I look at him strangely. "Is that what you think I'm doing here?" I asked ironically.

"*Bfarmayyed Khanoom*, come in," he said pointing to the open door. "Where we are going is a surprise."

His warm and simple demeanor relaxed me. As he pulled away, he asked, "Did I tell you why I became a taxi driver?"

"No," I said, "please tell me, Aqa." Truthfully, I had wondered about this, but never asked. On our first trip, I'd expected him to know the local gossip and be able to tell me more about Menejeh's fate, but I hadn't expected him to speak to me so articulately about *qisas* and its basis in the Quran. The only man who had ever spoken to me so freely and respectfully about such religious matters was Hajji Aqa Ayatollah. Surely, my cab driver didn't appear to have Hajji's education.

"I will tell you," he said. "I taught physics and chemistry at a high school until I retired. But outside of the laboratory, I love my community. I like to meet people, talk to people. So, when my friend retired, I bought this car from him. I work here and there, mostly in the summer when there are travelers."

"You are a very resourceful man," I said.

"Maybe," he said. "I don't drive this car for the money I earn, that's for sure."

As we drove on, he told me stories about his children. He was most proud of Ahmad, his eldest son. When Ahmad got married, he had managed a small orchard, making just enough money to get by. Now, ten years later, he managed several orchards and provided a comfortable life for his wife and two children, soon to be three. I thought of Mrs. Berenji and wondered if Aqa's son plowed any of the agricultural land himself.

"What about you, Khanoom?" he asked me. "Do you have any children?"

"Yes, of course." I replied. Why did I keep lying to him? His sincerity made such an impression on me. I felt wrong lying to him, but I wanted him to respect me.

"I have a son, Alireza," I heard myself saying. "He is eight years old."

I gave Aqa driver a few details about him, all based on Batul Khanoom's grandson, who was just about eight.

"Only one?" he asked, "I am sorry."

"Yes," I said.

"But you are lucky you have a son to carry his father's name to the future."

A few moments passed. I didn't want to tell him any more lies, nor did I wish to hear about how lucky I was. I let him think I felt very lucky. I thought about how lucky Baba was, for having two sons to carry his name into the future.

"We are almost there," he finally said.

We went to what appeared to be a meeting point on the corner of one of the major intersections. We pulled behind three buses that were filled with people of all ages.

"We are going to follow these buses to a wedding," he explained. "The bride's family home is in a nearby town not far from Nahavand."

"A wedding?" I asked, grinning with excitement. "Are you serious?"

"Yes, Khanoom. I thought you'd be happy."

Suddenly I thought of the poor bride in the *qisas* case. "Oh, no," I said. "Aqa, this is not a *qisas*, is it?"

"No, no, Khanoom," he said. "Please trust me."

As the buses started moving, we followed them. After about twenty minutes of driving, we pulled in behind them as they stopped on the side of the road. I looked out the window and saw that we were on a hill of breathtaking green fields with the Zagros mountains in the background.

"What happens now?" I asked.

"You will see," he said.

I watched as everyone stepped out of the bus and onto the field.

Some began forming a line. Three men stood next to each other and uncovered musical instruments, which they began to play as everyone began to dance. One played a large drum that rested on his shoulder, which he beat on each side with two large sticks. Another played a large, long, flute-shaped instrument known as a *shaypoor*. The last was a violinist. All were dressed in vibrant tribal clothing. The women wore brightly colored, long dresses with flowers printed on them and long slits open on both sides. Under their dresses were long skirts with many pleats that opened as they moved side to side. They had sensuously painted their eyes with *sormah*, an eyeliner made from charcoal. They had rosy cheeks and beautiful dark curls cascading from colorful silk turbans on their heads.

"Do you wish to dance with them?" Aqa driver asked.

"Yes!" I exclaimed.

He went and talked to the bridegroom's family and came back to me with a few of the older women.

"This is the modar of the young man getting married," he said. "She is also my first cousin on my modar's side."

I got out of the car and extended my arm to shake hands.

"*Salaam Khanoom*," I said, very politely and respectfully. She came close, and instead of reaching for my hand, she kissed me four times on my cheeks, welcoming me.

"*Salaam azizam*, hello my dear," she said. "*Tehranee hasty*, you are from Tehran? *Khosh amady*, welcome."

When these women saw my enthusiasm, they went back to one of the buses and returned with a package. The next thing I knew, I was wearing a long dress like theirs with sides that opened to show my jeans underneath.

The red color of the dress reminded me of the gypsy dress at the boutique across from the registrar's office building nearly fifteen years ago.

Then the women wrapped a large, colorful silk shawl around the top of my head and asked me to take off my shoes. Soon I was hand-in-hand with men and women, following their dance steps as closely as possible in my bare feet. I felt intoxicated; like the poet Molana,

177

Rumi, when he heard the sound of rhythmic beating coming from a bizarre in Konya... Rumi was walking through the town marketplace one day when he heard the rhythmic hammering of the goldsmiths. It is believed that Rumi heard the dhikr, *la elaha ella'llah,* "no god, but God" in the apprentices' beating of the gold, and was so entranced in happiness, he stretched out both of his arms and started spinning in a circle. With that, the practice of Sema and the dirvishes of the Mevlevi order were born.

The Mevlevi believe in performing their dhikr in the form of a dance and music ceremony called the Sema, which involves the whirling from which the order acquired its nickname, "whirling dervish." The Sema represents a mystical journey of man's spiritual ascent through mind and love to perfection. Turning toward the truth, the follower grows through love, deserts his ego, finds the truth, and arrives at "perfection." He then returns from this spiritual journey as a man who has reached maturity and a greater perfection, so as to love and to be of service to the whole of creation.

Dancing barefoot in the dirt, I felt carefree and light as if I were on clouds. I danced and laughed with people I hardly knew. I was filled with joy as if I were dancing in that red gypsy dress I saw at the boutique years ago. I looked up at the perfect, deep blue evening sky, which even at this early hour was beautifully studded with shining stars. "God is great," I thought. I will never forget that day. I had never been to a ceremony such as that one. At the wedding parties I had attended in Abadan and Tehran, the families so often focused on impressing the guests with lavish food and decorations. Conversation among those in attendance always consisted of comparing this year's wedding to last year's, which bride received better jewelry and gifts, and whether or not the pair was a good match.

What I saw here before my eyes was an expression of joy.

After a good couple of hours of dancing, everybody went back to the buses and started driving to the bride's parents' house, twenty minutes from Khoramabad.

We followed behind them, and after we reached the wedding place, Aqa told me to wait in the car for a moment. He stepped out of the taxi and said something in the local dialect to one of the younger women I had danced with.

The young woman disappeared quickly. I wondered what was going to happen next.

After everybody had gone inside the brick and clay house, nearly identical to the other village houses we passed, the young woman came back carrying a hand-carved water decanter specific to Hamadan region.

Grandma Jamileh had told me that when she lived in her in-law's village, guests' feet and hands were washed with fresh water containing rose petals, as part of showing hospitality. I was thrilled.

I raised my feet happily as the young woman poured the refreshing water over them. With every drop of water on my tired but happy feet, I thought of Bejan, and how after we made love for hours my body was tired in the most pleasurable way.

Aqa introduced me to some members of the family as a distant cousin from Abadan who taught in Tehran. My darker, olive skin indicated that I was not from Tehran itself.

There was a large spread in the middle of a long hallway with people sitting crossed-legged next to one another, eating. Taking me in as their guest, some elderly women offered me food and drink. The family had been so hospitable to me that when the time came for me to go I felt terribly rude leaving early, but I knew the General expected me to be waiting for him when he came home. It took me a long time to convince them that I had to go, and I was very sad to leave because more music and dancing were going to follow the feast.

On the ride back to Khoramabad, I thanked Aqa.

"I know what kind of stories you must read about us in Tehran," he said. "I wanted to show you something you don't read about. We are not as uneducated as some Tehranys might think. As simple as we are, we respect traditions and customs.

"I know you might still be questioning our wisdom in carrying out *qisas*," he continued, "but the alternatives are not any better. Murder leaves the family of the victim and aggressor feeling unjust and empty. *Qisas* fills in some of that emptiness."

179

I sat there quietly as he continued.

"I was one of the elders consulted in the *qisas* you'd asked about the first day I met you. I took part in the tribunal reaching the decision. The decision to give the girl in marriage to the victim's brother was in the best interest of our community. As harsh as it may sound to you, it prevents further bloodshed."

I could not bring myself to argue with him. For once, this wasn't about *aberue*. I still didn't think the ends justified the means, and I felt much sympathy for brides in *qisas* cases. But I could not doubt this man's good intentions.

When the car came to a stop in front of the hotel, Aqa turned around and asked, "Do you still want to see and talk to Menejeh?"

"What?"

"The girl in the most recent *qisas* case. I have talked to her and her husband. If you wish, they are willing to talk to you." Then he got out of the car and opened my door.

"*Bfarmayyed*," he said politely.

I was too tired to respond.

"I will be waiting here tomorrow morning if you decide to visit them," Aqa said before he got back to his taxi.

As I entered the hotel room I was startled by the General's voice. "Khanoom, we are going to be late for the dinner party given by General Falahi," he said with a trace of authority and anger. "Did you forget?"

I jumped back into my position of temporary wife, and did what I was supposed to do. I never did meet with Menejeh, but returned to Tehran with a better understanding of *qisas*.

With the wedding still fresh in my mind, I returned to Tehran feeling renewed and hopeful. Graduate school was more difficult than my previous courses had been, which in turn motivated me to work harder. Since the General's contract was well behind me, I dove into my studies and started teaching part-time.

While I still had a few days left before the start of the new semester, I decided to take a break from my studies and visit Tanaz at her studio. It had been a while since I saw her, and she had invited me to see what she was working on. I stopped to pick up some pastries on the way.

Her studio was a storefront she rented within a much larger building. It was lined with windows where she displayed paintings and sculptures by local artists. After we greeted each other, I complimented the pieces she had on display.

"Oh, Ateesh, thank you," she said. "But to tell you the truth, they aren't very good, but they'll sell."

I smiled and nodded. Tanaz's husband had supported her decision to open a studio, but only if it could sustain itself financially. Tanaz knew it wasn't always great art that sold, but usually more ornamental pieces that would fit comfortably with the decor of an already decorated room.

After we chatted over pastry and sips of Nescafé, she said, "Let me show you what I've been working on."

I followed her into the backroom of her studio, which was always in disarray. There were sculpting tools all over the floor and everything seemed to be covered with a thin layer of dust.

In the middle of the room stood Tanaz's sculpture. It was a figure of a woman with long flowing hair, who resembled any number of Persian goddesses.

"Take a closer look," she said.

I did, and that's when I noticed the woman's expression. It was difficult to describe. She looked neither pained nor happy. Perhaps, like the material from which she was carved, the look was simply meant to convey lifelessness. Still, she was quite beautiful. As I ran my fingers along her to feel the texture of what I knew must have been the result of Tanaz's many painstaking scrapes and strokes, I was surprised at what I felt. Shallow grooves had been carved into her skin, and when I inspected them closely, I saw calligraphy, though it was difficult to read. I could only discern a few words here and there.

"What's this?" I asked. "I can't quite make it out."

"Good," Tanaz said. "You're not supposed to. They're verses, but they're meant to be imperceptible, distorted—exactly what some men, and women, have done to these verses."

I inspected the sculpture more closely and recognized some of the verses from Chapter Two of the Quran, which is dedicated to women. The engravings didn't make her skin look wrinkled, but cut up, fragmented, almost as if she'd been dropped on the floor, broken, and then skillfully glued back together.

That's when I realized. "Oh my God, Tanaz," I said, as I felt the tears coming, "you made this after the case in Buffalo, New York, of the woman whose husband forced her to tattoo his name on her body, above her genital area."

She nodded and said, "I thought you might recognize it earlier. It's not exactly something I can put in the window."

Then she stepped away. "Come on, let's eat. Stress makes me hungry."

"Wait…"

"You heard me! Let us eat." Her face was unreadable; devoid of any expression.

"Tanaz," I said, "let's talk."

"Come on, Ateesh, don't get so emotional over things," she said. "Men are hurting women all over the world. How about that case in Buffalo? The husband who committed that crime was a young Moslem man, born and raised in America! There is no hope for women asking for equal treatment. Any of us who are vocal are called whores. Because that is the ultimate character assassination of a woman: To call her a whore! Ateesh, did you hear about the other Moslem man who slit his wife's throat?"

"You mean the one in Orchard Park, New York?" I asked.

She nodded. "It was in the news that she had asked him for a divorce and had a restraining order against him. Some called it an 'honor killing.' We don't know whether this was honor killing or not because the trial has not begun, but it won't be the first time a woman is killed, asking for a divorce."

For a second I thought she was going to cry, and at first it seemed that her deeply held hurts were starting to surface. But as she continued speaking, I realized there was something missing. The strength I usually heard in her voice was gone, and seemed to be replaced with a tone of surrender, which was frightening to me. It was as if she had become indifferent to the sufferings of women, and in a way, of herself. How awful it must be for her to pretend she is heterosexual year after year, and to be married to a man. I realized how similar our lives had become. Tanaz and I were living lives full of pretenses, right along many other women who were in marriages and had no choice but to prostitute themselves to maintain the marriage status.

"Tanaz, we cannot give up hope," I said. "The case could also be domestic violence. The husband had prior incidences of such behavior toward her, and his previous two wives. There was nothing honorable about it."

"Oh, really! She indeed must have dishonored him by her behavior!"

She turned around and headed toward the exit.

"Do you want to eat with me?" she asked. "That's all I want to do right now."

I quietly followed her out of the studio, closing the door behind me.

By the time we sat down to eat, our conversation had changed to other topics. She had always shown such interest and excitement in my studies, and asked me to tell her everything. But throughout our light, casual talk of graduate school, I couldn't seem to shake the uneasy feeling I had inside.

As I played around with the eggs on my plate, I thought of the verses on the sculpture.

"Tanaz, if we surrender, what is going to happen to our daughters?" I asked softly, trying hard to hold back tears. "What kind of future are they going to have? What are they going to think of us as mothers?"

"That we got tired of discrimination and bias and a culture full of pretenses," she answered.

"We as women and mothers cannot give up our fight for equality with men," I said. "I am not." Then I gave a faint smile and reached out for her hand. "Tanaz, do you ever wish you were born a man? It appears much easier to be a man than a woman, does it not?"

Her soft fingers touched mine and she just nodded. I got up and went around the table and held her.

～～～～～

On the way home, something in the window of the bookstore on Pahlavi Street caught my eye: A new English translation of famous Persian poems. I was so excited that I momentarily forgot about the visit with Tanaz that was burdening me, and I ran inside.

I had studied enough English at the university to judge the translation, and I was thrilled to do so with works I knew by heart. I found the volume on the top shelf, but as I was in the habit of buying the book straight from the display, I went over there and waited. The employees were busy with students purchasing books for the new semester.

"Khanoom, we'll be right with you," the clerk said.

"Thank you," I replied, and just then I noticed a man, also standing next to the display. He was a little taller than me with broad shoulders, and penetrating, dark brown eyes with long lashes. He reminded me of Omar Sharif, whom I had seen as a very young girl in the film, *Doctor Zhivago*.

"Can I reach something for you, Khanoom?" he asked.

I realized then that I was staring. "Yes, please," I said. "The display."

I noticed his cute accent and wondered where he was from. Also, the strange way he addressed me as Khanoom seemed overly formal.

"Oh, I have this one," he said, as he handed the book to me. "My Farsi is not good enough to read the original, so I can only read the translation."

"You like Persian poems?" I asked. "Where are you from?"

"I'm American born and raised, but my parents are from India."

He was a visiting scholar from the United States, teaching courses in American literature at the University of Tehran. He was also a converted Moslem.

Then he must be circumcised, I thought, as I felt myself blush. *Shame on you, Ateesh!* Although my time with the general was done and my three-month waiting period was over...

He had initially come to Iran to visit the holy cities, but had decided to stay longer when he was offered a position at the University of Tehran. "You remind me of Omar Sharif," I heard myself saying. "Is it okay if I call you Omar?" I felt myself blush as I realized I was flirting with this man.

He smiled pleasantly and replied, "You can call me anything you want. Just call me."

His smile made me feel warm all over.

"Actually, my name *is* Omar," he said. "Dr. Omar Gobta."

He was staying at the university guesthouse located not far from the campus. I told him I was a graduate student at the law school.

"A woman with such beauty and intellect," he said, as he took a half step toward me, took my hand, and gently kissed it. "I'd better be careful."

I was totally charmed by him. I glanced around to see if *mardom* was watching!

"Let me see what your palm says, Khanoom," he said. Omar then turned my hand and gently traced the lines. "There are three lines here, each representing different characteristics about you."

I tried to pull my hand back, but he held onto it. "You have secrets you do not wish to have revealed," he said.

His dark eyes were penetrating and I wanted to let go of every defense I had built around my feelings. I thought of Bejan and what might have been if I hadn't run away. I closed my palm but Omar still didn't let go. I enjoyed feeling his warm hand touching mine, but it instantly made me feel vulnerable and that was something I didn't want.

"Let go of my hand and I will tell you everything," I said.

He immediately let go. "Sorry, Khanoom," he said. "Please tell me your secrets."

"Secrets? What secrets? I want to tell you your fortune."

He held out his hand and said, "You have to hold my hand to read the lines, yes?"

"Not really, I can see the lines from here."

"But I bet it is more accurate if you hold my hand. Then you can trace the lines with your eyes closed, through feeling alone."

"Is that what you want me to do?" I asked softly. "Hold your hand and trace the lines with my eyes closed?"

I could see how he was melting with every word that came out of my mouth, just as I was with him. I moved closer to him, so close that I could feel his fast heartbeat. "I need to pay for the book of poetry I have been holding under my arm before they think I am trying to steal it." Then, I took a step back and looked at him. He was still standing in the same spot with his hands held out for me.

"Khanoom," he said, as he slightly bent his head, "I am absolutely enchanted."

I relaxed. I was in control again.

"If you would not be too offended by my asking," he said, "would you consider having tea or coffee with me? Water? Anything?"

I hesitated. There was something so different about him. He had a quality that I had never detected before in Iranian men.

"I am so sorry," he said. "I did not mean to insult you."

I didn't know what to say. It was the first time a man had ever really asked me out.

"Please say something, Khanoom. This is my first time asking out an Iranian girl here. Help me out, please?"

His smile revealed his beautiful white teeth. When the professor had asked Suzan and me for lunch, he was looking only at me. If Suzan had not said yes for me, I wondered what would have happened.

I heard myself saying, "Okay."

"Okay what? When? Perhaps today? Tonight?"

I could no longer contain myself and started to laugh. I was totally amused by him. An Iranian man would never be so straightforward and obvious.

"I could have dinner with you at the Maharaja Indian restaurant next week," I said. "It's right down the street."

"But not tonight?" he persisted.

The more he talked, the more I liked him. His questions conveyed a sort of naïve confidence, and I loved the way he pronounced "khanoom." What would he think if he knew this khanoom was a practicing temporary wife?

"Pardon me," he said. "Next week is fine. I will keep every night open, just in case. But tonight is better. Maybe? Yes?"

I heard myself again, "Okay, I'll see you tonight at Maharaja at eight." Then we shook hands and parted.

I purchased my book in a daze and caught a taxi home. What had I done? I knew exactly what I had done. I was following my heart, and I knew better than that. It could only get me into trouble. I must stick with my plan of using men to maintain my independence!

After Bejan, I hadn't dated anyone else. How could I? I had become a professional *sigeh* instead. I had successfully separated my heart from my job. So why did it feel so good to be with this American?

So what? There was nothing wrong with having dinner with him! I was going to enjoy myself.

187

But I was a *siqeh*, which is "to give pleasure." *Don't you forget that,* the voice in my head reminded me.

~~ ~~ ~~ ~~ ~~

At Maharaja's that night, the American led me into a different world. Omar was respectful without being prudish, and he possessed a gentle sincerity that he often conveyed by the way he looked at me when he spoke. Time seemed to fly by as we talked about our lives, our careers, and our families. I told him about my family and my childhood in Abadan. He was the first man I had ever talked to about my past. Of course I didn't tell him everything, but I found myself talking to him about things I had never talked about before. I felt like I had known him a long time.

"A young, beautiful, vibrant woman like you must have broken many hearts!" he said.

"I was married as a teenager," I found myself saying. "It was an arranged marriage, which resulted in my own broken heart."

He nodded and smiled at me kindly. I couldn't believe those words had come out of my mouth. It felt good to say it.

Before dinner, the waiter brought over two silver bowls filled with water and red rose petals. "To rinse your hands," he said.

He explained that it is a tradition to bring water bowls before and after the serving of food. "When I visit my relatives in India, they follow the same tradition. Typically many Indians use their hands instead of utensils."

I had to tell that to Grandma Jamileh. She had gone through the hand-washing tradition in Grandfather's village.

I thought about the wedding Aqa driver had taken me to and how they had rinsed my feet in Khoramabad. How happy and festive everybody had been that day! Dancing barefoot and carefree in the dirt with majestic mountains and fields of dusty green grass in the background. As if *mardom chi megan*, what people would say or think, didn't matter at all. That wedding was so rejuvenating. But then there was that visit with Tanaz.

We spent five hours at dinner that night, and were the last couple to leave the restaurant. During dinner, he chose Canani as our wine. It was very sweet and tasted like Iranian sherbet.

This was my second experience with wine.

"I have read and heard," I said, "that alcohol makes men and women misbehave."

I was flirting with him again, and it was fun. He didn't quite know how to respond. When I smiled and tossed my hair, I could feel his desire for me. That's not wise, the warning voice in my head tried to remind me, but I brushed it off.

When the waiter came back and poured our wine, we toasted.

"*Bsalaa mati,*" he said, stumbling a bit over the words. To this I said, "Cheers."

Unlike when I'd been taken out to restaurants by my temporary husbands, whom I'd viewed as business clients, I felt like I was on a real date. Though he was nothing like Bejan, the first man in my life I had feelings for, he roused my emotions the same way. I was being swept off my feet and I was allowing it to happen. Was it wrong? Having fun with him meant letting go of who I had become, independent not only financially but emotionally, intellectually, and physically. I never allowed myself to be physically satisfied with any of my temporary husbands. I kept my true emotions and needs hidden. I had strictly trained myself not to let go with any of them, regardless of how badly I wanted to be satisfied. All I had known about relationships was that as soon as women let go of themselves, men usually betrayed them in one way or another. I would run fast before I would ever allow that happen. How long did I have until I had to run from this American?

We were close to finishing our bottle of wine when he told me that he was separated from his American wife after a very short marriage.

"Where does she live?" I asked.

"In San Diego, California," he said. "We're still friends."

Knowing this made me feel comfortable telling him a little more about my own short marriage, telling him how difficult it was to get my divorce.

"May I ask why you got a divorce?" he asked.

"I just couldn't stand him touching me. His touch made me sick."

It felt so good to talk to him, and I realized how tired I was of keeping secrets. For a second, I even thought of telling him about my profession.

Then I had second thoughts. Sure, he would understand. What made him so different than rest of them? I was just fooling myself by thinking I could be so open and truthful with a man. But I liked him. He was waking things up in me that had been asleep for a long time. If I wanted this to be different, I would have to be honest with him. No matter how ashamed I was of what I had chosen as my profession, I would have to come clean, wouldn't I? I didn't know how to go about any of this.

Luckily, the wine took over, and I heard myself saying, "Let me become your *siqeh*." But this wasn't the voice of "independent Ateesh," as I had planned. This was another side of me, brimming with unfulfilled desires, aching to be touched by him.

For a second, he looked puzzled, then his expression briefly turned to shock, then he said, "I accept!" Then he smiled and raised his glass, "Let us drink to that, Ateesh!"

"You know about *siqeh*?" I asked.

"Oh, yes! It is being practiced in Los Angeles among some Iranians." He paused before adding, "I've had two Iranian-American girlfriends. One insisted on *siqeh* rather than a regular relationship. It is all the same to me. It is about being together. I am attracted to you, Ateesh."

I knew I shouldn't have let myself go. I never thought I would meet someone from America who would tell me about the practice of temporary marriage over there, much less someone who had actually practiced it himself. I was shocked and disappointed. Here I was thinking about a real relationship with him. Something I longed for with man. Honestly, I didn't expect him to know what *siqeh* was. So, he was just like the others.

But if that was true, then why did it feel so good to sit across from him? He aroused and touched a hidden part of me.

I admired American women for being frontrunners in the struggle for equality, and I had expected better of Iranian-American women. Surely, I thought, Iranian women exposed to American culture would be demanding more equality. Apparently not.

"Why do Iranian women practice temporary marriage in America?" I asked him. "And why would you do that?"

"Please," Omar interrupted, "don't get the wrong idea about me. I saw how it was practiced when I went to Mashhad and Qom. Both of these holiest of cities are almost equally notorious for their available *siqeh* women. The only difference is the contract. In America it is normal to have a relationship before marriage.

"I never even talked to those women," he continued, "and I felt embarrassed by the men who propositioned them. In the States, it is different. The woman I dated said she couldn't openly date me unless we made it legitimate religiously. Isn't that your reasoning, Khanoom?"

I had proposed in such a flirtatious way that he must not have suspected that I was doing it professionally. I decided then and there I could never tell him about my profession.

"Well, it is too late to go to a registrar tonight," I said. "Why don't you think about it for a few days? It is not permanent, of course, but maybe we should see each other a few more times. Don't you want to make sure I'm worth it? It is going to cost you."

"I have no doubt, Ateesh Khanoom, you are worth it," he said. Then he thought for a minute and said, "Worth what? Don't tell me you have a contract price too. You are kidding right?"

"But that is part of the religious belief," I said.

"Okay, Khanoom, we'll play it according to your belief. Do we have to wait for a third party to say the words of the offer and acceptance? Don't you think you are taking this too far?"

I thought how different the love story of *Dr. Zhivago* was from the relationships I had experienced. But perhaps this Omar that I sat across from represented what I really wanted and desired.

"Yes, let's do it tomorrow, properly," I said.

We both sat there quietly. He seemed as disappointed as I was. But I was not going to break the *siqeh* rules.

"I have to ask for one more thing," I said. "Nobody can know this is a *siqeh*. It's one of those things that everyone knows about but never talks about. We must be discreet. It could do us both a lot of damage professionally."

"For your sake, I will be discreet," he said.

"I have to make sure it is all done within the parameters set by Islam. I hope you understand."

"I agree," he said. "As long as I don't have to wait after tonight."

The effects of the wine combined with the fact that I was having so much fun with him inspired the next conversation. I took a sip of my water and asked, "How many camels do you have, Omar?"

He almost spit out his wine. "I am sorry, Khanoom, what did you say?"

"Camels," I said, "you know the custom here in Iran."

He shook his head.

"Well, when a man asks to go out to dinner with a woman, her family requires him to show how many camels, goats, and hens he has. It is also important for the family to know how many humps the camel has."

Then I took a deep breath and asked in a desperate voice, "You do have camels, right?"

He stared at me with his mouth open and waited for me to explain.

I took a sip of my water and continued, "No camel? No goat? No hen?" Then I shook my head.

"Khanoom, where can I buy some?" he asked. "If this is traditionally required, then tell me where I can get them."

He sounded so sincere that I couldn't control myself any longer and started laughing.

∿∿ ∿∿ ∿∿ ∿∿ ∿∿

The next morning I called Hajji Registrar. When I couldn't reach him, I called Ali. Ali was the only person outside of Hajji Registrar who knew about my profession. He was a long-time clerk of Hajji's who agreed to witness all of my marriages for a cut. In all of our dealings, he had proven himself to be reliable and discreet.

"Khanoom, you are over twenty-five years old!" Ali said. "Doesn't your American know he can get a much younger woman at a lower price?" Then he laughed and said, "Better yet, for a little bit more, he could take a trip to Dubai!"

Of course, based on experience, he knew that Dubai had become the center of pleasure and delight for many men interested in very short duration temporary wives. He often acted as the escort for those young, poor girls, accompanying them to Dubai.

"Ali," I said, ignoring his attempts at humor, "I'm not asking my usual price. And when we get there, act as if this is the first time I have ever done this. Please."

"Okay, okay," he said. "So you want to do this today? At a discount and with no health certificate? Ha! Don't tell me you care for this guy. You are a heartless woman with no feelings! Or has that changed? I can't wait to hear what Hajji has to say about that, Ateesh. Does this mean my cut is lower too?"

"You and Hajji will get your usual cut." I said coldly. "Take it out of my share."

I didn't want anybody to know that this time I had feelings for who I was marrying. This time I would have to pretend.

"Well, I must say I can't wait to see this American," he laughed again. "Does he realize what a deal he's getting? I will see if I can get Hajji to marry the two of you today. It should not be a problem."

When Ali called me back, he said Hajji wasn't available to marry us until the next day. He had gone out of town to officiate a wedding.

I hung up the phone. I couldn't wait for the next day. I had butterflies in my stomach. I was afraid that if I waited too long to do this Omar would slip through my fingers and I might lose this feeling forever. I picked up the phone and asked him to meet me for cappuccino.

When I saw him, he looked more handsome than ever. I noticed then his taste for expensive designer clothes, his cologne, and his kissable lips. This was starting to feel like some sort of fairy tale. I hoped this wasn't a mistake.

"Are you still sure about this?" I asked him.

He nodded and smiled. "It's all I can think about. You are worth it, Khanoom,"

It occurred to me then that maybe he thought of himself as just another client. I was something he was paying to enjoy while he lived in Tehran. I was the only one romanticizing our transaction. Perhaps, as an American, he felt it was necessary to court me first. Then again, I had proposed the marriage. Was I simply making his conquest easier? What was happening? I wasn't sure. Was this real or I was making it up?

"But there is something you should know," he said, suddenly becoming serious.

I held my breath and waited for him to continue.

"We both know I am only here for a year, and I don't want you to get hurt," he said.

My heart sank into my stomach.

"If this goes public it will only hurt your reputation," he said. "I don't want to pretend we're not together when we're at school and then have to sneak around in the city, fearing we might run into someone. I don't behave that way in the United States, and I don't want to here. I respect you and I already care for you tremendously."

What was he saying? Did he not want to do this? Did he not want to see me at all? The voices in my head fell silent and I anxiously waited for him to explain.

"I bought you this," he said. He took a small box out of his pocket and handed it to me. "I understand if you need some time to think about it. You can keep it as a gift or return it to me when I leave. It is up to you. No one has to know it is only temporary but us."

I opened the box. It was a simple, delicate gold band with diamond cut, but at that moment, it was the most precious ring I had ever seen.

"I would rather people think we are crazy for marrying so fast than have them gossiping about us behind the scenes," he said. "I am familiar with the art of gossiping among Iranian people, especially women. What do you think, Khanoom?"

Unable to speak, I put my hands over his and looked deeply into his eyes.

I nodded. I thought of my wedding at twelve years old. Nobody had asked me what I thought then.

"Is that a yes?" he asked.

After we parted that night, I went back to my apartment and lay on the bed. When I closed my eyes I could still see him there sitting in front of me. I was lost in visions of his light brown skin. The top button of his shirt was opened, and he had the perfect amount of dark hair on his chest. I wondered what it would be like to touch him. I fell asleep with that vision of him fresh in my mind.

Early the next morning, I called him to go over the details of our wedding. This was my wedding night, and I wanted this one to replace that first wedding night at age twelve.

Hajji Registrar would marry us later that afternoon, and all we needed to bring to the ceremony were the two required passport-sized photos for the marriage booklet.

Before we hung up the phone, I made Omar reassure me one more time that he wanted me to be his *siqeh*.

I called my hairdresser for an appointment, and then I took a long bath. I chose to wear a red dress with pleats at the bottom. The dress was similar to the one I had seen on display many years ago, as I rode away from the registrar's office for the very first time. I had found the dress in a small boutique in a plaza in Oktoban and had kept it for the right occasion. This would be the first time I would wear it.

On the way home from the hairdresser, I picked up a fancy cake from the famous Bibi bakery, not far from my apartment. I asked them to write on it, *mobarak bashad*. I wondered if Omar knew that phrase. It meant, "congratulations."

Back at my apartment, I placed a tablecloth on the small table on my balcony. I put flowers in a vase on the table and chilled champagne in the refrigerator. I changed my bedding to a silky set of pink bed sheets with a matching comforter that I'd bought on my last trip to Abadan. As I spread the comforter on the bed I remembered what the sales person had told me: *"Mobarak basheh, barayeh arouseh,"* hinting it was for a bride. And indeed I was a bride! I was so happy and wanted to share it with Modar and my grandmas. But I knew they wouldn't approve of our separation a year from now.

I left the red dress on the bed to wear as soon as we came back from the registrar.

Before I knew it, the time had come to meet Omar. With sweaty palms, I checked my watch. I had never been this nervous before. All of my previous marriages were business transactions. This was different. I was thinking about being in bed with Omar, being held by him. My naked back against his naked chest, real close…I couldn't wait.

By the time he stepped into the room, I was completely flustered.

"How beautiful my bride looks!" he said, as he handed me a bouquet of fresh yellow and orange flowers.

"They are beautiful," I said, as I took them from him with shaking hands. "Thank you."

He took my hand and gently kissed it, "You are welcome, Khanoom. Are you ready?"

He had a taxi waiting to take us to Oktoban, an area not far from Shahyad Monument Square, within walking distance from Hajji Registrar's office and Ali's home. Hajji Registrar had my photo on file but Omar needed a photo for the *siqeh* certificate, so we stopped at a quick service photo shop along the way. While the photos were being processed, we walked to a nearby sweet shop for some ice cream.

Ali insisted on coming along, joking with Omar in his broken English, "You get good bargain," to which Omar replied, "Don't I know it!"

"Why are you so happy?" Ali asked me. "You are behaving as if you love this guy."

"Why do you care?" I asked, with a big grin on my face. "You're getting your usual share. You are just a witness. Don't forget that!"

I looked over at Omar. Fast music was playing in the background, and as romantic as everything was, I tried not to think about what I was doing. I was acting as if this was a real marriage, a permanent marriage. The reality of it didn't hit me until I heard Hajji Registrar pronouncing us husband and wife for one year.

After signing the marriage certificate, we rushed into the waiting taxi and back to my place. As he poured the champagne, I changed into the red gypsy dress. At first we sat on my balcony overlooking the Alborz Mountains, drinking champagne. I wanted time to stop and record everything very slowly so that these new pleasant memories would replace the old hurts and wounds.

Maybe it was the early fall sky, or the champagne, but the mountains had never looked more beautiful.

Omar held my hand as we walked to the bedroom," I want to take my time with you, Khanoom," he whispered. That's what I wanted him to do. First he gently lowered the strap on my shoulder. Then he started to kiss my neck and shoulder gently, until I felt his tongue on my breast. It was intoxicating. We made love that evening as the setting sun shone through my window. The beautiful magic of that night made me wish our day, our night, would be endless.

The next day was my first day back at school, and I immediately submitted a letter to my department requesting an increase in my part-time teaching position. I wanted to make sure I would remain financially independent. My credentials, along with various honors I had received, qualified me for the position. But, as I well knew, even in the minds of my liberal professors, the greatest credential was the ring I now wore on my finger. Somehow marriage elevated a woman's status among my colleagues.

Between studying, teaching, and coming home every night to a man I loved to be with, I felt content for the first time in my life. I tried not to think about what would happen a year later when our contract was up. I found myself pretending we were in a permanent marriage, and imagined what it would feel like to have something good like this, forever.

On a crisp winter morning some months later, I awoke to the sun shining brightly on my face. The air in my bedroom was cold, though, so I stayed in bed, keeping myself warm under the blankets. I dozed off and on, thinking, in my state of semi-consciousness, that I should get up, make some coffee, sit down at my desk, and start writing... when the phone rang.

Modar wept softly as she told me the news: Baba was dead.

I felt numb. "I'll be home on the next flight," was all I could think of to say.

I cleared my short leave of absence with Dr. Goodarzi, and said goodbye to Omar. He offered to come with me, but we agreed that his presence would only raise questions and make life complicated. Besides, I told him, he had his responsibilities at school, and Modar would need me.

I took the first flight to Abadan that afternoon. I hadn't been there in a long time. Though I had visited on holidays, my studies and professional obligations kept me in Tehran more often than my family liked.

When I stepped out of the taxi in front of Grandma Jamileh's house, I could hear the voice of a cleric reading Quranic verses over the wailing and moaning of women in mourning. As is the custom during *azaadary*, mourning, Grandma Jamileh's front door was wide open. It was the second day of mourning, and everybody who knew Baba would go to pay his or her respects.

I walked through the front door in a daze. Men and women sat around in different rooms and servants and young family friends were serving halvah and other refreshments. Everyone was dressed in black. The entire back of Grandma Jamileh's courtyard was filled with huge pots and pans while cooks discussed what food should be served for the occasion. A charcoal-burning oven was brought in to accommodate cooking large quantities food.

This was the first time since I had left Abadan that I was appearing in front of such a large number of friends and acquaintances back at home. When I walked into the parlor, there was Grandma Jamileh, looking much more wrinkled and sadder than I could ever remember seeing her. Next to her sat my father's second wife. I turned away and pretended I didn't see her. There were many other women sitting in the room, but none I recognized at first glance.

With the aid of a cane I never saw her use before, Grandma Jamileh got up from her sofa and embraced me. I felt like a lost child and wanted to remain in her arms forever.

"Ateesh Joon, it is so good to have you home," she said. "We miss you so much."

"I miss you too, Modar Bozorg," I said. "I am so sorry."

As I uttered those words, I looked at Baba's second wife from the corner of my eye. Some time ago I had forgiven Maheen in my heart, though I never spoke a word of it to anyone. I had tried to understand her position as a woman. She had no choice but to get married when the best offer came along. Financially, she would have been a fool to decline Baba's proposal so many years ago. I let go of Grandma Jamileh and helped her back onto her sofa.

Maheen stood up and took a half step toward me as if she were going to kiss my cheek. Instead, I reached for her hand and shook it gently. No words were exchanged between us, perhaps for fear of breaking down. But she nodded knowingly, and the look on her face expressed gratitude.

After all, it was her hatefulness toward me that had sent me to the university, I thought.

I looked around the room. "Where is Modar and Grandma Tuba?" I asked.

"They were waiting at the front door for you," Grandma Jamileh said. "They must be in the kitchen."

I went into the kitchen but they weren't there. There were women making halvah and other delicacies for the occasion. Grandma Jamileh's regular samovar had been replaced by a giant one, but the framed poetry about Padeshah Khanoom was still hanging on the wall. I smiled.

I found Modar and Grandma Tuba, and before long we found ourselves sitting together with Grandma Jamileh and Maheen. We spoke nothing of the past, but only of funeral arrangements and the events of the week.

Baba's heart attack had been wholly unexpected by Modar, but his second wife had seen a change in his health over the past few years, or so she said. We tried not to pay too much attention to her.

If nothing else, Baba had always been a hard worker. Since I had left for Tehran, he had opened two other restaurants in the nearby cities of Khorramshahr and Ahvaz. The long hours he spent working paid off financially, but finally had taken a toll on his body.

Suddenly I found myself missing my grandfather.

"Where is Grandfather?" I asked.

"He must be sitting with the men in the other room," Grandma Tuba said. "Don't go there, we'll call him here."

But by then I was already on my way to him. I stood at the entrance and saw him right away. He immediately got up and rushed toward me. "Ateesh!" he said.

I went to him and held his tall, skinny body. He immediately opened one side of his beautiful, black cloak and held it around me. Then he faced the men who were sitting around in the room. "Look here, this is my granddaughter Ateesh Khanoom, from the University of Tehran. She is a girl but as good as any boy."

He said those words so lovingly. I remembered that as a child, I always daydreamed about being in Grandfather's cloak. He would place me under it and poof! I was in another world. In that other world, I was carefree. In that fantasy world I could do whatever I wanted and be whoever I wanted to be. I would hop instead of walk. I would dance and play without any boundaries. I remembered praying and hoping that one day that would be my reality.

"Ateesh!" Modar called from the other room. "Where are you?"

Her voice brought me out of Grandfather's cloak and back into reality: Baba was dead.

Before I left that night with Modar and Grandma Tuba, Grandma

Jamileh handed me a box. "Your baba gave this to me a few weeks ago," she said. "He wanted me to keep this for you, Ateesh."

I looked at the sealed box and saw my name scribbled in black ink. I recognized Baba's handwriting right away.

"I don't know what is in it, but I'm sure he gave it to me thinking that *she* wouldn't," Grandma Jamileh said, nodding her head toward Maheen.

What could Baba have possibly kept for me in a box? The last time I saw him, he was so angry with me, he didn't even look at me. I had wanted him to look at me just once, the way he looked at his sons. I thought I was over that, but as I stared at the box now, I realized that I wasn't.

I felt Modar's arms around me. "Azizam, my dear daughter," she said.

She took the box from me and handed it to Grandfather. "Keep this for Ateesh so she can open it back in Tehran," she said.

Grandma Tuba held my hand as we walked through the narrow alley back to her house. We looked at each other and smiled, both remembering the last time we walked through that very same alley.

The burial service took place three days later. My father's body had already been taken to the funeral home, washed thoroughly and, according to custom, wrapped in several meters of new white cotton. His body was then placed in a wooden casket and carried by four men to the cemetery. I recognized two of the men as Karim and Alireza. It had been years since I had seen them. They were boys then, and now they were full-grown men. I realized then that they were both staring at me. I almost looked away, but didn't. I kept my head up and stared right back at them. For the first time, I did not feel any less significant than they.

They both had Baba's curly dark hair, like me. I wondered what other characteristics we shared.

Grandma Tuba leaned toward me and whispered, "Talk to them after the funeral if you wish. It might make you feel better."

I didn't respond. Emotions were piling up and I was trying hard to contain them.

As Baba's body was lowered into the grave, Modar, both grand-modars and I sat on a bench under a large willow tree. Maheen stood close by. I looked at Modar and gestured toward the empty space next to us, to see if we could invite her to sit with us. Modar shook her head and continued to stare at the grave through teary eyes.

Then Karim and Alireza came over and handed us flowers to be thrown into Baba's grave.

Alireza extended his arm toward me with a flower, "Salam Ateesh Khanoom," he said.

Grandma Tuba squeezed my sweaty hand, which reassured me. I shifted uncomfortably on the bench. "Salam," I said, but I didn't take the flower. Grandma Jamileh reached out and took it, giving him a faint smile.

"My brother and I would like to see you before you go back to Tehran," he said.

I didn't know what to say. I stood up to stretch my legs and sat down again. I felt sick to my stomach. All I kept thinking about was that night, all those years ago, when Karim told me he hated me.

As Alireza and Grandma Tuba made small talk, I looked around for Karim and found him staring at me again.

I held back my tears and let my eyes meet his. I thought back to when we played in the garden together and swam in the pool. We were so young and innocent, and didn't know there was supposed to be so much friction between us. I remembered climbing the fruit trees in the orchard, racing to the top, laughing. Then I turned nine years old and everything changed.

After my divorce, when I had moved in with Grandma Tuba, I received a number of letters from him, but I told Grandma Tuba to send them back unopened.

Grandma Tuba elbowed me, bringing me back to the present moment.

"Karim and Alireza want to spend some time with you while you're here," Grandma Tuba reminded me, gesturing towards Alireza, who was still standing there.

"No," I said. "I don't want to see him."

Later that night when Modar and I were alone in her bedroom getting ready for bed, I started to cry. Modar held me until I fell asleep.

For the next several days, Modar, Grandma Tuba, Grandma Jamileh, and I spent most of our time together at *majleseh tarheem*, mourning gatherings, where memorial services continued from morning until late at night. Maheen was present at all the gatherings, but stayed in the background, somewhat alienated from us.

On the eve of the seventh night, there was a large dinner gathering where loud religious and customary chanting was performed over loudspeakers. I moved through all the ceremonies in a daze. By the next morning when I left for the airport, I was totally drained.

I had been in Abadan for seven days, and though they said they understood, I knew Modar and Grandma Tuba and Jamileh were disappointed that I didn't stay for the required forty days to mourn. I disliked the idea of mourning in public and for such a long period of time. Despite having been raised in a culture that emphasized public appearances, I had learned to mourn and cry privately. I didn't want to, but I promised to return for the fortieth memorial service. I knew I needed to be strong for Modar and especially Grandma Jamileh.

~~ ~~ ~~ ~~ ~~

Through a bequest outside of his will, Baba had left me several acres of undeveloped land with an orchard filled with fruit trees on one of the parcels. It was one of the orchards that Karim and I used to play in. He left the other half of it to Karim.

The significance of this eluded me. He must have known that I had no interest in returning to Abadan. Was this his way of making sure I got my share of inheritance, despite his will in which I had been disinherited? How valuable the land was did not matter at all. What mattered was that he had given me the exact same piece of property that he had given to his eldest son, Karim! I was completely shocked. Had he loved me as he loved his sons? If so, then why hadn't he treated me that way? He scarred me for life with the way he had brushed me off when he was alive. Now was I supposed to understand and forgive him? How would that be possible?

When I stepped off the plane and found Omar there anxiously waiting for me, I found him more desirable than ever before.

I hadn't talked to him the entire time I'd been in Abadan. As soon as he saw me, he pulled me close and held me in his arms, and then right there, out in the open, he kissed me passionately on the lips. It felt so good to be with him again. I missed him so much and just wanted to hide in his arms forever, just like Grandfather's cloak.

He didn't ask any questions nor did he complain that he hadn't heard from me.

When we got to the apartment, he carried me upstairs to the bedroom. There were long-stemmed, red roses all over the bed.

"It has been exactly 168 hours, 23 minutes, and 62 seconds since I was deprived of you," he said, as he gently placed me on the bed. Again I allowed myself to submit to him completely. He took his time, kissing every part of my body as he slowly undressed me. When he finally got to the last piece of clothing, I found myself in a state of vulnerability that I had never before experienced with a man.

A few days later when I was alone in my apartment, I decided I was ready to open the box from Baba. I had placed it under the bed in the guest bedroom the night I returned and had been avoiding it ever since.

I pulled the box from under the bed and went outside to the balcony. I sat on the chair that faced the great mountains and listened for any sound of wisdom from their majestic presence. Not even a whisper. I took a deep breath and opened the box.

What I found was a memoir by Charlie Chaplin that contained personal letters to his daughter, Geraldine. It was titled, *To My Daughter*.

I stared at those words, not knowing what to think. Then I opened the book and began to read. The letters talked about Chaplin's belief that his daughter's virtue would survive despite a world of sex and drugs and where having orgies and getting high on drugs were fashionable. Baba knew I loved Charlie Chaplin's movies. He must have been worried about my virtue, but did he worry about it even after my divorce, and so many years later? I was confused.

In the box was also a great lithograph of a Sufi woman by a re-nowned Persian artist, which read, "Oh God, if I worship you for fear of hell, burn me in hell; If I worship you in hope of paradise, exclude me from paradise; But if I worship you for your own sake, grudge me not your everlasting beauty."

Immediately, I felt as if I were back in Grandma Jamileh's kitchen reading the poetry by Padeshah Khanoom. I fell in love with this message, and hung it next to where I hung the other poetry, by the entrance of the apartment.

I do not know what had prompted Baba to set these gifts aside for me. Perhaps he had forgiven me for bringing shame to him in my youth. But more than that, why was he showing me a side of himself I had never seen before? Baba was a university dropout who had be-come a shrewd and successful businessman. His intellectual side was unknown to me, but it became evident when I saw the other book he left for me: *The Book of Great Mawlawiyah*, by Balkhi, who is known more commonly in the west as Rumi. I just had so many questions. One of them being, could I ever forgive him?

I found myself desperately trying to understand Baba's lack of compassion for Modar and me. As soon as I became old enough to get to know him and enjoy his presence in my life, he stopped loving me. Now he had left me with Rumi and mystical love. Rumi was a thirteenth-century poet, Islamic jurist and theologian, whose love for God expressed through his mystic poetry brought spiritual ecstasy to his followers. Rumi's love for another man, Shams Tabrizi, was seen as mystical and divine by their followers. I remember reading a passage about their relationship by an Iranian writer. Rumi and Shams would sometimes disappear for days, weeks, or months searching for divine love and mystical awareness.

As a graduate student, some of my classmates and I had talked for hours about the claim that Rumi and Shams' relationship was divine. In line with the culture that mystified and glorified Rumi and Shams' relationship, and which Baba apparently accepted, my father never-theless would never have believed such mystical relationship between two women could exist.

Rumi had described his love for Shams as: "Too great to be called human experience; but if I was not afraid of God, I would have called it from the divine."

Underneath this book, there lay an old tambourine with Baba's initials on it. The tambourine is an important musical instrument in Sufi gatherings. Had Baba been a Sufi at some point in his life?

Sufis are Moslems who seek a very close, personal relationship with God. The origin of the name is not known, but it is believed to come from "suf," which is the humble, rough garment that early Sufis wore. Sufism is generally understood to be the inner, mystical dimension of Islam. Another name used for the Sufi seeker is "dervish." Classical Sufi scholars have defined Sufism as "a science whose objective is the reparation of the heart and turning it away from all else but God." Clearly, Baba had turned away from Modar and me. Was this reparation of some sort for him?

I started to wonder if I ever really knew Baba. Then again, Baba was also a polygamist. Was that practiced by Sufis as well? I still saw his second marriage as the ultimate act of betrayal of Modar and me. I recalled asking Modar many times if Baba loved me then why did he need to have boys? Isn't that why he remarried? Did he really love me even though I was a girl? Every time I asked, poor Modar assured me of his love.

Now Baba left me his most private belongings, even though his sons were alive and well. Why had he given it to Grandma Jamileh? Surely, he hadn't foreseen his untimely death. I did not know what to make of any of this.

The last item contained in the box was a small, decorative box with a key attached to it. The box had ivory inlaid in the typical style of Persian miniatures. I unlocked it and saw the most beautiful jeweled pin in the shape of a large bird called Simurgh. I looked at it closely. According to the Sufi, the Simurgh symbolizes an endeavor for unity with the divine.

As I was looking at the jeweled Simurgh, I read the poetry Baba had copied on the back of the lithograph. It told that when other birds heard of the Simurgh's splendor, they elected him as their king and searched for him. Only thirty survived the journey, and as they reached the mountains where the Simurgh was supposed to have lived, they realized that he and they were all one.

I looked out at the mountains outside my balcony. Looking at their majesty, I hoped that Baba left those things to me because he loved me as if I were his son.

That night when Omar came back, I was already in bed.

I kept my eyes closed as he came into the bedroom and sat on the bed. I felt his fingers and hands running gently through my hair. "Ateesh," he whispered, "I have fallen in love with you."

He'd never said that before. I didn't move. He kissed my head, then, gently lifting my hair, nibbled the back of my neck. Only he knew how much that aroused me.

After a few minutes, he stood up and walked into the bathroom to get ready for bed. After he closed the door behind him, I heard myself say, "I love you, too."

One of the first trips Omar and I took together was to Mashhad, one of Iran's holiest cities, to visit the shrine of Imam Reza, the eighth Imam. We stayed at the Hotel Homa. I didn't care much for it because I had stayed there several times before with my Arab temporary husbands, but of course I didn't mention that to Omar.

As soon as we registered, the manager of the hotel brought us two invitations. As a foreigner and Shi'i Moslem, Omar had been offered a special dinner as the guest of the Imam's foundation.

After we checked into our suite, we took a taxi and went to the shrine. As we approached the entrance, the enormous gold dome atop the building, which holds the Imam's tomb, glistened in the sun, in sharp contrast to the white marble floor on which we walked. There were many other pilgrims there, and apparent newlyweds made wishes into a fountain as we passed. Inside, the ceilings, walls, and floors were made of marble decorated with *minacari*, colorful and geometrical carvings, many of which contained verses in calligraphy. They reminded me of Tanaz and her sculpture.

Magnifying the vivid colors were ornate crystal chandeliers that hung from the ceilings and small mirrors of various shapes and sizes, which covered the spaces between the *minacari* in regular patterns.

I had visited this shrine by myself a few times, and only once with one of my temporary husbands. He was an Arab, and had insisted that

I remain very close to him the entire time we were together to ward off any unwanted approaches by men. At a religious shrine! He also insisted on a full-style Arabian chador for me, which only showed the eyes. I objected, and told him that eyes are even more sensuous when only they remain uncovered. He agreed with me and then decided on a full-face cover. I just played along, remembering my wise Grandma Tuba's advice, not to be afraid to become invisible. In the end, his hypocrisy had astonished me, for it was not my chastity he was concerned about in covering me, his *siqeh*, but the public perception of him.

I looked up at Omar. He was such a different man than the others were, and I loved him for that. I didn't share that experience with him just then, although I made a promise to myself that I would try to be as honest with him as I could about my life. I grabbed his hand and held it. Then I told him a story that Grandma Tuba had told me once, about a trip she took to this very same shrine when my modar was only nine years old.

I missed Grandma Tuba. Talking about her comforted me, and I found myself laughing when I remembered how angry and animated she had been when she told me this story.

"Grandfather had gone to the men's section for prayers," she said. "So I took your modar and we sat along with the other women in the women's prayer area. All of the sudden, this middle-aged woman approached your modar and asked, 'Are you married, daughter?'

"'No,' your modar answered her. Now, I was spreading my prayer rug, but also watching this woman very closely."

Grandma Tuba continued, "'Is this your modar here?' the woman asked. Your modar nodded, and then this woman sat down and made herself comfortable right there, in between us! '*Qhaboul bashed*, May your prayers be accepted,' the woman said to me. 'I am a marriage broker with several proposals from a list of available, interested, and of course, honorable men. How old is your daughter?'

"'She is nine and not interested in your honorable proposals!' I replied in anger. Then she said the customary well wishes for visiting the shrine, and left.

"Soon after, a man in his forties approached me and asked if he could take a few minutes of my time. He was carrying books, so I thought he was selling religious blessings. Next thing I know, *be pedar*, the bastard says, 'I am interested in marrying you for a short period for a certain sum. I am an honorable man traveling without my family. My proposal is an honorable one.'"

At the time this had happened, Grandma Tuba was in her early twenties. I saw pictures of her. She had long, dark, curly hair, a beautiful smile, and a distinctive look. Even covered under the white, floral-patterned, cotton chador that women wear during prayers, I was sure she had appeared desirable, especially to the "honorable" man.

Grandma Tuba was so angry that she hit the man over his head with her prayer rug. "What kind of a woman do you think I am?" she yelled at him.

"I am married. Besides, this is the house of God! You should be ashamed of yourself!"

"Please stop hitting me, sister!" he said. "I didn't know you were married!"

"Get lost, *be pedar*!" Grandma Tuba said.

Grandfather told me that he had heard a commotion, and looked over and saw Grandma Tuba hitting this man. So he rushed over as the man ran away.

When Grandma Tuba told Grandfather about the man's proposal, he said he was glad she hit him. Then Grandfather had started to laugh.

"Why are you laughing?" Grandma Tuba snapped.

"You see that woman?" Grandfather pointed to the same woman who proposed to Modar earlier. "She asked me if I was interested in marrying her for a short time."

"What? She also proposed marriage for our daughter! Stop laughing! I am angry! This is a place of God, a sanctuary to cleanse our hearts and thoughts! Unfortunately there are more than enough places outside here for this kind of dishonorable behavior."

She collected her prayer rug in a huff, took Modar by the hand, and said to Grandfather, "Not another second here. We are leaving!"

I looked at Omar then, and tried to read his face for his reaction, but couldn't tell what he was thinking. "Such stories were not unusual then," I said to him, "and are even less so now. Women unaccompanied by men receive propositions from 'honorable' men everywhere."

"Why are these men called 'honorable'?" he asked. "How did the word 'honorable' get attached to them?"

I shrugged. "I'm not sure. It could just be a selling pitch, or a way to tell others it's honorable, because it is believed to be religiously endorsed. What do you think?"

"I think you're right. If a bad Moslem can fit it under the name of Islam, then it gives it validity. Those who only follow without thinking convince themselves it is honorable."

Omar reminded me that he had visited Mashhed and Qom before, and he knew that some men made regular pilgrimages, mainly to obtain temporary marriages. "This behavior is not honorable," he said. "We should call it what it is: extramarital sex."

I nodded in agreement.

"Make sure to stay very close to me, Khanoom," he said jokingly. "Honorable men and women are watching!"

I thought for a moment of Hajji Aqa Ayatollah. Of course, when Grandma Tuba told me the story of her trip to Mashed, as with so many of her stories, there was a warning to be wary of men. "Even in the sacred space of the shrine, Ateesh, you must be careful," she said. "You don't need to be alone in a dark alley for a man to find you and want to harm you." She was so right.

We walked by the shrine of Imam Reza, made entirely of 24-carat gold, accented with silver. It is believed that the Imam acts as a mediator between people and divinity, and his tomb is covered with pieces of blessed green thread that pilgrims tie into knots, representing their personal requests. Pilgrims throw small pieces of writings containing certain *duaa*, a prayer, or money, on top of the tomb, which is surrounded on all sides by a silver grate through which the tomb can be seen. The sterile ask for fertility; the blind, for sight; and the married, for blessings. After making requests, pilgrims also promise to give certain sums of money to the Imam's charity, one of the largest in Iran.

The dinner we enjoyed later was elegant and plentiful. It was attended by many. Omar and I were seated apart from one another in adjacent rooms. Afterward, he teased me that many *siqeh* brokers had propositioned him at dinner.

"How many?" I asked.

"Three different ones," he said proudly.

"Do you know how many men asked me if I would be their *siqeh*? Five!" I said, of course omitting the detail that one of them had been a former client.

We stood outside on the balcony overlooking the beautiful outdoor restaurant, listening to soft, instrumental music.

"I want you to dance for me with your sensuous Persian moves, Princess," he commanded.

I obeyed.

Back in Tehran, I had a conference to plan. Omar was giving a lecture elsewhere on campus the day of my conference, but he helped me organize it. He'd been learning about the difficulties women face in Iran every day, and had been appalled when I told him about my childhood marriage. Being from the West, he had heard some horror stories, but the hospitality that Iranian people had shown him since his arrival made him think maybe he had heard exaggerations, or just very rare cases of brutality against women in remote areas.

He was also surprised to learn that my father had been married to two women. I explained to him that there were more than a handful of men with multiple wives in Abadan at that time. They were all middle to upper class businessmen and not terribly religious, but they followed rituals. Many had children from the first wife as well as subsequent wives, so it wasn't procreation that was the driving force for polygamy. Nor was it the requirement for Moslem men to "rescue believing women from destitution." I had heard this justification from Hajji Aqa Ayatollah.

Upon hearing of this, Omar contacted a feminist scholar he had met briefly during a workshop at the University of Shiraz. He had only met her once, but she was held in high regard by some professors he knew. We invited her to my conference to discuss the state of polygamy in Iran. The result was disastrous.

Most attendees were students who had taken classes with Omar or me, but there were some faces I did not recognize from any of the classes on campus. I was pleased to see some unfamiliar faces. Word of the conference had obviously gotten around.

My excitement quickly faded as soon as our speaker began.

"Men are not monogamous by nature," she said, setting the tenor of her lecture right then and there. I was disgusted. It took all of my willpower to sit quietly and wait for her to finish.

When she finally did, the audience applauded politely, if insincerely.

"Any questions?" she asked.

This was when I stepped in. "The threat of a husband's ability to take another wife overshadows every marriage," I said. "It is like a permission slip in the husband's hand that can be used at will."

One of the attendees, a well-dressed, bleached blonde woman in her mid-thirties, dripping in jewels, replied, "If a woman keeps her husband satisfied at home, he will not go out looking for other women!"

Others nodded their heads in agreement.

"Men's sexual needs are greater than women's," someone said. "That is why God has allowed men to have more than one wife. But it is not allowed for women to have more than one husband."

"Holding onto a husband is a skill, which obviously not everyone has," the blonde woman said.

"In my opinion, feminism has undermined the dynamic of Iranian families by bringing in the Western ideas that women's sexual needs are the same as with men," the speaker said, using the word, "feminism" in English as there is no word for it in Farsi.

I sat back in my chair as a few bland questions were asked and duly answered. I was disappointed that none of my students had spoken up.

The next day back in the classroom, I asked them why, and was told they felt uncomfortable and intimidated by the speaker.

"Because she was standing on a stage speaking into a microphone?" I asked in disbelief. "That makes her viewpoint more legitimate than yours?"

"No, Professor," one of my students answered. "But what we talk about here in our class is the minority view. Out there in real world, what the speaker said and what almost everybody agreed with is how things are."

A few nodded in agreement.

"Then things are going to just continue without change," I said. "We have to start some place. The more we talk about it, the more our voices are going to be heard."

"Maybe we shouldn't invite speakers who hold such beliefs," someone suggested.

One of my brighter students asked, "Is it culture or religion that has had the most negative impact on our attitudes about gender equality?"

"I think they're both intertwined in a way that is impossible to separately weigh their effects," someone answered.

As my students bounced these ideas off each other, I thought again of Tanaz's sculpture. I saw the woman's face, devoid of expression, and all of those distorted verses etched deeply into her.

That evening at dinner with Omar, I was still thinking about my students' comments on culture and religion. "Omar, do you think it is culture that is responsible for misinterpretation of religious texts?"

"Please, Ateesh," he said. "No more laws here. I am tired of this subject." Then he added, "Just for tonight...please."

After that, I tried not to bring the issues home too often, but found myself staying late at work, trying to deal with the issues there.

It was nearly the end of the semester, and Omar and I had both been spending a lot of time in our offices grading papers and advising students. We hadn't seen much of each other, so we decided to have lunch together one afternoon. It was a beautiful day and we decided to eat outdoors.

"I just have to meet one of my students in a little while," I told him, as I sat down across from him.

He sighed. "You're cutting our lunch short?" he said.

"Please, Omar," I said. "She's going to meet me here. It shouldn't take long. She's a good student. I'm not even sure why she needs to speak with me."

Nazaneen was one of my best students, and she never ceased to surprise me. She was from Arak, a small city about 300 kilometers from Tehran, and from what I imagined must be a conservative family. I wondered how she even made it to the university, until one day she explained: Her family was poor, and her father had completed a few years of college, but had lost much of the family's money in failed investments. They moved out of a much more urban area because they could no longer afford it. They could live a better life in a smaller town, her parents had reasoned. Still, her parents had sent her to the university primarily to make her more suitable to marry a successful husband.

As I was telling Omar what I knew about Nazaneen, she walked over to us.

"Nazaneen, this is my husband," I said, introducing them to each other. "Do you mind if he stays while we talk?"

"No," she said, as she sat down at the table. "I just need some advice."

She explained that a friend of hers from a much more conservative family had lost her husband in a car accident. Apparently, when he was put on a stretcher and carried into an ambulance, he blurted out that if he should die, his older, unmarried brother should inherit his young wife of two months. Later on, he died from internal bleeding. His older brother had honored his dying brother's request and married his sister-in-law.

"The worst part, Professor, is that neither one of them wants to be married to the other," she said. "She doesn't even know why her husband made this request. Maybe to make sure she was taken care of? Or maybe he felt guilty because he was married and his older brother wasn't? But why is this allowed? Why can her husband decide how she is going to spend the rest of her life?"

I understood her frustration. "I am so sorry, Nazaneen," I said.

"She is pregnant too," she said. "All she is being told at home is that she is lucky to have the brother-in-law there doing the right thing. Everyone is happy for her. I thought you might have some advice."

"Let me consult with Dr. Goodarzi and get back to you with some answers," I promised her.

"Thank you, Professor," she said. "There is no one at home we can turn to. You know how it is. It is much easier to give in to what is expected."

I knew exactly what she meant.

"It was nice meeting you," she said to Omar.

When she was out of earshot, Omar spoke first.

"What will you tell her?" he asked.

"I could write a paper on verses that contradict such a custom," I said. "One of the clearest verses in the Quran is about the pre-Islamic practice of inheriting a woman after a husband's death. The Prophet stopped the custom. Moslems who practice such unjust customs are not practicing Islam."

"Let's leave early tonight, Ateesh," Omar interrupted. "I'm simply tired of all of this. Can we forget about the problems of the world for one night? We'll have dinner and go to bed early."

I nodded, and that's exactly what we did.

For every student I had like Nazaneen, there were a dozen others from more modern cities with wealthier, more liberal-minded parents, at least among the female students. Even religious women who wore more conservative clothes were among my most vibrant and creative thinkers when it came to Quranic interpretation. I saw proof every day that young, educated women were able, even if not always willing, to interpret their faith in new ways and critique the discriminatory practices we experienced all the time. The difficulty was in making an impact outside of the university walls, in helping women like Nazaneen's friend.

But what could I tell them? I, too, had failed on many occasions. I had been able to help my friend Azita get out of a marriage, but had been unable to help her avoid it altogether. I had met five bright young women in Khoramabad, all of whom desired to attend the university, and I had been unable to help them do so.

In the face of what I perceived as failure on so many levels, Omar was a great comfort to me.

"Think of yourself as a pioneer, Ateesh," he said to me. "Without you, they might only have sympathy for victims. You give them the ability to diagnose the disease."

I never shared with Omar the extent to which I had been a practicing *siqeh*. I told him about my financial situation when I first arrived in Tehran at the age of eighteen, and about a few of my clients, but I presented them more as boyfriends. He understood my financial need, and naturally thought that since I was now working at the university, such business ventures would no longer be necessary. I let the matter rest there.

In my darkest moments, I questioned my own role as a perpetrator of injustice against women. I knew most of my clients were married, just as I knew all too well how their wives would feel if they'd ever found out about me. Was I any better than my father's second wife? Or was I worse because I had made the choice to become a *siqeh*, because I somehow rationalized the financial benefits and had perceived my career as a route to empowerment? I never shared these thoughts with Omar, and I'm not sure how he would have answered me if I had. Omar had been with me through the death of my father, and I was eternally grateful to him. He had no words that comforted me though, when six months later, I witnessed the terrible murder of my friend, Sherin.

I met Sherin on a doctor's visit. She was the doctor's wife, and worked in the office at the front desk. During the long wait for him to see me, we began chatting and found we had much in common. She was not college educated, but she was very well read. She also fulfilled my fantasy for shopping at some of the most exclusive boutiques uptown. For various reasons, I never made another appointment with her husband, Nasser, but Sherin and I went shopping together as often as we could.

She confided in me over lunch one day at the end of a costly adventure at Banu. She told me that Nasser was a pathologically suspicious man in desperate need of some sort of psychiatric help. Unfortunately, going to a mental health professional, especially for a man, carries a heavy stigma. She said he'd been making her life a living hell, and had recently forced her to stop working at his office.

I started to see less and less of her, but we continued to speak over the phone, and occasionally I went over to her house to visit her while Nasser was at work. She told me he began reacting violently every time she left the house, and that she couldn't go anywhere without his permission. When she showed me her bruises, I told her to leave him. I told her to stay with me as long as she wanted, until she could figure out a way to divorce him.

Knowing how laws of divorce are applied, I knew that it would be very hard for her to divorce Nasser unless he agreed to it. I had been through this before. Both Sherin and Nasser were from prominent families, and she was under a tremendous amount of pressure to remain in the marriage to save face. As a prominent physician, Nasser did not want any negativity associated with his name or that of his father, a well-known judge in family court. It was widely known that Nasser had many affairs with women on his staff, but divorce would bring a much more malevolent kind of attention.

Sherin's modar had encouraged her to give it some time, maybe even have a child with him. These things would make him behave. When Sherin was not convinced, her modar simply said *mardom chi megan*. Leaving the marriage was not an option. "Make it work," she had said.

One night when Omar was working late at the university, Sherin showed up at my house unexpectedly, crying and covered with bruises. In the past, Nasser had been smart enough to avoid hitting her face, where people could see the evidence of his abuse. This time, he had lost all restraint.

I got some ice and a towel for her to hold on her swollen cheek.

"That's it," I said. "It's over, Sherin. You're not going back there."

"He will have me arrested if I leave!" Sherin said through her tears. "I cannot leave. He thinks I am having an affair, Ateesh. An affair! I never leave the house. He telephones me all day to make sure I am home."

I held Sherin in my arms while she told me about their fight. Apparently she missed one of his calls. She didn't know how it had happened. She had done some laundry, taken a nap, but she hadn't left the house. How could she have missed the call?

A little while later, I got up to get more ice for her face when I heard Omar coming in. Sherin jumped at the sound of the door opening.

Omar sat with us and I explained what had happened.

"It's okay, Ateesh," Sherin said. "I will take a taxi to my modar's house."

"Sherin, he will find you there," I argued. "He is probably there now."

"You are safe here," Omar said. "I can leave if you want. Or I can get the police."

"No, I will be okay," she insisted.

"Thank you, Ateesh."

Sherin kissed my cheek quickly, and then she was gone. Omar and I just looked emptily at one another. He stood up and walked over to the kitchen to make some tea, and that's when we heard the shouting. We ran outside on the balcony and found Nasser down on the street, confronting Sherin.

"Stop it, Nasser!" I hollered. "She was with me!"

But he didn't seem to hear me. He looked up at Omar, and then looked back at Sherin. He must have followed Sherin to my house and saw Omar come in a short while later. Seeing Omar standing up on the balcony must have sealed her fate.

On our way down the stairs, we heard a gunshot. Omar grabbed me by the arm and held me back. I pulled away and continued running.

Nasser was crying as he sat next to her body on the asphalt. I yelled for help and an ambulance. Omar picked up the gun, which had been lying on the ground a few feet away. I knelt by Sherin's motionless body and held her in my arms. Blood was running through her beautiful hair and into my hand. She died before the ambulance got there.

When the police arrived, they helped Nasser stand up and directed him to their car for questioning. One of the officers asked Omar and me if we saw what had happened. We were asked to go to the station to give an account of the event. But I needed to get cleaned up first.

A few moments later, I stood in the shower, numb, as I watched Sherin's blood swirl down the drain. When I finished, I opened the closet and pulled out a black dress and black stockings. I dressed quickly and brushed my wet hair back into a ponytail. Omar held my hand as we left for the police department.

In the taxi, Omar told me he didn't want to bear witness to what he had seen. He was in Iran as a visiting professor, to build his resume, and to visit the holy cities, not to get himself entangled in a foreign criminal justice system.

"I am an outsider, Ateesh," he said. "I cannot testify! You must do it without me."

I was enraged. How could he sit next to me, holding me, and tell me this?

"What do you mean, you aren't going to testify?!" I demanded. "You saw what happened! You saw him shoot her in the street in cold blood! What kind of man are you?!"

"I can't!" he said. "I can't get involved in this! You saw it too. They don't need to know that I saw anything."

Tears suddenly began to spill from my eyes.

"Omar, please," I said, as I struggled to regain my composure. "If you love me, you must tell them what happened. You don't understand! My testimony is worth only half of yours. In a homicide, it is worth nothing at all!"

"What?!" Omar shouted. "This fucking backward country of yours!"

He had let go of me during our fight, and now he fell back against the seat of the taxi. Rubbing his eyes, he cursed under his breath.

What I didn't tell Omar was that even his testimony, that of only one man, might not be enough to give justice to Sherin. Nasser was from an influential family and had political connections. It was possible that Omar would pay a price for his testimony. Nasser might be able to have Omar's teaching privileges or even his visa revoked.

In the end, Omar did speak to the police. We held each other that night but did not sleep nor speak. The scene kept replaying in my head. I blamed myself for letting her leave my apartment. I should have helped her get a taxi. I should have convinced her, long ago, to leave him and never look back.

Nasser later confessed to killing Sherin. Omar and I sat with Sherin's family in court as he slandered her. He claimed that she was unfaithful, that she had committed *zina*. It was an *honor killing*, he argued. Nasser was acquitted on the basis of justifiable homicide..

〜〜〜〜〜

In the weeks that followed, I felt closer to Omar than ever before. Knowing how he felt about everything, I hadn't expected him to testify, but he did. He was courageous to do so, and I told him that. At least the truth had been heard, even if Nasser was acquitted.

Meanwhile, Omar became more and more disillusioned with Iran. Like most people from the West, he heard about cases like Sherin's, but never believed it could happen in Tehran.

Because of Nasser's status in the community, the case made the news. When my students brought it up in class, I did something I had never done before as a professor. I let my students debate each other on the details of the case. They were surprised and took it as a sign of my confidence in them and their understanding of justice. In truth, I was simply afraid of breaking down.

"First of all, the verse that says the testimony of a woman is worth half that of a man is clearly meant for business transactions. It is misinterpreted when it is applied to other types of cases," one student said. "Of course, in the mid-sixth century, women would have been intimidated to testify against men."

"Maybe it was to encourage women to come forward in support of one another in cases against men," another student suggested. "To think otherwise would be insulting to the Prophet. His wife Khadigeh was a successful businesswoman who was also his boss."

"It is no different from any other laws on testimony," one student said. "You always need a man, whether it is for homicide, *zina*, business transactions, and even in most family law cases. Even male children, let alone females, cannot testify without their fathers present."

"The point is that Prophet Mohammad had intended to help women escape injustice," another student finally said. "If we look at the context of the verses concerning women in the Quran, they were necessary at that time to lessen the social injustices against women; we should not have difficulty seeing the wisdom behind such verses in the mid-sixth century."

I had to speak up, though I was afraid my voice was going to crack.

"Imagine that you are in charge," I said to them. "You have been given the task of *ijtihad*. How would you interpret these verses and codify them into law?"

For a few moments, there was silence. I sat back on the chair behind my desk. Was this the end of the discussion? Could we only criticize misinterpretation? Were we incapable of creative resolution?

"Talk about it amongst yourselves," I said finally. "See what you can come up with. I'll give you ten minutes."

I pretended to look through my notes. If they thought I wasn't paying attention, maybe they would allow themselves to think more freely, to test their ideas with each other before trying them out on me. Shortly, a few voices began to emerge. Young men and women were discussing different approaches to eliminate bias and discriminatory interpretations of verses on women. I knew some of them might have heard these discussions growing up in Tehran, but for others, it was the beginning of a new consciousness.

While the students went on with their discussion, I thought about my own life, my own consciousness. I found myself staring at a photograph on my desk, which was taken of Omar and me on our wedding day.

My relationship with Omar started out as a temporary arrangement, a mutual infatuation. Over the course of a year, it had become serious. But after the murder of Sherin, talk about extending his visa and his contract with the university had dwindled.

"I've been thinking about this for a long time," he said. "We can go to the States. We can get married. You don't belong here. Why would you want to stay? Once you are in the States, it will be easy to bring your family over too."

"And not finish law school?" I asked furiously.

"Ateesh, don't you want to get married?" he asked. "A real marriage? You must come with me. I cannot stay here in Iran. I want us to have children together. Don't you want to have children together?"

I had no answers for him.

It did not escape me that he loved me deeply, in spite of all we had been through together. Part of me was tempted to say yes, to embrace him with all of my might, to leave the university and my country behind. But a feeling I could not comprehend was stopping me.

"I need some time to think about it," I said finally.

His disappointment was obvious. But I couldn't overcome what I felt at that moment. It was the same feeling that had compelled me to leave Bejan. I was still not independent enough as a woman to make a difference in other women's lives in a more meaningful way. And because of my experiences with men from early on in life, I was vulnerable to meaningful relationships with them.

Modar, Grandma Tuba, and Grandma Jamileh were here too. How could I just get up and leave, and start a new life in another country?

Not to mention that I'd just challenged my students to do more than criticize the misinterpretations that had led to Nasser's acquittal on the basis of justifiable homicide.

I couldn't just walk away.

"**J**ust think, Ateesh!" Omar said. "By this time next year, we could be in California. You have to see it. There is everything: mountains, oceans, vineyards! Oh, and high fashion! You will fit right in!"

We were at the airport. He was leaving for the United States, and I still hadn't the heart to tell him I was never going to join him. We just left it open as something I was still thinking about and would probably do in the near future.

"Do you love me?" he asked.

I looked away. As much as I loved him, I was protecting myself by not acknowledging it out loud. When I had come to know that Baba had taken another wife to have a son, because I, as a daughter, was not good enough, that had destroyed my heart. I was afraid I couldn't take the pain anymore.

I kept the ring that Omar gave me. For a while, as far as everyone in Tehran was concerned, Omar and I were still married. I was bombarded with questions from friends and colleagues. Was I going to America with him? Wouldn't I be crazy not to? I avoided them carefully, trying to be as vague and noncommittal as possible in my answers. That was not too hard in a culture where a lot of pretense goes on, especially when it comes to marital relationships.

In the months that followed, he wrote me many letters and emailed as promised. He even sent tickets for a U2 concert in New

York that year. I never answered his emails and soon I stopped open-ing them. I was so afraid that reading anything from him would send me into a deep depression. I tried hard to remain in the present and not the past. *He is gone.* I had to repeat that again and again.

I moved through my days listlessly, doing what I had to do to get by. Then, in the midst of my sadness came Nowruz, the Iranian New Year.

Nowruz is by far the biggest celebration for the Iranian people. Literally, it means new day, new beginning. A non-religious holiday celebrated by everyone, Nowruz starts with the beginning of spring, as snow glistens on Mount Demovand and the cherry trees in our courtyard begin to bud. Iranians do not follow the Western calendar, but lunar months, which means the holiday could fall on different days each year. It typically falls on March 20 or 21, which is the day of the vernal equinox.

According to ancient custom, there must be a table spread with seven items that begin with the letter "s," and each item must sig-nify something related to life. We start by growing different kinds of sprouts. Never wanting to prepare too much in advance, Modar would usually grow lentil sprouts, called *javanayeh adas*. Grandma Tuba grew mung bean sprouts, *javanayeh mash*, which required more time, and Grandma Jamileh grew wheat sprouts, *javanayeh gandom*. Apples, *seeb*, considered the fruit of health, were also always included, along with garlic, *seer*, vinegar, *serkeh*, and dry berries, *senjed*, all of which are believed to have medicinal and health values. Gold coins, *sekeh*, would always be placed on the spread, since they represent wealth. Hyacinth, *Sonbol*, the flower of spring, and *samanu*, a sweet paste made from wheat germ and freshly painted eggs, signifying re-production, finished off those items. We always bought or prepared other essentials as well, such as goldfish to symbolize life, candles to signify light, and various sweets and candies.

As a child, I always stayed up until the New Year was broadcast on the radio. Modar, Baba, and I would sit around the table with the seven items a couple of hours before the Nowruz bell was announced on the radio. As soon as the bell rang we all kissed, and Modar served sweets and freshly made tea. Then Baba and Modar gave me a crisp, fresh bill, as elders giving money to the young is part of the tradition. After exchanging pleasant conversation on renewal and rejuvenation, we would go back to bed, if it was not already morning.

On the first day of celebration, we always went to Grandma Tuba's house first, then to Grandma Jamileh's house. On the second day, we held open house for others to visit. After that, every day we visited distant family and friends and acquaintances. On the thirteenth day, the last day of Nowruz, we removed the items from the table, packed our picnic baskets, and went to lavish green fields near a river. After lunch, each family gathered around by the river, and as they threw out their bean sprouts they chanted, *sisdah be dar!* Out with 13! Then, young unmarried girls sat on the ground knotting two long blades of grass, symbolizing their wish to be in a husband's house by the next Nowruz. Boys never took part in this, and neither did I.

Throughout the holiday, the schools were closed, and between the first and last day of Nowruz, we would see everyone from Baba's employees to our cousins to neighbors. They would usually stay for an hour or so depending on relation and closeness to us. During the evening, we saw close relatives and friends, usually for dinner.

During my childhood, I always looked forward to going to Batul.

We went to Khanoom's house for one of these nights, as she held the biggest party in our community every year. She had the most children my age among her family and friends, and I always stayed up late and played with them. But after the birth of her second grandson, her daughter Farah had taken over the duties and began to hold the gathering at her house.

The last time I was there was some years before I left for Tehran. Now after nearly fifteen years I was going there again. I hadn't stayed home for the entire thirteen days in a long time. This time I felt I needed to stay. I was still hurting and mourning the loss of Omar and I needed to keep busy. Although Baba was dead, being in Abadan made me feel as though he was still controlling my emotions. I was very self-conscious and worried about what others would think and say about me.

As soon as she came to know that I was in town for Nowruz, Farah called Modar's house and asked me to help her with some last-minute preparations the morning of the party.

"I think it is more to find out what is going on with you," Grandma Tuba said.

"Modar, is it okay with you if I go?" I asked.

"Sure, my Ateesh, just give the taxi driver the address. Their new house is about a half hour ride from here." She scribbled down the address on a piece of paper and handed it to me. "Grandma and I will come together later on." Then she smiled at me. "You know, my daughter, how good I feel when people who have not seen you for years say you look even more beautiful than ever?"

I smiled and kissed her good-bye.

"If you feel you need to take a break from Farah, come back here and we'll go back together later," she said as I walked out the door.

Farah's husband was there when I arrived, and in him I saw no sign of the monster that had threatened her on their first night of marriage. Perhaps he had mellowed. More likely, he was just maintaining appearances in front of me.

I helped Farah arrange some flowers while her husband and their two young sons went out to take care of some business.

"How has your modar been, Farah?" I asked.

"Oh you know, she is getting old. Aches and pains, this and that," she said. "She complains about her health all the time. You are lucky to live in Tehran, Ateesh."

"I'm sorry to hear you say that," I said, surprised to hear her speak this way.

"My husband has been my savior," she said. "Without him, I'm not sure I could stand all of my mother's complaining. If she isn't complaining about her health, she is complaining about my father's behavior and character."

"Has your father's treatment of your mother changed at all?" I asked softly, trying not to offend her. After all, the last I'd heard anything was fifteen years ago when her father had pushed her mother into a wall.

"Well, you know men don't change," she said. "We just have to adjust to them if we want to keep our marriage." I wondered if her husband physically abused her as her father abused her modar and that is why she would make such a statement.

So much for her good husband and perfect marriage. I didn't know what to say. I felt sad that another one of my sisters had been caught in this trap of marriage. I wish she would realize she didn't have to stay. She had a choice.

Or did she?

Farah broke the awkward silence. "But I have to say I don't know how you get along without a husband, especially at your age and in a big city like Tehran. It must be so expensive. Don't you get lonely? Who is looking after you?"

I wasn't sure how to answer. Once upon a time, when I was younger and had lived at home, I would have had a lot to say in response to these questions. But not anymore. I had learned the hard way that sometimes saying less was wiser. How could I explain that we as women could and should look after ourselves, that women should be with men only if they wanted to and not because they needed to be?

Not many women there, including Farah, would understand me or appreciate what I was doing.

She was staring at me, waiting.

"My work keeps me very busy," I said, "and I have many good friends."

But in that moment I suddenly felt like my life was poor in comparison to the one she was leading. She had adjusted herself to fit into her husband's character. She looked happy. Who was I to question and judge that?

I fought this feeling and eventually made an excuse to leave. I told Farah I would be back later. Modar must've seen this coming. I had no doubt that she and Grandma Tuba had been fielding the same questions since the day I left. Farah was just the first person bold enough to ask me directly.

This was probably the reason Baba had discouraged me from attending the university. Why was everyone so concerned about my lack of a husband?

Surely I did not have to marry to have love in my life. But not according to them. Why did I have to prove my womanhood? How little they knew, or would ever know, about my ability to please a man! Of course, I could not say any of this. I was forced instead to occupy a role to which I was unaccustomed: a poor, pitiful spinster. Because I was a woman, my education and achievements were meaningless in Abadan if I didn't have the shadow of a man over my head. I was my own shadow, thank you!

For the first time in my life, I wasn't looking forward to a party. I knew who I was and what I needed, and it was not marriage. I felt very out of place.

∿ ∿ ∿ ∿ ∿

Persian people are known abroad for their hospitality and lavish parties, Omar had told me, but Farah had truly outdone her modar. I suspected that the money her husband made was, in fact, Farah's savior, and not the man himself.

There were purple, pink, and white fragrant flowers like Hyacinth everywhere, and the spread was abundant, containing all the Nowruz specialties as well as many others.

I arrived back at the party with Modar and Grandma Tuba, dreading the airs I would inevitably have to put on, which were vital in those gatherings. Nowruz celebrations are about renewal, but in typical fashion, many women were dressed more for the runway than a party held at someone's house, trying to out-do one another.

Many of the guests were Batul Khanoom's friends, people I saw only at Nowruz. To avoid answering too many questions about my own life, I asked all of the questions they would be most eager to answer. In this way, I got my annual update on children who were inevitably doing exceptionally well in school, dutiful sons who held promising and successful positions, and beautiful, obedient daughters who had married well.

I couldn't wait to get back to Tehran.

I went into another room that was populated mostly by the older women. They sat around smoking qalyan. I felt less out of place here, and I found Grandma Tuba and sat with her and Batul Khanoom.

"Ateesh, it is so good to have you home," Batul Khanoom said. "When are you coming back to Abadan? There are many bachelors here. It isn't too late for you, you know."

Grandma Tuba just looked at me and smiled. Batul had meant no harm.

"Look at what my daughter Farah has done," Batul Khanoom continued. "I thank God every day for my son-in-law. He takes such good care of her! And, finally, another grandchild is on the way! *Allaho Akbar!*"

All of the women in the group congratulated Batul Khanoom on her good fortune. I joined in too. God willing, I thought, she would have another boy.

The next day, I told Modar I was off to the market to pick up more jasmine tea because it was my favorite. She understood. I was accustomed to living by myself, and so I took the chance to go somewhere alone to think and clear my head.

"Okay, Ateesh Joon. Meet me at Grandma's later," Modar said. "Be careful."

Walking through the market, I lost myself in thought. It always gave me a warm feeling to walk the streets I had walked so many times with Grandma Tuba. I thought of Omar. I imagined what it would have been like to bring him here to Abadan. He would easily fit into the city, filled with many highly educated engineers and foreigners who worked in the oil industry. I was lost in these thoughts until I reached the teashop we had been going to since my childhood. Totonchi was the name of the shop, after the name of the owner. It was fifteen years later and I recognized him right away. He was grayer and still kept his head down as he asked, "How much and what quality?" For a second I felt as if I had gone back in time and was a child again.

I made my purchase and stepped out the door when I heard a familiar voice call my name. "Ateesh!"

I looked in the direction of the voice and saw a woman about my age with two young children walking beside her. It took a second for me to recognize her.

"Oh my God! Behrook! It is you?" I cried, embracing her. "It has been so long!"

"I wondered what happened to you!" she said. "You seemed to have fallen off the face of the earth!"

I explained to her that I was still living in Tehran and going to law school.

"I always knew you were different from the rest of us," she said. "Obviously, I got married. It happened right after graduation. He is a big businessman."

"Well, you look wonderful, just like you did back in school," I said. "I'm so happy for you."

And I was. Behrook, like Farah, wanted nothing but a husband and children. She seemed content.

"You must come to my son's circumcision party in two days. It is his ninth birthday," she said proudly.

He would be circumcised, and implicitly the expectations and privileges of manhood would follow. There would be many guests, and he would receive gifts and money. The whole ceremony signified quite the opposite of a girl's ninth birthday. I remembered my own. Grandma Tuba's words rang in my head: "You must stay away from boys, Ateesh." No gifts, no presents, but responsibility to keep the honor of the family by staying away from the opposite sex. That was all I remembered.

I couldn't wait to witness another glorious incident in a man's life. "I will be there," I said. "I hope we get a chance to catch up more."

"Yes, and bring your modar if you want, unless you got lucky and have a husband to bring?" she asked hopefully.

"We'll be there," I said, leaving her to wonder whether I was lucky or not. What happened to the Behrook I knew, I wondered. The one who talked to me about her desire to be touched by a man, who got me thinking about my own desires? I'd spent many restless nights over her provocative question.

⹊⹊ ⹊⹊ ⹊⹊ ⹊⹊ ⹊⹊

Two days later, I went to Behrook's house. Her "big business-man" husband turned out to be a much more humble provider than I expected. Her house was modest, as was everything in it, but it was clean and obviously well cared for. I was surprised to see that among the guests were some of our old classmates from night school. Like Behrook, they had remained in Abadan, married, and were now raising families of their own. I sat down with them as Behrook was busy receiving guests.

"My husband is such a kind man," I heard someone say. I recognized the woman from school, Soraya, whom I remembered as a quiet, studious girl. It wasn't often that I'd heard a woman speak of her husband like this, so I moved a little closer to hear more.

"He is a Sayeed," she explained, "a direct descendant from Prophet Mohammad."

Immediately I thought of Grandma Tuba's first husband.

"He cares for three orphans who lost their father to a long illness. He acts as their father and visits the children at their house, which they share with their poor young widowed modar."

My old classmates and I looked at each other skeptically.

"What do you mean?" someone asked. "Has he taken her as a *siqeh*? Because otherwise he couldn't go to her house."

"No," Soraya said. "I mean yes, he had to in order to be able to go and visit the children."

The room was quiet. A few women shifted in their chairs uncomfortably and waited for Soraya to continue.

Grandma Tuba had explained to me when I was growing up, that there was only a small group of male relatives before whom a girl can appear without covering herself. For me, it was Baba or Grandfather. Later on, Hajji Aqa Ayatollah explained further: There are a group of men which girls are prohibited to marry because of close blood relation, but that she can appear in front of without the religiously required covering. However, outside this very small group of males, she must cover up, and association with men outside this group must be legitimized by *siqeh mahrami*. This type of *siqeh* does not involve sexual relations.

"Anyway," Soraya continued, "The other day he asked me to go buy gifts for him to bring to the orphans."

She looked around the room. It seemed she had been anticipating a reaction she wasn't getting. Did she expect us to be impressed with his kindness, when obviously this was just another example of a typical lying and cheating man? Or was it just that I had become cynical?

"When I realized I left the money for the presents at home, I had to go back and get it," she said.

So this was when she would see the truth about her husband!

"When I walked in the house," she continued, "I heard him from the guest bedroom on the second floor, reciting a beautiful verse from the Quran about righteousness in this world resulting in paradise in eternity."

We all waited.

"When I walked up the stairs, he rushed out of the room and explained, 'We have a guest who is performing her midday prayer.'"

"Guest?" I blurted out, incredulous.

She nodded and continued. "'My dear wife,' he said, 'she is a traveler and was passing by our door at prayer time. Being a true righteous woman she knocked at our door requesting permission to come into our home.' So I went into the bedroom, and there I found a woman covered from head to toe in a black cloak, standing in prayer position performing the mid-day prayer!"

She couldn't be serious, I thought. The verse discussing travelers stopping to pray in the middle of their journeys dated to sixth century Arabia, and a traveler's route was through the Sahara desert. Nowadays, in the twenty-first century nobody stops and knocks at a stranger's house to pray. Also, the residential neighborhood that Soraya lived in was not located along the route for travelers' stops. And even further, unrelated men and women are not permitted to pray together. Surely Soraya would know that.

Now, here this woman traveler was "praying" in their bedroom!

"Sayeed told me, 'God is showing mercy on us by sending this woman to our home to perform her prayers, and for sure *savab* has been noted by the angels on our accounts.'"

I knew as well as the others that she was performing something with Sayeed, but far from what poor Soraya believed.

"So what did you do?" one of the women asked.

"I went to make her tea."

Her trust in her husband was never questioned, and Soraya continued to believe her husband was truly worthy of his namesake. In a way, I admired her blind trust in her unworthy husband.

⚬⚬⚬⚬⚬

I didn't really have much of a chance to catch up with Behrook at the party, but I was able to spend some time with her a few days later. I suggested that we meet at the ice cream shop, where I used to dream about marrying the ice cream man. In spite of the many years that had elapsed, I was able to speak much more candidly with her than any of the others. When I told her I was studying law, she seemed truly impressed.

"Who would've thought, Ateesh" she said, "I, and everyone who was at the party, we are all married and settled. And you are...are you looking to settle down, Ateesh?" Then she lowered her voice and for a brief second I saw the Behrook I knew over ten years ago, "Have you been touched? I mean more like, have you felt the electricity all over your body?"

She looked at me and waited for an answer. I couldn't lie to her. I thought of Bejan, then Omar, and said, "Yes, I have."

"Excellent! Stay with him, marry him!" she said.

I had to change the subject. My wounds were hurting. So I said, "I thought I saw all of the old faces, at least the ones of our friends, at your house."

Behrook's face suddenly became serious. "Maybe you didn't hear. I'm surprised your modar didn't tell you. Do you remember Golbarg?"

"Yes! She wasn't there, was she? I thought she married one of her cousins after we graduated," I said. "Whatever happened to her?"

"She did marry one of her cousins, but, Ateesh, it was horrible.

Once she moved into his house, his uncle used to come over and harass her. She used to call me crying all the time."

"What do you mean, harass her?"

"You know, he visited her house when her husband wasn't home. Poor girl told her modar and she told her father but nobody took it seriously."

I had that uneasy feeling in my stomach. The same feeling of anxiousness I used to get whenever my husband would come home. With the sound of his footsteps on every one of the five steps into the house, I became more nervous in anticipation of what was to come.

"Where does she live?" I asked in a low voice, "Let us go and visit her."

"Ateesh, she is in jail."

"Oh God, no!" I cried.

"Even a lawyer would be no use to her now. When she finally told her husband about the harassment, he spoke to his uncle, or at least that's what he told her he did. Before we knew it, she was accused of *zina*. She sits in prison as we speak."

"No! *Zina*?" I asked, "How?" But I knew the answer.

"Don't go to visit her, Ateesh," Behrook said sadly. "It won't do any good. I went to see her once. She is resigned to her fate."

But I could not stop thinking about it.

Later on that night as Modar was busy preparing and setting the dinner table, I sat at the kitchen table and just held my head.

"Modar," I said in angry frustration, "I'm so sick of women always getting the blame, even when they are raped!"

She stopped setting the table and came closer. "You heard about Golbarg?" she asked softly. I nodded. "Grandma Tuba was going to tell you, but we decided to wait. There is nothing we can do. *Zina* is the highest degree of criminal offense. Grandma Tuba has visited her in prison."

I felt her warm hand on my head. "Ateesh, you cannot continue to feel responsible for all the injustices done to women. I am worried about you."

Between the news of this injustice and the pain of missing Omar, my heart was hurting. I felt physical pain.

"I feel sick to my stomach about the unjust interpretation of verses on women, Modar. Where is the protection for the weaker sex, which Islam is built upon?" She didn't know how to answer that.

"Modar, do you know a lawyer here in Abadan?" I asked. "I need to hire someone to defend Golbarg." She knew there was nothing she could do to stop me.

I got my laptop and started typing a letter to the leading women's magazine, *Zaneh Rooz, Today's Women*, about Golbarg's case, and the stringent requirement of four witnesses to the adultery. Cases like Golbarg's were not common, but they were also not unheard of.

By the time I was finished typing Modar had some of my favorite dishes on the table, and Grandma Tuba, Grandfather, and Grandma Jamileh were at the door.

"Partying without us?" Grandma Jamileh said with a wink, as she came in. Something was different about tonight's dinner, I thought.

I looked at Modar and she smiled. She had set the table fancier than usual. Then I noticed the good china, which was only used for special dinners. Who was coming next, I wondered? A suitor?

Grandfather must have read my mind, "This was not my idea, Ateesh, and I want you to know that."

Then Grandma Tuba came closer and scolded in a hushed voice, "They are right behind us, Hajji." Then she took one look at me and said, "With that sad face, they are going to leave right away. That is a good plan."

I knew what was going on but I couldn't blame them or be angry with them. "All right," I said. "I'll play along. Let the suitor in."

"But you are not carrying the tea tray, Ateesh!" Grandma Jamileh said with a smile on her beautiful, chubby face. "I will serve the tea!"

Grandma Tuba gave her a stern look. "Go on and freshen up quickly, Ateesh," she demanded.

I rushed into my room and put on some light pink lipstick.

"No, that is too light," Omar would have said. "You look fantastic in red, Khanoom. Put that color on." For a short second, I saw his reflection in the mirror.

I wiped off the pink lipstick and went for the red he liked. "I wish I was putting this on for you, Omar," I whispered.

"No you don't, Khanoom," he said in response. "You pushed me away. You are afraid of letting go. There is something inside you…"

"Ateesh Joon, please come and join us!"

"Coming, Modar Bozorg!" I said as I walked down the hall toward the dining area. I passed the large mirror hanging on the wall and stopped to look at myself. Even the red lipstick could not hide the sadness on my face, and especially in my eyes. I closed the top button on my shirt and quickly tucked it into my jeans.

~~ ~~ ~~ ~~ ~~

When I walked into the room I saw an older couple sitting down with a younger man with a buzz-cut. I was too old for this kind of introduction, but one look at Modar, Grandma Tuba, Grandma Jamileh, and even Grandfather, made me think my night might be enjoyable.

"Salam," I said.

All three people stood up. I went toward the woman first.

"Salam Azizam," she said. "I am Mrs. Morady, and this is my husband, Mr. Morady." Then she pointed to the younger man who stood next to Grandma Jamileh. "That is our son, Mehdi. He lives in America but he is visiting us for Nowruz."

I shook hands with her husband and then walked toward their son. "Where in America do you live?" I asked as I reached out and shook his hand, which was soft, but not warm.

Grandma Jamileh quickly moved from her seat and said, "Ateesh Joon, sit here so you can talk with this handsome young man." There was a sparkle of hope in her eyes.

"I live in New York but I'll be moving to L.A." he answered.

"Because of your job?" I asked.

"Yes, I am a computer specialist and my company is transferring me to L.A. Of course, I am happy about that."

"Because of the weather or because of the large Iranian community living there?"

"You seem to know a lot about America," he said. "Have you been there?"

"No, but I do meet people at the university who are from different states in America." Then I looked around the room and realized all eyes were on us.

"How about we eat? My modar makes the best kebab in the world. I bet the recipes for my dad's restaurants came from her." As I sat at the dinner table, I noticed that they had intentionally arranged his seat next to mine.

I looked at Mehdi and asked in English with a hushed voice, "Do your parents speak English?"

"No they don't, but I see you do."

"Oh thank God. Listen, the truth is that I really did not know you guys were coming until just before you arrived. I am not interested in getting married at all. No offense. But why did you agree to come? You don't believe in this kind of matchmaking, do you?"

"No I don't, but they kept insisting. Then I thought, why not? So I just came along."

We both laughed.

"I just broke off with a friend I think I was in love with," I heard myself say, "and I am hurting quite a bit."

Did I actually say "in love with?"

"I have a couple of girlfriends back in America but my family hopes I will marry a girl from my hometown," he said. "They believe girls who have remained in Iran are virgins, unlike those who live in America. That is why they suggested I come here."

I almost choked on the piece of kebab. The hypocrisy of Iranian parents! I thought of the surgeon back in Tehran whose specialty was reconstructing hymens.

"How about we make it an enjoyable evening for our families and try to have a good time?" I managed to say with a smile, knowing I was being watched.

"Now I can relax!" he said. "I thought I was going to be forced into marrying a girl without really knowing her." We both laughed. Our families looked relaxed and hopeful.

243

As we ate, we continued our conversation in English. Nobody objected.

"What are the relationships like between young boys and girls in America?" I asked.

"You mean Iranians?" he asked.

I nodded.

"No different than Americans, with one big exception: Iranians date but pretend they don't. And families pretend their daughters are all virgins! You know how image conscious our culture is and it becomes even clearer when you encounter people like that overseas."

I laughed so hard that I almost fell off the chair onto him. He caught me and I immediately pulled away and sat myself up straight in the chair. We both looked at each other and in English I said, "We better stop here, or else our families are going to start printing the wedding invitations."

Looking at their faces, I could see that at the same time they were happy, they were questioning my giggling behavior. What a scandalous headline that would make: Ateesh, a desperate thirty-year-old maid-divorcee ends up on the top of a suitor!

The rest of the evening was nice. We all made small talk about everything and nothing. My family kept giving me loving looks from time to time. I could see how happy they were to see me interacting with others, but especially with Mehdi. It did feel good talking with him.

"Do you have a boyfriend now?" He asked me as we sat together with tea in the sitting room. Our families were intentionally in the background, not too far and not too close, yet right there.

"I do. Well, I did." I stopped quickly before tears found their way to my eyes.

"I am sorry," he said." I know how hard it can be. I have gone through it. How about I tell you something funny?"

"I'd love that!" I said quickly as I wiped at the tears that were forming in my eyes.

"The first time I went out with an American girl, her family had no idea about Iran and Iranians. They were a lovely family but had a stereotyped image of Iran. The first time they finally agreed to meet me and invited me to their house for dinner was during the hostage crisis in 1980. My girlfriend Sue took me to the house at dinnertime. The whole family was there to celebrate Thanksgiving. This was my first one.

"'Dad this is Mehdi,' she said. Her father came out of the kitchen with her two large, older brothers on each side. Her father was holding a big knife in one hand. He extended the other hand and said, 'Come on in and meet the rest of the family.'"

I chuckled. Poor Mehdi! What a way to be introduced to your first Thanksgiving dinner!

Omar was the first to tell me about Thanksgiving. We made a turkey together back in Tehran. I felt my mind wandering back to that time and had to force myself to focus on what Mehdi was saying.

"I got a little nervous because they were all sitting around the Thanksgiving table staring at me," he continued. "'Everybody, this is Mehdi. He is from Iran,' her father said, still holding the knife. It was the kind of knife I had seen only here in Abadan in the butcher shops. All through that miserable dinner, I was questioned as if I were the son of one of the hostage takers or if I were the ambassador of Iran! As time passed it got better, though. By the time dinner was over, they finally believed that I had no better idea than they did about what was happening in Iran."

I shook my head and laughed. I truly couldn't believe the way the world was sometimes.

Mehdi took a sip of his tea and looked at me. "So, Ateesh, when my parents told me to come to check you out for possible marriage, I thought I was going to see an all made-up woman dressed to kill with her nose high up. Instead, I see a down-to-earth, intelligent, unpretentious woman who is confident and kind enough to just go along with this whole thing so she doesn't disappoint her family."

"You are so sweet," I said. "I appreciate your kind words. I enjoyed talking with you very much, and if this was a different time in our lives maybe something could have happened between us."

Then I turned around and saw Grandma Jamileh coming toward

us. "It is very late in the evening, kids. But if you want to continue chatting…"

Mrs. Morady came in behind her, "Mehdi, at first you did not want to come; now you don't want to leave?" Both Mehdi and I laughed. His mom and Grandma Jamileh looked at each other.

"All right Modar, we can go," he said. Then he lowered his voice and said in English, "Ateesh, I am not really sleepy, are you?"

"No, but I guess you have to go or those wedding invitations are going for printing!" I said as we both started laughing again. I extended my hand and told him, "I thoroughly enjoyed my time with you."

He shook my hand and said, "I did too."

After they left, we all went into the kitchen. Grandfather had fallen sleep on the recliner already with a blanket on him.

"I'm going to bed," I said. "I'm tired."

"Oh no, Ateesh Joon!" Grandma Jamileh said. "After talking for hours to that handsome young man, you have to talk!"

Modar and Grandma Tuba didn't say anything but I could see that they were all eager to hear what had happened.

"Well, he is a nice man," I said, "but…"

"But what, Ateesh?" Modar asked lovingly. "It's okay, child."

I thought of telling them that Mehdi has a girlfriend, but I was sure that would get back to his parents and they would be upset with him.

"Neither of us was interested," I said.

"You guys were laughing the entire time!" Grandma Jamileh said. "That's a sign of having a good time! I called my tailor and ordered a special custom-made outfit for the wedding!" I knew she was joking but I could tell that she was hopeful.

"Azizam, my dear, you are old enough to make your own decisions," Grandma Tuba said. "We love you. But we're concerned that you might be lonely out there all by yourself without a husband."

Modar looked at Grandma Tuba and said, "We know many women who are married and still lonely. A husband might not be the answer for you, but perhaps companionship is? We want what is best for you."

I smiled at her gratefully. That was what I always wanted: Permission from my family to do what is best for me, even if that meant not getting married.

Grandma Jamileh came closer to me and whispered, "Did you get the tingling feeling in your body when you intentionally fell on him?"

I shook my head. She looked at Grandma Tuba and Modar and said, "I am canceling the dress order! Goodnight." She kissed me and she walked to the guest bedroom.

One thing I had to admit to myself, though, was that it was nice to laugh with Mehdi that night. I needed that.

When Grandma Jamileh was out of hearing range, Grandma Tuba looked at Modar and said, "As Jamileh gets older, she gets worse! I'm not sure if she even prays regularly."

"Grandma, you are harsh on her," I said. "She is a kind, good-hearted, loving person who has her own style."

Since the death of Baba, Grandma Jamileh had been spending more time with Modar in her house. I was so happy to see this. Of course, I also knew that after Baba's death and the division of his estate, his second wife had disconnected from all of his family. Although Grandma Jamileh often talked about Baba's two sons, she never had to reassure me of my place in her heart.

A little while later, I fell into bed exhausted. Thoughts and images swarmed through my mind, of Golbarg, Mehdi, Omar... I thought of Golbarg in a prison cell, Mehdi standing across from a man with a big knife in his hand, Omar walking away from me at the airport, his back to me, the distance between us increasing with every step. Even Karim and Alireza made an appearance in my mind before I finally fell into a restless sleep.

~ ~ ~ ~ ~

One night after dinner, as we were sitting in the garden having tea, Modar suddenly stopped speaking mid-sentence. When I followed her gaze, I saw Karim and Alireza walking in through the garden gate, heading toward us.

I froze as they approached.

"Salam," Karim said. He was holding a large basket of yellow roses. "Ateesh, these are for you."

Looking at him this closely for the first time brought sad emotions to the surface. I saw love in his handsome eyes as he looked at me, but I also remembered his hurtful words from long ago that had caused such a sharp pain in my heart: *Your modar is less than a woman because she could only give birth to a girl.*

"Ateesh," Modar said, "It is late in the evening and they shouldn't be here. They are not welcome in this house."

"I am sorry," Karim said. "I am here to speak to Ateesh, and I am not leaving until I do. Please!"

"It's up to Ateesh," Grandma Tuba said.

Modar stood up and walked back inside, slamming the door behind her.

"You should have called first, son," Grandma Jamileh said to him.

"I did several times, Grandma, but they kept hanging up on me. At the funeral I sent Alireza to talk to Ateesh. That didn't work either."

"Ateesh," Grandma Tuba chimed in, "how about we go inside and let you and Karim talk for a few minutes?" Then she turned to Grandma Jamileh and said, "Jamileh, let us go inside."

As they both stood up to leave, Grandma Jamileh called out to Alireza, who was still standing at a distance, "Come on inside with us, son. Have you had dinner?"

Alireza looked at Karim. Karim looked at me.

"Come with us inside," Grandma Jamileh said again. Alireza finally followed her in, and Karim and I were left alone there in the garden. My heart was beating hard and fast. I remembered Grandma's words not too long ago at the funeral: *This might be the time to heal your pain.*

I took the flowers from Karim and said, "You at least remembered I like yellow roses." I nervously stared down into the yellow petals.

He kneeled down in front of me and said, "Look at me, please. I know that when you are hurting you avoid eyes. Please look at me."

I couldn't. I still felt hurt over how Karim had taken my place with Baba after he was born.

"Ateesh, I was only a child when I repeated what my modar had said. I didn't even understand what it meant!"

I never guessed that he ever thought twice about the words he had spoken to me that night, and how hurtful they were to me. Now he was kneeling here in front of me, trying to apologize.

I still couldn't look at him because I was afraid if I did, the tears would come.

"I swear on Baba!" he continued. "Do whatever you want to me! Say whatever you want! Hit me, but please talk to me! Please look at me!"

Then he gently lifted my chin with his hand. With the other hand he brushed some long curls away from my cheek. Then he wiped the tears from my face.

I raised my eyes and looked at him. For a few minutes, no words were spoken. We were both lost in the past. That's when I realized that there was a bond between the two of us. Up until then, I hadn't realized it existed.

I stood up and removed my shoes. "I'll race you to the top of the apple tree!"

When he didn't respond, I said, "I beat you then and I will do it now!"

He quickly began to remove his shoes when suddenly it started to rain. He hesitated.

"Scared?" I said.

"Not a chance!"

We both ran. There were a number of fruit trees in the backyard but Karim and I had always climbed the strongest and tallest. I was determined to get to the top first, but he beat me to it.

"I can still beat you!" he said from the top. "Admit it!"

I laughed and found a comfortable place on a branch next to him. We sat quietly there in the tree for a few minutes, listening to the rain hit the leaves.

More than twenty years had passed since I had climbed that tree with Karim.

A lifetime of holding hatred and grudges were disappearing from my heart within minutes. How could it be? How could I let go so easily of something that I had carried for what felt like forever?

"Ateesh, talk to me this time," Karim said.

Keeping my balance on the tree, I reached my hand out to him. He took it. I looked at the sky and then at him.

"I am sorry, sister," he said lovingly as he squeezed my hand.

Sister! I was his sister!

"You know, Ateesh, you have always been my hero," he said. "I always admired your strength and determination. I always wanted to be like you, I mean as a person. You refused to give in to expectations after your arranged marriage."

Then he was quiet for a minute. I didn't say a word and waited for him to continue. I wanted to hear more of what he knew about that.

"I am so sorry," he said. "I knew all about it. I knew my modar was planning it all along. I used to hear her shouting at Baba at night that he had to get rid of you because you were becoming too much to handle. She hated you and was jealous of Baba's love for you."

"Baba's love for me?" I said in disbelief. "He didn't love me."

"Even I was jealous of his love for you," he said. "He used to always compare me to you and how smart you were."

"Don't play with my emotions, Karim," I said, as I pulled my hand away from his. "I will never speak to you again."

"What are you saying, Ateesh? Baba used to tell me all the time that you were his first born and your place in his heart was special."

I sat there quietly, trying to absorb his words.

"Ateesh, you are my idol," he said, as he reached out for my hand again. "I wish to be independent and strong like you."

Suddenly I felt tears come to the surface again. This time I didn't try to fight it. I let them pour down my face.

"Let's climb down," he said.

I climbed down and followed him to the cement area by the pool, where we used to lay down and look at the stars after we went swimming. He took my hand and we lay there together in that same spot.

"All is forgiven but not forgotten," I said softly. I felt connected to him and did not want to let go of this moment in my life. He gently kissed my hand. It was a beautiful warm, wet night.

Then I thought of poor Modar, and the way the door had slammed behind her. I knew she wasn't happy about Karim's presence at our house. He was a sore reminder of what Baba had done. From where I was laying, I could see the large bay window opening to the backyard and into the garden. Modar was sitting alone. I knew I would be still thinking about her and her pain even after I got back to Tehran.

※ ※ ※ ※ ※

Two days before my flight back to Tehran, I was sitting by the bay window doing some paperwork when I realized that my period was more than a week late. I threw the papers off my lap and ran over to the calendar.

What if I was pregnant? I couldn't have a child! Look at how miserable Modar has been all her life because she had a child! She was linked to Baba all these years because she had a baby with him. She was hurt badly by him because of me. I stared blankly at the calendar on the kitchen wall. Baba wouldn't even have had a second family if I'd been born a boy. He would've had the boy he wanted and then our family would never have been torn apart. Or maybe it would have been. It seemed that if a man didn't beat his wife, then he married someone else, or had a *siqeh*, or lied, or something. It was all a mess, and if this is the way the world was, I didn't want to bring a child into it.

Suddenly I couldn't think of anything else. I became nervous and distant.

Almost immediately my family noticed a change in my mood. I told them maybe I was not used to so much partying. They all laughed.

"A-ha!" Grandma Jamileh said. "In Tehran, you stay home every night with your books! Isn't that right, Ateesh Joon?"

Grandma Tuba gave her a look of disapproval. Then she turned to me and waited for me to explain. When I didn't, she offered to go for *esteqareh*, religious consultation, on my behalf.

"Modar Bozorg, you know I don't believe in *esteqareh*! And nothing is even wrong! I am fine," I said. "Anyway, isn't *esteqareh* usually taken when an important decision is being made, like a marriage? I am not getting married."

"We know that, child!" Grandma Jamileh said, "I have canceled the dress order!"

"No," Grandma Tuba said. "It can guide more than a marriage decision. I will go consult the cleric. Let us see what he has to say."

So off Grandma Tuba went, but not before she looked at Grandma Jamileh and said, "For once you should behave your age!"

Grandma Jamileh ignored her, and as soon as Grandma Tuba was gone, she asked Modar to bring the poetry book of Hafez.

"Hafez knows better," she explained. "Let us take her *Faleh Hafez*, telling of the fortune, through Hafez's poetry. This is more accurate than whatever comes from those clerics."

Modar handed her the book.

"Place your hand here on the book," Grandma Jamileh instructed me, "and make a wish silently."

"Modar, do you believe in *Faleh Hafez*?" I asked, as I put my hand where she told me.

"I don't believe in those superstitions anymore," she said. "I believe in the spirit that is in art, especially poetry. Not what Grandma Tuba is doing right now."

"Make your wish!" Grandma Jamileh prodded.

I closed my eyes and suddenly Omar appeared. I remembered how badly he wanted us to have a child together. I opened my eyes immediately.

Grandma Jamileh then randomly opened a page.

"You are torn between feelings and wisdom in your situation," Grandma Jamileh read. "In your present state of being there is no unity between the two."

So I will have the baby and be the laugh of the town? Or will I abort and kill part of me? What kind of choice is that? Just a few days earlier, I was thinking about the choices women like Farah made for themselves, and how they got themselves into their situations.

"I wonder how long before Grandma comes back with an answer from the *masjid*," Modar said, her voice breaking the silence.

"She might have to wait in line to consult with a cleric," Grandma Jamileh answered. "There are many people who actually believe in consulting with clerics about the most private matters of their lives."

Modar shook her head in disapproval. I could see that neither one of them had Grandma Tuba's religious conviction.

"Of course, Tuba Khanoom is a true believer," Grandma Jamileh said carefully.

Modar looked at her and said, "Even Grandfather does not have her conviction."

As they were going back and forth on the subject, I stared at my tall, beautiful, glass filled with hot jasmine tea. I thought of Omar again and how happy he would be if he even heard about the possibility of us having a child. It was three in the afternoon, so it was three thirty in the morning in L.A. For a brief second I thought of calling him. I missed everything about him.

Everything.

I saw my reflection on the top of the tea glass; the steam from the tea was forming water in my eyes as if I'd been crying. I looked up and saw that Modar and Grandma Jamileh were both staring at me with worried faces.

Suddenly Grandma Tuba burst in the room. "Trust in God and leave this decision to God!" she announced. "*Allaho Akbar*, God is great!"

The three of us stared at her until Modar said, "I hope you did not pay any money for that." Then she stood up. "I'm going to get more tea and snacks."

As Grandma Tuba sat down next to me, her words rang in my mind: *Allaho Akbar, God is great.* She patted my knee and smiled. *Trust in God and leave this decision to God.* Yes, leave this decision to God. What about all of my other decisions? Was I doing what was right in my life? Was I going in the right direction?

That night I asked Modar if I could sleep in her bed with her. I told her I wasn't feeling well. She offered me some sour cherry sherbet, but I declined, shocked that she had offered me this remedy that was traditionally used to cure an upset stomach, which usually accompanied early pregnancy. My mind was too active. I hated myself for the world of secrets I was living in. But the life I was leading would have been so hurtful to the ones I loved the most. No, I couldn't tell them, but I needed to talk to someone.

"Ateesh, what is the matter?" Modar asked as we lay next to each other. "Are you still hurting from the past?"

"It's a combination of past and present, Modar," I managed to say. "I am just missing you already and I haven't even left yet. I also am missing Grandma Tuba and Jamileh."

"Why don't you come for another visit soon? You know you don't have to stay in Tehran as much as you do."

"Maybe," I said. I could never, ever tell Modar what I was going through. Modar had stayed out of my personal affairs since the night she caught me coming home late from Bejan's apartment. Surely, she must have felt left out of my life. But she never asked questions. Suddenly I started sobbing. It had been years since I had cried in front of Modar. And although I had mourned inside a number of times, I remained stoic during Baba's funeral. But this time, as Modar held me in her arms so lovingly, I lost control.

"Ateesh Joon, it will be okay," she said soothingly. "Where are all these tears coming from? You know we are all very proud of you. Do not listen to what people say if you don't share their beliefs. I don't anymore. If you desire not to marry, then don't. Maybe it is in your fate to control your own destiny. You are a strong woman, Ateesh. Your grandmas and I fully trust your judgment. *Doayeh khereh ma poshteh toh*, our blessings are with you!"

Perhaps Modar was right, but how strong she must have been all those years, dealing with Baba's remarriage, my disastrous child marriage, and my move to Tehran. I had been strong, but I had also been selfish. Had I simply remarried, I could have spared her so much pain. I was crying uncontrollably for my selfishness. As she had done a number of times when I was a child, she held me and told me this story:

My name had not been selected beforehand, but was chosen at the time of my birth. As soon as Modar saw my eyes, she told Grandma

Tuba, who was at her side, that she was naming me "Ateesh." Grandma Tuba objected and proposed "Zaynab," the name of one of the Prophet's granddaughters. Grandma Tuba was a great admirer of Zaynab for her courage and suffering in keeping alive the story of her entire family's brutal murder in Karbala, and her passionate speech to unify and energize the followers of her father's faith in their battle against their oppressors. My father settled the matter by giving me both names. Zaynab would appear on my birth certificate as well as legal and formal documents. Ateesh was to be used at all other times. It means fire.

I slept soundly in her arms.

By the time I returned to Tehran, I was well over a week late and resigned to the fact that I was pregnant. My periods were usually on time, and I had kept a thorough record of the start and end of my menstrual cycles. Since I had started my profession, I used both birth control pills and condoms, which were widely available. Although the more traditional method of withdrawal was used by many Moslem couples to avoid pregnancy, I did not want to leave such an important decision in the hands of any of my temporary husbands.

Many times I thought about being pregnant and having children, especially daughters. I imagined that I would raise them like princesses, but also intellectuals who would not allow any man to control their lives. On one hand I felt that I should be celebrating the power of creation in me, but on the other hand, I was afraid and nervous. In this instance I was somewhat glad that Omar was gone, so that I alone could make this decision. I was missing him so much though, especially lately; probably because I was feeling so vulnerable. I will be fine, I told myself unconvincingly. This was my decision alone.

I was too emotional to think objectively about my situation. I needed to consult with a wise friend. Then I thought of Dr. Goodarzi. Just recently, I had spoken to her at length about possible legal reform after Sherin's murder. In spite of much effort, Dr. Goodarzi had not been able to prevent Nasser's acquittal. I had gained a friend in her through years of discussions, as we discovered our common passion for achieving justice for women. I looked at the clock. It was four in the afternoon, and she could still be at home finishing her afternoon rest. Some people take a long lunch break, which gives them enough time to eat and take a nap before returning to work. Many businesses shut down during these few hours.

I dialed her home number, but before it rang, I hung up. What was I going to say to her? I decided to say that I was inquiring for someone else, and dialed the number again. After a few rings, I heard a child's voice.

"Allo," the child said. My heart sank. This child's sweet voice could be the voice of my own child.

I introduced myself and asked, "Is your modar home?"

"No, Modar is still in her office," the child answered.

"How old are you?" I asked.

"I am six years old!" the child said proudly. "How old are you, Khanoom?"

My child would be as intelligent as this one!

"Make sure to tell her that I called," I said.

When Dr. Goodarzi called me that night, I asked her to meet me the next morning at the university for Nescafé.

I tried to chase the little child's sweet voice out of my head that night as I tried to figure out what to do. I went back and forth for hours until I finally decided to look at the Quran one more time to find its stand on abortion. The thought of killing my baby was cruel and disgusting. But what else could I do? How could I bring a child into the world who would be stigmatized by everyone because she was born not from a permanent marriage? Even if the baby was from a permanent marriage, I still wouldn't have parental rights to her. As a mother, my rights would be limited to nurturing her only up to age seven. That is all, and only if her father would allow it. To be born and raised as a child without a shadow of a father, *be pedar*, bastard, is what everybody would call my child.

I closed my eyes and lay on my bed without sleeping.

I met Dr. Goodarzi the next morning as planned, and immediately asked her about any cases on the rights of unwed mothers.

"None," she said. "These things are handled away from the public, and you should know that. Are you okay, Ateesh?"

My decision was made, even before I heard her confirming my belief that giving birth under my circumstances was a disaster.

Dr. Goodarzi asked me how law school was going, and I told her that was why I had called. She then offered me an internship at her family law office and said there was a good chance she could hire me after I graduated. Under normal circumstances, I would have been elated at this news. Working with a woman like her would be a dream come true. But just then, I had too much else on my mind to fully appreciate what she was offering.

"Make sure to call me if you need me for any reason. I mean it, Ateesh." Before we parted, she gave me a big hug. "Ateesh, we women must support one another in all of our struggles, personal or professional. I am here for you."

Later that afternoon I went to my gynecologist, Dr. Rumana, and took a pregnancy test. It was positive.

I walked home in a quiet daze.

As soon as I heard my apartment door close behind me, I began to sob uncontrollably. All of those back in Abadan who thought I had a lonely life were right. I had never felt lonelier. All these years I had been working so hard at being strong and independent, but now I felt so fragile, and at this moment I was breaking.

I went out to the balcony and looked up at the sky. Oh God, you can punish me, but not this innocent baby!

That night, I went to bed crying. I just couldn't accept what so many women in my situation believe in: *sarnewasht*, destiny. I kept repeating to myself, "I am in control of my destiny," again and again. I was afraid that if I stopped reminding myself, I might become like Farah and the others, resigned to their fates and surrendering to abuse.

Later, as I fell asleep, I heard a voice say, *"Are you having second thoughts, Ateesh?"* It was Dr. Rumana. *She was standing over me in the operating room, preparing to start the procedure. "You are not that far along, you know. You can think about it for a few more weeks."*

As I felt her warm hand on my head, caressing my hair, I thought, am I doing this for my sake or the baby's? Didn't I want children? I remembered how good it felt to be held by Modar the last night I was in Abadan.

"Are you ready?" Dr. Rumana asked.

"No!"

I was awakened by a sharp pain in my abdomen and with blood all over the bed. Through the pain and confusion I realized what was happening, and remembered what Grandma Tuba had said: Leave this decision to God. *Allaho Akbar.*

My bank account was nearly empty again. There had been the attorney bill for Golbarg in Abadan, and the cut in salary when I took leave to help with the defense of the several temporary wives who had been accused of prostitution and killed as a part of cleansing the shrine of the eighth Imam.

I desperately needed money, but I couldn't be a temporary wife anymore. Not after everything that had happened, and especially after being married to Omar. I was a different woman now. I wanted to take care of myself the right way, but I didn't know how. My stipend from the university was barely enough to cover my living expenses. How would I support myself? Then I remembered the parcel and the orchard Baba bequeathed to me in his will. I ran to the phone and called Modar.

"Modar, do you know the value of the land, including the orchard, which Baba left for me?" I asked.

"I am not sure, Azizam, but I have something to tell you!" she said, her voice filled with excitement.

"What is it?"

"One of Grandma Tuba's friends is a nurse, and she contacted us to see if we could help set up a place for abused women right here in Abadan. Grandma Jamileh thinks that the location of the land that Baba has given you would be perfect to build such a place. We were going to call you. We are just so excited, Ateesh! Grandma Tuba and Jamileh both think that this would be so important for women in Abadan."

"Wow…," I said, as I tried to soak in everything she just told me. "But where would you get the money to construct the building and for all the other expenses?"

"This just happened yesterday, so we're still trying to figure all of that out. Baba left money for Grandma Jamileh and me. We wouldn't hesitate to put all of it toward such a great cause. Grandma Tuba is coming here shortly and we were going to call you about it and ask your opinion."

She sounded so happy, just as she had been back in the days we spent in the pool swimming together.

"Why do you want to know the value of the parcel?" she asked. "We can easily find out."

"Oh, no, Modar." I managed to say. "Don't bother. I was just curious. No reason."

"Grandma Jamileh thought of asking Karim to do the same. Because it is one huge parcel divided between the two of you equally. But we thought we should wait to talk to you first. After all, we are doing this to honor you and what you are doing. It is perhaps our way…" She started to choke up on her words then she stopped talking.

"Your way to what?" I asked.

"To try to make it right for the mistake we made." She stopped again. I knew she was crying and my eyes began to fill with tears, too.

"Is that your phone ringing, Joon?" she asked.

"What?" I asked.

"Your phone is ringing," she said. "How many phones do you have?"

"Oh…it's my business line, Modar."

"You have a business line? Oh, Ateesh, we're so proud of you! Go and get that, Ateesh. We need the money! I'll let you go. We'll talk later." Then she hung up.

I stared at the other phone for a few seconds, knowing exactly who it was. Finally I picked it up.

"Salam, Hajji," I heard myself say.

"Salam Ateesh, why haven't you been answering your phone? I've been trying to call you! I have your old Arab client asking for you. I told him you are not accepting clients anymore."

I didn't say anything. I gripped the phone in my hand and re-membered the last conversation I had with Hajji Registrar. We were in his office. I had given the last of my income from the General to the parents to use as blood money to revenge the murder of their daughter.

"Hajji, I need the money," I'd told him. "I have no choice. Can you find me a client? What about some of my regulars?"

"I'm going to tell you the truth, Ateesh," he said. "There are many younger women out there. This is what men come to me asking for. Especially at the price you want, it will be difficult. I'm sorry. I have nobody right now who wants a woman over eighteen. Especially a woman like you, who challenges everything they're doing!"

Then he must have felt bad, because he softened and said, "Are you sure you want to get back into this, Ateesh? You know this isn't for you anymore. Look at you, you're leading a double life! Finish your school. Find a real husband. Get married and have a family before it is too late."

"I will call you if anything changes, Ateesh!" He called out behind me after I had turned to leave. And now here he was, calling me.

"Ateesh, are you there?" he asked.

"I am here, Hajji. Who is the guy?"

He started laughing. "He is the Arab Sheik from the Gulf region whom you told is misreading the Quran!" Laughing again, he contin-ued, "I am sure you remember him. I told him there are others but he wants you. I think he is crazy wanting you back after all of that!"

The Arab Sheik that Hajji was talking about used to come twice a year to Mashhad for a pilgrimage without any of his four wives. I had been part of his pilgrimage for the past few years.

Every time he came he would stay for one week. He would always call me in advance to make sure I was available before he would make his final arrangements. He always wanted us to stay at the Hotel Homa and always in suite 501. But now that luxurious hotel reminded me of Omar and the time we went there to visit the shrine. I couldn't go back there again.

I never enjoyed the Sheik's company but I was able to tolerate him because he was very generous and always paid above the contract price.

He was good at performing all the Islamic rituals, too, and it was puzzling to him that I would challenge him on his practice of the Quranic verses in his personal life. He believed rituals were the essentials of the faith. I told him that performing rituals was just a small part of being a good Moslem.

"How do you know all of this?" he asked. "You are just a *siqeh*."

The last time I was with him, he became furious with me because I'd gotten my period five days into our trip to Mashhad. He accused me of planning it that way.

"Are you crazy?" I asked him. My cycle had occasionally been irregular. I couldn't have planned it if I wanted to.

He was more obnoxious than usual on that trip. "Now I can't have sex with you!" he snapped. "You're unclean!"

Something in my mind had exploded then. "Do you know why you shouldn't have sex with a woman during her period?" I asked. "Because it could be damaging to her fertility!"

"What are you talking about? You are absurd. I could have sex with you right now if I wanted to," he said. "But I don't want to touch you."

"You can't have sex with me if I don't want you near me!" I snapped back. I remember feeling so tired of being in these situations with men like him over and over again. But then there was the money. The money I received from him as my marriage gift paid for my expenses at the university for a full semester. He used to bring belly-dancing music and outfits for me to wear while I danced for him. Each night that I danced for him, I received a gold coin.

Yes, the money was good. So now, if I could tolerate him for one week, I would receive enough money to take care of my financial needs until I finished my Ph.D. Then I could find a full-time job easily. This way, there would be no need to sell my parcel in Abadan. Modar's excited voice was still ringing in my head. This was the right thing to do.

"Listen carefully, Ateesh," Hajji Registrar said. "You simply cannot afford to antagonize him. Do you understand? He is one of my best clients."

"I know, Hajji. I hear you," I said. "Okay, ask him to call me. Tell him to pay half up front and the other half after two days. I need the money now."

He sighed, "Ateesh, what do you do with all of your money? You're always in need!"

~ ~ ~ ~ ~

Going back to Mashhad and staying at Hotel Homa was going to be painful. Even looking at the beautiful mountains from the balcony that overlooked the lush hotel grounds wasn't going to make me feel any better about having to spend time with the chauvinistic Sheik. This was going to be the last time I did this! I was going to get a full-time job and never have to go through this again. I repeated this promise to myself over and over.

That night Modar called. "Ateesh, both of your grandmas are here and we are all so excited!" she said. It was so nice to hear her sound so alive. I wished I could see her beautiful face. "How did it go with your business call?"

"Ateesh!" Grandma Jamileh's voice called out in the background, "you have to come here and see what we're going to build! A real shelter for women!"

Tears came to my eyes. "That's great!" I said.

Then I heard Grandma Tuba's voice on the phone. "Joonam, we are putting together a business plan, and on Thursday evening after the prayers at the *masjid*, we are going to announce the project. We have decided to ask the community to get involved. We think this way we can also raise some money."

Then Modar was on the phone again, "Ateesh, we were just thinking that perhaps someday you may decide to come back here and run the center, but no pressure. It is your decision."

"Some pressure is not bad!" Grandma Jamileh called out.

I joined in their laughter and after about half an hour of talking back and forth with the three of them, I said goodnight. Before I hung up the phone, I told them I would call Karim myself to ask him about his share of the land and the orchard.

Seeing the three of them working together as a team to help other women warmed my heart. But the brief elation I felt from all the talk of a women's shelter quickly evaporated when I remembered that I was going to be a *siqeh* again.

That night I couldn't sleep. I just lay in bed for hours staring at the ceiling. Finally I got up and went to the kitchen to make some hot tea for myself. It was three in the morning. I took my cup of tea and walked outside to the balcony and sat on the chair. The sky was clear with thousands of stars. Remembering my cousin Saeed, I searched the sky for the prettiest of all. I felt as if he was looking down at me. *Ateesh, don't be so sad,* I heard him say. *Everything is where it's supposed to be.*

"I wish you could hold me now," I said aloud.

My prettiest star of all, you cannot change what has happened in your past, but perhaps you can make new decisions for your future.

"You know, Saeed, with the money I have inherited from Baba, we are going to fight the very attitude and culture that Baba embraced. I hated him and defied his culture. Now with his help maybe I can make a difference."

I stared into the deep, star-filled sky. I threw a kiss toward the sky and realized I was crying. I wiped the tears off my face, rushed back inside, and looked everywhere for Omar's telephone number. I had erased all his texts and messages. Where else could I look for his number? He had received an offer from New York University. I wondered if he had taken the position. And if he had, would he still be in the office at that late hour? It was 3:00 a.m., which meant 6:30 p.m. the previous night in New York. I found the telephone number for the university and dialed his extension through his last name.

"Dr. Omar Gobta," a female voice said.

"I am calling from Tehran, Iran." I said nervously. "Is the doctor available?"

"Oh, you must be Ateesh Khanoom!" she said.

I almost dropped the phone. She knew about me? He talked about me?

"I am pleased to hear your voice," she continued. "I am Sakura Yashicomy, his wife. He is teaching the evening class. He should finish in a half hour. I will tell him you called."

His wife. Suddenly all the sparkling stars in that big blue sky turned into arrows aimed right at me. They were stabbing me in the heart over and over again.

"Thank you," I managed to say.

I hung up the phone, lay on the floor, and closed my eyes. I wished I would never wake up.

But I did wake up the next morning, to the business line ringing. I knew exactly who it was. This was the reality of my situation.

"Allo," I said, dreading the sound of his voice.

"*Salam Aleikum*, Ateesh Khanoom. This is your Sheik!" I felt nauseated by the lust in his voice.

"Yes, Sheik. *Ahlan va Sahlan*, how are you?" I asked in broken Arabic.

"*Marhaba*, bravo. I love it when you speak to me in Arabic. What else do you remember?"

"*Sabahal kheer habibi*, good morning my dear," I said.

"*Sabahal noor habibat*, good morning my dear, and I can hardly wait to see you in Mashhad. *Enshallah*, God willing."

"*Enshallah*," I said.

The plan was for me to leave that night for Mashhad, and the Sheik was to arrive the next morning. After I hung up the phone, I went to the shower and stood under the hot water for a while. My body and mind were numb.

I arrived in Mashhad and took a taxi to Hotel Homa. As always, the Sheik had reserved suite 501. After I checked in, I went to the Mezzanine level, which faced the large entranceway to the hotel. I sat in the café area and ordered a cappuccino. I tried not to think of the last time I was there sipping coffee with Omar. I couldn't help it. I remembered there were a few young Asian men and women sitting not far from us. They smiled at us and we smiled back. One of the young women started speaking to us in her language, which I hadn't understood, but I was surprised to see that Omar did as he began conversing with her.

"You speak Japanese?" I asked. "How wonderful!"

"They are Chinese," he said. "I have many friends and several graduate students from different parts of China. I've traveled extensively through there. If you ever allow me to take another wife, she would be Chinese or Japanese!" he said with a wink.

"Just make sure she will attend to both our needs!" I said jokingly. We both laughed. The Chinese group didn't know what we were laughing at, but they smiled and laughed with us.

This time I didn't see many foreigners but more Arab men with their long white gowns and turbans. It was ten in the evening and I wasn't hungry for dinner, so I went upstairs to the suite and unpacked. As I was placing my toiletries in the washroom, I glanced at myself. I looked tired and pale, and the spark in my eyes that Omar had always talked about was gone. My eyes were puffy and red with dark circles underneath them.

"Oh, Ateesh," I said to myself, "don't pity yourself. This is all your doing!" I took another look at myself in the mirror and thought, "Hajji is right, there are much younger women available who can do this." There was no sympathy from the inner voice. I waited for a few minutes for the other voice—the strong, supportive, independent one. But it never came.

I called the hotel operator and asked to be connected to the beauty salon. I made an appointment for a complete massage and facial for the first thing in the morning. Then I went back to the shower area and started a bath. I put on some soft and sensual instrumental music, threw some sea salt and bubble bath in the Jacuzzi and undressed. I put my hair up and stepped into the hot, foamy water. This was to be my last act of economic dependency on men I reminded myself as I reached for my bottle of mineral water and immersed my body in the

Jacuzzi. As I rested my head on the headrest and stretched my legs out into the soapy water, I took a long sip. It was refreshing and delicious.

This was going to be the last time, I reminded myself again. I had to keep saying it. I was going to stay positive.

I slept well that night.

～ ～ ～ ～ ～

The next morning after breakfast, I went to my appointment. After nearly two hours of relaxing beautification, I got ready to go to the airport to receive the Sheik. As I dressed, I listened to the soothing, instrumental music that was playing on the radio. I wore an ice blue blouse with buttons in the back, and a black, above-the-knee length skirt with a belt. I fixed my hair and put on some makeup, with sheer pink lip-gloss. I put on my black heels, went downstairs and caught a taxi.

As the distance between the taxi and airport decreased, my anxiousness, which I'd been trying so hard to ignore, increased.

I had called earlier and was told that the plane had arrived. When the car pulled up to the airport, I reminded myself once more that this would be the last time. I asked the driver to wait for me to return, then I went to the receiving area and waited along with hundreds of people, until I saw him coming toward me. I stood up to greet him. He came close to kiss me and I offered my cheek. He handed me a small package, and with a big grin on his face he said, "I think you'll be happy with this."

I smiled and thanked him as I took the package. For the first time, I didn't even wonder how valuable of a gift I was receiving from a temporary husband or what worthy cause I could spend it on. I was too busy wondering how I was going to get through this one last episode.

Back in the hotel room, I watched blankly as he changed from his long gown into pants and a shirt.

"Come on, Ateesh," he said, "you have not opened your gift. You'll like it."

I sat on the sofa and opened the package, which contained a small box that sat on a beautiful, silk, black chador. I opened the box and saw the biggest diamond ring I had ever seen.

"This…must be five carats," was all I could manage to say.

"Put on the chador and let me see," he said.

I did as he asked.

"Do you like the ring? I bought it for you"

Was he proposing? The chador, that gigantic ring… But wait a minute, he couldn't be proposing. He already had four wives.

"These are very nice, expensive gifts, Sheik," I said.

"Ateesh, I am asking you to marry me permanently. You can still live here in Tehran and I will visit you whenever I can. Of course we'll have to cleanse you from your sins first, by doing ablution. Then of course you must wear the chador."

I looked back at the ring, and remembered the wedding ring Omar had given me: the simple, delicate, gold band with diamond cut. The most precious ring I'd ever seen.

What was I doing here in this hotel room with this man? Business, I reminded myself. It was just business. He had already paid half my contract price. The other half would be paid in two days.

"What are you thinking, Ateesh?" he asked.

"Well," I said, "the marriage proposal coming from such a good practicing Moslem who follows the Quran and its Prophet is—disappointing, Sheik!" I said this in a patronizing voice, as I tried to keep in mind that I only had to put up with him two days.

"Oh, Ateesh, of course I keep and follow the Prophet's tradition. I believe and follow the verse that allows men to marry up to nine wives."

"Nine wives?" I almost choked over those words.

"Yes! It says to marry 'two, three, and four.' If you count them, it adds up to nine!" Then, with a smirk forming on his face, he said, "You know, the Prophet himself had nine wives."

"I've never heard of that interpretation, Sheik. You're kidding right?"

I remembered then that Hajji specifically asked me not to antagonize this man, but I couldn't help it. I was disgusted and had a difficult time hiding it.

"No," he said. "There are many who follow the Prophet's traditions set by his own example."

It was so clear that he was enjoying himself. I took a deep breath. I just needed to bide my time for two more days.

"Well," I said, as I looked back down at the box. "I need to think about this, Sheik. You really took me by surprise. I will let you know by the end of our contract."

"All right," he said. "I know you must be overwhelmed. How about trying it on and seeing if it's the right size?"

"No, it would be bad luck, Sheik. How about I try it on after the ablution?"

"Yes, yes, that makes sense. I have to cleanse you first," he said with a smile on his face. "Let us go now to the best restaurant to celebrate!"

All of the positive energy I tried to summon up for this was quickly evaporating.

We took a taxi and went to a hilly area outside the city called *Kohsanghy*, about a half hour away from the hotel, and then to an outdoor restaurant in the middle of a garden that overlooked the entire city. The view was spectacular.

The Sheik never asked what I wanted to eat and always ordered for both of us. I had always objected to such behavior, but not this time.

"Ateesh, you have changed," he said.

"In what way?" I asked.

"You are quieter, as if you are thinking more than you are talking. You are scaring me. I think you're setting me up for one of your lectures on how as a Moslem man I'm misusing religion to abuse women."

"Don't you think you are?" I asked as softly as I could.

"How, Ateesh? Tell me. Until now, I have had four wives, yes. But I treat them equally, as it says in the Quran. I follow all the rituals, even when it comes to temporary marriage."

"You have never been with a woman outside of permanent or temporary marriage?"

"No, I swear. Never."

"Do you tell your wives about your temporary wives?"

"Why should I? It is not any of their business."

"Don't you think it would be hurtful to them to know their husband is sleeping around?"

"I only marry based on what is allowed by the Quran," he said.

The food arrived then, but I had lost my appetite. I ordered a pot of hot tea with lemon.

"Come on, Ateesh," he insisted, "eat some of this delicious kebab."

"Maybe we can take some with us back to the hotel and if I get hungry later, I'll eat," I said. "Sheik, what do you do for living? I mean, I know you are a businessman, but what kind?"

"Are you considering my proposal?" he asked. "Is that why you're asking all these questions?"

I nodded and shrugged. I found that I no longer had ready answers to these questions.

"Well, I lend money to people," he said.

"Do you charge interest?" I asked.

"Of course, how else am I going to make money?"

"Isn't charging interest forbidden, Haram?" I asked gently. "Based on the Quran?"

He shook his head and laughed, "I know you too well. Didn't I say you were setting me up for one of your lectures?" Then he stopped the waiter and asked, "Where is my water pipe?"

The waiter appeared a few seconds later with the *qalyan* and my pot of tea. When the Sheik started smoking the *qalyan*, it took me back to Grandma Tuba's house over twenty years ago.

"You want a puff?" he asked.

I shook my head. There was fast music playing in the background and I thought of the music in the ice cream shop where Omar and I waited for his photos to be developed for our marriage certificate. As the Sheik was talking about himself and his glory, I realized I couldn't go through with this. Not even for two days.

I would borrow money from someone if I had to, but whom? I didn't know, but one thing I was sure of right then and there: I was done being a temporary wife. How was I going to tell the Sheik this? He kept talking and smoking and I kept thinking and sipping my tea.

I would have to return the half he had paid up front. Whatever I had to do, I would do it. Now I just had to come out and tell him.

"Let's go back to the hotel, Ateesh," he said, as he waved the waiter over to bring our bill.

~~ ~~ ~~ ~~ ~~

All the way back to the hotel and up to the room, I kept opening my mouth to tell him, but he interrupted me every time. I wanted to get it over and done with but I didn't know how to go about it. Back at the hotel I was sitting in the bathroom trying to figure out exactly how I was going to say it.

"What is taking you so long?" he shouted from the other room. "Hurry up to bed! I want you!"

"I'll be right there!" I called back to him.

Okay, I told myself. I'll tell him, then I'll pack, go to airport, and sleep there until I catch the next flight out. Suddenly I heard him moaning.

I opened the door and went into the bedroom. "Listen, Sheik," I said softly, "I am so sorry, but I have to tell you that I cannot go through with this anymore."

He was lying on the bed quietly. He looked at me as if he hadn't heard me. I went closer. He was sweating profusely and looked as if he were sick. I sat on the bed next to him and touched his forehead. He seemed unconscious. I quickly picked up the phone and dialed the front desk and asked for an ambulance.

Throughout the ride in the ambulance, I held his hand. I felt bad for having been so harsh to him. The hotel nurse who was riding in the ambulance thought that his symptoms were of food poisoning. They asked where we had eaten that evening. As soon as we got to the emergency room, several doctors and nurses with white scrubs took over. One of the doctors came over and asked about the Sheik's general health and other personal information. I felt very uncomfortable answering. I was hoping that nobody would find out I was his temporary wife. They all seemed to assume we were husband and wife visiting the shrine.

The hours of violent vomiting finally subsided. As a precaution, they pumped the Sheik's stomach of any remaining contents and administered an enema to clean out his lower digestive tract. Now that the worst was over, the Sheik was just ill and weak.

There he laid, mouth open, ashen faced, attached to a monitor and a saline solution IV. He looked small and fragile. Framed by the window and behind the glass, there was a certain detachment, which made me feel as if I were looking at a person I had never met. As I stood there staring, I couldn't help but feel some compassion for him, though much like I would for any other person who appeared so sick.

I remembered Grandma Tuba's words on impure thoughts and how God hears them, so I was very careful not to make any wish but for the Sheik's complete recovery.

For the first time ever in dealing with temporary husbands, I was not thinking about the money at all. All I wanted was for him to recover and for me to leave. But I could not leave him in that condition.

I went into the room and stood near the bed and looked at him. His eyes were barely opened.

"How are you, Sheik?" I asked softly. "I was quite worried about you."

He opened his eyes and looked at me. "You don't have to stay here," he said. "You can go back to Tehran. I will pay your full price."

"No, Sheik, I am staying until you get out of the hospital. Then I'll leave."

"I will pay you," he said.

I gently caressed the back of his hand and asked, "Shall I call someone for you?"

He shook his head.

"The doctor says you'll be fine," I said. "It was a really bad case of food poisoning. But you must stay for a couple of days under observation."

He held my hand and I did not object. "I never saw this gentle, kind side of you, Ateesh," he said. "The doctor said if you had not called for help right away I could have died."

"It must have been God's wish for you to continue life," I said. "It's in Her hands."

"Well, yes," he said. "He is in charge of us. What do you mean by 'Her'?"

"What do you mean, 'He'?" I said, realizing that I was starting to antagonize him again.

"Are you questioning His gender?"

"Are you saying God has a gender?"

The Sheik was quiet for a second. Then he started laughing and I joined in.

One of the doctors came in and said, "I am glad you are feeling better. We will see how you feel tomorrow. Right now we have to make sure you get enough rest and liquid in you."

Then he looked at me and said, "I am afraid your wife has to leave."

"Yes," the Sheik said. "My beautiful wife, you go back to the hotel and I will join you tomorrow." But instead of releasing my hand, he gripped it tighter. I bent down to him and whispered, "Cut it out," and I gently pulled my hand from his.

As I walked toward the door, I said goodbye to him and the doctor, and I left the hospital.

Back at the hotel, I took a shower, put on my robe and went out to the balcony.

"God" I said as I looked at the night sky full of shining stars, "thank you for watching over me."

It was a beautiful night with a promising morning.

I went back in and went to bed. The next morning I woke up early and called the hospital. The Sheik was doing fine and was going to be released later on that afternoon. I decided not to see him back to the hotel. I called the front desk to find out the flight schedule for the day to take me back to Tehran and then I started to pack.

I tried to pack his belongings without going through his personal items. I repacked the chador and the ring he had bought for me and placed it inside his suitcase. I called the travel agency to see what flights were available for him. The first available was for the next evening. I wrote down all the information for him and placed it on the coffee table next to the bed. It was almost ten in the morning. I went downstairs, picked up a large cappuccino with an extra shot of espresso and then went outside and took a taxi to the hospital to check on the Sheik one last time before I left for the airport.

There was no turning back. "*Tubeh, Tubeh, Tubeh*, repentant," I said three times in accordance with Quranic traditions.

Oh God I have discovered love
How marvelous, how good, how beautiful it is
My body is warm from the heat of this love…

— Rumi

At the Mehrabad airport in Tehran, I picked up my suitcase and turned toward the exit when I was startled by a man's voice, "*Bargard*! Step back!"

Suddenly a suitcase cart hit me from behind. I spun around and fell backward onto the floor, landing on something sharp. I sat there on the cold, marble floor of the airport, dazed and with an excruciating pain in my tailbone.

"I'm so sorry!" the man said. "Are you okay?" He reached out to me and gently took my hand. Feeling his strong, wide hands and getting a quick glimpse of his wavy dark hair, he reminded me of Modar's description of Baba the first time they met. "Being trapped like a fish in a net," was the way she described how she felt.

Now, looking at my assailant, the words of Rumi suddenly came to mind:

I have fallen and unable to rise,
What kind of a trap is this?

"Does that hurt?" the stranger asked as he reached down and touched my ankle.

"No," I said, still reeling from the pain in my tailbone.

"I am so sorry, Khanoom." His deep voice was mesmerizing, and even through the haze of my pain I felt myself being drawn to him. I had never experienced such a strong feeling of attraction like this so quickly. I felt overwhelmed. I didn't know if I should be angry or happy. I almost forgot about the sharp throbbing in my tailbone as I stared at his fingers on my leg.

His hands were large and strong and he had neatly cut nails. I wondered if he worked with his hands. My heart was pounding. I felt as if I were caught in that same fishnet my modar had talked about. *This is crazy*, a voice in my head said. *Get hold of yourself, Ateesh!* But after everything I had been through, I felt so vulnerable.

That's when I noticed his wedding band, and I felt a wave of disappointment. I knew I had to say something quickly so he wouldn't catch on.

"Are you a doctor?" I asked, as I tried not to look into his eyes.

"No," he said with a smile. "Why?"

I didn't answer.

"I'm an artist," he said. "I make sculptures." Then he softly added, "You are not screaming as I am touching your ankle, so it's probably not broken. Just to make sure, I'll drive you to a nearby clinic."

I was so overwhelmed that I'd forgotten to tell him that it was my tailbone, not my ankle that was really hurting.

"Is your husband picking you up here at the airport?" he asked.

"No, I was going to take a taxi," I answered, intentionally leaving his inquiry into my marital status unanswered.

I saw him look down at my left hand on which I was wearing the wedding band that Omar had given me. At the same time I kept looking down at his wedding band. Then we both looked at each other and allowed our eyes to meet for the first time.

"I am not married," I heard myself blurting out to him, to my surprise.

By furrowing his eyebrows, it seemed that he was trying to appear indifferent to my marital status, but he couldn't maintain that facade for long. As he smiled, his entire face brightened and a twinkle came to his dark blue eyes.

"I was hoping you weren't married. I intentionally ran my cart into you to stop you from getting away without giving me your phone number."

I was stunned. I couldn't tell if he was joking or not.

"*Asabany nasheen*, don't get angry," he said. "I didn't mean to hurt you."

I just looked at him. Instead of getting angry or even questioning his motives, I found myself asking him, "What about you? I see you are wearing a wedding band."

It didn't matter if he was married or not, I told myself. I was not going to lose control of myself over a man who could easily marry many women at the same time. I was also finished being a *siqeh*. That was over and done with. I was going to let this one go.

I stared at his mouth to avoid looking into his eyes. I'd heard that my eyes say a lot, and I didn't want my assailant to know what was going on inside of me. But as I watched his lips, the thought of kissing him gave me goose bumps. I had to look away from him and pinch myself so I would stop thinking about it. But I felt completely overpowered by the thought.

In spite of my attempts to avoid eye contact, my assailant looked into my eyes and said, "My marriage ended a long time ago. I guess I just kept the ring because that is the only thing left from that relationship. What about you? Why are you wearing a ring if you're not married?"

Instead of answering his question, I tried to stand up, which I knew wouldn't be easy. The sharp pain in my tailbone seemed to scream louder as I moved, and I felt myself grimacing from the pain. He reached over to help me.

As he lifted me up to stand, my heart was charging forward in full gear. This man was the one that had caused this pain and I wasn't even mad at him! What was happening to me was like in the movies where everything around the actor stops and becomes kind of foggy as she tries to focus on what is in front of her. Then comes a greater force, which sucks her in like a tornado. The irresistible force of his presence was overpowering the wisdom in me. I was losing my self-control. I couldn't allow this to happen. *Come on, Ateesh, wake up,* I scolded myself. This couldn't be reality.

I heard my thoughts but wasn't listening to them. It was as if I was having an out-of-body experience. One part of me was fighting the other part. I stopped listening to my own voice and heard the words of Rumi instead:

What chains tie my hands and feet
How secret, how obvious it is
I am falling in love, and it is so obvious
My heart is pulsing with passion
And all can see that
I offer my salutation to the moon and to the stars,
To all my sisters and brothers,
I offer my salutation to the spirit of passion that
aroused and excited this universe…

∿∿ ∿∿ ∿∿ ∿∿ ∿∿

I had resigned myself to the idea of not experiencing love at the level that existed in books among lovers such as Yousoof and Zolyka or Romeo and Juliet. Was this feeling what those lovers had experienced? Of course I didn't believe in love at first sight, so this must be just a physical attraction. Or could it actually be possible to love someone you just met? A wide range of emotions was going rapidly through my mind. At times I felt resentful and almost angry. I think the innocence and carefree pleasure of being in love had been taken from me as a result of my arranged marriage.

"Khanoom, say something," he said. I felt his hand on my shoulder gently shaking me. "Are you okay?"

I nodded. He helped me to walk by having me lean against him. As he kept talking, I could hear him but not really comprehend much of what he was saying. I was feeling so much pain that I thought I was going to pass out. Was this all a dream? I wasn't sure.

I think I heard him saying that he had a car waiting, and that he was going to take me to a nearby clinic.

As we sat in the backseat of the car, I found myself leaning toward him and my head resting on his shoulder. He didn't seem to mind, but as soon as I realized what I was doing, I managed to explain, "It hurts to sit with my weight evenly distributed." He adjusted his body more towards me and brought his right arm around my shoulder to create more room.

When we reached the clinic, the driver asked if he should go and get a stretcher.

"No, it is not necessary. Just go inside and ask for my sister," he said. "Tell her it's family and to make sure we have a private room available."

Then he gently picked me up and carried me inside so easily it felt as if I were weightless. I floated in his strong arms. Then I felt another sudden, sharp pain. This time I let my head fall onto his shoulder and didn't offer an explanation.

For the first time since I'd seen this man, my mind was quiet.

He took me into a room that had the name Dr. Parvin Chenary on the door, and gently placed me on the examination table.

"*Chi shodeh*, what happened?" The voice came from a woman who had followed us into the room. The artist turned to her and said, "Parvin, I caused this beautiful woman's fall. I don't think anything is broken but please take a look."

The doctor came close to me and said, "Enchanted, *Khoshgel Khanoom*, beautiful one. I am the doctor in the family but my brother Javad apparently does the diagnoses."

So the artist's name was Javad and this doctor was his sister. He did not let go of my hand and stood right there as his sister tried to examine my tailbone and legs.

I didn't mind at all having my hand held by Javad and I also felt quite comfortable being called beautiful by him even though I really did not know him. I had a feeling that I knew him from the past. His hair reminded me so much of Baba, who was the last person I wanted to think of, especially now that I was holding hands with a stranger, something of which Baba would not have approved. I felt a connection to Javad that was difficult to comprehend. There was just something about him. His gaze had something in it and, although I could not identify it, it shot straight to my heart. I thought of Omar and our first meeting at the bookstore. Was I looking for him? Is that why I was attracted to this man? Was I longing for love?

"Give me space to examine her," the doctor said with a serious tone. Javad didn't move.

The doctor scratched her head and asked, "What has come over you? It looks like she is in a lot of pain, I have to examine her before I can give her some sedatives. "

I did not make any attempt to remove my hand from his grip. The doctor was imparting meaningful glances and smiling at both of us. Not a sound or a move came from Javad, and I only cried out once as the doctor touched my tailbone.

"The good news is that nothing is broken," she said, "but it is going to take some time to heal. I'll write you a prescription for some strong pain medication. Take it easy for the next few days. Do you want to help me see if she can sit up, Javad?"

"No, I can do it alone," he answered, gently pushing his sister from my side. He reached under my waist and pulled me toward himself in order to help me to sit up. I couldn't help but look at his lips again. That's when he lowered his head to get real close to my face. As I felt his breath on my lips, I was sure the intensity of feeling was mutual. The doctor turned her face away in embarrassment, which brought me back to reality.

I turned my face away just in time to avoid his kiss, even though my lips were agonizing for his. His lips reminded me of Omar and our first kiss. Then I thought his lips were traced with opium because as I tasted his lips only once I desired more. My entire body was aflame. His gaze was penetrating my resistance. Again I heard the voice in my head ordering me, *Don't be stupid, Ateesh.* I was trying!

You are not trying hard enough!

The doctor tapped Javad on his shoulder and whispered something to him. As he turned around to respond, he loosened his grip on my waist. Painfully, I tried to sit up but again I cried out. The doctor left the room and came back a few seconds later with a glass of water and two tablets.

"Take these two codeine tablets," she said. As she placed the tablets on my tongue, Javad took the glass from her and held it to my lips and poured the cold water into my mouth. I felt his gaze on my mouth, and with every drop of water, I imagined his tongue. I visualized all the things this sculptor and I could do… *help me*! I searched for that strong, independent voice inside me. She was gone.

"I want to go home," I said. I tried to step down from the examination table and suddenly felt dizzy.

"You can't leave on your own," the doctor said, "and a few days of rest are a must. Stay here and rest at least for a few hours. You are in no condition to leave. Do you have someone we can call?"

The doctor and Javad were both looking at me, waiting for an answer.

"All my family lives in Abadan."

"You live alone?" Javad asked.

"I don't live too far away from here," I said. "I can take a taxi."

"Oh no, I will drive you home," Javad said. "This is the least I could do."

I nodded, "Okay." The codeine was kicking in and the pain was starting to subside a little.

After Dr. Chenary gave me a week's worth of codeine pills, Javad lifted me up and carried me out to the car waiting outside the clinic. He was very firm and I tried not to hold tight to his muscular arms. He helped me into the backseat, where his sister had placed a pillow to go under my neck. Gently, he pushed away the strands of my hair that were all over my face. Then he turned toward his sister and they quietly spoke a few words before Javad got into the car and drove away from the clinic.

"Thank you," I managed to say to the doctor before we left.

I was quiet as I lay in the back of his car. He reached back for my hand and again I let him hold it without much resistance. I remembered the first time I'd sat in Bejan's car; my heart had pounded the same way when he had held my hand.

᭧᭧ ᭧᭧ ᭧᭧ ᭧᭧ ᭧᭧

I didn't want Javad to know which building I lived in, so I went and stood by a building on the other side of the street from my apartment. Painfully, I watched him drive slowly away. It felt as if my heart was desperately trying to jump out of my chest to follow him. I could feel the flames of yearning desire to be with this man. "*Baseh, Baseh,* enough, enough," I said out loud, with anger and resentment at my heart's vulnerability. I felt weak and wished I had never met him. *This is just infatuation and physical attraction. Give it some time and it will die off.*

I nodded, hoping the voice was right.

As soon as I closed my apartment door behind me, I took two of the pills the doctor had given me. I went directly into my bedroom and lay down on my bed. I closed my eyes and Javad appeared right there on the bed with me. My bed was filled with the smell of his cologne, which had so aroused me right at the airport as he got closer and closer. I could still feel his hand on my ankle and the sensations within me that Omar had created before.

I started to sob. I did not want to feel whatever it was I was feeling! I could not go through the pain of losing someone I cared about again. I had to control it. I had to avoid it before it went deeper. What was this? Love? It was something, and it might just be love. I remembered Omar and how miserable I felt when he'd left, and as much as I'd wanted to be with him I had resisted. I hated to feel so weak and vulnerable over the very gender that I was trying to be independent from. I sobbed harder than ever before. I missed Modar and wished I could cry in her comforting arms.

The effect of the codeine was numbing, and eventually I fell asleep despite my feverish state. I dreamt of Javad all night. In my dreams I heard the voice of the poet, Forugh Farrokhzad:

> *I know that one-day, from far away*
> *A highborn prince will appear*
> *The hooves of his fleet-footed steed*
> *Strike the cobblestones of the streets*

Sunshine rebounds like a flame
Through the top of his crown.
His garment is golden, warm and wool
His chest covered by strings of pearls and gems
The breeze bends the feathers on his crown
Now this way, now that
And caresses the curly tufts
Scattered on his beaming forehead.
People whisper in each other's ears:
"Wow! So lofty, so strong, so majestic
He is peerless in the whole world, no doubt!
Must be a most noble prince!"
Girls rear their heads from behind low windows
Their cheeks blush at the sight
Their chests heave in tumult
Hearts beating at the thought:
"He might be—coming for me!"

When I awoke early next morning, Javad was still fresh and strong on my mind. I told myself very clearly, *You are not going to fall in love! You will not lose control of your heart.*

I could not control my dreams, but I could most certainly control my heart. I had done it in the past and was determined to do it again.

I took a long shower, hoping it would drive him from my head, but the heat from the water only seemed to fuel my desire. I would first tease his lips with my tongue, lick around his mouth and mustache with short wet strokes, and bite his lips gently, yet firmly and passionately. The thought of his lips weakened me. This was crazy. It had to stop.

I called the university and told them of my fall and the possibility of a few days of absence.

I went back to bed and stayed there for the rest of the day with a lot of pain in my tailbone but in a state of tranquility from a combination of the painkillers and thoughts of Javad.

A couple of days later, the powerful surging in my heart began to overcome the fears I had about men. I asked myself, "Would I deny myself this love because of the risk that someday he might break my heart?" The independent voice inside me quickly answered, *Yes*.

I was determined to make myself busy in the hope of getting over the burning desire to see him. I went back to work even though I could not sit for very long. I kept taking painkillers and each day I spent a few hours lying down on the floor. Wherever I was, I could feel his presence with me. Every evening as I went back to my apartment, I could see him. Was he following me or was I imagining it? I kept wondering.

It was the end of the fall semester and two months since I'd met Javad in October. I spent many long days staring at papers and I couldn't concentrate. I avoided friends and colleagues. I didn't feel like socializing with anybody.

"What is happening, Ateesh?" my friends would ask. "Why are you losing so much weight? Are you sick?" When this had happened after Omar left, I'd made excuses for feeling so down, but this time around I didn't even know how to answer.

Every night as I lay in bed and closed my eyes, Javad would come to me and undress me one piece of clothing at a time. I laid on the bed in anticipation of the ecstasy of being underneath him. He had evoked something in me more than sexual attraction. I couldn't articulate what it was, yet it remained strong within me.

Then one morning after another long night of thinking about him, I found myself heading toward his building. When I arrived, I walked through the front door, took the elevator to the second floor and walked right into the studio bearing his name.

He was talking to a woman behind a desk. I immediately caught sight of his dark, wavy hair. For a few moments, I just watched and listened. His voice was deep and smooth. Words came out of his mouth like long notes played on a stringed instrument.

For the first time since I'd met him I realized how much he resembled and sounded like the Baba I'd known as a very young child; before things had changed because of his second marriage. Was I longing for Baba's love?

The woman behind the desk that I came to know later as his assistant saw me first and kept looking in my direction until Javad lifted his head and looked over at me. Our eyes met again after all those long days since our first meeting and I felt our hearts melting with joy.

The wise and independent voice in my head was totally quiet this time.

"*Khanoom!*" he exclaimed happily. "I can't believe my eyes!"

He walked toward me, pulled me close to him, and then lifted me into the air.

"Please put me down," I said with embarrassment.

"I can't believe you are here!" he said as he gently put me down.

I quickly pulled down my shirt, which had curled up, showing my waistline.

"*Bebaksheed*, excuse me," I told the secretary who was watching us with a big grin on her face.

"I knew something was going on with him," she said. "He hasn't been acting like himself since you left the clinic two months ago."

I looked at her and blushed, but I didn't remember seeing her in the clinic.

Javad scolded her for talking too much. She got up from behind her desk, and as she was walking toward the exit she said, "Everybody at the clinic talks about it. I am going there right now for a tea break."

Javad didn't say anything, but just stood there and waited for her to leave. After she closed the door behind herself, he led me into a room with pictures of foreign places covering the walls. There were vibrant pictures of landscapes from all over the world decorating one wall of his busy, large, warehouse-looking workroom. The lush green fields and mountains of Switzerland, the majestic Himalayas, the mysterious Nile, the ice blue Tibetan skies, and the ever-magnificent Grand Canyon. I was trying to take it all in. *Wow*, I thought, *he has seen the world!*

"How are you feeling, *goleman?*" he asked, and without waiting for a reply continued, "What kind of pain brings you back to my studio?"

The way he called me *goleman*, his flower, was intoxicating. I felt a rush of blood from my head to my toes. I felt feverish and dizzy. He pulled a chair out for me. I sat down and he stood very close to me. On a huge table next to me, there was a sculpture of a naked woman. I stared at her face. It looked familiar. I thought of Tanaz's sculpture of the naked woman with the Quranic verses on her.

As I continued to stare at the sculpture, he knelt down, just as he'd done at the airport, and touched and caressed my ankle. I moved on the chair but remained silent in a daze. He started touching and massaging my legs gently.

"I hope you are not feeling much physical pain at the moment," he said in a seductive whisper. "And if it is not the pain that brought you back, then what?" Suddenly, he leaned forward and I thought for sure he was going to kiss me. Instead, he blew out a few strands of curl from my cheek. Then his face got really close to mine and I felt the warmth of his mouth on my lips. I even felt his moustache. His cologne smelled like a mixture of early spring flowers. I felt a sensation on my left breast where my heart was beating like a volcano starting to erupt. I saw and felt the same level of passion and desire in him for me as I had for him. We were both fully aware of that.

Then he pulled away from me and smiled. He locked the door and walked back to me, lifted me up from the chair and laid me gently on the very large table next to the statue.

He started tracing my face and neck with his fingers. "After I dropped you off at your place, I came right back here to my studio. I was afraid I would awake in the morning and you would not be real. I thought by sculpting you right away I would have your image and know you were not just a dream—and that I would see you again."

I looked again at the sculpture. It *was* me. "Wow!" Was the only thing I could say. Again I thought of Tanaz's sculpture. I got an uneasy feeling in my stomach.

Javad lay next to me and we held each other, silently, for longer than I can remember ever being held without a word. He kept caressing my hair and smelling my neck, kissing my eyes. I couldn't remember ever being with a man alone in that position without having sex. This was not going to be just that. This was something more powerful than just physical attraction. He traced my entire face with his fingers and kept looking into my eyes. Every time my eyes shied away, he would gently tilt my chin up until I looked at him.

Several hours must have passed by before we heard a knock at the door and the assistant's voice, "It's time to leave for lunch," she said. "Are you leaving too?"

"Yes," Javad called back.

"Okay, goodbye!" she called out before we heard her footsteps moving away.

Then he whispered into my ear, "*Goleman*, let us go to my place. I want to hold you for the whole day and night and every other night after that."

I did not have to say a word. We drove to his apartment, which wasn't far from his studio. As we stood in front of the entrance to his apartment, I read, "Javad N. Jawady 1125G." Once we got inside his two-story apartment, he lifted me up and put me on his strong, wide shoulders and carried me upstairs into his loft-like bedroom. Mirrors covered two sides of his loft and on the other side a large window overlooked a garden below. The large swimming pool in the middle of garden reminded me of my childhood, where I had swum happily with my modar.

As I lay on his bed with lacy canopy matching the cushions, he put new age music on his CD player, then he lit the three candles, which were held on a long wooden pedestal. All in different sizes yet joined at the bottom in a pool of already burned wax. Then he joined me in bed and lay next to me, embracing me. He started kissing and gently biting me all over, first with clothes on and then within a few minutes, he began undressing me one piece of clothing at a time. I started undressing him too. There was an element of pleasant surprise on Javad's face at my full participation. No words were exchanged, only the passion and ecstasy I'd thought and dreamt of since our first meeting. I felt his wet kisses all over my body. I returned them with longing and desire, totally submitting, and was surprised suddenly to feel tears escape my eyes and wet my face.

"*Goleman, chieh*, what is it?" he asked me.

"It feels so good and right at the same time," I said. Omar's face kept coming back. It had been too long since he'd left and my repressed desire had intensified. For the first time I didn't feel the pressure of obligations and appearances and I felt a tremendous sense of relief. No more feeling guilty and ashamed of what I was doing. No longer did I need to care about the watchful eyes of *mardom*. I felt liberated.

He kissed my tears away. "The first time I saw your eyes, I saw a world of love and desire. You are my perfect match.

"I want to take your picture like this, naked in my bed, and I want to carry it everywhere with me," he whispered, as he climbed on top of me.

After reaching climax several times, we finally lay quietly together, snuggling, as we faced the beautiful garden and swimming pool. My back was against his chest and his arms were around me, warm and tight. We fell asleep just like that..

~~ ~~ ~~ ~~ ~~

When I awoke hours later, we were still in the same position. All the candles had burned down and some wax had fallen on the pedestal. But the instrumental music still played.

I stayed there quietly in his arms and listened to him breathe. The weight of his arms around me felt warm and comforting. I never thought I could feel so safe with a man. I felt somehow as if I'd known him forever.

Then I heard the front door open downstairs, keys jingling, and a woman's voice say, "It's me!"

I sat up, and in that split second I realized I hadn't really known this man forever. All my fears came flooding back. "Who is that?" I demanded.

"It's my cleaning woman," he said, laughing. "Don't worry. She will not come upstairs."

In relief I fell back into his arms. "Just hold me, don't let go of me."

He started kissing my neck and breathing in my scent as if I were a rose. Snuggling and kissing passionately, I whispered, "Make love to me again." And again, our bodies became one.

Javad was more than a willing partner; he also liked letting me take control. I enjoyed that tremendously.

The next night, we had plans to go to a restaurant that overlooked the mountains in the north of the city, and after dinner we had tickets to go to the opera house, *Talareh Roudaki*, to hear the famous opera singer, Pari Zangeneh.

Javad came over at 7:00 p.m. to pick me up, but we never made it to the opera house or to the restaurant. After several hours in my bedroom, we were both starving. We took whatever was in the refrigerator and put it on a large tray to bring back to the bed. Simple whole wheat bread and sheep's cheese with a few strands of fresh cilantro and basil had never tasted so delicious. After we were done eating, there were crumbs all over the bed. We laughed as crumbs attached themselves to our naked bodies.

It was amazing how our taste for food was alike. We were both almost vegetarian, which for Iranians was unusual, as some form of meat or poultry is eaten at least once a day.

I discovered how much fun it was to cook and create dishes. There was nothing I made that he did not taste with pleasure.

"Ateesh, you are the best cook!" he said.

I blushed and smiled proudly, remembering how I used to cook with Grandma Tuba as a child and how I wanted so much to be good at it. I remember being told that one day I would make a good wife. I thought about what it would feel like to be Javad's wife…a real wife, not a temporary one. I shook the thought out of my head as quickly as it came.

"I've always cooked myself and was told I was pretty good," he said. "But now with you to cook like this for me, I am retiring!"

"Okay," I said. "I'll do the cooking, and you can be my sous chef!"

"What is that?"

"You know, you will take care of small things for me, like kind of a busboy! Things that are not as creative I will assign to you. Deal?"

"Like what?"

"Well, you just will do as I tell you. Like being under me, in a way."

He lowered his voice and asked, "Is that what you like?"

"Yes, I like to be in charge."

"Then that's how it's going to be. You tell me what to do and I will oblige."

The chemistry between us was incredible, like nothing I'd ever experienced.

Javad was also an excellent ballroom dancer. He shared with me that he had taken hours of lessons from an American dance teacher who happened to be a colleague of Javad's sister.

"Please teach me how to tango and salsa and all those romantically sensuous moves, Javad," I said. "I love dancing. It is really a passion for me."

Then I put on some slow instrumental music and began to dance and move toward him. I lost myself again; it was so easy to do that with him.

"Ateesh, when you dance, I feel your passion," he said. "But I don't want you to dance like that in front of another man. I would be jealous."

I walked over to him and sat on his lap. "Oh Javad, please don't be," I said. "Dancing is my stress reliever remedy. When I dance I really don't see or look at anybody. It is just music and body movements for me. It is the ultimate ecstasy combined with passion."

He curled his arms around me. "I want to be all that for you," he said." Come on, my private dancer, dance for me again."

And I did.

We danced almost every time we were together. Following his moves and steps in ballroom dancing was a challenge for me, but he was patient and taught me one step at a time. On the dance floor, he lead with pleasure, yet in the bedroom, he followed my lead. In all my years of being a temporary wife I had learned how to arouse a man and to give pleasure. To see Javad satisfied under me made me feel good. Finally I had found pleasure in my heart-wrenching years as a temporary wife to men who'd been absolutely nothing to me but a vehicle to my independence.

There were a number of things I'd always wanted to do but had kept putting off because I didn't want to do them alone. Now I had Javad to do these things with, like ballroom dancing, skiing, even walking in the rain or in snow.

The Dizin sky resort is one of the highest natural ski resorts in the world, located only two hours north of Tehran in the Alborz mountain range.

"Are you sure you want to ski?" Javad asked.

"Yes!" I answered, unable to hide my excitement.

"I'll ride the ski lift with you," he said, "but do you mind if I don't ski? I'm afraid I might break my legs."

I agreed. "How about after I ski for a little bit, we walk in the snow for a long time?"

He courted me unlike any man I had ever known.

Whispering, people ask each other:
"Who then is this lucky girl?"
Suddenly the knocker echoes in our house
I fly off to open the door
It is him, yes, him.
"Ah, my prince, you are the beloved of my dreams
I have seen your face midnight deep in sleep!"
He smiles a shy, most childlike smile,
And lowers my eyes with passion-filled eyes
"Ah—your eyes, they shine," he sweetly says
Will they light my path to the abode of bliss?
Will your lips pour wine on mine with a kiss?
Hurry up, beloved of red ruby lips!
Our palace is far, hidden from our sight
But in your honor it's festooned with light."
Without uttering a word I set foot in the stirrup
Crawl in the shadow of his chest, and rest in those arms
I am in a swoon.

That magical time together was followed by many more, and as the months passed, I discovered Tehran with him. For as long as I'd lived there, I had never known of its magic, its romance. I discovered with him so many alleys and tucked away romantic spots frequented by lovers hidden from the eyes of *mardom*.

One night we went to the Maharaja restaurant for dinner and I ordered Canine wine, which Omar had introduced me to. "Now, *goleman*. Indulge me. I know a lot about wine from traveling all over the world," Javad said somewhat ostentatiously. He introduced me to wine tasting and fine dining. He was a renowned sculptor, well-known throughout the world. Through his eyes I was able to discover and explore that world.

He lit a spark in me as well as aroused a love I'd never known I was capable of. I told him everything about myself, leaving out one detail—my history as a *siqeh*.

And, in turn, he shared his life with me. He was a few years older than me, with no trace of gray in his hair. We had actually attended the university at the same time. His two prior marriages had ended in divorce and he still carried a lot of pain inside him, which he always tried to hide with humor.

"What took you so long, *Jooneh Delam*, to find me?" I asked him affectionately.

He cleared his throat. "*Goleman*," he said, suddenly becoming very serious. "I must tell you something."

Tell me what? I wondered nervously. I sat there still and quiet, and waited for him to continue.

"I have applied for a visa to go to America," he said.

He was leaving me, as Omar did.

"It has not been approved yet," he continued, "but it is just a matter of time. I can get you one, too. I want you to come with me."

"Come with you?" I asked. "You mean leave here for good? How can I?" I took my hands out of his and caressed his cheeks. "Are you serious?" I asked softly.

He took my hands away from his face and kissed them gently. "How much do you love me?" he asked.

"More than anybody could ever love," I answered him.

"Then just follow your heart," he said. "Everything else is secondary."

Javad had totally overcome all logic in my head and I took that as a sign that I was in love. It was not that he treated me better than Omar did. It was not that intellectually he was more challenging or more compatible. I couldn't explain it. I only needed to hear his voice or to feel his touch to lose control and submit to pure feelings without much participation from my brain.

A few days after my graduation with a Ph.D. in Law, I flew to Abadan to be with my family. My grandmodars didn't feel comfortable flying to Tehran. Modar had come to my graduation but I couldn't persuade her to stay with me in Tehran longer.

"Tehran is your city, Ateesh," she'd said. "Mine remains Abadan. You never know, Abadan may become yours one day, too."

I was proud that Modar had come to see my graduation from the university. She had flown there and stayed with me in my apartment. She was amazed at how well I was doing. But she was an intelligent modar, and this time around, as soon as we sat in the plane to Abadan, she asked me who the man in my life was. She said she could see it in my face since she'd arrived. She was hoping to meet him or for me to at least tell her something.

Had she asked me such a question at any other time, I would have immediately started cooking up different stories in my head, as I had nearly fifteen years ago, when I'd come home from Bejan's house and found her waiting outside my apartment.

This time I let Modar into my life without limits. As I told Modar how good I felt, she cried with happiness.

Javad couldn't be at my graduation because he was at a show in Europe presenting some of his sculptures, including the one he'd made of me.

I realized then just how much I missed him. If I closed my eyes I could feel him as if he were right there with me. I could see his eyes sparkle as he laughed and even feel his warm lips against mine. The taste of his kisses lingered on my mouth and his fragrance remained on me.

I opened my eyes. Suddenly I felt nervous and found myself shifting in my seat. Yes, I'd reached the goal of economic independence for myself, and I had made my family proud; nevertheless, I didn't feel as if I was truly independent. I'd become dependent on a man emotionally. Yes, there was so much I loved about Javad and our relationship: I loved the sharing, the anticipation of being together, the chemistry, the unity of two bodies without inhibition. But I hated needing him. I needed him emotionally and physically, and I didn't like that at all.

"Ateesh Joon, you are deep in thought," Modar commented. "You have everything a woman could possibly want. Aren't you happy? You should be."

I shrugged. "I'm not sure," I answered. "I feel as if I have to make a choice between independence and love. Love to me means boundaries around intellectual and emotional growth. Also, in a way it is a form of control and dependency. I mean, emotionally."

Modar just looked at me. I couldn't tell from her look if she understood what I was saying. I wasn't sure myself. I didn't trust my feelings of happiness with Javad. I think that was it. I felt panic.

"I know Tehran is your city, Ateesh. But you can always come back to Abadan. You are free to do as you want. You have freedom of choice, which none of us as women had," she said with a sparkle in her beautiful eyes. "Live your life. Find a balance between freedom, independence, and love. Don't lose sight of one over the other."

The warmth and softness of her hand comforted me.

The main reason I was taking this trip back to Abadan with Modar was to tell the most important people in my life all about Javad and our plans to move abroad to America, but now, suddenly, I wasn't sure.

"Karim has a special graduation present for you, which I think may heal some hurts in your heart."

"You talked to Karim?" I asked. "When?"

"Well, I asked Jamileh to call him about something and he told her to tell me," she said.

"Wow," was all I could say. Modar was healing, too, I thought.

"But you just have to wait." She squeezed my hand gently. I looked at Modar and noticed that her angelic face was shining like it had when I was only a few years old. She looked absolutely beautiful. She had put on makeup and her dark hair had some traces of burgundy highlights.

"Why are you staring at me, Ateesh?"

"Modar, you look so beautiful as if you are so content. If I didn't know you better I would have thought there was a man in your life!"

"Shame on you, Ateesh. Don't you ever say that."

"But Modar…"

She did not let me finish my sentence. "No more nonsense."

"*Bebaqsheed*, forgive me." We held hands until the plane landed.

As soon as we picked up our bags, we took a taxi and went directly to the women's shelter. All the old memories passed through my mind as we rode through the streets. Most were painful, yet valuable.

Luckily, I had inherited Modar's strength, which amazingly seemed to get stronger as I got older. Both grandmas and Modar came together to give me a much better chance in life than they would have individually. I was very fortunate. But regardless of how these attributes had helped me achieve the goal of financial independence, it hadn't prevented me from becoming emotionally and physically dependent on a man and love.

Perhaps I had overcome the biases and prejudices of my culture, but would my culture accept me?

Modar couldn't wait until we got to the center to tell Grandma Tuba and Jamileh my news. She called them from the taxi and said, "We're on our way! And we have news!" She went on to tell them that there was a wonderful man in my life. Then she handed me the phone.

"*Allaho Akbar!*" Grandma Tuba said. "I wish you had brought him with you to Abadan so we could meet him."

"Is he handsome?" Grandma Jamileh's voice chimed in. She must have grabbed the phone. "Is he worth having waited for all these years?"

As the taxi approached the shelter, they were both standing outside waiting for us. Both were more wrinkled and gray than the last time I saw them.

As I held Grandma Tuba, I hugged her tiny frame closer to me. I remembered the great comfort those hugs had given me throughout my life, and especially during the six years I had lived with her and Grandfather. Her hugs were often a warm escape from the harsh reality of my situation. From her I inherited conviction for God and the Prophet.

Going to Grandma Jamileh's was an escape as well, but this time into the world of poetry and "The Epic of Kings" with Ferdosy, who recorded history as the great Persian Empire began. A time when love and lovers were not shunned, but instead were written about. From Grandma Jamileh I had inherited passion for life and poetry.

Grandma Jamileh, as plump as ever, had a big grin on her face as she whispered in my ear as I hugged her tight, "You got butterflies in your tummy?"

"And more," I whispered back.

She started laughing and squeezed me tighter, and I felt her tears on my face.

They walked me inside and suddenly all the lights turned on at the center.

"Surprise!" many voices yelled. I found myself surrounded by several familiar, smiling faces. Grandfather was standing right up front with two clerics with white turbans whom I remembered seeing at Baba's mourning ceremony. They were wearing the religious light cotton cloak, as Grandfather was. Grandfather looked proud, as if I were a boy. Then I saw Karim. He walked toward me with a little girl in his arms and a woman next to him. He reached out to hug me, and I hugged him back tightly, without any trace of the resistance that had been there for all those years.

"This is my wife, Yasmin," he said. "She knows all about our tree climbing and other mischief, sister."

It was the first time I was meeting his wife. "Salam," I said, and kissed his wife on both sides of her cheeks, as is customary.

"This is my daughter," Karim said, and he handed me the beautiful little girl with dark curly hair that he was holding. "We named her Ateesh," he said with a big smile, "simply because she resembles her *Aameh*, sister-of-father."

She was holding a yellow rose. "For you, Aameh Joon," little Ateesh said.

I held her tight to my chest for a long minute, without saying a word, the way Grandma Tuba used to hold me. She just rested her little head on my shoulder and whispered, "You smell good!" as she continued sniffing my neck.

Alireza was there, too, with his pregnant wife.

From the corner of my eye I saw Baba's second wife. I turned around and looked at Modar. She had become herself again, perhaps by letting go of the past. Our eyes met and we both smiled. Modar nodded her head at me. I extended my hand to Maheen and said, "Salam."

Everybody I knew was there, even Behrook. If I could have captured that moment, it would have become the backdrop of my life itself from that moment on. There must have been about thirty or forty young women there whom I did not know, but who were residents of the shelter. As I stood there, I realized this was absolutely the happiest moment of my life.

On the plane back to Tehran, I realized that I hadn't told Modar and my grandmas about my plan to move to America with Javad. That was the big news I was planning on telling them while I was there. It must have been all the excitement over the graduation that made it slip my mind…seeing everyone I hadn't seen in a while, meeting all of those women at the shelter. Now I wondered, was it really that? Or was it that I truly didn't want to go?

As I stared out the window, I realized that I suddenly had all these questions that I hadn't had before. Or was it that these questions and doubts had been inside of me all along and I'd just been ignoring them?

I wanted to be with Javad, didn't I? Didn't I want to be happily married? Modar and my grandmas wanted me to be. But it was through them, however, that I'd also come to know about how much we women suffered in my country. Leaving Iran would mean ignoring that suffering, following my own happiness instead. Was that being selfish? If I simply left for America, I would be abandoning my dream of fighting for equality for women in my country. Going to America had become Javad's dream because all his family had moved there. His goal was to join them. My goal was not just about me being happy.

"Once you give me four boys, they will take care of your passion!" he had joked.

"Boys?!" I'd said. "I want girls!"

"No way!" he'd said, becoming serious. "I need boys to carry on my name."

"*Jooneh Delam*," I'd said. "We're both well over thirty years old. Do you think having four children is even feasible?"

I couldn't believe I was even talking about having children when I'd been so against it all these years. But I'd realized that deep inside, I did want a child.

"Four is a good number," he'd replied determinedly. "You deliver them, then we will worry about their upbringing."

"What about my career and my work to try to narrow the gap of gender inequality?" I'd asked.

"*Goleman*, after you raise our children you can do whatever you want. But I think your purpose in life for now should be to raise children."

What did that mean? I'd wondered. But deep down I knew what it meant. It meant my role as a wife was to produce children, preferably boys, and as a modar, to raise those boys.

We'd talked about getting married in America. I didn't care for an extravagant ceremony, desiring instead something small and tasteful. "You never know, *goleman*, you might feel differently when the time comes. Life is full of surprises. We will see where it takes us," Javad said. "There are no guarantees," Javad had said a number of times, referring to other life events. Sitting in the plane on the way back to Tehran, those words kept echoing in my mind.

I think it was at that moment on the plane that I realized why Javad had reminded me so much of Baba. He thought the same way Baba had. Remembering and thinking about some of our conversations made it more obvious than before. I had fallen for a man who believed in things I hated.

I had no doubts that he loved me as much as I loved him. But now that I had found love, I needed to believe that it would last forever, that one day he wouldn't leave me as Baba had. My heart would not take it this time around. I told myself. *You have to leave him before he leaves you.*

⩗ ⩗ ⩗ ⩗ ⩗

Tack in Tehran, Javad was busy closing his studio as the last step in preparing to move to America. Consequently, I had a lot of time to myself and that was exactly what I needed.

I'd spent the last few days at my favorite places, knowing that it might be a long time before I saw them again. I visited my friends who still lived in the city and invited all of them to my wedding in America, but few of them could commit. They now had families of their own.

It was late in the afternoon one day, and I decided I had enough time to walk the streets of my old university neighborhood for a while. I re-lived the taxi ride I'd taken to meet Bejan for the first time. I looked in the windows of the Pahlavi bookstore where I'd met my Omar. I passed the place where Tanaz and I used to meet for Nescafé, and walked past the restaurants I used to frequent with my girlfriends. My memories were happy, but more than once, I felt as if the streets were haunted by the memories of my ten marriages. Some were as short as one month and others as long as two years. None of them forgotten.

Finally, I decided to hail a cab. As I opened the door of the taxi to get in, I heard someone calling my name. I turned and saw Dr. Behi Goodarzi running toward me, waving. I hadn't realized I was right in front of her office. I apologized to the driver and asked him to wait a minute.

"I have great news for you, Ateesh!" Behi said over the passing traffic, as she approached me. "A full-time job that actually pays well! I have lots of cases right now that need a woman like you. The sooner you can start, the better! Please come into my office. We need to talk."

Without waiting for a response, she turned on her heels and headed toward the front door of the building.

With my hand on the door of the cab, I stood on the sidewalk, hesitating. By now, Javad would surely be wondering where I was... the man with whom I was planning to move to America, marry, and have children.

"*Khanoom*, are you coming or not?" the taxi driver asked in an irritated tone.

"*Bebaksheed*," I said, and let go of the door.

I turned and headed toward the building, where Behi stood holding the front door open for me. As I hurried toward her, I thought of Golbarg, sitting in her prison cell. I would start with her.

As Modar said, it is my choice what to do with my life. *Allaho Akbar!* I thought, as I walked through the open door..

~~ ~~ ~~ ~~ ~~

My name is Ateesh and I am a thirty-plus-year-old Iranian woman. I am the director of *Khaneyeh Zaneh Bepanah*, a home for women without homes. I did it for Modar, Grandma Tuba, Grandma Jamileh, Sherin, Golbarg, Marjon, and all the other women whose paths I crossed. I know I made the right choice.

Author's Note

The tragic events of September 11, 2001 were the beginning of my quest to learn more about Islam, my religion, and shortly after I focused on the position of women within the text of the Quran. As an attorney I soon began examining the available evidence to look for a correlation between the intention of Islam from its inception and its effect on the current poor status of Moslem women. I found much evidence of misogynous interpretations of the Quran by the historically androcentric Arabs. It became no longer comforting to me to hear the excuse, "this is not religion but culture," when those words are used as a justification for the ill treatment of Moslem women.

Culturally accepted biases continue to harm Iranian women in family and criminal courts. Divorce in particular is one of the areas in which Iranian women are most affected by these male-biased Quranic interpretations. During my visits to courts in Iran, I met many vibrant, strong women who had learned to use their religion positively as a tool of empowering them to insist upon the original Islamic intention to promote fairness for women. But they fight an uphill battle because the male-centered misinterpretation of Islam has been codified into Iranian law, rather than the gender fairness that is actually to be found in the Quran.

Temporary marriage is one of the those practices, which at its inception 1400 years ago might have been beneficial to women, but which now clearly serves the interests of men. Here, as with so many other laws in the Islamic world, what was originally done to emancipate women has been twisted into a means to oppress them. My goal in writing this novel is to work towards eliminating the great gap between the religion of Islam as it is written and the way it is practiced.

Part of the proceeds from the sale of this book are being donated to a foundation that provides support and assistance for Moslem women suffering the effects of domestic violence.

— Nadia Shahram

Partial Historical and Religious
Justification for Temporary Marriage

Temporary marriage (*siqeh* in Farsi or *muta* in Arabic) is a type of marriage practiced by the followers of the Shi'i sect of Islam. It differs from a regular marriage by its specific time limitation. At the outset there are three requirements: a proposal by a man (married or single) and an acceptance by an unmarried woman; a specified sum of money; and a fixed duration. The legitimacy of temporary marriage is debated among different sects of Islam. The Quranic sanction of *siqeh* can be found in Chapter 4 Verse 24 (hereafter 4:24).

After the death of Prophet Mohammad in 632, the Muslim community established government and laws in keeping with the Quran and the Sunna, the Prophet's spoken and enacted response to divine revelation. The law, known as the Sharia, was compiled by religious experts, and relates to all individual and communal activities. Muslims look to the Sharia for guidance on morality and faith. Various methods and schools of interpretation developed, of which four have had a lasting influence on Muslims. Maliki, Hanafi, Shafi, and Hanbali are the four slightly different systems of legal methodology named after, and based on, the interpretations of the four leading legal experts in the early Islamic period. Their regulations provide individuals with the basic tenets for living a righteous life. Shi'i Muslims differ from Sunnis in that they also follow the teachings of their Imams, descendants of the Prophet whom they believe to be inspired by God to give authoritative instruction. Since the ninth century when the line of Imams ended, individuals at the highest clerical level known as "Ayatollah," or Sign of God, have guided Shi'i Muslims. An Ayatollah is to be a source of wisdom and an example of righteousness for Shi'i Muslims to follow.

The Quran is comprised of 114 chapters, and Chapter Four: Al Nisa ("The Women") is devoted to the relationship between men and women and their treatment of each other. The verses on the treatment of men and women are directed towards men only. The verses on the relationship of men and women towards God are gender-neutral and directed to mankind. Chapter Four is the main source of authority on the formation of family law, which is commonly known as the Islamic Law governing all aspects of family relationships.

Chapter Four, The Women, opens with one of the most humanistic verses, which if followed should remove any patriarchal notion of gender inequality in the creation of Islam:

O mankind! Reverence Your Guardian-Lord, who created you from a single person, created, of like nature, His mate, and from them twain Scattered (like seeds) countless men and women fear Allah, through whom Ye demand your mutual (rights). And (reverence) the wombs (that bore you), for Allah ever watches over you. (4)

The main support for temporary marriage comes from the following verse: And all married women except those whom your right hands possess (this is) Allah's ordinance to you;

And lawful for you are (all women) besides those,
Provided that you seek (them) with your property, taking them in marriage not committing fornication. Then as to those, whom you profit by, give them their dowries as appointed;
And there is no blame on you about what you mutually agree after what is appointed;
Surely Allah is knowing, wise. (4:24)

Shi'i Muslims pay special attention to the words "Then as to those whom you profit by, give them their dowries as appointed; and there is no blame on you about what you mutually agree after what is appointed."

This verse was revealed towards the beginning of the Prophet's stay in Medina, the migration or *hijra* that marks the start of the Islamic era. At that time the men of Medina used to "seek pleasure/enjoyment" from women for a limited duration in exchange for a specified sum of money. By its revelation this verse in effect confirmed an existing custom. It emphasized that men must fulfill their promises to women concerning the agreed-upon sum of money. At that time in Medina, this custom was a kind of temporary marriage and was referred to as Istimta, which is the same word used in the Quranic verse. The literal meaning of this word is "to seek benefit" or "to take enjoyment." Hence the meaning of the Quranic verse must be understood in terms of the conventional usage of the time. It is well-known in the science of Quranic commentary and Islamic jurisprudence that the Quran follows the conventional usage of the people in all statutes and legal prescriptions.

On the other hand, Sunnis agree that temporary marriage was permitted at the beginning of Islam but argue that it was later forbidden and abolished after the death of Prophet Mohammad. Their argument relies heavily on Quranic verse 23:1-6:

> The believers…who refrain from sex, except with those joined to them in the marriage bond, or whom their right hand possesses…

There are at least two undisputed historical incidents that sanctioned the use of temporary marriage. The battle of Hunain and the conquest of Mecca were both occasions where temporary marriage was permitted. The Sunnis stopped practicing temporary marriage after those occasions when the successor of Prophet Mohammad, Caliph Omar, declared an outright ban on temporary marriage.

Over the next thirty years, four men, Abu Baker (632-34), Omar (634-44), Uthman (644-56), and Ali (656-61) led the Muslim community as Caliph (which is the title for the leader of the Islamic community). Sunni Moslems regard this as Islam's golden age. Shi'i Moslems hold that Ali who was the Prophet's son-in-law and cousin should have been the first Caliph. Although both sects agree on the fundamentals of the religion, the dispute over the rightful successor continues to this day. It is this division that has caused slightly different rituals between the two sects.

Temporary marriage has become almost an exclusively Shi'i practice and was given great amplification by a famous commentary of Imam Jafar al Sadiq. The late Imam Jafar was the sixth Imam and the chief jurist of his time.

Shi'ism relies heavily on Imam Jafar's thinking. Shi'is follow his advice in regard to temporary marriage: "I do not like a man to leave this world without having married temporarily at least once." The encouragement, promotion, and rewards for temporary marriage are not only physical, but are also for the perceived *savab*(religious blessings one collects in this life to be redeemed in the next) and revival of the traditions of Prophet Mohammad, which were forsaken by the majority of Muslims. Imam Jafar refers to this verse to further the holiness of temporary marriage:

> What Allah out of his mercy doth bestow on mankind, there is none can withhold: What he doth withhold, there is none can grant... (35:2)

Imam Jafar emphasizes the first part of this verse, declaring that temporary marriage is indeed part of that mercy.

The following verses are a few of the verses that have been used in the formation of many laws in Muslim countries that are severely biased and discriminatory towards women. The women in the stories told throughout this book all have been affected by the culturally accepted usage of these verses.

> Permitted to you, on the night of the fasts, is the approach to your wives. They are your garments and ye are their garments. Allah knoweth what ye used to do secretly among yourselves... (2:187)

> .... Ye may approach them, in any manner, time, or place, ordained for you by Allah. (2:222)

> Your wives are as a tilth unto you so approach your tilth when or how you will; but do some good act for your souls beforehand; and fear Allah... (2:223)

> O ye who believe! When you deal with each other, In transactions involving Future obligations... And get two witnesses, out of your own men; and if there are not two men, then a man and two women, such as ye choose, for witnesses, so that if one of them errs, then the other can remind her. (2:282)

> If you fear that you shall not, be able to deal justly with the orphans (widows) marry women of your choice, two, or three, or four; but if you fear that you shall not be able to deal justly (with

them), then only one, or (a captive) that your right hand possess. That will be more suitable, to prevent you from doing injustice. (4:3)

If any of your women, are guilty of lewdness, take the evidence of four (Reliable) witnesses from amongst you against them; and if they testify, confine them to houses until death do claim them, or Allah ordain for them some (other) way. (4:15)

O ye who believe, ye are forbidden to inherit women against their will... (4:19)

If a wife fears cruelty or desertion on her husband's part, there is no blame on them. If they arrange an amicable settlement between themselves; and such settlement is best.... (4:128)

You are never able to be fair and just as between women, even if it is your ardent desire: but turn not away (from a woman) altogether, so as to leave her (as it were) hanging (in the air). If you come to a friendly understanding, and practice self-restraint, Allah is oft-forgiving, most merciful. (4:129)

And those who launch a charge against chaste women, and produce not four witnesses (to support their allegations) flog them with eighty stripes: And reject their evidence ever after, for such men are wicked   transgressors. (24:4)

And for those who launch a charge against their spouses, and have (in support) no evidence but their own   their solitary evidence (can be received) if they bear witness four times (with an oath) by Allah that they are solemnly telling the truth. (24:6)

Although this story is fictional, all the references to the Quran are direct quotes from various translations/interpretations:
"Holy Qur'an" Translation into English & Persian by A. Iranpanah
"The Holy Qur'an" English translation by Abdullah Yusuf
"Partoyyee as Qur'an" by Sayeed Mahmood Taleghany
"The Gracious Qur'an" by Ahmad Zaki Hammad

For those who want to learn more about the practice of temporary marriage in a scholarly written text, *Law of Desire* by Shahla Haeri is recommended.

Qur'an and Woman: Rereading the Sacred Text from a Woman's Perspective by Amina Wadud offers a much-needed explanation.

Discussion Questions

1. The novel begins with Ateesh's memory of riding in the ambulance and the conversation between her grandma and modar. What impact did that particular memory have on her?

2. What correlation did you find between the title and the way the story unfolds?

3. Which characters in particular had an impact on you?

4. *Mardom chi megan* and *bi-aberue*, are two phrases repeated throughout the novel. What are their meanings and significance on the lives of Iranian women?

5. The story of struggle for independence is also an issue facing women here in the United States. Ateesh attained her independence through temporary marriage. What do you think of her struggle and her choices?

6. Iranian culture placed a great deal of pressure on Ateesh with significant consequences. Did this seem at all real? What are some of the cultural effects facing women here?

7. What were some of the religious pressures placed on Ateesh? Are there similar religious pressures and expectations here?

8. In your opinion what affected her life the most?

9. How do you assess the status of women in Iran? Give examples.

10. Do you believe that Ateesh gained independence through her temporary marriages or was she imprisoned by it?

11. How would you describe Nadia Shahram's style of writing? Did it strike you as unusual/different?

12. How would you have liked the story to end? If there is a sequel, where do you think it will begin? Why?

Acknowledgments

Marriage on the Street Corners of Tehran is a novel about the socially acceptable practice of "temporary marriages" in Iran. The main character Ateesh is my own creation, but her story is a composite from my many interviews of real-life women and their experiences. In 2004 and 2005, I visited my native country, Iran, to research the treatment of women from a social, cultural, and religious perspective. There in Tehran, Mashhad, Qom, Khorramabad, and Brojeerd, I met with many women whose stories I have woven into the novel. Their names and personal descriptions were changed to protect their privacy.

During my two visits to Iran some of my cousins from my father's side of the family traveled with me and helped me interview the women I write about in this novel. In particular, the familiarity of Dr. Golareh Mahigear from Boroujerd, and Mrs. Maleheh Rumana and Shahnaz Jorbozehdar from Tehran, with the culture, customs, and day-to-day lives of Iranian women from all walks of life was invaluable to me.

Once I returned to the States, I received a tremendous amount of encouragement from the faculty of Hilbert College, where I was an adjunct faculty member in 2004-2005. In particular, Dr. Edson, Dr. Snow, and Dr. Degnan offered unreserved inspiration and support during the early days I was working on this book.

I thank:

Michael Lee Jackson Esq. and Dr. Bruce Jackson for advice and help.

My friends and colleagues, Dr. Sue Mangold, Dr. Sue Tompkins, and Dr. Isabel Marcus at the University of Buffalo, who have always been great supporters of my work.

Dr. Hai, Dr. Karimi, and Dr. Korashi for their overall help throughout the various drafts of my manuscripts and their religious point of view.

Dr. Andrey Kuzmin, Dr. Alexander Kachynski, and Ms. Margie Weber for their assistance in many areas.

Thank you to Beth Seilberger from Buffalo and Tracy Spleeman from Fiction Critiques. I thank my new publisher Megan Hunter for trusting my work by republishing it through Unhooked Books. I also thank Julian Leon from New York City for the new book design and another round of editing by Patti Frazee from Minneapolis.

I am grateful to:

My assistant and close friend Ms. Terri James who, among many other things that were beyond the call of duty, helped to copy and stuff envelopes for publishers as we drank tea and joked about life.

My friend Jamshid Vafai who provided expert media support, including the cover and back photo and design for the first publication. He has been a tremendous supporter and help with the overall project, as well as many other projects throughout the years, many of which are available for viewing on Youtube.

My close friend and colleague Ms. Pamela Thibodeau, and James Ginnane, both of whom played many roles, including acting as readers and commentators. I am appreciative of their assistance and guidance throughout the writing and publishing process.

My friend and old classmate Sebastian who is a big supporter of my projects and has timelessly critiqued my style of writing and, at the end, before publication, provided many hours of crucial proofreading and dedicated his time generously.

Special gratitude to Dr. Paras N. Prasad, father of my two precious daughters Melanie and Natasha and, at the time I was writing the book, my husband of twenty years. During the last five years I worked on this novel, he has supported me emotionally and unconditionally, encouraging me to complete the book. He showed me endless patience throughout the process.

Finally, I thank God for my father from whom I learned writing with much passion, and my mother from whom I learned selflessness in raising daughters.

The Author

Born in Tehran, Nadia Shahram, along with her five sisters and parents, moved to the small town of Borojerd. After she was sent to Canada in 1978 to finish high school, she developed a vision for her life that included moving to the United States, becoming an Iranian version of Barbara Walters, and then returning to her home country. Although she did eventually move to the States, the rest of  her dream was interrupted by the 1979 Iranian revolution and the long war that followed. Shahram currently lives in Amherst, New York, where she practices family law and matrimonial mediation. This is her first novel. Contact Nadia at attorneynadia@gmail.com.

Glossary

Aameh: Sister-of-father.

Aberue yeh man meereh: I will lose face.

Ahlan va Sahlan (Arabic): How are you?

Allaho Akbar: God is great

Asabany nasheen: Don't get angry.

Ateesh pareh: Sparkle of fire.

Bargard: Step back.

Bebaqsheed or Bebakhsheed: Forgive me.

Be pedar: Without father, bastard.

Be sharaf: Without honor.

Chador: A long material worn from head-to-toe that usually covers the whole body but not the fae. This particular style of covering is limited to Iranians.

Chi shodeh: What happened?

Dan don ru gigar mi zareh ama he chi ne me geh: Bite your tongue and don't say anything.

Doayeheh ma poshteh toh: Our blessings are with you.

Enshalla: God willing.

Esteqareh: Religious consultation.

Faleh Hafez: Telling of the fortune through poetry by poet Hafez.

Gendeh khanoom: Prostitute, in a sarcastic way that is degrading to a woman whose behavior is outside of the norm.

Goleman, chieh: What is it, my flower?

Hajji: An honorific title given to those who have completed their pilgrimage of the holy. It could also refer to an old man.

Hajjieh: Female equivalent to Hajji. It could also refer to an old woman.

Haram: Forbidden.

Imam: Usually the religious leader of a community who guides the prayer and sermons.

Joon: My dear, in an informal way.

Jooneh Delam: Dear to my heart.

Kareh vajeeb: A serious matter.

Khaneyeh Zaneh Bpanah: House for women without homes.

Khanoom: Lady.

Khosh amadeed, bah safa awordeed: Customary greetings, welcome, you brought pleasure by your arrival.

Khoshgelam kon: Make me beautiful.

Mardom: People.

Mardom chi feker me konand: What people would think.

Marhaba (Arabic): Bravo.

Masjid: Mosque.

Mehman habibeh khodast: A guest is God's gift.

Metarsam: I am afraid.

Mobarakeh: Congratulations.

Modar Bozorg: Grand mother..

Mohalal: The man who is hired for a sum of money to marry a wife who has been divorced by her husband three times.

Qalyan: Hookah, water pipe.

Qisas: Blood money.

Sabahal kheer habibi (Arabic): "Good morning my dear," male.

Sabahal noor habibati (Arabic): "Good morning my dear," female.

Shahvat: Desire.

Siqeh: Temporary wife.

Sofreh: A white cotton tablecloth usually thrown in the middle of a room where families sit around to eat.

Zina: Sex outside of marriage.

Zoroastrians: Parsees.

CPSIA information can be obtained at www.ICGtesting.com
Printed in the USA
LVOW11s0521200716

496899LV00002B/10/P